NO
PLACE
FOR
WOLVERINES

JENNY WILLSON MYSTERIES

Full Curl
No Place for Wolverines

NO PLACE FOR WOLVERINES

A Jenny Willson Mystery

DAVE BUTLER

DUNDURN
TORONTO

Cover image: istock.com/Hämta härifrån
Printer: Webcom

Library and Archives Canada Cataloguing in Publication

Butler, Dave, 1958-, author
    No place for wolverines / Dave Butler.

(A Jenny Willson mystery)
Issued in print and electronic formats.
ISBN 978-1-4597-3983-3 (softcover).--ISBN 978-1-4597-3984-0
(PDF).--ISBN 978-1-4597-3985-7 (EPUB)

    I. Title. II. Series: Butler, Dave, 1958-. Jenny Willson mystery

PS8603.U838N67 2018   C813'.6   C2018-900726-5
                                              C2018-900727-3

1 2 3 4 5   22 21 20 19 18

 Conseil des Arts du Canada   Canada Council for the Arts   Canada   ONTARIO ARTS COUNCIL CONSEIL DES ARTS DE L'ONTARIO
an Ontario government agency
un organisme du gouvernement de l'Ontario

We acknowledge the support of the **Canada Council for the Arts**, which last year invested $153 million to bring the arts to Canadians throughout the country, and the **Ontario Arts Council** for our publishing program. We also acknowledge the financial support of the **Government of Ontario**, through the **Ontario Book Publishing Tax Credit** and the **Ontario Media Development Corporation**, and the **Government of Canada**.

Nous remercions le **Conseil des arts du Canada** de son soutien. L'an dernier, le Conseil a investi 153 millions de dollars pour mettre de l'art dans la vie des Canadiennes et des Canadiens de tout le pays.

Care has been taken to trace the ownership of copyright material used in this book. The author and the publisher welcome any information enabling them to rectify any references or credits in subsequent editions.

— *J. Kirk Howard, President*

The publisher is not responsible for websites or their content unless they are owned by the publisher.

Printed and bound in Canada.

VISIT US AT

 dundurn.com | @dundurnpress | dundurnpress | dundurnpress

Dundurn
3 Church Street, Suite 500
Toronto, Ontario, Canada
M5E 1M2

CHAPTER 1

DECEMBER 1

Sue Webb paused. The forest was silent around her, deep snow muffling all sound. The crisp morning air, so clean it could purify lungs in a single breath, smelled and tasted of wild places.

A curious grey jay landed with a squawk on a branch above her. She looked at the bird but couldn't shake the disconcerting feeling, like a subtle electric current humming at the back of her neck, that something else was watching her. She scanned the trees, searching the dark places between branches for movement — the blink of an eye, the flick of an ear. *Is it tracking me? Will I see it if I keep walking? Or will it remain in the trees, studying me, waiting for another time?* She pushed the questions from her mind, slid her gloved hands into the straps of her ski poles, then shuffled higher into the forest, picking a safe route through the conical canopies that avoided tree wells, those deadly spaces between fallen snow and the trunks of trees that can swallow a person whole.

The early snowpack, a blanket of unconsolidated powder, covered the uneven ground to a depth of almost two metres. Webb's snowshoes, wide and long, offered much-needed floatation above the deep snow. But as a result, her inner thighs complained, and her knees and hips protested with each repeated motion. Sweat dripped down her flushed cheeks. She understood why the *coureurs de bois* — the early fur traders known as "runners of the woods" — walked with bow legs, even in summer. Yes, she had volunteered for this. And yes, it had seemed like a good idea at the time. Despite that, she was in agony.

After five long kilometres, all uphill, in a forest dense with Engelmann spruce and subalpine fir, Webb looked back at her supervisor, Albin Stoffel. He was a hundred metres behind — and below — her and was clearly struggling, his head down, his pace slowed. *Suffering is easier to take when it's shared*, she thought. *But is it okay to enjoy the fact that Albin seems to be suffering more than I am?* She smiled. *Absolutely.*

"Are we having fun yet?" she yelled.

"Jesus," said Stoffel between deep breaths, "I remember why I love my touring skis … and why I hate these goddamn torture racquets. What a tough way to travel."

"It is," said Webb, "but there's no way we could get up here on skis. The forest is too dense, too tangled."

While she waited for Stoffel to catch up, she sucked on the plastic tube connected to the bladder full of thirst-quenching sports drink in her pack, fuel for her engine. She squinted at her cellphone as the GPS app recalibrated their position. "Less than a kilometre to go," she said.

"Excellent," Stoffel said. "At least we'll be on a packed trail going back. By the time we get back to the truck tonight, every part of me will be sore. I may never walk like a human again." He grabbed the front of his jacket and shirt with a fist, flapping the two layers to vent the moist, warm air coming off him. "Shite, I think I pulled a groin muscle coming up that last hill," he said with a grimace.

Thirty minutes later, they stopped in a small natural clearing, where subalpine fir outnumbered spruce and light overwhelmed shadow. They were near the headwaters of Collie Creek, in a basin just below the treeline, the amorphous boundary between forest and alpine meadow. To the south, Webb could see slices of the upper valley shining in the sun. Above, a fantail of spindrift blew off the craggy ridges of Mount Collie.

These December days were short, so Webb and Stoffel shrugged off their packs and immediately got to work. They needed to get back before nightfall. After searching for recent tracks in the fresh snow, Stoffel waddled on his snowshoes over to a spruce tree, its lower branches pruned to a height of about four metres. A single strand of barbed wire spiralled up the trunk. He peered at the wire and then slowly, carefully, pulled a couple of hairs from some of the barbs, placing them follicle-end first in a clear plastic bag labelled with date and location.

Webb crossed to the far side of the clearing, where, in late October, just before the first snowfall, they'd strapped a surveillance camera to the trunk of one of the fir trees, two metres above what they'd estimated the eventual snow depth would be here. Motion triggered, it captured a 120-degree view of its surroundings. Webb opened the waterproof case, replaced the batteries, and popped the memory card out onto the palm of her hand, staring at it for a moment as if she could see its contents. After sliding an empty card into the camera, she tucked the used one into a plastic bag in her breast pocket. "I can't wait to see what's on this baby," she said. "It'll be like Christmas."

She turned to see Stoffel wrestling a fourteen-kilogram skinned beaver carcass out of her pack. Frozen solid, it had been tightly wrapped in plastic bags, yet the musky aroma was unmistakable. They'd picked it up that morning from a local trapper who had no use for it once the body and the valuable pelt had parted company. As the volunteer on the team who was lowest in the pecking order, Webb had landed the job of carrying the carcass up the hill. Now it was time for the next step in the process, so she stepped out of her snowshoes.

Stoffel, stronger and taller than Webb, boosted her up the tree, trying not to snag her or her clothing on the barbed wire. Grunting with the effort, Webb tied the carcass to the tree with baling wire, and then, with the flat end of an axe, she pounded a long spike through it, deep into the scaly trunk. The pounding echoed around the basin. To a branch above the carcass she added a scent lure that stank of rotting meat, designed to attract hungry carnivores from kilometres around. With a whisper, a cloud of snow slid down from the tree's upper branches and entered every opening in their clothing.

"Okay, I'm done," said Webb. "It's not going anywhere." She dropped to the ground and turned to face Stoffel. She had tree sap smeared across one cheek and spruce bark and snow on her toque, face, and shoulders. The arms of her jacket, its chest panels stained and smelling of rancid beaver, had been shredded by the sharp barbs of the wire. "If I didn't already have a husband," she said, "there's no way I'd get one looking like this."

"I don't know, Sue, you look and smell like the kind of woman that old trapper would love to snuggle with during the long winter."

They both laughed.

"Jesus," said Webb, grinning, "I'm going to burn this jacket when the season's over … and stay the hell away from that trapper."

"Good idea on both counts," said Stoffel.

Later that evening, Webb and Stoffel huddled at a desk in their office in Golden, B.C. It was an old log building on the north bank of the Kicking Horse River, the cheapest place they'd been able to get as a home base for the research project. After the long trip down the Blaeberry River valley to town — partly on snowshoes, partly on snowmobiles, the rest in a pickup truck — they'd picked up, then devoured a fully loaded pizza. The stained empty box now sat abandoned on a table behind them. Taking a final sip from a bottle of beer, Webb pulled the memory card from her pocket and pushed it into a slot on the laptop that was open in front of them. "Let's see if we had any visitors," she said. The light from the screen reflected the anticipation in her eyes.

With Stoffel peering over her shoulder, Webb clicked steadily through the images on the card, creating the effect of a rough animation. The camera's shutter had not only opened whenever the sensor detected movement, but also every twenty seconds until the motion had stopped for longer than a minute. Each image showed the date and time it was captured.

In the darkened office, the two researchers watched as a parade of animals investigated the first carcass they'd staked to the same tree five weeks earlier. Because the camera was inactive when there were no animals around, the hundreds of time-lapse photographs, erratically strung together like an early black-and-white movie, made the tree look like Grand Central Station for wildlife.

Some animals visited during the day and were easily identified. Others came at night, like ghosts; shadows and shapes and glowing eyes. Some, like a wolf pack in mid-November, circled the tree, looking up, their tongues lolling, unable to reach the carcass. Defeated, they moved on, not to be seen again. Others — martens, weasels, and fishers — climbed the tree often, gnawing on small bites ripped from the frozen carcass. A lynx appeared three times to do the same.

Finally, in an image captured just the previous week, they saw the beast emerge from the forest. It paused, staring directly at the camera, unblinking, fearless, as if it knew it wasn't alone and didn't care. In the next, it was in mid-leap to the frozen beaver. Next, it had grabbed the carcass in its powerful jaws, doing its best to rip it from the tree. For ten minutes, the beast went up and down the tree, trying to wrest the prize from its perch. The intermittent images made it appear hyperactive, easily distracted, but its goal was always clear. The second-to-last picture showed the animal hanging from the carcass with its full weight, its jaws sunk deep into the icy meat, its head and limbs blurred with motion, scrambling, tearing. In the last image, taken forty seconds later, the carcass had been torn free. The beast stood over it on the ground, staring directly at the camera. In that stare they saw tenacity, ferocity, and perhaps a hint of smug satisfaction.

Webb and Stoffel turned to look at each other, in awe of the beast, its power, its intelligence. They smiled and bumped fists.

"Excellent," Stoffel said. "We've now got proof they're in Collie Creek … and I've finally got the first solid pieces of data for my project." As one, he and Webb turned back to the screen. There stood a full-grown male wolverine in startling clarity, the dark-brown coat thick and gleaming, a light patch across its face and chest, two light stripes running down its flanks. Black eyes glared at them.

Stoffel pulled his chair back from the desk and raised his arms toward the roof in a noisy stretch. "That was a good day, Sue, but I'm going home. Lyndsey said she'd wait up even though she starts on early shift tomorrow at the hospital. What are you going to do?"

"I'll finish my report and then probably crash on the couch here. It's too late to drive home tonight. I'll text Bruce to let him know I won't be home."

"You're welcome to stay at our place."

"Thanks, but I'm happy here. You don't need me as a third wheel. Do you want to take the memory card and hair samples with you?"

"Yeah, I probably should. I'll send them to the lab first thing in the morning."

With a start, Sue Webb awoke from a nightmare in which she was being smothered by a large, dark mass, unable to breathe. Before she had time to process where she was or what was happening, she began to cough. When she tried to inhale, her lungs filled with acrid smoke. She coughed again and instinctively rolled to the floor. Looking around the large office, she saw that one entire wall, once a floor-to-ceiling bookshelf filled with textbooks, scientific papers, and magazine articles and divided by the only door in or out of the building, was engulfed in flames. Her brain and heart racing, she crawled awkwardly across the rough wood floor toward a window, her lungs desperate for oxygen. In the confusion of the flames and the dark rolling smoke, she slammed headfirst into the corner of a desk, then slumped to the floor, dazed, a gash in her forehead pumping blood across her eyebrow and into her eye. With a final choking cough, Webb's nightmare became her reality.

CHAPTER 2

NOVEMBER 24, ONE WEEK EARLIER

The Parks Canada administration building oversaw the town of Banff from an elevated perch south of the Bow River. It was a dominating presence, facing north along the congested length of Banff Avenue toward Cascade Mountain. It spoke of permanence, authority, tradition. Constructed as a Depression-era make-work project, the three-storey structure was completed in 1936 and symbolized Canada's emerging need to manage the wilderness for people. Built of limestone, with sandstone trim and cedar shakes and surrounded by sweeping gardens, it projected an air of calm control, efficiency, and strong management.

For Park Warden Jenny Willson, the castle-like building sat in stark contrast to the wilderness of Banff National Park. And it represented all she hated about a bureaucracy that often served itself instead of the citizens who paid the bills. She knew there were many good people here dedicated to the park, their efforts valiant *despite* the system rather than because of it — those weren't the people she despised. Her disgust was reserved for the men and women whose sole objective was to climb the career ladder, rung by slippery rung, tossing aside their morals and ethics as they did so, who changed directions with each passing political breeze, and who clawed their way up while shovelling steaming piles of blame onto the hapless rung-climbers below them.

Willson paused below the stone archway at the building's east entrance, her face reflected in the original stained glass panels, one hand gripping a brass door handle worn and discoloured from eighty years of contact with palms and fingers. She'd gone for a bike ride that morning and, because it was her day off, hadn't bothered with the tan shirt, dark-green pants, and bullet-proof vest that she normally wore on duty. Instead, she had quickly pulled on jeans, hiking shoes, and a blue fleece jacket over a flannel shirt. Her long brown hair was pulled back tight in a ponytail.

The last time she'd been in this building, she remembered, two senior officials from Parks Canada's Calgary office had tried to derail her investigation into wildlife poaching in the park. Despite their attempts to impede her, to prevent her from doing what she knew to be right, Willson had relentlessly chased an American hunter and his accomplices back and forth across the international border. She'd eventually won the race. Then, in classic government style, campaigning politicians took credit for her actions, while one of the two obstruction-ist bureaucrats resigned quietly and without fanfare. The other crawled up another rung on the government ladder, proof that the Peter principle was alive and well.

Willson took a deep breath. Every time she passed through this door, her life changed in some way, and never for the better. She could walk away from the agency, but to do what? Reluctantly, she pulled open the heavy door and walked down the empty hallway to the office of Banff Chief Park Warden Frank Speer, her footsteps echoing on the tile floor.

A thirty-year veteran of the agency, Speer was one of the few people above Willson in the parks hierarchy whom she truly respected. He'd supported her through the tortuous poaching investigation, putting his career and his pending retirement at risk. In fact, he'd been the only one to stand by her.

Willson pushed open the windowed door to Speer's office and greeted Pat Scott, a plump, no-nonsense woman in her sixties who'd worked with the chief in one capacity or another since he first became a warden. Her job title was now executive assistant, but she still referred to herself as his secretary. Old habits. Pat was short enough to be the same height standing up or sit-ting down — or so it seemed to Willson, who towered over her by nearly a foot.

"Hi, Jenny, it's been a while. The chief's waiting for you." She winked. "Keep up the good work."

"Thanks, Pat. I appreciate that more than you know."

Willson entered the inner office and sat down in a creaky old chair facing an older man with a grey crewcut.

"You wanted to see me, Chief?" she asked, stretching her legs out.

Behind the desk, Frank Speer pulled the wire-framed reading glasses off his face and looked up from a stack of documents. Willson noticed the dark circles under his eyes and the creases at the corners of his mouth — exhaustion from the bureaucracy, perhaps?

"Thanks for coming up, Jenny," he said with a weary smile. "I know how much you love this place."

"To be honest, Chief, I'd rather be at a kid's birthday party with balloons and a friggin' clown than in this place. But I came because you asked me. What's up?"

"I'm on the horns of a dilemma … and I'm interested in getting your perspective."

"Okay …" said Willson, intrigued. She took a sip from her travel mug filled with Kicking Horse's Kick Ass coffee, strong and black. Until the poaching investigation, she'd consumed anything that looked or smelled like coffee, be it from a fast-food place, a plastic pod, or even a jar of powdered instant; she hadn't cared. But hanging out with a coffee snob had forced her to see the error of her ways. Kick Ass was the only coffee for her. It reflected her approach to life and to her job. Now, she would kick ass whenever possible.

"Before I start," Speer said, "you should know that what I'm about to tell you is not only highly unusual, but also extremely confidential."

"I love a mystery, Chief. Lay it on me."

"Well, do you remember when we talked earlier in the fall about the rumour of a ski area being proposed near the boundary of Yoho Park?"

"I do. But that was just a rumour, wasn't it?"

"Not anymore."

"Are you serious?"

"I'm afraid so. We now have an application. I'm surprised you haven't heard, actually."

"I'm not much for water-cooler gossip. But why the hell would a proposal even be accepted? Wasn't the Parks Act changed back in 2000 so no new ski areas would be allowed?"

Speer leaned back in his chair, his hands linked behind his neck. "Ah, yes. It so happens that our federal government made another change to that same act about three months ago. The change was buried in a mammoth omnibus bill with everything in it from soup to nuts, and it now allows for no more than *two* ski areas *per* mountain park. So, any park with one or none is now open to proposals."

"Are you kidding me?" said Willson. "Why the hell didn't anybody notice?"

"People noticed. By the time they did, though, it had been jammed through Parliament with no discussion or debate. That's what happens with a majority government. A few senators raised a stink when it reached them, but they were outvoted by their colleagues. It's a done deal."

Willson shook her head. "Un-friggin'-believable. Do you think they knew there was a proponent out there in the weeds, waiting to drop this idea on them?"

"I don't know," said Speer. "But you *do* have to wonder. Regardless, an American developer from Idaho — a guy named Stafford Austin — made a joint proposal to

Parks Canada and the government of B.C. shortly after the legislation was amended. He wants to develop a new ski area in Collie Creek, on the northwest boundary of Yoho. He's calling it Top of the World Resort. Part of it's inside the park, part outside. That's why he had to approach both governments."

"I know Collie Creek," said Willson. "There are back-country huts in the two adjacent valleys, and Collie Creek sits between the two. We used to ski and hike there when I lived in Golden. And didn't we recently approve a new CMC hut in that area?"

"Yes, we did. When Austin dropped the idea on the two governments, they tried to keep it quiet. That didn't last long. The Mountain Club members were seriously pissed when they got wind of it. But Austin's already telling the media there'll be millions of dollars invested, more people will visit the park, Golden will get a whack of new jobs, and its reputation as a world-class winter playground will grow. He's selling it as the best thing since the internet."

"But it's in the middle of nowhere. What the hell is he thinking?"

"You know the drill. It'll be gondolas and lift towers and ski runs and a resort base — potentially even a town-site. People will come from all over the world to ski there, he says. On paper, the project looks damn impressive."

"Sounds to me like a dumbass idea for all sorts of reasons," Willson said. "No one's taking it seriously, are they?"

"You know how these things can take on a life of their own. Once the review processes start and politicians get involved, it's like an avalanche, gathering speed and power, burying everything in its path. This one is already moving, and I'm getting strong indications from my sources in Ottawa that federal ministers are interested. And with the parks legislation out of the way, it's suddenly become a possibility."

"Forgive a stupid question, Chief," said Willson, "but why are we talking about this? It's a problem for Yoho Park, not us, right?"

Speer smiled, but there was no warmth in it. "You know that Jack Church is the park superintendent for Yoho. You may not know that his father was my first boss when I joined the Warden Service thirty-four years ago. I have all the respect in the world for Church Senior, but I don't quite feel the same about Church Junior."

"Why?"

"Because he's one of those ladder-climbing pissants that you and I hate so much, and he'll do whatever our bosses tell him to do, no matter how asinine.... I trust you won't repeat that."

"Of course not," said Willson. She wondered where this rant was leading.

"Well, my sources have already raised questions about the ski area proponent," Speer said, "about his background and his ability to make the project happen — the kinds of questions whispered behind cupped hands rather than asked aloud. And there's also a pile of questions about the impact a resort would have on the park, on its environmental and recreation values. But Church seems willing to ignore them all. From what I hear, he's rapidly become the project's biggest cheerleader inside Parks."

"What does it matter what he thinks?" asked Willson. "Won't all those questions be answered by the federal and provincial review processes? The ultimate decisions will be made above him, won't they?"

"Some, but not all of them. From what I can see, Jack's too much of a keener to understand what he's getting into … or what he could unwittingly do to the park."

"I get that a ski area would have huge negative impacts on the park, but why are you concerned about Church?"

"I don't give a rat's ass about him, really. It's all about the park. But he's a symptom of a much deeper problem in the system. The more people there are like him, the less likely it is a project like this will get a thorough, unbiased assessment."

"What are you thinking?"

"I don't know. At this point, I'm venting, just thinking out loud. I'd love to find a way to expose the project for what it is: a tremendously dumb idea that would have major impacts on Yoho." Looking uncharacteristically lost, Speer stared at her. "Any thoughts?"

Willson stared back, her mind racing from one potential plan to the next. Some were crazy and easily discarded. Others were over the line, and would surely end up with her in jail. And some were too complicated, with too many factors that could go sideways. But then she thought of her mother living alone in Golden, struggling with depression. "You need someone on the inside," she finally said. "Someone based in Yoho who could quietly turn over a few rocks and see what's really going on."

Speer's expression slowly changed from confusion to anticipation. "What do you have in mind?"

"If a certain Banff warden were seconded to Yoho, maybe to take an existing vacant position there, perhaps under the pretense of strengthening their law enforcement capacity, that individual could then do what few others could or would be willing to …"

Speer smiled, his eyes sparkling. "Do you happen to know such a person, Jenny? Perhaps someone whose mother lives in Golden and would benefit from some time with her daughter?"

"I do … and I'm guessing you could make it happen with one call to Jack Church."

Willson watched Speer swivel his chair around to stare out the window. After a moment, he turned back. "How does six months sound, with an option to go to twelve if you need it?"

"Sounds good, Chief."

"Consider it done." He sat forward in his chair, hands clasped, his forearms on the desk. "Now … I've already told you this is highly confidential. You won't quite be undercover, but no one except you and me will know why you're there. If Church gets wind of what you're up to, he'll send you packing so fast your head will spin. And because you wouldn't be reporting to me, I'd have a tougher time protecting you…. If this goes bad, it could be career-ending."

"I'm not overly concerned," said Willson, shaking her head. "I'll keep things low-key. If there's anything going on, I'll let you know. And what I'm doing will be none of Jack Church's business."

"I'll phone him now to get you an interview for the position. Once it's confirmed, we can set you up with a place to live in Field, or in Golden, if you prefer. Unless you want to stay with your mother."

Willson sat back in her chair, unconsciously mimicking her boss's earlier body language by linking her hands behind her neck and fixing her gaze on the ceiling. The swirling patterns in the wood mirrored her thoughts. "No, I'd rather have my own space."

"Speaking of your mother, how is she?"

"She hasn't been doing too well recently. It's coming up on the day my dad died twenty years ago."

"Sorry to hear that," Speer said. "Will you give her my regards next time you see her?"

"I'll do that, thanks." Willson looked out the window, taking a moment to compose herself. It was always hard, damn hard, to talk about her mother's depression. Willson thought about her, worried about her, every day.

"What will you do with the information I dig up?" she asked, changing the subject to something less painful.

"At this point, I'm not sure yet," said Speer. "We'll have to decide. If it matches what comes out in the review processes, we won't need to do anything. But if you uncover something different or new, then ... we may need to take a different approach."

"I'm ready to get started. But I do have one request."

She could see that Speer hadn't expected her to request a quid pro quo. His eyebrows lifted and the corners of his mouth turned down slightly.

"What is it?"

"You remember Tracy Brown from the U.S. Fish and Wildlife Service in Spokane? I worked her with on the Castillo-Eastman poaching case. Well, she wants me to join her on a secondment to Namibia to teach investigative techniques to wildlife officers. The government there's working on multiple fronts to conserve wildlife, including doing a better job of convicting poachers. They're willing to pay for us to go over there, including our salaries. I'm excited about it. My grandmother travelled to Namibia many years ago. Her stories always made me want to go. I still have one of the postcards she sent me."

"Where the hell is Namibia?"

"It's on the west coast of Africa. It's the next country up from South Africa."

"How long have you known about this?"

"She only told me about it six weeks ago, a few days after we wrapped up the poaching case. I haven't mentioned it because it was still a big maybe, but it seems more definite now."

"It sounds great, Jenny," said Speer. "And I can see why you'd want to do it. But this ski area project is happening now, so —"

"Timing shouldn't be an issue. The application and visa processes will take a while. From what I've heard from Tracy, it may not happen for another year. What I need from you, please, is a letter of support so I can submit my name with Tracy's and get the ball rolling. I also need you to run interference so the bigwigs in Calgary don't get in the way. There shouldn't be any reason for them to, anyway; it won't cost them a cent."

"Well, if that's all, I'd say we've got a deal. I'll phone Church and set it up. I can't thank you enough for this." Speer stood and held out his hand.

Willson gripped it. "I just hope it all works out. How about holding off on the thanks until we see where this leads us?"

"Fair enough," he said, walking her to the door. "Go turn over some rocks. See what crawls out."

Willson said goodbye to Scott and closed the outer door to Speer's office. She paused in the hallway, her hand still on the doorknob. Had this truly been her own idea, her ingenious response to Speer's dilemma? Had he really shared it with her only to clarify his own thoughts, without expecting a resolution? Or had the crafty old warden been nudging her toward suggesting this inside-woman plan from the start? With a wry smile, she acknowledged it could be a little of both — it didn't matter. She was ready to protect some wilderness and kick some proponent ass.

CHAPTER 3

DECEMBER 2

Stafford Austin stood motionless in the centre of the bank's spacious lobby. He was a big man at six foot five and three hundred pounds. Currents of people flowed around him like water around a massive midstream boulder.

Moments before, his account manager had beamed a professional smile when Austin slid the certified cheque across the desk, his fingers lingering on the edge of the paper. But the banker's attempt at nonchalance was betrayed by his wide eyes. It was a substantial initial deposit, and made with the hint of more to come.

Through the lobby's floor-to-ceiling windows, Austin watched a parade of cars on Burrard Street waiting to escape Vancouver's downtown. Water streamed down the glass, distorting the headlights and tail lights into blurs of colour and motion. The blasts of car horns were sharp, impatient. A sense of urgency expressed itself as a pressure deep in Austin's chest.

For a moment, he considered hailing a taxi. But he knew his chances of getting one were slim in the midst of Friday afternoon rush hour. Instead, he chose to walk. By the end of the first block, he realized he'd made the wrong decision. Horizontal pulses of rain were coming at him as if thrown from a bucket, apparently unmitigated by the tall buildings all around. He'd grown up in Florida, so he knew rain and wind. But there, it had always been warm. Here? He didn't understand how people could live like this. It was grey and dismal, cold and wet; the damp crept into his bones. Standing beside him at an intersection, people huddled in raincoats and under flapping umbrellas, their faces resigned. He'd been told that Vancouver's rain started in November and kept coming in depressing, persistent waves until March. The streetlight changed and he continued walking, shivering at the thought of the months of suffering ahead.

Two blocks more and he'd reached the Terminal City Club on West Hastings Street, at the edge of Vancouver's financial district. He shook the water off his umbrella and pulled open the heavy glass door, his hand slick on the round handle. The lobby was warm and inviting, living up to its billing as the one of the oldest and most respected private member clubs in the city, a refined place where one could transition seamlessly from business to pleasure.

He greeted the friendly concierge as he passed and smiled when she responded to him by name. *This place knows how to do things right*, he thought. But when he looked down, he was embarrassed to see his leather boots were water stained, his lower pant legs sodden. He looked as though he'd walked through a shallow pond.

Leaving dark, wet footprints in the rich carpet, he squished along the hallway, up a set of stairs, then turned left, water still dripping from his raincoat. Hearing the clink of glasses and the hum of relaxed conversation coming from the Cuvée Wine Bar, he paused and stared at himself in a tall mirror. As one of the club's newest members, he still felt like a visitor on foreign turf. But early on, he'd decided to do all he could to be part of this world, to be respected and admired, slapped on the back and recognized as one of them. These were his people, whether or not they knew it yet. By being accepted as a member, Austin had gained a shortcut to new connections. Money in search of more money. He had to make it work — and he knew he could. He pulled his shoulders back, smiled, and proceeded to the bar.

Passing his raincoat and umbrella to the waiter, Austin spotted the man he was looking for seated at a small table across the room: He was a solid six-footer in a bespoke suit and polished shoes, with blond hair, designer eyeglasses, and a five o'clock shadow. In his left hand he gripped a glass of amber liquid.

Austin had researched the man carefully before requesting this meeting. Matt Merrix was a thirty-five-year-old Vancouver-based agent for a sports management company in Toronto. After an NHL career just long enough to have had a cup of coffee, he'd played ten seasons with professional teams in Finland and Italy. Now Merrix had an MBA from a prestigious business program and an impressive list of contacts. He represented hockey players and other sports figures around the globe, handling their contract negotiations, tax compliance, insurance, endorsements, and marketing plans. For many, he also handled their accounting and banking.

Austin also knew that Merrix, despite the claims on his website, was at best a second-tier agent. His clients weren't the elite stars, although it was possible that one of them might graduate from junior or university hockey to become the next big thing. Instead, he represented third- and fourth-line NHL players, players on the rosters of European teams, players who rode buses in the American Hockey League or the East Coast Hockey League, players whose NHL dreams had been crushed by the realities of supply and demand. Still, many of them received salaries and endorsement cheques to rival those of corporate CEOs. It was this access to large amounts of capital and Merrix's ability to influence where and when that capital was invested that intrigued Austin.

"Matt," he said, offering his large right hand as he reached the table, "thanks for your time today."

"I'm pleased we could do this, Stafford," said the agent, standing to shake. "It's good to finally put a face to the voice on the phone."

"Agreed," said Austin, as he sat and ordered a beer from the attentive waiter. He glanced down at his sodden pants. "Another wet one out there. What's your schedule like tonight, Matt?"

"I've got an hour before I'm off to Rogers Arena for the Canucks game. Two of my clients are playing. I have an extra ticket if you'd like to join me."

"Excellent." Austin was a baseball fan and, until a few weeks ago, had known little about hockey. But he wasn't about to tell Merrix that. He'd spent days studying books, stats, and game films to gain enough information to play the role of average fan rather than clueless hick. "I haven't had time yet to watch a game this season, and it would be good to see that new kid on the Oilers' roster, the one everyone's talking about."

When Austin's drink arrived, they toasted to a Canucks victory. Then Merrix quickly shifted the talk to business. "So, you said you had an interesting investment opportunity that some of my clients might like?"

Austin paused before responding, taking a slow, thoughtful sip of his beer. Even though in his mind his pitch was a perfect balance between science and art, numbers and passion, he understood that guys like Merrix would be approached dozens of times a month about new business opportunities. And although Merrix's clients were often seen as wealthy and largely uneducated — ideal targets for get-rich-quick schemes — that's where mistakes were made and doors slammed closed before they'd opened more than a crack. Austin knew that today's pro athletes surrounded themselves with lawyers, accountants, and business advisers: perceptive people like Merrix. Austin's approach had to be professional, credible, and compelling.

"I do," he said. He lined up the edge of his cocktail napkin with the edge of the marble tabletop, then placed his glass in the centre of the linen. Everything had to line up. "It's a little-known fact that a recent change to federal legislation allows for new ski areas to be built in some of Canada's national parks. The investment community has yet to pick up on it. While ski hills in parts of B.C. and Alberta and even in Europe are suffering the effects of climate change, I've found an intriguing high-elevation site in Yoho National Park that gets lots of snow and has some of the biggest glaciers in southern Canada. It's on the north edge of the park, between Banff and Jasper, on the border between B.C. and Alberta. The number of skiers in the world is growing each year, so there's going to come a time, sooner rather than later, when an undeveloped, high-quality location like this will be extremely rare. It may already be. And rare means valuable."

"And you're looking for investors."

"I'm looking for investors who want to get in on the early stages of a project that will, by completion, be worth something in the order of five hundred million. It won't just be a ski hill. There's a base resort component with condos and hotels, and there's also significant potential for summer activity. I'm calling it the Top of the World Resort."

"You've probably heard that some NHL players were burned in the Bear Mountain project near Victoria," said Merrix, his eyes narrowing. "A lot of money disappeared in that one, Stafford, something like thirteen million dollars. Everyone in my world is nervous about that kind of investment. How is this different?"

"I heard about that," Austin said. He'd known Bear Mountain would come up. "There are two key differences here. The first is the unique nature of this project. Bear Mountain was a golf course development that started at the same time as many other similar projects, just before the economy took a nosedive. It was one more project among many at a time when the market was already saturated with golf courses and golf resorts. Whereas Top of the World is a unique project that, if we get the approvals, will meet a growing demand others can't satisfy. Instead of being late to a party that's already over, this is an opportunity to be first in the door."

"And the second difference?"

"You mean aside from the fact that I won't be taking millions out of the business to buy an NHL team?"

"Yes, aside from that." Merrix smiled.

"This will be an investment fund, a fund that will not focus solely on the ski resort," Austin said. "I don't want all our eggs in one basket, and I want the level of risk to be low. There will be other investments to support guaranteed regular returns to investors. These include shares in other businesses, commercial mortgages, dividend stocks, etc. The resort project, as one of the core holdings in the fund, will be phased in over a number of years. So initial investors can, if they wish, take their money out, plus interest, at specified intervals. Or they can reinvest their earnings and grow their ownership stake in the larger fund."

"You mentioned guaranteed returns. What are you thinking?"

"I'm looking at guarantees in the range of 10 to 12 percent per annum for initial investors."

"Huh. That's very attractive, especially with interest rates so low," said Merrix. "How are you setting up the investment structure?"

"The resort application was submitted under the name of Collie Creek Resorts Limited, but all investments will flow through the Collie Investment Fund. It's registered with the B.C. Securities Commission. Initially, investors will receive certificates of deposit to confirm their investment and their rates of return. Later, they can also choose to become owners in key components of the resort project as it unfolds." Austin reached into his briefcase and passed two documents across the table to Merrix. The first was a promotional brochure for the ski area filled with facts, figures, and dramatic colour images. The second was the formal prospectus for the investment fund.

"We'd better get going," said Merrix, looking at this watch. "You can tell me more on the drive over."

Three hours later, after the Vancouver team had beaten Edmonton, Austin was introduced to two of Merrix's clients in the hall between the dressing rooms. One was a Canucks veteran defenceman on the verge of a new contract, the other a young forward in his first stint with the Oilers. At Merrix's request, a passing equipment manager captured a photo of the four of them together. The men were all smiling, each for a different reason.

"I like what I heard from you tonight," said Merrix as they parted company outside the arena. "And it's good to deal with someone who knows hockey. I'll call you in the next few days once I've spoken with a few of my guys."

It was still raining. Austin wasn't going to make the same mistake twice in one day. He climbed into a waiting taxi, cautiously optimistic that his sales pitch had gone well and the agent would recommend the investment fund to his clients. But nothing was certain until the money flowed. As the taxi worked its way through traffic back to the Terminal City Club, Austin, pleased with the evening's efforts, chatted with the young driver as if he cared what the man had to say. All that mattered was that the first element of his business plan was in motion.

CHAPTER 4

DECEMBER 2

As soon as Willson walked through the front door of the library, she grasped the important role it played in the community of Golden, B.C. It was a physical space where locals gathered, learned, and caught up on local news. She saw people of all ages scattered around the large room, from seniors reading newspapers to a group of children gathered around a librarian who was enthusiastically telling them a story, holding the picture book to face them and pointing to the illustrations as she read.

A bank of computer stations, all occupied, lined the wall on the west side of the building. As Willson circled behind the users, she saw faces intent on the screens, fingers picking hesitantly at keyboards. Mesmerized by what they were looking at, they ignored her. She understood that these machines might be these users' only connection to the internet, perhaps to the rest of the world, either because they couldn't afford a computer or because they were strangers to technology.

Willson had grown up in Golden, a town of 3,700 in the Rocky Mountain Trench on the eastern edge of British Columbia. Back then, logging and the railroad had driven the economy, and the community had been predominantly white, so she was surprised by what she observed now: a Filipino family sat in the corner reading together, two elderly women pointed at a grainy photograph in a Cantonese newspaper, a middle-aged East Asian man studied the back of a hardcover book in the mystery section. Things had changed.

Willson joined the queue at the front desk, standing behind a mother and three young children as they checked out their books. Gone were the index cards to be date-stamped and tucked into pouches in the front covers of books. Now the process was all vigorous swipes across digital chip readers, electronic beeps, and paper receipts, like from a store till. She smiled to see the three children's flashing eyes, their eager movements. Their excitement to get their new treasures home was palpable. She fondly remembered feeling the same way on summer holidays and winter weekends, clutching a pile of new books tight to her chest. That hadn't changed. One of the kids, a young boy, sat cross-legged at his mother's feet, already reading, unwilling to wait. Once the books were checked out, the young mother corralled her children toward the door, and the boy continued reading as he wandered behind her, unaware of anything but the world between the covers. His mother gently steered him out of a near collision with the doorframe.

Willson stepped forward as the librarian turned to look at her. "Hi, Mum," Willson said. "Ready for lunch?"

"Oh, Jenny," said Anne Willson in a librarian's whisper, a smile breaking across her face, "I'm *so* glad to see you."

She came around the desk and gave her daughter a long hug. She was thin, much thinner than when Willson had last seen her, her sandy blond hair now completely overtaken by grey. Her face had also thinned, and in contrast to her bright smile, her eyes showed lines of sadness and fatigue. Willson was troubled that Anne looked much older than her sixty years.

"Can you get away for lunch?"

"Yes. Let me tell Heather I'm leaving. Then I'm done for the day."

The two women walked the four blocks from the library to Jita's Café, crossing Highway 95 near the Kicking Horse River. They sat facing each other in a high-backed booth with a view of the Purcell Mountain Range to the west and the Rockies to the east. Both ordered chicken curry wraps and chai tea. Around them swirled the usual lunchtime collection of athletic post-yoga mothers, dirtbag skiers fresh off a morning run on the local hill, and late-season tourists who'd wandered in on their way down the Rocky Mountain Trench. But in the booth, just the two of them, they were in a world of their own.

"Jenny, I'm happy you're here … and *so* pleased you might be moving back."

"Me, too, Mum. But nothing's decided yet. I have a meeting with the park superintendent this afternoon, so I should know by tomorrow."

"It'll be nice to have some company," Anne said, a tear suddenly running down one cheek, "and just in time for Christmas. It's been years since we spent time together. But I do know you'll be busy, so I don't want to be a burden. *If* you move here, that is …"

Willson reached across the table to grab her mother's hand. "I'm here now," she said softly, "and you're never a burden. Tell me how you're doing, Mum."

That one small prompt punched a hole in Anne's emotional dam. She started slowly, strained words trickling through the breach. "I just can't believe that soon your father will have been gone twenty years. I still miss him terribly. Some days are better than others, but there are lots of mornings where I struggle to get out of bed. When I really can't cope with things, Heather, the head librarian, lets me spend my shift reshelving the returned books so I don't have to talk to people. It's very understanding of her. And, oh —" she said, changing track before Willson could fully process what she'd said, "I finally got my widow's pension from the railway sorted out. They'd stopped it for two months because of a clerical error in head office! It was tough, I had to make do on just my part-time salary. But at least it's coming in again."

"Wait," Willson interrupted, "they stopped your pension cheque for two months and you didn't tell me? You should have called, Mum, I could have helped."

"I didn't want to bother you. I know how occupied you were with your investigation."

Willson held her mother's hand and let her talk. She was starting to realize just how bad Anne's depression had become. Things like going out to buy groceries or making an appointment at the bank, simple tasks for most people, were insurmountable challenges for Anne on a bad day. Worse still, her daily routine had become isolated and unvaried, apart from the library, and devoid of any activities to look forward to or enjoy. It sounded almost as if her life had lost meaning, as melodramatic as it sounded, and that scared Willson. Though Anne had struggled with chronic depression on and off over for the last couple of decades, she had still moved through life with purpose and curiosity. But now it seemed she was merely going through the motions. Gazing into Anne's troubled eyes, Willson was relieved she'd come up with the plan to spend time in Golden. It had been the right decision for all sorts of reasons. Her presence here, even if only temporary, might give her mother something to focus on besides her sadness. But Willson was also sure that her mother needed more than just her company; she needed professional help.

By two in the afternoon, the café was quiet. They were the last customers left, and Anne had run out of steam. Willson paid the bill, and they began the slow, cold walk back to the library, where they had both left their cars.

"Are you seeing anyone?" Anne asked, her eyes lifting from a damp café napkin still clutched in her gloved hand.

"Not right now. I haven't met anyone yet who's worth a second date."

"I'm sorry to hear that. You deserve to find someone nice. Are you still doing that internet thing?"

"If by 'that internet thing' you mean online dating, Mum, then yes, I'm still doing that. It seems to be the most common way to meet people these days."

"I can't imagine what that would be like. Is it a good idea to have your personal information online for anyone to see?"

"I choose what I share," said Willson, "and not everyone in the world can see it."

"It's just there are lots of wackos and perverts out there. You know, I've mentioned you to some of my friends who have sons. We could introduce you to them."

"We'll see, we'll see." *Shit. Time to change the subject.* "So, Mum, while I'm here, what are we going to do together?"

"We'll have a special dinner tonight to celebrate your possible return. Tomorrow night, there's a thing in town up at the senior centre I'd like to go to. I wouldn't go by myself, but with you here, I think I can do it."

"A thing?"

"Actually, it's an open house about the new ski hill proposal up the Blaeberry River."

"Why would you want to go to that?" As Willson asked the question, a thread of guilt wormed its way into her thoughts. She hadn't imagined having to be dishonest with her mother on her first day back in town. This was going to be tougher than she'd imagined.

"Everyone in town is talking about it," said Anne. "People are asking me about it when they come in to the library — what I know about it, whether I think it's a good idea or not. I don't have enough information to answer their questions."

"If you want to do that, then sure, let's go. If I'm going to be a new warden in the park, I guess I should know something about it, too." She hadn't lied, but neither had she told the truth. Back outside the library, she hugged her mother.

"See you about six," Anne said, looking over the top of her car. "Good luck with your interview."

"Until then, Mum," Willson said, looking back and waving.

With an hour to spare before her meeting with Jack Church, Willson decided to circle the town to see what had changed since she was last there. Still on the south side of the Kicking Horse River, she cruised past her old high school, then the provincial government buildings and city hall. She crossed the river on the narrow two-lane highway bridge and toured the small but vibrant downtown, noticing new stores, restaurants, and coffee shops alongside others that had been there since she was a teenager — a good sign.

She turned in to a back alley that paralleled the river and was shocked by what she saw. What she'd remembered as a charming but ancient log building was now a smoking skeleton of burnt wood criss-crossed on blackened concrete, everything sealed with a thin layer of ice. The entire area, including a burnt-out vehicle, was circled with yellow police tape. Small red flags waved from scattered spots throughout the debris; Willson knew these marked key evidence locations. A van from the provincial fire investigator's office was parked to the north. Nearby, an RCMP officer sat in his cruiser, head down, tapping on the car's computer.

Willson got out and approached the cruiser. "Hi there," she said from a distance, trying not to startle the Mountie.

"Sorry, miss, this is a crime scene. Can I help you?"

His expression changed when she pushed her badge toward him. "I'm Jenny Willson. I'm a law-enforcement specialist with Parks Canada."

The officer levered his long, muscled body out of the car and pushed his hand toward hers. Willson took it, gripped it hard, and looked up all six foot five of the man to his craggy face and deep-blue eyes.

"Corporal Benoit Fortier. Pleased to meet you, Ms. Willson."

"It's Jenny, please. I'm in town visiting my mother and noticed the scene as I drove by," she said, finally letting go of Fortier's hand. "I hope no one was hurt?"

"That was our hope, too. But unfortunately, we found a body inside buried under a collapsed wall. It's too early to determine a cause of death. It was so badly burned that we can't even confirm who it is."

"That's awful. Any idea what happened?"

"I'm fairly certain there was a fire," the Mountie said, smirking. Dark humour like that was common to law enforcement. "We've got a few theories about cause, but the investigators are still working on it." He pointed to a man taking pictures inside the charred ruins, his yellow coveralls a stark contrast to the black wood and white ice.

Another man was sitting on the ground just outside the line of yellow tape facing the smoking ruins with his arms across his knees. His features were blocked by a shock of wild black hair and a beard. "Who's that?" Willson asked.

"Albin Stoffel," said Fortier. "It was his office. He's a wildlife researcher working in the mountains around here. I spoke to him when he arrived here first thing this morning, and he's been sitting there ever since. He's certain the deceased is his research assistant, a woman by the name of Sue Webb. He says that's her car. He's also convinced it was arson … and he keeps saying he knows who did it."

"Who?"

"Well, he claims it was the guy who's proposing the ski area, a guy by the name of Stafford Austin. You've heard about the project, I assume?"

Willson nodded. It was only her first day in town, not even on the job yet, and Fortier was the second person she couldn't be completely honest with about her presence in Golden. And now she'd learned of an unexpected connection to the ski area. If the researcher's accusations were true …

"Could Stoffel himself be responsible?" she asked.

"It's possible, I suppose, but not probable. He was clearly devastated when he arrived this morning. If he did do it, he's a talented actor."

"So why does he think Austin did it?"

"He claims Austin didn't like his research," Fortier said, "and that he did it to silence him."

"That's one hell of an allegation."

"It's a pretty drastic way to make a problem like that disappear. Last summer, Stoffel did lay a complaint against Austin and his partner, though — a guy by the name of Hank Myers. Said they'd threatened him with a gun. I talked to them, but it was a classic 'he said, he said' — no evidence to prove anything. They knew they were on my radar, though, so to go from an alleged threat to arson and murder would be a huge step."

Willson turned toward the burned building, her mind ablaze with questions. And one of them had nothing to do with the fire — she found herself wondering whether this tall, rugged Mountie had a wife or a girlfriend.

"Can I ask what your interest is in all of this?" he asked.

Besides you?

"Nothing at this point," she said, turning back to him. "I'll find out later today if I've got a job in Yoho Park. If I do, and there's a criminal link between this situation and the proposed ski area, I'd like to know about it."

"Fair enough," said Fortier. "I've probably already told you more than I should, but it was colleague to colleague, right?"

"Got it," said Willson. "What did Stoffel lose in the fire?"

"Everything in the building was destroyed," said Fortier. "I was in there last summer when I first met him, and that building was a tinderbox, a firetrap filled with shit from one corner to the other. But he told me today that he keeps digital backups of all his research off-site, and that all his hair samples — whatever they're for — were at his house and are being couriered to the lab today."

"So, we've got an incredibly tragic loss of life for no apparent gain," said Willson, thinking like the investigator she was. "Stoffel will have to find a new office, I guess. What do you know about Stafford Austin?"

"Good question," he said. "I ran background checks on him before I met with him. The only blemish on his record is a pair of charges for fraud in Idaho. No convictions. As far as I can tell, this seems to be the first time he's done business on this side of the border."

"Fraud?"

"Yep. But his partner, Myers, on the other hand, is even *more* interesting. He was discharged from the U.S. Marine Corps for an alleged off-base assault, a serious one, from what I can tell. Wasn't convicted in court, though, military or civilian. His record shows he worked for a series of private security contractors after he left the Corps. I'm wondering what any of that has to do with building a ski area."

"It's not a set of skills I would look for if I were starting a project like that. The only thing those two men seem to have in common is that they both have good lawyers."

"That's exactly what I was thinking," said Fortier, breaking into a wide grin.

Willson's knees almost buckled at the brilliance of Fortier's smile, but she continued calmly. "Because of the possible links between this and the park, could you keep me posted as the investigation evolves? *If* I move here, that is."

"No problem," said Fortier. "I'll tell you as much as I can." He handed Willson his card, and she returned the favour. "Will you be living here in town, or up in the park?"

"I'll be here in town," she said. "My mother lives here." *Why is he asking?*

"Good. It'll be easier to stay in touch." He took her hand again. "Thanks for introducing yourself. I'd better get back to my notes. My boss will want to see them by the end of the day."

Willson watched him fold himself back into the police car, then she turned to again look at the smouldering ruins.

CHAPTER 5

DECEMBER 2

As the sun dropped behind the Purcell Mountains, splashing the sky with vivid streaks of red and yellow, eleven people settled into old couches and mismatched chairs in the basement of a home on the McMurdo Benches. Like many houses in the rural subdivision south of Golden, it sat on a rocky knoll surrounded by trees, linked to Campbell Road by a long gravel driveway. Through a gap in the forest, the house offered its resident a western view of a slice of the Columbia River wetlands that stretched 180 kilometres, north to south, at the bottom of the Rocky Mountain Trench.

Some of the evening's visitors clutched mugs of tea; others sipped something a bit stronger. An ancient wood stove crackled and popped in the corner. The conversation was quiet and subdued.

The owner of the house remained standing. Fit and vibrant in her sixties, with grey hair cut short and parted in the middle, Sara Ilsley stood with the confidence of someone who'd spoken in public many times and was comfortable taking charge. As a retired forestry professor and consultant who'd moved to the valley three years earlier, Ilsley was respected by everyone in the room, not only for her intelligence and background, but also for her passion about their shared values. Behind her, wedged in the corner, a stack of blank flip charts sat on an easel, with a rainbow of felt markers nearby.

"Let's get started, people," she said, pausing to look at each person in turn. "In my opinion, this issue will define the Columbia Valley Environmental Society for decades. More importantly, it has the potential to change the nature of our whole area, to alter the quality of our lives. Personally, I can't think of a more important reason to work together."

Ilsley looked at her audience's nodding, earnest faces and continued. "To do that, we have to get our shit together — pardon my French. Now, I'll bet that when you first heard about the Collie Creek ski area, what the developer is calling Top of the World, you all laughed. You probably thought it was ridiculous, a hare-brained scheme that made no sense. You thought, I'm sure, that it wouldn't go anywhere. But things have changed. The monster is now among us. Governments and their legions of bureaucrats are now involved. And when that happens, we know from previous experience that logic and common sense go out the window. None of them — not the proponent, not the government staff who run the review process, not the senior bureaucrats and politicians in Victoria, Calgary, and Ottawa who make decisions — none of them cares about us, our valley, the place where we live and work and play. Our organization must take this project seriously, because the monster has momentum. And momentum is dangerous. We've got to actively engage in every stage of the review process, as flawed and one-sided as it may be. We must play the role that no one else is playing, speak for values that can't speak for themselves. And to do this, we have to be smarter than the proponent. They've got money behind them ... and they seem to have the ear of both the federal and provincial government. I don't think I'm overstating the situation by suggesting that this is going to be an uphill battle of epic proportions."

For a long moment, she was quiet, staring at the wood stove, her face lit by its orange, flickering light. Her mouth was a tight line, her hands steepled under her nose as if in prayer. She was clearly in her element. She'd been the ideal candidate for executive director of the Society. She knew it, and the board of directors had come to know it in her first interview.

"In my opinion," Ilsley said, "the work we undertake together to oppose this project, starting tonight, will be more important than anything any of us has ever done. If we're going to succeed, we have to throw everything we have at it. Each and every one of us has to commit to this, and we have to find others willing to do the same."

She paused. "Before we start, Albin Stoffel sends his regrets. Many of you know about Albin's wolverine research, and some of you know that, tragically, his office burned to the ground last night. Albin wanted to be here tonight, but he's busy finding a new office and dealing with the aftermath of the fire." Some heads were shaking; many in the room were likely thinking about the body found in the ruins. "Who's ready to get started?"

"Count me in," said a bearded man sitting in the corner. He was in his early twenties and his eyes shone with excitement. "But what the hell do we do?"

"I've got some ideas," said Ilsley, "but if we're ready to work together, I think we should start by talking about what *you* think we should do."

The young man slid so far forward that he was barely in contact with the chair. "I don't know," he said. "I've never done anything like this before. I guess we could use Facebook to get the message out, to let people know that the ski resort is a crazy idea. And we should all attend the project open house tomorrow night so we can get more information. Even though we know it'll be mostly bullshit."

"Great point," said Ilsley, chuckling. "We should all be there."

"We need slogans," said a mother of three who lived next door. "And I refuse to use the developer's name for the project. In my mind, that somehow legitimizes it. So, how about "Keep Collie Wild" or "Conserve Collie"?

"And what about rallies?" asked a younger woman beside her, sitting back deep in a couch. "Let's demonstrate in front of politicians' offices. In front of the town hall. Let them know we oppose the project. Get the local newspaper there. Make them listen to us and our concerns."

Ilsley began taking notes on a flip chart. Facebook. Social media. Slogans. Rallies. "This is good," she said, "keep the ideas coming." She wanted them to engage, brainstorm, find their way as a group to the big picture, to a course of action. But there was one idea bouncing around in her own mind that she wanted to get on the table. Finally, she couldn't wait any longer. "What if we submit a competing proposal?"

The young woman who had suggested rallies looked at her with confusion. "But we don't want a ski area up there! What good would that do?"

"It would mean," said Ilsley, smiling, "that the government couldn't immediately work with Stafford Austin. They'd have to decide which proponent had the right to proceed. If they chose us, then we could string them along for a while until Austin moved on. Then, when he was out of the picture, we could withdraw our interest. But even if they didn't choose us, it would still cost Austin time and money." Her idea was met with nods, so she added it to the flip chart.

"I think we should set up a blockade at the bottom of Collie Creek," said another, much older woman. "We did that to stop logging on Vancouver Island back in the eighties and nineties."

"You mean like a protest camp?" one of the women asked.

"That's exactly what I mean. We would not only stop them from getting in there to do their studies, we'd also prevent them from building the resort if, god forbid, they ever got approval. And a blockade is a good way to get media attention, get people to hear to what we're saying. Standing in a determined line across a road, arms linked, makes for a great front-page photo."

"If you want do that," said Ilsley, "you've got to be willing to be arrested."

"Not a problem," the woman said with a grin. "I got arrested three times back then, and I'll do it again if I need to. I can think of worse things than strolling down a logging road arm-in-arm with a pair of handsome Mounties."

Everyone laughed. Everyone, that is, but a middle-aged man in the corner. "With all due respect," he said, "we're talking about small actions that, on their own, won't make a bit of difference to a project of this scale. What we need to do is to develop a strategy … a campaign … a battle plan … like we're going to war. These guys are smart and they appear to have money behind them. We need plans and backup plans. We need to understand what resources we'll require, and that will include money. Lots of money. We need to consider every side of this, and we need to hit it from many different angles. We've got be smart and coordinated."

"You're right," said Ilsley. "What I'm trying to do is get as many ideas as we can think of down on paper. Then we can organize them into a campaign plan, just like you suggest. This is going to take lots of work, and we're going to need more than just the twelve of us to make this happen. Tonight is only the first of many meetings."

"Okay," said the man, "I want to be sure we all understand that this is a big deal; we can't go off like we're shooting a pellet gun in the air, trying to knock the project down with sheer luck."

By late in the evening, Ilsley had filled many flip chart pages with ideas. One led to another, which led to another.

"And we have to start calling it a mega-resort," said the older woman, smiling.

"What does that even mean?" asked Ilsley.

"I have *no* idea ... probably nothing. But people won't take us seriously unless they know it's not just a ski resort, but a *mega*-resort."

Smiling herself, Ilsley wrote *MEGA-RESORT* at the top of the paper.

Looking around the room, she sensed that the energy had begun to wane. People's batteries were running low. "Perhaps it's time that we —"

"I've got a question," said one young man, interrupting Ilsley. He was sitting in a darkened corner of the room, dressed in worn blue jeans and a long-sleeved camouflage shirt, a ball cap pulled down over his eyes. It was the first time he'd spoken all night. "Do we have to follow the rules?"

Ilsley turned to him. "What do you mean?"

"Earlier," he said, his arms folded across his chest, "we started talking about blockades and getting arrested and stuff. If we want to stop the project, if we all believe that a new resort will be bad for the community and bad for the environment, then how far are we willing to go to stop it?"

"What do you mean?" Ilsley asked again, more alert than she'd been all evening.

"I'm not thinking about anything specific ... yet," said the young man, his eyes still hidden. "But we've all seen it before. The review processes for big projects like this are always slanted in favour of the rich, not people like us. It's like being in front of a fucking steam roller. If we stay there too long, playing by their rules, we get flattened. If we jump out of the way, it rolls past us to where it was going anyway. We lose either way. We're stupid if we think otherwise. Our only real option is to put sugar in the gas tank of the process ... or blow the fucker up."

The warmth of the wood stove did nothing to dispel the sudden chill that enveloped the room. Ilsley shivered. "You're talking about breaking the law," she said, shifting to professor mode. "Let me explain something to you, and to everyone here. Civil disobedience is the public, non-violent, and conscientious breach of law undertaken with the aim of changing laws or government policies. We saw that in the forest industry — blockades were common in B.C. for a while — and we've seen them on pipelines. You've all heard of the Standing Rock blockade in North Dakota. Perhaps we'll end up doing that as a tactic in our campaign. It's an important part of taking a stand. If we do, we must be respectful, and whatever we do has to be non-violent. And we'll have to think carefully about the implications, not just for our campaign, but for us as individuals, too."

She paused, crossing her arms across her chest. She looked at each person in the room in turn. "Let me also remind you that anything beyond civil disobedience is criminal activity. It's nothing more than eco-terrorism. I can't and won't condone our being part of that. Not only is it against the Society's constitution and bylaws, but someone could end up in jail for a very long time. And most importantly, we'd lose all public support that we might have gained for our cause. Eco-terrorists who resort to violence are dealt with harshly in this country, both by our courts and in the court of public opinion. As they should be. We saw that when protestors spiked trees and destroyed logging equipment. Am I clear?"

"Hey lady, chill," said the young man, holding up his hands and showing his palms. He tilted his head to one side. "I was only asking a question."

Ilsley looked at the man for a moment. As experienced as she was, the question had shocked and surprised her. And she was angry at herself for not anticipating it, or something like it. She realized then that everyone in the room was staring at her, confused, as if they were children waiting for direction. The young man's outburst had dramatically changed the mood of the evening.

"Uh … I think it's time we called it a night," she said. "We've made a good start. Thank you all for your participation. I'll organize these notes and then get them out by email. Let's get together here again next week, same time, same night."

Eleven people shuffled out the door into the frigid darkness, leaving Ilsley standing in her open doorway, frozen in place with the heavy wood door at her back. Unconsciously, she again folded her arms across her chest as she watched the procession of red tail lights disappear down her driveway. A truck, the young man's, was the last to leave. She glimpsed his face as the truck slowly passed her house with its lights off. After locking and bolting the door behind her, Ilsley leaned against it, pondering the young man's question … and the dark pits where his eyes should have been.

CHAPTER 6

DECEMBER 3

"Hello, and welcome to the Top of the World open house," said the man standing inside the front door of the Golden Senior Centre. "My name is Hank Myers. I'm with Collie Creek Resorts Limited. Feel free to wander around the display boards. I or my partner will answer any questions."

Myers was a tall, muscular man, with tightly curled black hair and a skier's goggle tan. His dark slacks were pressed, his brown loafers shined, and his blue blazer looked new and expensive. To Willson, he seemed more like a bouncer at an exclusive club than a land developer hosting an open house.

"Thanks," she said, taking a brochure without introducing herself or her mother.

"Could I ask you both to please sign the visitor sheet?" Myers asked.

"You could, but we'd rather not," said Willson, moving past him.

Willson and her mother slowly circled the bright room, moving from one display to the next. Willson paused at a large wall map showing the project's location. As expected, a bold line captured the upper Collie Creek drainage. But the map also showed that the proponent had his eye on parts of the Ayesha, Des Poilus, Yoho, and Wapta glaciers in the Yoho River valley, as well. She carefully traced her finger along the boundary of Yoho National Park and stopped at the point where she knew the new Mountain Club hut was located. She tapped the map once, twice. *Shit, at least a third of the project is inside the national park, and the hut is in the centre of it all.*

Willson's mother, oblivious to her daughter's musings, pointed her own finger at the adjacent drainages. "This is so close to the huts in Wildcat Creek and Amiskwi River, Jenny. You remember when your father used to take us hiking and skiing there? I wonder what they think about this."

"I can't imagine they're happy," Willson said. "If the idea goes ahead, it might create better access for them and their guests, but that whole area is going to be a very different place."

As they circulated around the room, she was surprised by how many of the people there knew her mother. She was introduced many times. "This is my daughter, Jenny. She's a park warden and just found out today that she's moving back to town …"

The two Willsons continued their tour, reading charts about the local economy and graphs showing how the global ski market was changing. They looked over lists of site details like vertical drop, aspect, and snowfall; artist renderings of lift towers and cables crossing ridges and peaks; a map showing the overlap with traditional territories of the area's indigenous peoples; and a stylized illustration of a future resort base. In the absence of a critical eye, it may have seemed exciting, full of hope and promise, like Disneyland for skiers. A magic ski kingdom.

But Willson was a cynic. Instead, she saw a significant change to the park and to the wild area to the north of it. The project was no longer a rumour, no longer something conceptual casually discussed across a desk with her boss. And she could tell that the applicants had put impressive amounts of time, effort, and money into the proposal. It was no half-assed scheme sketched on the back of an envelope with a crayon. *These guys really are serious about this*, she thought. And with that, the implications of her deal with Frank Speer took on a new reality.

Her meeting with Jack Church the previous afternoon had confirmed her fears. After he'd approved her secondment to the park, he had, without any prompting from Willson, expounded on the benefits of the proposed ski area, showing himself to be as much a champion of the project as Speer had painted him to be. She'd had to use every ounce of self-control to not question or contradict him.

She felt her mother's touch on her arm. "Are you okay, Jenny?"

"I'm good, Mum," she said, her trance broken. "I'm trying to decide how I feel about this." She was supposed to be her mother's security blanket for the evening, comforting and calming in this public setting. She was fine with that. Now, with a gentle hand on her arm, her mother had returned the favour.

They moved on to a display about the environmental impacts of the project. Willson mentally ran through her own checklist of items she thought the proponent should address. Wildlife and habitat issues? Check. Fishery issues? Check. Water quality and quantity? Check. Vegetation? Check. Geology and soils? Yup. Impacts of new road access and traffic on Collie Creek and the Blaeberry River? Nope. Missing. Climate change and receding glaciers? Nowhere to be seen. *Are they only going to tell us the good news?* she wondered.

Suddenly she felt a tap on her shoulder. "Hi, ladies," said a bearded man, his voice revealing the lilt of a Swiss accent. "I'm Albin Stoffel." He glanced over his shoulder and lowered his voice. "I don't work for the proponent. I'm actually studying wolverines in the central Rockies." He was wearing stained Carhartt pants and a badly pilled fleece jacket, and he had a wild shock of curly, dark hair that looked as if hadn't seen a brush in days. "I'm trying to speak with everyone who comes in tonight, even though the proponent would prefer I not be here."

"Hi, Albin," Willson said. "I'm really sorry about what happened to your office ... and your assistant. Have they confirmed that it was her?"

"Not yet," Stoffel said, his face darkening.

"I wanted to ask you some questions when I saw you there yesterday, but I figured you had other things on your mind."

"What did you want to ask me?"

"There must be wolverines in the project area, right?"

"There are," he said. "From hair samples, we know we have at least one male that uses Collie Creek as part of his home range. He moves in and out of the park. And we have GPS collars on two females in the main Blaeberry drainage. There's likely a den site in there somewhere."

"Interesting," Willson said, turning back to the display. "I don't see that mentioned here anywhere."

"No, you don't. I think the proponent wants me *and* the wolverines to disappear." Stoffel stopped speaking for a moment. Willson guessed he was thinking about the fire and its fatal results. "The animal is endangered under federal species at risk legislation, and that creates a problem for the project," he continued.

An older couple joined them at the display board. Stoffel turned his attention to them. "Hi, I'm Albin …"

Leaving him to his pitch, Willson and her mother moved to the final display, completing their circuit of the room. This one was titled *Project Benefits* and consisted of three panels. Standing beside the display was a very large man wearing pressed blue jeans, polished cowboy boots, and a black western-style blazer over a checked blue shirt. His skin was pale, his red hair showing the telltale ring of a hat recently removed. "Thanks for coming to our open house tonight," he said. "I'm Stafford Austin, and I'm proud to be the proponent for Top of the World."

He launched into a speech about the project benefits, the investments, the jobs, the new tourism profile for Golden. He talked about the five hundred million dollars to be invested over the life of the project. He mentioned the many organizations that were already supporters. He waved his hands for emphasis as he spoke, making his two large gold rings, one on each hand, glint in the light.

Willson watched him through narrowed eyes. *So you're the guy,* she thought, *my target, the focus of my waking hours for the next while. You don't know it yet, buddy, but I'll be poking and prodding and peering into places you don't want me to go.*

At that moment, Stoffel appeared. "All you ever talk about is benefits," he said to Austin loudly. "This is a crazy idea and you know it!"

The room went quiet as all heads turned to look at the two men. Willson saw her mother's face flush as she moved away to avoid the confrontation.

"What about the wolverines? What about the grizzly bears? What about the mountain goats?"

"Mr. Stoffel. I assumed you would show up tonight to disrupt things," said Austin, his smile like that of a jackal.

"I'm not here to disrupt anything," said Stoffel. "I want to make sure people understand that not everything about this project is good news. There are many issues that people should be concerned about. It's a bad project in the wrong place." He pointed to the display board. "If this ridiculous idea goes ahead, there'll be serious environmental impacts — which you're trying to hide."

Like the good interrogator she was, Willson studied Austin carefully, watching his reaction to Stoffel's outburst. His smile did not waver, but his eyes narrowed and his face flushed slightly. His arms were still and tight against his side, his fists clenched. He was *not* a happy man.

"We've been open about the project impacts *and* benefits," Austin said, more to the onlookers than to Stoffel. "We believe that the significant benefits of a development in this area will far outweigh a few minor impacts. But the beauty of this process, Mr. Stoffel, is that *you* don't get to decide if the project goes ahead or not. That will be left up to experts, people who know what they're doing."

"*I* know what I'm doing," said Stoffel, his voice more strident. "I'm talking about science. I'm standing up for the environment. I'm making sure that everyone knows about the importance of the Blaeberry and Howse River drainages to wolverines and other wildlife, and to the parks next door. About the value of large, wild places."

Austin's smile was gone. "Feel free to do that," he said. "I know that your little study, with your little team of volunteers, all well meaning I'm sure, will be just one small piece of the information about Top of the World to be reviewed. We've hired a reputable environmental consulting firm to study the wolverines, bears, mountain goats, and lots of other things. They're professionals. They'll be following standards created by federal and provincial government scientists, not by some left-wing university. In my humble opinion, that's where the truly useful and accurate information about this project will come from."

"No one is going to believe anything that comes from someone *you* hire," said Stoffel. "I want you and everyone here to know that we're going to oppose you, every step of the way." He turned and walked out of the hall, staring at Austin and bouncing off Hank Myers as he passed him.

"I apologize for that unfortunate disturbance," said Austin, his smile returning. "As you can tell, Mr. Stoffel is passionate … and I must say, misinformed. Are there any questions I can answer for the rest of you?"

"Why another ski hill in this area?" asked one middle-aged man who was standing beside Willson. "We've already got Kicking Horse and Panorama and Kimberley in the valley here, Lake Louise and Sunshine just over the border in Alberta, and then Revelstoke to the west. Won't you be poaching skiers from our existing resorts?"

"Great question," said Austin. "We've done detailed market analyses. Based on those, we know that there are thousands of skiers around the world who don't come to British Columbia. We believe that many of them will choose to come visit for a new resort of this calibre. Wealthy skiers like trying new experiences. It will be unlike anything else in the area, with great snow and glaciers and incredible views. And we'll operate year-round. Because of that, we don't see those hills competing with this project in any way. In fact, I believe they'll all benefit from having more skiers in this area in general."

"Hmm," said the man, looking less than convinced.

"The site is far from here," said the woman beside him. His wife? "Who's going to pay for the road to get there?"

"That's something we'll have to talk with government about," said Austin. "But it's my understanding that taxpayers won't be on the hook for any of it."

"I don't buy that for one minute," said the woman. "We taxpayers always end up paying for projects like this."

Austin did not respond.

A young woman stepped up beside Willson. She was red-haired, thin as a rail, and wore a black T-shirt with *Keep Collie Wild* scrawled across the front in what appeared to be white paint. "Was it you who burned down Stoffel's office?" the woman asked, pointing right at Austin, her eyes blazing.

"I had nothing to do with that," Austin said. "And you should be very careful about making accusations, young lady, or you'll end up in court."

Myers stepped toward the protestor with his arms out like he was trying to herd an angry farm animal, clearly intending to usher her out. But she took one look at him and started to head for the exit on her own.

"We'll see you in court, all right," she retorted. "The same day your idiotic project gets booted out of town." She turned back at the door to yell at Austin, "We're coming for you!"

"I've got a question for you," Willson said. She waited for Austin to turn back to her, and when he did, he looked rattled. "This appears to be an ambitious project, one that'll be very expensive to build and operate. Where's the money coming from?"

"Ah," Austin said, "the money question. We're a private company created for this project. Our initial investors are excited about it. As it proceeds through the approval processes, more investors will come on board."

"Do you have any of your own money invested in the project?"

"What did you say your name was?" asked Austin.

"I didn't," said Willson with a smile. "Call me curious."

CHAPTER 7

Enjoying the wind in her face and the sound of the fat tires humming on hard-packed snow, Willson savoured riding her mountain bike for the first time in weeks. Golden was like that. It could be full-on winter elsewhere in the mountains, but if there was enough sun by noon to burn off the valley fog, then the town — at just under eight hundred metres elevation in the Rocky Mountain Trench — could be balmy and pleasant by comparison.

After Jack Church had given her secondment the nod two weeks earlier, Willson had quickly moved into an old house in Golden. It was owned by Parks Canada and needed lots of work, but she had no intention of doing anything besides live in it for a year. She'd been able to get her clothes, bike, skis, and beloved Bose sound system from Banff in a single tight load in her Subaru. It was all she owned and all she needed.

Over two evenings, she'd helped her mother decorate for Christmas. It was the first time in five years that they had hung ornaments on the tree together. During the day, Willson patrolled every main and side road in the park, walked through now-closed campgrounds, met the owners of most of the park's commercial businesses — hotels, lodges, restaurants — and reviewed a large stack of old case files and court documents. She wanted to understand the law-enforcement issues she might be facing in Yoho, and she needed to get a read on the experience and capabilities of the other wardens she would be working with.

Now, on her first day off since arriving, she cruised through her new neighbourhood. Swinging by her old high school brought a flood of memories rushing back — some good, some less so. The best memories were of sports, at which she'd excelled: track and field, volleyball, cross-country skiing. Then there was the supportive biology teacher, Mr. Baumbrough, who'd been a father figure to her after her dad passed away. He'd given her much-needed advice at a time when her life could have gone downhill. Uncle Roy, her father's brother, had done the same. With their constant encouragement and timely words of wisdom, she'd found her way through months of grief and uncertainty. Her most difficult memory was of crossing the stage to receive her high school diploma without her father there to see her, her mother a teary mess in the front row and barely aware of what was happening.

She continued west along 9th Street, passing the hospital where she'd said her final goodbyes to her father, then cut north along 8th Avenue to the Kicking Horse pedestrian bridge. It was Canada's longest free-standing timber-frame bridge, and because it hadn't been there when she was growing up, she marvelled at the Douglas fir beams stretching across the river. Strong, beautiful, it was as much art as it was engineering. Now, it was the second crossing of the Kicking Horse River, which cut the town of Golden in two. Most of the residential area was on the south side; on the north were the commercial and industrial area and the busy highway corridor.

She walked her bike halfway across the bridge, then stopped to look down into the river. The fast-flowing water was milky with silt scoured from glaciers high in Yoho Park. Two kilometres downstream from where she stood, the Kicking Horse joined the much larger Columbia River, which picked up the waters of the Blaeberry River and dozens of other drainages along the way as it flowed toward Astoria, Oregon; there, it emptied into the Pacific Ocean.

On the north side of the river, only a dozen pedal strokes from the bridge, Willson passed the blackened skeleton of the wolverine research team's old office. She remembered that the building had been a private residence for many years before it became the offices of an engineering company for many more. An image flashed in her mind of herself and her friends sitting here along the riverbank, sneaking a beer after a track meet.

Willson turned onto Golden's main downtown street and found the address she was looking for. She locked her bike to a metal stand on the street side of the sidewalk and climbed up a narrow staircase that creaked and complained with each step. She banged twice on the only door on the second floor.

"Yeah, come in," said a voice from inside, "door's open."

Willson pushed her way in and then paused in surprise. It was a small room, no larger than one might find in a shabby motel, but with considerably less charm. It was dominated by a single wooden desk, behind which Albin Stoffel sat hunched over a MacBook, his fingers motionless on the keyboard. File boxes were piled in one corner.

Stoffel stood when he saw her. "I apologize for the poor manners," he said. "I get so few visitors that I forget to be more welcoming. I'm Albin Stoffel." He shook Willson's hand warmly and gave her a double air kiss, his beard scratching her face. "Didn't I talk to you at the open house a couple of weeks ago?" he asked as he pulled back, still holding both of her hands in his.

She smiled. "Yes, you did," she said, "I'm Jenny Willson."

"Pleased to meet you, Jenny … again. Have a seat." He pulled a rickety chair from behind the door and placed it in front of the desk. "Would you like a tea or a coffee? I can run downstairs to the café."

"No, I'm good, but thank you anyway." Willson put her jacket on the back of the chair and then sat while Stoffel returned to his seat.

"Once again," she said, "I'm sorry about the fire. Have they confirmed the identity of the … victim yet?"

"No. But I know it was Sue. I haven't seen or heard from her since that night, and neither has her family. She texted her husband that she would be crashing there for the night, and her car was there when the firefighters arrived. Her husband and parents have been phoning the RCMP and me almost every day to see if we've heard from her, or if there's any news." A tear rolled down his cheek. "We hadn't worked together long, but I really liked her. She was a great volunteer who worked hard. And she was passionate about wilderness and wolverines. She didn't deserve to die. I wish I could have done something ..." He stared out the small window. "She chose to stay in the office that night. I could have insisted she come to my place ..."

"I understand how you feel," Willson said, putting her hand on Stoffel's arm. "But this is not your fault. She made her own decision. Neither of you could have known how it would turn out."

"I know. That's easy to say, but not so easy to believe. Maybe we'll find out it wasn't her after all ..."

To shift the discussion, if even only slightly, Willson pointed to the file boxes in the corner. "Did you lose all your work in the fire, or were you able to salvage some of it?"

"We lost almost everything. All our research papers, written reports, our skis and snowshoes and outdoor gear, cameras, GPS units, two computers, and a bunch of hard drives. Luckily, I always took backups home with me every night. That's all I have left now, other than the hair samples we got that day in Collie Creek."

"Has the RCMP kept you posted on its investigation?"

"Corporal Fortier has been filling me in as much as he can. I told him they should be looking at Stafford Austin and Hank Myers. I assume they're on the list of suspects. And speaking of Austin, I'm sorry you had to see my outburst at the open house. That guy really pushes my buttons. And I let him do it every time I see him."

"No problem," said Willson. "I see how committed you are to your research. In fact, that's why I'm here today. When we met at the open house, I didn't yet know whether I would be the newest park warden in Yoho. But now I'm confirmed and living here in Golden. I'd like to learn more about your project and the wolverines that live inside and outside the park. And after what happened at the open house, I'd like to understand why you're so opposed to the ski area."

Stoffel looked at her with the expression of a man who had just been asked to have sex right there on his desk. *Uh oh, this guy doesn't often get asked about his research.* It was too late to take back the question, walk out the door, race down the stairs, and escape on her bike.

For the next two hours, Willson learned more than she'd ever imagined it possible to learn about wolverines, their biology and sexual habits, their teeth and their main prey species, their massive home ranges covering thousands of square kilometres, how Stoffel had used hair traps made of barbed wire to capture DNA samples, and how he could tell individuals apart by the shape of the patches of light hair on their chests. And she learned that wolverines didn't leap from trees onto unsuspecting passersby, like they were described doing in early literature. Instead, they showed their displeasure by savaging the interiors of cabins and mountain huts. She remembered a warden cabin she'd once visited while on boundary patrol in the upper Red Deer River in Banff Park. Not only had a wolverine torn apart the interior and consumed everything edible, it had also sprayed the bedding and mattresses with a foul-smelling musk. When they realized what had occurred, she and her partner had been tempted to burn the cabin down. Instead, they rode an extra thirteen kilometres to the next one.

Eventually Stoffel began to wind down, as though running out of manic energy.

"*Gulo gulo*," he said with a sigh. "The Latin name means "glutton glutton," and they have earned that name honestly. Members of the Shuswap First Nation call it *qwilqen*. It's a mysterious but truly amazing species that few of us know much about. I want to understand them, to learn all I can. I want to see them survive and thrive. And what they need for that to happen is large wild places, places with no humans. Highways and ski areas and settlements don't work for them."

"I can see why you're so passionate. They're like the proverbial canary in a coal mine." She rotated her chair around so she was straddling the seat and leaned her chest forward against the chair back, her forearms resting along the top. The talk of wolverines and wilderness had finally wound down. It was safe to stay. "You sound like you were born in Switzerland, Albin. How did you end up in Golden doing wolverine research?"

"You're right, I was born in a village in Switzerland called Saas-Grund. It's one valley to the east of Zermatt. My older brother came here twenty years ago to be a heli-ski guide. He and I were always close. After he left, I looked for ways to follow him to Canada. I got my master's degree at the University of Zurich in ecology while studying the wolves that were moving back into Switzerland from Italy. I decided that getting a Ph.D. would be my ticket to Canada, and I was accepted for doctoral work with a University of Calgary professor who was studying wolverines in the central Rockies. And here I am."

"How's your project funded?" Willson asked.

"I've got money coming in from a federal science research grant and from Parks Canada. British Columbia and Alberta have also thrown in money because of the wolverine's species at risk status, and the local environmental group tops it up as best they can."

"Was it just you and Sue doing the research?"

"No. I have access to grad students when my supervisor can spare them, but most of the legwork is done by volunteers. They're called citizen scientists. I've got a team of twelve, some in the Canmore-Banff area and some here in Golden. They're the ones who regularly check and re-bait the hair and photo traps so we get a sense of how many different animals we have and where they're moving. Sue is … was … one of them. She lived in Canmore. I've already got twenty camera stations spread out in a grid pattern across the Rockies, with more to come. One of them is up Collie Creek, where they're proposing to build the ski area."

"That's a lot of work," said Willson. "With all that, do you see your brother more now?"

"Only when he has days off from guiding," said Stoffel. "And then we go backcountry skiing together. No chairlifts, no helicopters — just us under our own power. I don't see him as much as I would like to. But somehow, being in the same country, even if it's a really big country, feels like we're closer."

"I'm happy for you," said Willson. "Sounds like everything has worked out. If you don't mind me asking, why did you get into it with Austin at the Senior Centre? You two don't seem to like each other much."

"You're right. I don't think we'll ever be pals."

"Why?"

Stoffel pushed his hands through his hair in a distracted attempt to bring it under control, but it immediately popped back out like a balloon. Willson sensed that he was frustrated, angry, perhaps even a little embarrassed by his earlier outburst.

"I first ran into Austin up the Blaeberry River early last summer," he said. "He and Hank Myers were stopped on the road near the Mummery Glacier trailhead. They were fixing a flat tire on a rental vehicle that shouldn't have been up there. I was on my way to Golden after spending a week up the valley doing habitat assessments. I stopped to see if they needed a hand. We started talking. They were pretty cagey about what they were doing up there, but when I told them I was studying wolverines, they started asking questions. At first, I thought they might be prospectors, poking around to see if there was anything up there worth mining. They asked about Collie Creek, and when I said we'd found wolverines there, their questions became increasingly critical and condescending. It was more like an interrogation. And no matter what I said, they thought I was full of shit, I could tell."

"I know what *that* kind of conversation is like ..." said Willson, thinking about many of the conversations she'd had with senior government officials in Calgary.

"What was troubling," said Stoffel, "was the gun I saw in the truck. Myers tried to throw a coat over it, but he knew I'd seen it."

"A gun isn't unusual in this part of the country," said Willson. She remembered the conversation with Ben Fortier.

"A pistol sure as hell is," Stoffel replied. "And having been in the military for two years, I know a 9mm semi-automatic when I see one."

"Have you encountered him since then? Before the open house, I mean."

"He came into the old office a couple of times demanding to see my research results. I told him they weren't ready yet and that he'd have to wait until they went through the university peer review process before they'd be available to the public."

"How did he respond?"

"Not well. It seems he's the kind of guy who usually gets what he wants. He threatened to call the university. I encouraged him to do that. The last time he came in, about a month ago, he was angry and aggressive. Myers was with him. Even though he never says much, he's an intimidating guy."

"Why was Austin upset?"

"I guess the letters I sent to provincial and federal authorities, and to local politicians, pissed him off." Stoffel smiled. "All I did was remind them that they had a legal responsibility to protect wolverines under federal species at risk legislation and that approving a ski resort in an area with occupied habitat wasn't doing that."

"He took it personally, did he?"

"Did he ever. His face was flushed and he called me every name in the book, most of them ones I'd never even heard before. He said I should stop meddling in something that wasn't my business."

"Did you take that as a threat?" asked Willson.

"I did. It made me nervous, especially since he had his goon with him. I had no idea what he'd do."

"Did you tell the RCMP about it?"

"Yes. I talked to Fortier. That was the first time I met him. He took a statement from me and I told him about the gun. He said he would have a chat with both Myers and Austin."

"That probably didn't make Austin dislike you any less," Willson said, leaning back in her chair. "Tell me why you're so opposed to the project."

"For all sorts of reasons," said Stoffel. "Most of my concern goes back to growing up in Switzerland. Not only did my own home valley have three ski areas, but Zermatt is right next door. There are other resorts in the same area — Brig, Bürchen, Eischoll, Lötschental. It seemed that every valley in the Alps had at least one ski area, each with lifts and roads and hotels and condos, trains and trams, restaurants and huts up on the ridges, trails everywhere. And people, thousands and thousands of people. They ski there in the winter, and they're there the rest of the year, hiking and mountain biking and trail running and hang gliding. There are few wild places left there anymore, few places where animals can survive without human interference. I don't want to see Collie Creek turn into another Zermatt. The fact that Austin is using the name Top of the World turns my stomach. And I haven't even started on the impact a ski resort would have on wolverines and other wildlife. If this project goes ahead, they'll be pushed out, forced into smaller and smaller chunks of habitat. I think it's a bad idea in the wrong place."

"I understand," said Willson, making notes as he spoke. "Are there wolverines in Switzerland?"

"No. We think there might have been centuries ago. But today, apart from Canada and Alaska, they're only found in Russia, Norway, Sweden, and Finland."

"No disrespect, Albin, but why are you so focused on fighting Austin? Why not just do your research?"

"You sound like my supervising professor. He keeps telling me to focus on my work and let the review process run its course," said Stoffel. "But I can't. It's something I feel strongly about. I can't sit by and let it happen. Even with the threats against me. And with Sue likely dead, I'll never back down."

"Do you know who else opposes the project?"

"The Columbia Valley Environmental Society certainly does. They've come out strongly and publicly against it. I agreed to work with them, but they're only getting started. Like many of us, I don't think they believed this proposal would actually go anywhere."

"What about the rest of the community?" asked Willson.

"In my view, the project has split the community in half. It's a real shame. Many people, including most of our local politicians, I think, seem to support it for the jobs and investment. There's even a local ski society that has formed to support the project. I can't help but think they've been bought off somehow. But many people are opposed, mostly for environmental reasons, or because we already have enough ski areas. Even the local First Nation bands can't agree. One of them likes it because of the jobs it would create. The other sees Collie Creek as a sacred valley and doesn't want anything developed in there. But as you saw at the open house, I suspect many locals simply don't know where they stand."

With this one visit, Willson had picked up more information than she'd ever hoped for. She stood to leave, picking her coat up off the back of the chair. She'd have to talk more to Ben Fortier about Stafford Austin. But this was a good start. She had some new avenues to pursue, but her first step was simply to learn as much as she could about the ski area application.

"Thanks, Albin," she said. "I appreciate your time and your patience today. I've got a much better understanding of the situation than I did before I came in here. Can I drop in on you from time to time to see how the research is going?"

"Absolutely," said Stoffel. "There aren't many people who're interested in it … and it's an important story."

More important than you know, thought Willson.

CHAPTER 8

JANUARY 5

First thing on a Tuesday morning, in a small windowless boardroom at the Parks Canada offices in Yoho National Park, Willson sat across from Tara Summers. Bleary-eyed, Willson clutched her third coffee of the morning as she stared at the table, which was covered in binders. She'd been called out the night before to investigate suspicious activity on the road to Takakkaw Falls. It had turned out to be nothing more than a gaggle of high schoolers from Lake Louise and Field enjoying a premature grad party, but she'd lost three hours of precious sleep.

Summers represented Parks Canada on the inter-agency team reviewing the Collie Creek proposal. A young redhead with acne-scarred cheeks, she was energetic and full of wide-eyed idealism about saving parks from the marauding hordes outside the ramparts. Willson knew that spending time in government would eventually bleed that enthusiasm out of Summers like a slow leak from a balloon. For now, though, after an hour of listening to Summers describe her education, her background, and her job, Willson saw that Summers excelled at talking … and talking and talking. What she didn't do was listen. Ever. Because she was always talking …

"Okay, Tara," Willson interrupted, wanting to bang her forehead against the table, "let's talk about the ski area project, the so-called Top of the World Resort. My mum talked me into attending the December open house in Golden, so I figured I should learn about the project and what we're doing. As far as I know, there aren't any law-enforcement issues with it, so this is just background for me, in case people ask me about it —"

"No problem, Jenny!" said Summers. "It came at us out of the blue. Like I said, I'm getting up to speed, too, so it's good to talk it through with someone."

"So, where's it all at?"

"The proponent, Collie Creek Resorts Limited, submitted its formal proposal to the Province of B.C. and to Parks Canada. Because the project is in these two jurisdictions, we're trying to sort out the process we'll use to ensure that both levels of government get what they need. As you can imagine, there's a long list of regulations, policies, and processes that have to be satisfied."

"Sounds like a clusterfuck before it even gets out of the gate," said Willson.

Summers guffawed. "Like I said, you don't know the half of it. Along with us and the provincial department in charge of ski hills, there's also the local regional district that will deal with land-use zoning, and then there are at least two First Nations bands involved. And a long list of other agencies and departments that want a piece of the action. The public will also want its say."

"Jesus. Why is this even going ahead?" asked Willson. "It seems like such a huge uphill battle — not something you want for a downhill ski area. And on the surface, it appears to be such a far-fetched idea —"

"I'm wondering that, too," said Summers, nodding. "There *are* more questions than answers at this stage. But you know how these things work better than I do. Governments these days tend *not* to turn things down early in the process, particularly not economic development projects … no matter how crazy they seem. We have to follow our policies and procedures so the processes are seen to be fair. In this case, the ball is rolling."

Or the avalanche, thought Willson. She pictured a mass of snow moving out of a starting zone along a rocky ridge, with Stafford Austin standing at the top, the large human trigger. The mass would slide slowly, then, as gravity took hold, pick up speed, threatening to smother everything in its path — including unsuspecting humans. *Large amounts of anything moving downhill is rarely a good thing in the mountains.*

"The proponent submitted an expression of interest to government very soon after the park legislation changed, so you can think what you want about that. He's been using the label Top of the World since he first submitted it. It's now moved on to what's called the formal proposal stage, which is why we're starting to get more detail," Summers said, indicating all the binders on the table.

"And what are the next steps?" asked Willson, bracing herself for the loss of another long, irreplaceable chunk of her remaining time on earth listening to Summers.

"Honestly, that's a mystery. This isn't something any of us have ever dealt with. We've got an interagency team set up. Like I said, I sit on that for Parks Canada. Together, we'll have to figure out the process and then, I assume, we'll review their submission to see how it stacks up against a long list of fiscal, environmental, and social criteria. This won't be a fast process, and it'll cost the proponent a pile of money."

Willson thought of her conversation with Frank Speer. "Do you know if Parks Canada has taken a position on it yet?"

"Not officially." Summers looked toward the door and lowered her voice. "But between you and me, I'm getting the sense from Calgary that there's support for it both there and in Ottawa. And maybe you've heard that our park superintendent is supportive."

"I have. But why do you think Parks Canada likes it?"

She shrugged. "You've seen more of those subtle messages come down the food chain than I have. Where the people who sit on the fence between bureaucracy and politics talk about encouraging investments in parks, getting more visitors into parks, looking for new sources of revenue to cover the costs of parks … You know the kind of message I mean …"

"None of that gives me confidence," said Willson. "In my experience, if politicians want this bad enough, they'll make it happen. And if they don't want it, it'll die a slow, painful, and costly death in the black hole of process." In that moment, she recalled one of her favourite quotes from the American wilderness enthusiast and all-around shit-disturber Edward Abbey: "A patriot must always be ready to defend his country against his government." Willson realized that she was starting to embody his prediction.

"You're probably right," Summers said. "Do you want me to walk you through the binders?"

"No, no, that's fine," replied Willson quickly, knowing she might be here for hours (or days or weeks) if Summers got started on those binders. "What do you know about the proponent?" she asked, shifting gears. "I met him at the open house in Golden."

"Then you're ahead of me. I don't know anything more than what's in the proposal. Like I said, the proponent is a B.C.-registered company. The president is Stafford Austin, a land developer originally from Boise, Idaho, now based in Vancouver. He claims to have experience in developing ski areas. I guess we'll be looking at that once the process begins."

Willson had noticed Summers's tendency to say *like I said* even when she hadn't previously said that thing. *Maybe I'll bang* her *forehead on the table instead of mine.*

"Austin seems confident that the project will go ahead," she said. "But I'd expect nothing less." She thought about the fire, the body found in the blackened building, Austin's response to the female protestor at the open house, and his alleged threats against Stoffel. Was he willing to bully and burn and even murder his way to a yes?

CHAPTER 9

Stafford Austin and Hank Myers sat on opposite sides of the desk in their Vancouver office ten floors above the corner of Granville and Hastings. It was a small, sparse space rented month-to-month, a place to keep files organized, track money flowing in and out of the investment fund, prepare client statements, and plan next steps in the business. A part-time assistant sat in the outer office, talking on the phone. The sounds of the city floated up from below: the hiss of cars, the whine of electric buses, the shouts of passersby. The office also included a small boardroom, but Austin preferred the Terminal City Club for client meetings. It was a more inspiring location for persuading wealthy people to invest their money.

"C'mon, Stafford," said Myers, "if I'm going to find more investors, I need news about the project."

"I wish I had something for you," said Austin, "but these goddamn government processes are slow as glaciers."

"I know there are advantages to the process taking longer," Myers said. "I get that. But I've got three people on the verge of investing, and I'm talking to more this week. Between them, they represent over two million dollars in new capital. Two of them came to us via your Matt Merrix. They're *this* close to signing," he said, holding his thumb and index finger less than an inch apart, "but they need confidence that this thing is moving in the right direction."

"That's perfect timing, because the first quarterly payments are due to initial investors by the end of this month."

"Exactly. So what can I tell them?"

"How about we make a phone call to Paul DeSantos and see what he's got for us." Austin reached for his cellphone. "We haven't talked to him in a while. It's important to stay in touch."

"Good afternoon. Resort Development Branch," said the female voice that answered.

"I need to speak to Paul DeSantos."

"Can I tell him who's calling, please?"

"No, you can't," said Austin. "But I guarantee he's expecting my call."

DeSantos came on the line about twenty seconds later. "Paul DeSantos speaking."

"Paul, it's Stafford Austin. You're on speaker. Hank Myers is with me. We'd like an update on our Top of the World project. Where're we at?"

"Oh. Hello," said DeSantos.

Austin detested wasting time on pleasantries. He saved that ridiculous dance for dealing with people with money, and only then because it was a necessary part of the courting ritual. Low-level government staffers weren't on his dance card. Instead, he waited in silence.

"Uh ... okay ... you want an update," said DeSantos awkwardly. "Here's what I can tell you. We've got the multi-agency review team set up, the process to review your proposal is under way, and we've contacted both First Nation bands to find out how and when they want to be involved."

"Is it looking good, Paul?"

"It's too early to tell, Mr. Austin. We're only starting to hear what the other agencies are thinking."

"When are we going to get an answer, Paul?"

"I can't tell you that. It's much too early to know."

"Paul," said Austin, "we've got potential investors lined up who will bring millions of dollars in capital to this project. We need to give them some good news."

"I wish I could give you more —"

"I need you to do more than fucking wish here, Paul." Austin chose to play a major card in his deck. "Do you remember when the three of us were on-site last fall? Do you remember when we talked about how important it is that this project keep moving ahead, *why* that was important, and *what* we needed you to do?"

Austin knew that DeSantos's mind would jump back to their conversation in Collie Creek in late September of the previous year, and, more importantly, to his family. They'd sat on the shore of a glacial lake in the upper part of the drainage near where the resort base was planned. It had been a long and exhausting field day, with Austin and Myers showing DeSantos where each part of the project would be located. DeSantos had made several notes, taken lots of pictures, and asked many questions. Compared to Austin, who was out of shape and easily winded, DeSantos had looked as if he could hike the area all day.

The three of them had sat alone in a patch of alpine heather, waiting for the helicopter that would take them back to Golden. Prompted by a nod from Austin, Myers had pulled a photo out of his briefcase. In it, DeSantos was standing in the doorway of a house, passionately kissing a woman who was not his wife. Staring at DeSantos, Meyers spoke with no emotion in his voice. "We need you to keep this project moving, Paul, not too quickly, but not too slowly, either. We'll tell you what we need and when we need it. We'll also need you to give us updates on who is saying what ... whenever we ask for them. The why of this is not your concern, but I'm certain you'll do what we ask so that this picture, and others even *more* interesting than this, do not get shown to your wife and daughter. You'll do that, won't you, Paul?" Myers had drawn out the single syllable *Paul* with chilling emphasis, with each repetition of DeSantos's name delivering a jab of intimidation — just as Austin was doing today on the phone.

"I suggest that you don't speak of this to anyone," Myers had continued. "If you do, we'll deny it, you'll be removed from the project for appearing biased ... and you will still face the loss of your family, at least half of your government pension, and your reputation." Myers glanced down at the picture, then back at DeSantos again. "You'll agree, I'm sure, that the consequences of doing anything other than complying with what we want would be devastating to you and your family. Do you understand, Paul?"

They'd watched a confident, experienced bureaucrat transform into a pale, shaking shell of a man, too shocked to ask how they'd gotten the photo. After a long moment, DeSantos had nodded in response to Myers's question, then remained silent for the rest of that afternoon.

Through the speaker now, they could hear DeSantos's breathing, quick and sharp. "Okay," he whispered. "There seems to be some political support for the project, but I'm guessing you already knew that. There's also local opposition. But so far, I'm not hearing about any showstopper issues, at least not from the provincial side. A big point of discussion is road access, but I understand you have something in the works there. The feds, however, are a different beast, and I have no control over them. They're concerned about the resort's impact on the national park and a Canadian Mountain Club hut they recently approved, and they're raising red flags about wilderness and wolverines. As you know, that's an endangered species they can't ignore."

"And?" said Austin.

"And you'll probably be asked to undertake more detailed environmental and geophysical studies of the area."

"No problem there," Austin remarked.

"You're okay with having to do more studies?" DeSantos's voice reflected his confusion.

"We are, and you don't need to know why. Nor will you tell anyone that we are. Understand?"

"I won't say anything."

"Good. Now, I need your honest opinion, Paul," said Austin. "Do any of the issues raised by the feds so far have the potential to derail our project completely?"

"I don't know," said DeSantos. "I haven't spent enough time with their people to get a solid read on how serious they are. But there's no doubt that political support high up the chain will make a difference."

"You can leave that to us."

"Yes, I expected so …"

"Good, Paul, good," said Austin. "That wasn't so hard, was it? We'll talk to you again soon. Keep up the good work."

He pushed the end call button on the phone and turned to smile at Myers. "That went really well, don't you think?"

CHAPTER 10

JANUARY 12

The sun was still an hour from rising. Willson sat in her warden truck in a dark parking lot midway between Lake Louise and Field. It was the same parking lot used as a staging area for the lodge and trails at Lake O'Hara. Hers was the first vehicle in the lot that morning; the truck's tracks were obvious in the new snow.

It's always coldest just before the dawn, thought Willson, *and it's freakin' cold this morning.* She turned the truck's heater up a notch and took a long sip of the still-steaming coffee in her travel mug. On a ridgetop to the east, a line of coniferous trees was backlit by the first hint of sun like a craggy saw blade.

As she waited, Willson pondered the call she'd received from Benoit Fortier the previous evening. Initially, her heart had jumped at the thought that he might have other things on his mind than the fire investigation. But he was all business. He'd phoned to tell her they'd confirmed that the deceased in the fire was indeed Sue Webb.

Willson's thoughts turned to the young woman, a volunteer who'd unwittingly paid the ultimate price for her commitment to wildlife conservation. She'd never met Webb, but she knew that somewhere, a family was grieving the loss of their loved one.

Fortier had also confirmed that this was now a homicide investigation. "We found evidence of glass on the inside of the building, which suggests that something was thrown through the window from the outside," he had said. "And we found traces of accelerant in one corner. It looks like someone tossed a Molotov cocktail through the window. With all that shit in there, and the old dry logs in the walls, it wouldn't have taken much to get a fire raging."

"Do you know yet how Webb died?"

"No. I'm not sure when we'll get the coroner's report."

"Why's it taking so freaking long? It's been like six weeks."

"Yeah, we're still getting the 'we're backed up' excuses."

Willson had asked if they had any suspects.

"Not yet, but we've got a long list of people we need to interview. Based on the threats to Stoffel, Austin and Myers are at the top of our list."

Willson's thoughts were interrupted by a vehicle turning into the parking lot from the east. Headlights illuminated the surrounding forest in jerkily moving circles until the vehicle slowed and stopped parallel to Willson's, facing in the opposite direction, with the driver-side doors almost touching. The headlights clicked off. Willson rolled down her window while the other driver did the same. She looked across at Chief Park Warden Frank Speer. Engine exhaust drifted up around them.

"Morning, Chief," said Willson. "Is this secret agent stuff, or what?"

"What have you got for me, Jenny?" said Speer. No nonsense and no idle chatter.

Willson began the first briefing she'd given to Speer since accepting the special Yoho assignment. "I haven't dug up anything new about the project besides what's in the written submissions that I assume you've read. There are lots of environmental questions, and people are asking about the cost of the road to the proposed site and who'd be responsible for that. Austin said he's talking to government about it, but suggested that it won't cost taxpayers anything."

"You've met Austin?" asked Speer.

"Yup. At an open house in early December. I went with my mum. I asked him where the money for the project was coming from and he didn't answer, other than to say it was from what he called 'initial investors.' He hinted more money would be coming in later."

"Does he know who you are?"

"I didn't identify myself then because it was a public open house and I was there as a local resident. It's unlikely he knows I'm a warden, unless he's taken the time to ask around."

"What's your read on him?"

"He's big and brash, with a classic salesman's personality," said Willson. "From what I've seen so far, he strikes me as a con man, a huckster who's shown up selling a miracle cure. He's got lots of compelling reasons why this is the best thing to hit Golden in a long time. You can probably tell from the project name that he's saying it'll be the highest, the biggest, the best. His so-called colleague, the guy who seems to be working most closely with him, has a sketchy background after time spent in the military. It's very strange."

"Huh. Any specific intel on Austin so far?"

"I've picked up three things," said Willson. "The first is that he seems to have done a masterful job at building a support network in the community. It's mostly businesses and local politicians. He's also created a local ski society to act as project cheerleaders. At least, I think he created it — it's an interesting mix of people, lots of backcountry skiers and snowmobilers, people who wouldn't normally support a ski area. They say they're a bunch of interested citizens trying to help the project succeed, but I've heard rumours that some of them are on his payroll."

"He's clearly being proactive. What else have you got?"

"The second thing is that, while he claims to have a background in ski area development, he was charged — though not convicted — of fraud in Idaho. I don't know the circumstances yet."

"That matches up with those whispered questions I was telling you about," said Speer. "Anything specific?"

"Nope," Willson said, "but I have a suggestion I'll get to in a moment. The third point is that he allegedly threatened Albin Stoffel, the wolverine researcher who's working in the area. Austin seems to view the research as a threat to his project, so he's obviously not happy about scientists poking around in Collie Creek, stirring up concerns — scientists who aren't on his payroll, that is. You may have heard that the research office in Golden burned down in early December, killing a woman who was inside. Now it appears the deceased was Stoffel's assistant. With both arson and homicide investigations underway, Austin's definitely on the suspect list."

Speer smiled. "You've dug up a lot in a few short weeks, Jenny. Good work. What next?"

"That's what I wanted to talk to you about," said Willson. "Because both the RCMP investigations and the project review process are going to take a while, I'm thinking this would be a good time for a trip to Boise — Austin's old stomping grounds. I can dig up more on him, talk to people who know him or have worked with him."

"How do you see doing that?"

"I've still got some vacation days left from last summer, and I've racked up some OT with a string of middle-of-the-night call-outs. So, in about two weeks, I'll head to Boise, and I'll take my mum with me. It'll just be two women on a ski holiday. Bogus Basin ski area is only twenty-five kilometres from Boise. While I'm there, I'll spend some time in the local library and see what pops up. I can access newspaper articles, court documents, you name it. Once I gather more background info, I'm sure I can find ways to run into people who've done business with Austin."

"I like it," said Speer. "Have you talked to Church about it?"

"I told him I wanted time off to spend with my mother, but obviously I didn't say what I was going to do, or where."

"That means you can't claim any travel costs. You understand that?"

"I do. But Mum and I need a holiday, so I'm good with it."

"Make it happen, then," said Speer, his eyes bright in the light of his dashboard. "I'm keen to see what you find hiding out there."

"Thanks," Willson said. "While we're here, have you got anything new that would help my investigation?"

Speer smiled, but it was ironic rather than joyful. His eyes were dark and weary. "Funny you should ask. I've been hearing rumblings via Calgary that this project has caused some people in Edmonton and Ottawa to resurrect the idea of a highway through Howse Pass."

Willson's eyes widened at the mention of Howse Pass. She'd been there once while on a resource management course with some other wardens. It was a relatively low pass in the Rocky Mountains connecting Alberta's Banff National Park with the Blaeberry River drainage to the west, in B.C. She and her colleagues had ridden horses in from the Banff side, following an old trail that dated back to 1806, and stayed overnight at a warden cabin. The valley was wide there, the river constantly changing course on its broad flood plain. The next day, they'd hiked the five kilometres up to the pass. Looking west from there on the border between Alberta and B.C., they'd seen the rugged valley of the Blaeberry River beyond. Knowing that the indigenous peoples had used the pass as a trading route for centuries before, she recalled that it had felt like they were standing in the midst of Canadian history.

"I thought that highway was one of those ideas people like the idea of but will never see happen in our lifetime, like jet packs, or flying cars, or a bridge to Vancouver Island," Willson said.

"Before I heard these recent rumours," said Speer, "I would've agreed with you. The scheme has been talked about on and off since it was first raised in the 1940s. It keeps coming up, like bad takeout, and it seems to be on the table again. I don't know who's brought it forward or who's supporting it, but with a possible ski area in the Blaeberry in the mix, the idea has been resuscitated. And what's disturbing is that the highway is being linked to the oil sands. The fact that a new route would cut off almost one hundred kilometres between central Alberta and the British Columbia coast seems to be a focus of the conversation."

"The oil sands? What the hell do a ski area and a highway have to do with the oil sands?"

"I have no idea. But someone is connecting them. And whoever that someone is, they're well up the food chain."

"You don't mean the Prime Minister's Office, do you?" asked Willson.

"I don't know, Jenny, I really don't. But if it is the PMO, that would explain why any of this is being taken seriously." Speer shook his head, a look of worry crossing his face. "When I first heard about the ski area, I was worried about its impact on Yoho Park. Now, with a possible cross-provincial highway rearing its ugly head, it's become about both Yoho *and* Banff. And it's a whole lot more political. Not good. Not good at all."

"Wasn't there legislation passed by a previous government that made it illegal to put a road through Howse Pass?"

"There was. It was designated as a National Historic Site in 1978. But we already know that the boys and girls in Ottawa have no problem changing laws with little or no debate. I'm afraid the idea of a highway could become possible again with the mere stroke of a pen."

"Jesus," said Willson, "every time I turn over a rock, more surprises crawl out. I wonder if Austin is aware of the highway discussion — he did say he was talking to government. Maybe he knows a hell of a lot more than he let on. Son of a bitch."

"I wouldn't be surprised if he's in the middle of it," Speer said. "But even if he isn't, think about how his project would benefit if someone else — like the taxpayers of Alberta and B.C. — paid for a paved highway that would run right past his doorstep." He looked at his watch, barely visible in the weak light. "I have to get to a meeting in Lake Louise. Let's connect again when you get back from Boise."

Speer's vehicle circled away, leaving Willson alone once again in the parking lot. She rolled up the window and turned the heater up another notch. She shivered, more chilled by what she'd just learned than by the outside temperature. Looking north, she saw the peak of Mount Bosworth, its eastern face now turning orange in the first rays of the morning sun. The sight should have warmed her, but it didn't.

CHAPTER 11

FEBRUARY 1

After an exhilarating day in fresh powder on the slopes of Idaho's Bogus Basin, Willson and her mother returned to Boise for an early dinner. When she saw Cynical Dark Ale on the menu at 10 Barrel Brewing Company, Willson's decision was instant. *It's as if they knew I'd be here*, she thought. The dark ale, nearly but not quite a stout, was a perfect companion to her mac and cheese: a bubbling sauce of smoked Gouda and tangy cheddar over elbow macaroni, bacon, and jalapenos, with pub chips as a side. She watched her mother enjoy a peanut butter and bacon burger washed down with sweet iced tea. Outside the window, streetlights illuminated the light snow falling on West Bannock Street. It was an ideal finish to their fifth day in the state capital.

It had taken the better part of two days to drive the 1,200 kilometres south from Golden to Boise, following

Highway 95 the entire way. It gave the two women time to catch up: while Jenny navigated the wintry roads, her mother talked and talked.

Like ocean currents, Willson's emotions ebbed and flowed as she listened to her mother reminisce about her father, a train engineer. The two of them had been married for only twelve years when the train he was operating left the tracks on the Golden side of Rogers Pass, plunging into the icy Beaver River. It had been a week before Christmas. Willson had been ten at the time, her mother forty. An hour after the derailment, rescuers had finally found her father on the banks of the river, hypothermic, clinging to rocks and to life. He'd died of a massive heart attack moments after the rescue helicopter touched down at the Golden hospital.

While the railway had paid her father well, at least in comparison to Willson's warden salary, the nature of the job had still made for a tough family life. He could be called out with little notice to take trains east or west, and his workplace was emotional and tense, with the union and management constantly fighting pitched battles for control. Willson recalled her parents' evening discussions around the dinner table, her father accusing "the billionaires who owned the company" of underpaying and mistreating their workers, of always trying to take things away from the people who made them their money. Whether these claims were true or not, those evening discussions had been the birthplace of Willson's own distrust of authority.

But when they could get away as a family, they had escaped to the mountains to ski or to hike. She remembered those times with fondness and longing.

Later, with her father gone and no siblings to lean on, Willson had relied on her uncle Roy and her biology teacher to fill the void, to offer her any perspectives on life that only men could. It was in her late teens that she'd begun to read the works of Edward Abbey, the American author and former park ranger known not only for his advocacy on land-use issues, but also for his deep distrust of institutions. By then, without some new age psychiatrist pulling it out of her, she'd come to realize that her father's untimely death had contributed to her becoming an independent hard-ass who struggled to trust others.

While Willson dealt with her own grief, her mother had spiralled downward in bouts of depression and anxiety. She suffered the most during the darkest months of winter. The fact that the railway had not offered her mother any support, and in fact delayed delivery of survivor benefits, did not help the healing process.

To break up the long drive south to Boise, Willson had reserved a room for them at a casino hotel in Bonners Ferry. She savoured the sweet irony of the overnight stop, knowing that the casino had previously been owned by Luis Castillo, her nemesis in the poaching investigation that had consumed two years of her life. Months after the case was over, Willson had decided that Castillo's murder, just as he was to start a life sentence in Washington State's Walla Walla Penitentiary, was a fitting punishment for the myriad horrific crimes he had committed. The fact that he'd died by hanging at the end of a dirty bedsheet, alone and on humiliating display in a prison cellblock, seemed incredibly fitting.

He had taunted, misled, and toyed with her and her colleagues on both sides of the border, at the same time coldly and without conscience executing trophy animals right under their noses.

Sitting in the hotel's hot tub overlooking the Kootenay River, Willson had taken great pleasure in toasting Castillo's demise, with her wine glass raised and her eyes cast down toward the fiery place where he no doubt currently resided. "Rot in hell, you son of a bitch," she'd hissed.

"Did you say something, dear?" her mother had asked from the other side of the tub, barely visible through the rising steam.

"I was just saying that this is a nice switch from Golden."

"It is," her mother agreed. "This is my first holiday in years."

With dinner done, the two women walked arm-in-arm to the main branch of the Boise Public Library, a nondescript four-storey brick building that seemed to be doing everything it could to conceal the collection of knowledge inside.

With her mother comfortably settled in the magazine section, Willson found an empty computer station and wiggled closer to the desk, the feet of her wooden chair scraping on the plank floor. An elderly man at an adjacent station looked up and scowled, momentarily distracted from his game of solitaire. Willson glared back until the man's eyes returned to his computer screen.

Thus she began her quest. For the first hour, using a range of search terms, she found a surprisingly short list of references to Stafford Austin. The first was the

2011 announcement of his hiring as a vice-president at Sawtooth Development Corporation, based in Boise. A media release indicated that Austin had come to Boise from Salt Lake City, Utah, with a background in ski hill construction. Willson saw that at the time of Austin's arrival, Sawtooth specialized in residential subdivisions. Other search results were more innocuous, showing Austin attending Boise Metro Chamber of Commerce events and announcing the completion of two new development projects on the boundary of the Boise National Forest. But when Willson jumped to Sawtooth Development's own webpage, Austin's name was nowhere to be found, not on current pages, nor in any company history.

That was weird. Based on all of this, Austin seemed to be nothing more than a fine, upstanding member of the business community — albeit something of a mystery man. But knowing what Fortier had told her, Willson knew there was something more lurking in the shadows. She just had to find it.

Only after searching the archives of the *Idaho Statesman* newspaper did she find what she was looking for.

Boise Pair Charged with Wire Fraud
Special to the Idaho Statesman
Michael Berland, Investigative Reporter
May 20, 2012

Jennifer Clarkson, assistant U.S. district attorney for the District of Idaho, Criminal Division, announced today that a grand jury has indicted

Stafford Lee Austin, 52, of Boise on two counts of wire fraud. In the same case, the grand jury also indicted Marie Antonetti, 48, of two counts of wire fraud, three counts of tax fraud, and five counts of conspiracy.

Until recently, Austin was the vice-president and minority shareholder of Sawtooth Development Corp. The indictment is based on allegations that Austin assisted Antonetti, the president and majority shareholder of Sawtooth, in submitting false and fraudulent applications so the company could partici-pate in two federally funded programs: the U.S. Small Business Success Administration program (SBSA) and a Department of Transportation roads program. Both programs are designed to help economically and socially disadvantaged businesses compete in the marketplace. To be admitted into these pro-grams, the owner/shareholder who qualifies as socially disadvantaged must demonstrate economic disadvantage by having a personal net worth below a certain statutory cap.

It is alleged that Antonetti took steps to artificially lower her personal net worth by fail-ing to report all of her income from Sawtooth and by transferring assets into the names of nominees in order to appear economically disadvantaged.

A person convicted of wire fraud faces significant potential penalties. A single act of wire fraud can result in fines and up to 20 years in prison. However, if the wire fraud scheme affects a financial institution, the potential penalties are fines of up to $1 million and up to 30 years in prison.

Clarkson advised that the investigation is ongoing and is being led by the Federal Bureau of Investigation and the Boise Police Department.

"Right friggin' on," said Willson, pumping her fist in the air. "Now we're getting somewhere."

"*Shh!*" said the man next to her.

"My apologies." Willson resisted her natural instinct to say something inflammatory and inappropriate. Being evicted from the Boise Public Library would not be a smart way to run a covert investigation.

Turning back to the screen, she dug deeper, following the manoeuvrings of the case in the pages of the *Statesman*. An article from September of that same year, using the same background material from May, stated that Austin and Antonetti were scheduled to stand trial in U.S. district court.

Next, she clicked on an article written two months later. At that point, Antonetti had been convicted of wire fraud and sentenced to twenty-four months in prison for conspiracy and tax fraud. She'd also been ordered by the court to pay restitution in the amount of nearly $150,000. But there was no reference to Austin.

Thinking she'd missed something, Willson went through the links relevant to the case again, but she could find no explanation as to why Austin was no longer connected with the fraud case. She did notice, however, that all of the articles had been written by the same reporter, Michael Berland. Talking to him was the obvious next step.

Michael Berland wasn't easy to reach. After Willson had left three messages for him the next morning at the newspaper's main number but gotten no response, she drove to the offices of the *Idaho Statesman*, which was were located in a commercial-industrial area just south of Highway 184. It was their second-to last day in town, and her mother was content to wander the aisles of a thrift store half a block away.

"Hi, I'm Jenny Willson," she said to the young receptionist, "and I'm here to see Michael Berland."

"Do you have an appointment?" asked the receptionist.

"I don't. But I left him three phone messages. I have information about a story he's working on that I think he'll want to hear."

"Let me see if he's available. You said your name was Willson?"

"Yup, Jenny, from Golden, British Columbia."

The receptionist picked up her phone and dialed. "Michael, there's a Jenny Willson here from Canada who wants to talk to you? She said she has information for a story you're working on?" She paused, listening to Berland. "Okay, I'll tell her."

Replacing her handset, the receptionist turned back to Willson. "He's working on a deadline, but he said he'd see you in about thirty minutes if you don't mind waiting?"

"Thanks, I'll wait." Willson walked over to a set of chairs in the lobby.

Berland came down to the lobby forty-five minutes later. He was tall, with a shaved head and the lanky physique of a runner. His pants were too short, as were the arms of his blue button-down shirt. Willson was the only one in the waiting area, so Berland immediately strode toward her. One large hand gripped a file folder and a reporter's notebook. A mechanical pencil was tucked behind his ear.

"Jenny?" he said. "Mike Berland." They shook hands. "I understand you're down from Canada. I'm not working on anything that touches north of the border as far as I know, so I'm wondering why you're here."

"Thanks for seeing me, Mike. Can we go somewhere to talk?"

Willson followed Berland to a small boardroom off the lobby, where they sat in hard plastic chairs at the corner of a wooden table. Berland's long legs took up much of the small space.

"So," he said, "what have you got for me, Jenny?"

"Does the name Stafford Austin mean anything to you?" she asked, studying the man's face carefully. It was a blank canvas devoid of expression. His brown eyes showed nothing. Either he didn't remember or he was a skilled actor. His silence was encouraging her to disclose what she knew, to keep talking. This guy was good.

"It doesn't …" he said. "Remind me."

"Sawtooth Development Corporation?" asked Willson. "Wire fraud charges?"

"Ah, now I remember. That was a strange case. There were more questions than answers. Why are you asking about Austin?"

"In short, he's formed a company in B.C. and has approached the provincial and federal governments for approval to build a ski resort on the boundary of one of our national parks. They're calling it the Top of the World Resort."

"A ski area? Now that *is* interesting…. But why did you come to me?"

"I saw your stories in the newspaper about the case he was involved in here."

"I appreciate that. But why are *you* talking to me?"

Willson was nearing a point of no return. Frank Speer had asked her to keep the investigation quiet, but finding out about Austin's background was contingent on building trust with this investigative reporter — a guy she'd met only moments ago. She decided to push Berland a little further.

"My mother and I are down here for a ski holiday," she said. "It's as simple as that. We live close to where the ski area might go. Austin is the talk of our town, and I'd heard he was from Boise. I found your name while reading the *Statesman* online and thought I'd ask if you knew anything more about the guy. I'm just curious."

"You don't really have new information for me, despite what you said to our receptionist?" He paused, tapping his pencil on the desktop, and stared at Willson, his brown eyes unblinking. "You're not being completely honest with me, are you?"

"I'm not sure what you're getting at. I wanted to tell you that Austin's proposing a business in our area … and to ask what you know about him. That's it."

"Let me summarize. You came all the way down from Golden, B.C., a town surrounded by some of the best ski areas around, to ski here, in Boise? At a time when the Canadian dollar is at seventy-eight cents against the American dollar? And then you just happened to find me?"

"That's right," said Willson. "You make it sound implausible, like you don't believe me." She stared back at Berland, hoping her expression masked what was going on in her mind. *Why is he pushing so hard? What does this guy know?*

Berland smiled. "Are you still a national park warden, Jenny?"

"How did you …" Willson watched as Berland opened the file folder on the table.

"You might recognize this from the *Calgary Herald*," he said, sliding a picture across to her. "I believe it's you and your colleagues receiving commendations after your poaching investigation took down Luis Castillo. Excellent work on that, by the way. I wrote an article on one of his businesses a few years ago." His smile grew larger, an obvious reaction to Willson's astonishment. "You forget that I'm an investigator, too. It's what I do. While you were waiting for me, I did some digging to find out who Jenny Willson really is."

Berland shifted forward in his seat, his right arm resting on the table, his gaze direct and challenging. "Now … let's start again, shall we?"

CHAPTER 12

The darkened ballroom of Red Deer's Black Knight Inn was quiet as Stafford Austin clicked to his final PowerPoint slide. It was a colour image of Mont des Poilus with the Yoho Glacier in the background and the rising sun washing the snow in a deep orange: a classic *you should be here* piece of destination marketing. He'd been invited by the Red Deer Chamber of Commerce to speak at this meeting. Although he couldn't see much beyond the front row of tables below him, Austin knew he was speaking to the best, brightest, and most engaged of the business community in central Alberta. Red Deer, an attractive community of 100,000, was tucked along the Red Deer River at the midpoint of the busy travel corridor between Calgary and Edmonton. It was also the largest city close to Howse Pass and to his proposed ski resort.

"Ladies and gentlemen," Austin said, his voice booming through the PA system, "*that* is why I believe that a new ski area in Collie Creek, the Top of the World Resort, will not only benefit people and businesses on the B.C. side of the border, but in your region of Alberta as well. I'm excited about this new venture, and I sincerely hope I can count on your support to make it a reality. Thank you very much."

The Chamber's president rose to join Austin on the podium. He was a young pharmacist whose independent drugstore outperformed all of the chain stores in town — Austin had done his homework before coming out.

"On behalf of our members," the president said, leaning over to the microphone, "I'd like to express our thanks to you, Mr. Austin, for your informative and inspiring presentation. Many of us have heard about your project, so it's been great to get more details from you." He handed Austin a cellophane-wrapped basket of local products as a token of appreciation. "Thanks again. I understand you've agreed to answer a few questions, so let's take a few moments for that."

As the lights in the large room came up, the president pointed to a woman in the audience with her hand raised. "Our local hardware store owner," he said to Austin by way of introduction.

She was a stocky blonde, and the name scrawled across the tag pinned to her chest was illegible. "You said you hope to invest about five hundred million in this project," she said. "Over what period of time will that happen?"

"The timing will largely depend on the approvals I get from the two governments, when and how they release land to us for base developments, and, of course, investor buy-in to the project. As an aside, did I mention that we welcome new investors in the project?" he said with a smile. "You can see me after if you've brought your chequebook with you." This prompted chuckles from the audience. "At this point, we're planning for investments to occur over a ten- to fifteen-year time horizon, perhaps slightly longer, depending on economic conditions."

The next question came from Jim Weslowsky, the Chamber's executive director. "Mr. Austin," he said, "I'm sure you're aware that this Chamber is on record as encouraging a more detailed analysis of a possible new highway through Howse Pass. From what we've seen to date, we believe that the highway would encourage economic growth in our area, reduce travel times from this region of Alberta to the B.C. coast by about an hour, and provide a low-elevation pass through the Rockies that would be a practical alternative to the Trans-Canada and Yellowhead highways. If we support your ski area, will you support the new highway?"

Austin smiled because Weslowsky had given him a heads-up that he was going to ask this question. "Thanks for the question, Jim. I understand that the idea of a highway through Howse Pass has come up a few times over the years." The crowd laughed again. "I've done my reading and I understand the history of the route. It's a history that leads back to explorer David Thompson and the year 1807. And before that, to the indigenous peoples who used it as a trade route for generations. I have also read your 2005 economic pre-feasibility study.

As many of you know, it estimated the net benefit of the Howse Pass route to be approximately two hundred and ten million dollars, with an internal rate of return of 21.2 percent. How many of us would like to see *that* return on investments in our own businesses? I know I would. Do I see the economic benefits a new highway would have on this area? And do I also see the value of a new highway to the Top of the World Resort project? Absolutely! And will you have my support if this Chamber raises the idea to the federal and provincial governments? Absolutely." As he finished his answer, Austin scanned the room to see if the two people he was about to meet with next were in the room.

"Mr. Austin," said a male voice. The president had pointed this man out to Austin beforehand, so Austin knew him to be a local newspaper reporter who was infamous for his allergy to facts and his resemblance to TV detective Columbo. "One more question," said the rumpled man. "Have you held any discussions with the B.C., Alberta, or federal governments about the Howse Pass route? Obviously, it would save you millions of dollars if taxpayers built a paved highway right past the front door of your project."

Austin again glanced around the room before answering. "As I said earlier, I recognize the value of a new highway to our project. But in response to your question, we have preliminary cost estimates in our proposal for a paved road that would connect the resort with the Trans-Canada Highway near Golden. Anyone can see those online, and they show our intentions. But no, as of yet, I haven't had any formal discussions with any level of government specifically about a route through Howse Pass."

With that, the young Chamber president once again thanked Austin for his presentation. As Austin stepped down from the podium to take his seat at the head table, he heard the president adjourning the meeting. But Austin's thoughts were fixed firmly on that reporter's last question and on the two people he was about to meet.

Austin moved his bulk in an awkward trot across the street toward Moxie's Bar and Grill, dodging four lanes of traffic rather than walk the extra block to a pedestrian crosswalk. When he opened the door of the restaurant, the sudden transition from the bright light of a blue prairie sky to the dark interior left him nearly blinded. He waited for his vision to return before responding to the sleek young woman at the front counter.

"Table for one, sir?" she said. "Or are you waiting for the rest of your party?"

"Thanks," he said, "I think my colleagues are already here."

"Feel free to look around, sir. If they're not here yet, please come back and see me and I'll set you up with a table." Her gaze, efficient and professional, shifted to a group waiting behind him. Austin turned to his left and began a circuit of the restaurant.

In a darkened corner, Austin found the people he was looking for. They were sitting on the same side of a massive booth, so he slid in across from them, the leather bench creaking as he moved his bulk into the narrow space. Isolated from the other patrons by the high seat-backs, dim lighting, and background music, the three of them had the privacy they required. It was an ideal spot for a clandestine meeting.

The woman spoke first. Austin had first met Wendy Thomas at an Invest Alberta event in Calgary six months earlier. On telling her about his resort project, he'd seen her eyes widen with what appeared to be excitement. She'd immediately pulled him by his elbow, like a misbehaving child, to a quiet hallway to tell him about the possibility of a highway through Howse Pass. Just from that quick, surreptitious conversation, they'd both immediately understood the potential for economic synergy between the two projects.

Broad and stern with her helmet-shaped white-blond hair, wire-frame eyeglasses, and brain hard-wired for politics, Thomas was the member of Parliament for the Yellowhead riding, a massive area of west-central Alberta wedged between the Rockies to the west and the agriculture, oil, and natural gas–dominated prairies to the east and north, with Red Deer at its centre. But most importantly, she was a key Alberta member of the federal government's right-wing caucus. That gave her access to the people who made the decisions that made things happen. Meeting Thomas had been a stroke of luck. Very good luck.

"Thanks for coming over, Stafford," she said. "I'd like to introduce you to Brian Cummings. Brian is a senior adviser in the Prime Minister's Office. Brian suggested we meet after I told him about what we discussed earlier."

Austin shook hands with Cummings, whom he guessed was in his mid to late thirties. He had curly brown hair and a face that was young and unlined, yet wise and discerning. Next they exchanged business cards.

"We thought about sneaking into the Chamber meeting to hear your talk and the Q and A," said Thomas, "but couldn't take the chance of the media seeing us and starting to ask questions. I wanted us to have a quiet talk. I've asked our server to leave us alone for a bit."

"No problem," said Austin. "It all went well. Just as we talked about."

"Good," said Thomas. "I'm sure you handled it well."

Austin shifted his gaze to Cummings. The young man had not said a word. "Mr. Cummings, I'm intrigued about what you want to discuss today."

"First," said Cummings, "call me Brian."

"What's on your mind, Brian?"

"I think you know my cousin, John Theroux."

"Yes, I do. John is the president of our Golden ski society and a great supporter of our project. He's been very helpful."

Cummings leaned forward, his eyes direct, his expression earnest. "You need to understand that I'm not officially here on behalf of the prime minister. But he is aware that we might be talking today and, very generally, of what we might talk about."

"And that would be?"

"The PMO has been briefed on your proposal in Collie Creek and on the overlap with Yoho National Park. We're watching that file closely. The concept of a highway through Howse Pass has been discussed, in some form or another, since the early 1800s. There's no doubt that a project like that would come with a massive price tag, and yet preliminary estimates do show a net economic benefit to this area of Alberta. But at the same time, we know it would face all kinds of social, economic, and environmental hurdles. Communities and businesses on the Trans-Canada to the south and on the Yellowhead to the north would likely oppose a new route through the Rockies, as it might draw traffic and economic development away from them. And proposing a new highway through thirty-four kilometres of Banff National Park would certainly stir up a hornet's nest of opposition from environmental groups."

Austin wondered where this was leading. "Seems like the highway is a pipe dream, to say the least."

"Funny you should mention *pipe dreams*," said Thomas with a sly smile, her eyes crinkling behind her glasses.

"An interesting and perhaps prophetic choice of words, Mr. Austin," Cummings continued. "The Canadian government, and some of the business interests who support it, are increasingly challenged in finding routes for pipelines to ocean ports — for both oil *and* natural gas. We're stymied by interprovincial bickering, delayed by environmental assessments, and blocked by some First Nations bands that seem intent on standing in the way of progress. In short, we're on the verge of what we view as a national crisis. Canada's competitive advantage and a key component of our national economy with the greatest chance for growth are at risk if we can't get our products to American and overseas markets."

Suddenly, as if he'd stepped back out into the brilliant prairie sunshine, Austin began to understand where this conversation was going. The implications for his project were overwhelming, he realized, his mind reeling. His eyes widened and so did Thomas's smile, as if to say, *See, I told you this would be worth your while.*

"Yes," said Cummings, noting Austin's reaction, "we've begun to talk about the Howse Pass route as a viable alternative. There's already a road in place through all but those thirty-four kilometres in the park. If we can find a way to build a highway from the current end of Highway 11 at Saskatchewan Crossing west to the Trans-Canada north of Golden, it could conceivably become a new corridor through the Rockies — not only for vehicle traffic, but also for a pipeline ... or two."

"Huh," said Austin. "This is not what I expected to talk about today."

"I'll bet," said Cummings. "But I can't overstate the confidential nature of what I've described to you. If either the media or the opposition catch wind of the fact that our government is talking about this, even thinking about it, it would be catastrophic for everyone involved. And it would likely mean the death of three potential projects — your resort, the highway, *and* a pipeline corridor — with absolutely no chance for resuscitation. Am I clear?"

"You can count on me to be discreet," Austin said. He looked at Cummings, at Thomas, then back at Cummings again. "But why, then, *are* you talking to me about this, here, now? What do you need from me?"

"Fair question," said Cummings. "I'd ask the same if I were in your shoes."

"Perhaps I can take a crack at Stafford's question," said Thomas, leaning forward to cross her hands on the table, looking fully engaged. "My riding is in a funny position, situated as we are halfway between Edmonton and Calgary. When one or both of those communities sneezes, we get pneumonia. If we can develop this new Howse Pass corridor for vehicles *and* one or more pipelines, our area would see all sorts of benefits in the short and long term. We could become a new economic engine in this part of the province, one that relies much less on the two big cities."

"That makes sense," said Austin. "Where do I and my resort project fit in?"

Thomas exchanged a look with Cummings before continuing. "In 2005, the highway was projected to cost two hundred and ten million dollars. It'll be a hell of a lot more now, at least double, I'm sure. Even though we're talking in the media about spending more on public infrastructure, there's no way that taxpayers will support the federal government spending that kind of money, not at a time when energy prices are so low."

"So ...?" said Austin.

"So, we believe that now is the time to invest in a project like this so we'll be in a better position when markets rebound. And they will. As a businessman, you'll understand that better than most. We also believe that the only way this idea can succeed is if we bring major investors to the table in a public-private partnership, if not a fully funded private-sector project. To do that, we need someone to bring those investors to the table. Someone like you."

The surprises were piling up for Austin. "Why me?"

"Because we've checked into you, your project, and your investment fund," said Cummings, "and we think you're the right person to make this happen."

"Interesting. But what's the revenue model for investors? That's a hell of a lot of money for someone to invest in a public transportation corridor."

Cummings smiled. "It's all about the tolls, Stafford, all about the tolls. In a public-private partnership or in the private sector model, investors would see revenues from vehicle tolls on the highway. And they would see revenues from per-unit charges on material flowing through the pipelines. Every day of the year, year after year, essentially forever."

Austin's mind was a blur of possibilities and questions, options and opportunities. Much of what Thomas and Cummings had said made little business sense, and he could see more problems than solutions. But what they didn't know was that this discussion had opened new avenues for his investment fund that hadn't been on the map mere hours before. Over the course of a single discussion in a dark restaurant in Red Deer, Alberta, his world had suddenly changed.

CHAPTER 13

With coffee cups clinking and latte machines hissing in the background, Willson and Berland sat in a corner of the District Coffee House in downtown Boise, their backs to a quilt-covered wall.

On the far side of the room, Willson's mother perched on a stool facing a ceiling-to-floor window, a book in one hand, a cup of tea in the other. While her mother had happily browsed alone in the thrift store the day before, a nameless visitor in a place that supported anonymity, Willson sensed that a day later, she was feeling less confident about being alone in a strange city. As a result, Willson was keeping her close.

"My apologies for ending our conversation so abruptly yesterday," Berland said, a line of foam on his upper lip. "My boss thought he had something urgent for me. It was far from it, in fact — but that's my world.

Anyway, it gives us a chance to take our time. Tell me again why you're down here, Jenny."

By asking the same question he'd asked the day before, Berland, like any good investigator, was testing to see if her story remained consistent.

"You already know I'm a park warden in Yoho National Park," Willson said, her mouth curled in a slight smile, "and that my mum and I *are* here skiing. Beyond that, it looks like I'm going to have to trust *you* … so that you'll trust *me*."

"That's how my business works," Berland said.

Willson paused. The moment of truth was here. But she still wasn't ready to divulge everything to the reporter. Not yet. With her boss's warnings echoing in her head, Willson considered Berland an unknown quantity, not worthy of her full confidence. She had no doubt he thought the same about her.

"I'm conducting an informal and low-key investigation into Stafford Austin's background, on behalf of my agency. It's part of the due diligence on his ski area proposal. Because Austin's the proponent, we — I — want to know everything there is to know about the man, his background, and his capacity to make a project like that happen. When I found out he was from Boise, this was an obvious place to start my digging. I found your name through archived *Statesman* articles, as I said."

"Have you met the guy?"

"I have, at an open house two months ago."

"What's your read on him?"

Willson sipped her Americano. "As I told my colleagues, he's big, overconfident, and, in my humble opinion, a snake-oil salesman flogging a remedy for an ailment we don't have."

Berland laughed. "From what I know of him, you're not far off."

"Okay, tell me what you know, Mike."

"Where to begin? Well, I first heard his name from a source in the Boise Police Department. He'd been implicated in a fraud at Sawtooth Development Corp. — he and a female colleague had allegedly conspired to defraud the government out of a big chunk of money. Without much effort and in record time, the assistant DA persuaded a grand jury to indict both of them on two counts of wire fraud. The crime had been accomplished via the internet and, because there was a clear digital trail, it looked like an open-and-shut case. There were whispers of something more, but neither the FBI nor the city police could find evidence to support additional charges."

"What changed?"

"What changed is that Austin's name suddenly disappeared from court documents."

"I noticed that when I was at the library. What happened?"

"I can only guess, but as far as I know, there are two possibilities. One: there was a confidential plea bargain in which the charges against Austin were dropped in return for information. Or two: there was insufficient evidence to move ahead. I couldn't get confirmation from my sources on which it was, but there were rumours that a key witness had disappeared."

"Disappeared? Does Austin have a record of violence?"

asked Willson, thinking of his threats against Stoffel and the body in the firebombed office.

"I didn't pick up anything like that, not in any of my research. Why do you ask?"

"He was accused of threatening a wildlife researcher who opposes his project. And that same researcher's office burned down a few weeks later. A research assistant was killed in the fire. The researcher is sure it was Austin."

"Jesus," said Berland, his eyes staring blankly out the window. "That would be a dramatic escalation, even for him. How big is the project?"

"It could involve hundreds of millions of dollars. So perhaps there's more at stake this time. When his name disappeared from the court documents, was that the end of it?"

"No. I kept hearing whispers from trusted insiders hinting there was more below the surface, that all was not what it seemed. I decided to dig into Austin's background myself. My gut told me there *was* something worth pursuing. I tried to interview him a couple of times, but he went underground. The receptionist at Sawtooth told me he'd left town for an indefinite period. So, I did what you're doing now. I drove to Salt Lake City, his previous base. It was an illuminating trip. Turns out it wasn't the first time Austin had been involved — or allegedly involved — in something like this."

Willson's right hand moved quickly as she scribbled in her notebook. "Tell me more," she said, her eyes eager.

"No matter who I talked to or where I looked, I heard the same things. First, Austin doesn't stay in one place for long. I think he was in Salt Lake City for only three years. Before that, he was in Texas. I also uncovered documents that hinted he'd been involved with something in South America prior to that."

"Bit of a vagabond, is he?"

"He is. And when people move around a lot like that, it makes me more curious. I found that most of his business dealings involved some kind of investment scheme — some legitimate, others less so. With that sort of thing, there's always a paper trail if one knows where to look. And when I dug deeper, I saw that Austin did leave a trail behind him, albeit a faint one. In most cases, by the time people figured out that something was wrong, he'd already left town."

"Seems like we're both on his trail now, although you're well ahead of me."

"It's always better to have two sets of eyes looking for clues."

An optimist, albeit a cautious one, Willson sensed Berland was starting to see her as an ally. "I agree completely," she said, "particularly if we share what we find."

"We seem to be on the same wavelength," said Berland. "As an investigative journalist, I don't normally work with anyone else. Few do in this business. Exclusives are our reason for living. But I think we might be able to help each other out."

"I agree. You seem to have picked up on a pattern in his behaviour; I can't help but wonder if he's continuing it in Canada."

"I wouldn't put it past him."

Willson turned to check on her mother. She was buried in her novel, oblivious to the busy coffee shop around her. "You didn't say what you found when you dug into Austin's dealings in Salt Lake City," she said, her attention back on Berland.

The reporter slid a small stack of documents out of a file folder and pushed them across the table toward her. "It was a whole different ball game. Seems that Austin and his business associates there were into gold mining."

"Gold mining? That *is* different." The fingers of Willson's right hand stroked the edges of the documents. They were tempting her, calling her name. *Read me. Study me.* But she kept her attention on Berland.

"And just like what happened here in Boise, it appears that Austin wasn't the main player in the project. From what I could uncover, he was more of a supporting actor."

"Where was the mine?"

"In Iron County, southern Utah."

"And the controversy?" asked Willson.

"It turned out to be a classic stock market play. Not a first for the mining sector. There *was* a mine, there's no doubt about that: the Silver Queen Mine. It seems that company officials from the Silver Queen Mining Corporation significantly over-reported the mine's potential production by a few orders of magnitude, including claiming that it would produce copper, silver, *and* gold for far longer than was actually the case."

"Which made the stock more attractive to investors."

"That it did. And not only that, they also sold more shares than they were legally allowed to by the Securities Exchange Commission. One family invested more than two million dollars in the company."

"Where did Austin come into the picture?"

"He was alleged to have been one of the people selling the stock, mostly to Mormon families. And he took a cut of those sales, although I never could find out how much."

Willson recalled her one and only conversation with Austin. He'd talked about initial investors and said more would be coming in later. Did he have the same kind of scheme planned? "Was he convicted of anything in that one?"

"No," said Berland. "It seemed that when the noose started to tighten, when the SEC investigators began putting pressure on him, he turned on his co-conspirators and acted as a witness for the prosecution."

"No honour amongst thieves?"

"Not this bunch. Once things got hot, they were like rats jumping from a sinking ship. It was an easy conviction for the feds because of the number of accused willing to spill the beans. The company president finally took the big fall. He was the last rat standing. When all was done, it was obvious the thing had been a scam. The president was permanently barred from participating in future offerings of penny stocks and was ordered to pay back two point six million dollars, the amount he made from the shares he'd sold plus interest. He and the company are still tied up in bankruptcy court."

"I assume Austin made big money on that deal? Did he have to pay any back?"

"I could never find that out. I bet he did ... but the details were buried in a plea bargain."

"A plea bargain. Where have I heard that before?"

"Exactly. There's that pattern again."

"And then he moved to Boise."

"He disappeared for a few months … but then, yes, he showed up here."

Willson flipped through the stack of documents in front of her — most were court documents and some were news stories from the *Salt Lake Tribune.* But her mind was racing. If Austin had been involved in questionable schemes like the ones Berland had described, what did that mean for the proposal? Was it legitimate, or another swindle? In the other frauds, Austin had always been in the background, not the main player or the frontman. Was there someone else, a mystery man or woman, behind the resort proposal? Or did Austin think he'd learned enough from his past brushes with the law that he no longer needed to work with or for someone else, but could successfully pull it off himself … whatever *it* was? He certainly had the ego.

"As I mentioned," said Willson, "Austin's submission to our governments implies that he has a background in building ski areas. In your research, did you find anything to confirm that?"

"I didn't. But to be honest, I didn't go any further back than what I've told you about. I'd heard rumours about South America, maybe Chile or Argentina. But my bosses wouldn't let me pursue it. I dug up a few newspaper articles, but they were in Spanish, so that was the end of it."

"Jesus," Willson said, "I came here for answers … and I feel like I've come away with more questions. One thing I'm sure of is that I'm more concerned than ever about Austin."

"You have a right to be. He's a guy I've had my eye on, but he's tough to track as he moves from one project to another. It was frustrating as hell for me to leave the trail when I did. I have no doubt he's still out there, moving from project to project. And now, it seems, from one country to another."

Willson studied Berland. He reminded her of an archer's taut bowstring, pulled back to the limit, fully loaded, ready to release. He was sitting with hands clenched, his eyes bright and brimming with the passion of an ambitious journalist. "On the surface, he's just another shyster who takes money from people crazy enough, or greedy enough, to give it to him," she said. "Why do you care so much about this guy, Mike?"

Berland raised his eyebrows, then smiled, visibly relaxing. "Is it that obvious?"

"You look like you might spontaneously combust right in front of me." said Willson. "I've spent the last five minutes wondering where the fire extinguisher is."

Berland chuckled and sat back in his chair. Willson's question had forced him to take a breath and relax.

"It doesn't take an investigator to figure out I'm passionate about this subject," he said. "When I came out of J-school at Boise State, I started as a junior reporter on the crime beat at the local paper. I was covering small-town stuff — assaults, thefts, domestic disputes. We all knew about Woodward and Bernstein and their role in uncovering Watergate, and I was fascinated by the investigative journalists telling the stories no one else was telling. I wanted to be one of those guys. I wanted to dig in the shadows, shine a light on the stuff that the politicians and business people didn't want revealed. When the global economy declined, all because of the despicable actions of the top guys at the Enrons and Goldman Sachses and WorldComs, I began to specialize in financial crimes because I saw that more people were being hurt by those than by so-called regular crime. At least it seemed that way."

Willson saw a look of melancholy pass over his face. "But there's more to this than that, isn't there, Mike? This is personal." It was more a statement than a question. She felt a pinch of compassion for Berland. It was a new sensation and it made her a little nauseated.

"My grandparents were taken for almost all their life savings by a guy just like Austin," Berland said. "As a result, their last years before they both passed away were very tough."

"But there's so much of this kind of thing going on all across North America — why Austin?"

"No, I know, there's nothing special about him per se; he's one of hundreds of people who make a living off the greed and ignorance of others. But Austin's trail has so many links to so many places that it seemed like a trail worth pursuing. Once I was on it, it was tough to quit." He looked past Willson toward the window, tapping his fingernail on his empty mug. "I hadn't thought about him in a few years, but with this new link north of the border that you've brought me, Jenny, that's changed. Quite frankly, this kind of story could be my ticket to a bigger paper in a bigger city, even if it isn't Watergate or Enron." He slid his chair back from the table and stretched his long legs out into the aisle beside them. The bow was now fully relaxed, the pressure on the string released.

"And what about you?" he asked. "Why do *you* care so much about this guy?"

"Fair question," said Willson. "I thought a lot about that driving down here. There are two reasons. The first is that the ski area, if approved, could have devastating effects on the park where I work and on the surrounding area, which is massive and wild and currently still free of human impact. Yes, a formal environmental assessment needs to be done, but I don't need to wait for the results to know a ski resort is the wrong thing for the area. It's a stupid idea. The thought of it going ahead sickens me. For me, this is about standing up for what's right, for what I believe in. 'The idea of wilderness needs no defense. It only needs more defenders.'"

"That sounds like Edward Abbey."

"That's right," Willson said in surprise. "It is. How'd you know that?"

"We studied him in journalism school. He's where I got the idea that our profession shines a light into the darkness."

"I like his reasoning on most topics," said Willson. "And I think I'm becoming more jaded, perhaps more of an anarchist, like Abbey was, than I ever used to be. That may come from working for government."

"I get you there," said Berland. "And your second reason for caring so much about Austin?"

"That might surprise you. In my short career, I've seen too many economic development projects come forward and, almost overnight, polarize communities, pitting neighbours against each other. Don't get me wrong, I'm no bleeding-heart liberal. I hate government bullshit and I hate useless process. But it seems like our system forces people to pick sides, what with every new development presented as a black or white, win or lose scenario. It's always destructive. It's always yes or no. Whether Austin's proposal is legitimate or not, I can already see this happening in my hometown, and it pisses me off. And after all that, if it's *not* a legitimate project and if it falls on its face, then the community— the people I care about — will be left to pick up the pieces."

Willson felt a hand on her shoulder and jumped.

"Jenny," said her mother, "I'm sorry to interrupt, but I'd really like to go back to the hotel now, if you don't mind."

Willson realized that in telling Berland how she felt about the ski proposal, she'd become as tightly wound as he'd been. And she hadn't even told him her real reason for starting the investigation. For that, she felt a momentary twinge of guilt.

By asking her the right questions and listening sincerely without judging, Berland had helped her to articulate how she felt. It was the first time in a long time she'd been open and honest with anyone. She looked at the reporter with new eyes. Sharing thoughts and emotions was a new and different experience for her, frightening. Nausea again tickled her stomach. The fact that they'd both learned from each other by probing and listening did not escape her. But neither did it make her more comfortable about being laid bare so easily.

"Okay, Mum," she said, putting her hand on her mother's. She turned back to Berland. "My mind's reeling from what I've learned from you, Mike. I need time to think about where to take things from here."

"And now that Austin has raised his head again, you've rekindled *my* interest in him," said Berland. "So we *both* have some thinking to do. Thanks."

"Mum and I are heading home tomorrow. How about if I give you a call in a week or so? We can talk then about if and how we could work together, and what the next steps might look like."

"I'd like that," he said, taking her hand in both of his.

She liked it right back.

CHAPTER 14

On her first full day back in Golden, Willson drove to the Service B.C. office on the north edge of downtown, passing the blackened skeleton that was once Albin Stoffel's office. It was now encircled by a chain-link fence likely erected by an insurance company worried about theft or children playing in the ruins. It was also a stark reminder to everyone about the power of fire. She saw a bundle of flowers, now brown and dried out, tucked against one corner of the fencing. Someone had cared for Webb, and that someone was now suffering her loss.

During the trip back north from Boise, Willson's mother had become increasingly silent. As they crossed the border into Canada, the weather worsened; a low-pressure storm was pushing in from the west. Willson hadn't needed to turn her head to see her mother wringing her hands in her lap, shifting uncomfortably in her seat. The anxiety was palpable. Was she worried about winter driving, or was it something else, a response to the cold weather and the memories it blew in? Time for an educated guess.

"How do you feel about coming home again, Mum?" she'd asked.

"I had a nice time with you, Jenny, and it was wonderful to be in a different place for a while, where no one knew me, or asked me how I was feeling … or watched or judged me."

"Do you like living in Golden?"

"I've asked myself that same question. I'm not sure anymore. I have friends, but the town reminds me so much of your father that I still see him everywhere. At the hockey arena, at the restaurants we used to go to, on the trail where we used to walk along the river. And every time I hear a train coming through town, I can't help but think about the horrible way he left us. Those trains set my heart racing."

"Mine, too. Do you see yourself ever moving somewhere else? You've lived in Golden a long time."

"I'm not sure. It would be nice to get a fresh start somewhere else. But I'd be leaving my friends. And it would feel as if I were abandoning your father's memory somehow, all that we built together. I don't know." Her hands moved quickly. "I don't know if I'm ready to do that. It scares me to think about it."

"It's okay, Mum. I'm not pushing you. You should do what feels right. You know I'm here to support you, whatever you decide." Without conscious effort, Willson's right hand had found her mother's left; their hands had remained intertwined across the centre console for the rest of the trip up the Rocky Mountain Trench.

That evening, they shared a light dinner of soup, crackers, and aged cheese at her mother's small kitchen table. Speaking little, they were content in each other's company. More than ever, Willson knew, her mother needed someone to talk to in order to help her through the worst of the depression and finally, after twenty years, fully come to terms with the loss of her husband. It was as if her mother had stayed trapped in the past for all this time with no way forward. And this time of year, with the cold, snowy, dark days, was obviously the toughest for her.

It occurred to Willson that she'd seen this before in warden colleagues who'd dug skiers from avalanche rubble, or located the battered bodies of dead rock climbers, or found missing hikers mauled and literally torn apart by grizzly bears. In their male-dominated world, it was common for wardens to ignore the horror they'd seen, push it to the far corners of their brains, get back on the proverbial horse, suck it up, and move on with life. But those horrible experiences, if not resolved, would lurk like a malignancy in the mind's hiding places, waiting to show themselves when least expected. Willson was no psychiatrist, but she thought it possible her mother had some kind of undiagnosed post-traumatic stress disorder to do with her husband's death. Willson vaguely recalled a checklist of symptoms one was supposed to look for … she should've paid more attention during that PTSD session at work. It would explain a lot. As soon as she could, she'd ask her human resources department for the name of a good crisis counsellor. They'd know where to start.

Thinking about helping her mother take that first step gave Willson a sense of relief. It was definitely past time for her to get her mother the help she needed.

"I'm Jenny Willson with the Yoho Warden Service. I'd like to do a company search, please."

The government agent was balanced on a stool behind the counter. She looked Willson up and down, taking in her warden's uniform. No judgment, just verifying. "Not a problem," she said. "As a government employee, it will cost you ten dollars per search. What kind of information are you looking for?" Her hands were poised over her keyboard as if ready to play a sonata on a grand piano.

"I don't think the company has been in existence long, but I need anything you can give me. I want to know who owns it, who the directors are, whether they're up to date on their corporate filings, office location info … the whole package."

"I can do that for you. What's the company name?"

"Collie Creek Resorts Limited."

"Ah … you're the first. I wondered when someone would ask for this."

"Why's that?"

"Well, the company and the Top of the World project are the talk of the town," said the agent, her fingers flying, "and because of the connection to the national park, I'm not surprised you're asking."

"It's all part of due diligence so we know who we're dealing with," said Willson. "Have you heard anything about them?"

"Nothing official," said the agent, "but I know that the folks in the resort development branch of our government are all over the proposal. And that provincial ministers and members of the legislative assembly are asking a lot of questions."

"Do you know if the Province of B.C. has an official position on the proposal yet?"

"It's probably too early," said the woman, "but I've seen this many times before. The formal government statements at this stage of a major project always express a degree of conceptual interest. Senior people know not to go beyond that because it could come back to bite them later, in the media, in a court of law, or in the court of public opinion. So any real interest is couched in paragraphs of political or bureaucratic double-speak. They have whole departments specializing in media releases that say nothing."

"Just like the federal government ..." said Willson with a knowing nod.

"Just like it ... and here we go," said the woman, pointing at the screen. "I'll print you a copy of the company summary. It should give you everything you need."

Willson absentmindedly passed the woman her credit card while she scanned the summary report. The two pages were a quick, superficial glimpse into Collie Creek Resorts Ltd. From having investigated other companies in earlier cases, Willson knew this information was just the face of the business that they were required to show to regulators. But it was never the whole picture. Not by a long shot.

Collie Creek Resorts had been incorporated for fourteen months. Its registered office was in Golden, just a few blocks away, while its records office was at an address in Calgary. From the number and street name, Willson assumed the office was a law firm, one of many specializing in people and businesses at the edge of both their budgets and the law. *No surprises here.* The company was in good standing, the annual report up to date, and there were no liquidation proceedings under way, nor any receivers involved.

On the second page, Willson found the key names in the company. Stafford Austin was listed not only as a director, but also the president. Hank Myers, whom Willson had also met at the open house, was a director and the vice-president. It seemed to Willson a strange role for someone who looked like he'd be more at home on the set of a military thriller than in a boardroom.

The corporate secretary was a Francine Rhodes, based in Calgary. Willson figured she was one of the Calgary lawyers. The remaining two directors listed were John Theroux and Sandra Jane Trueman, both with the same Golden address. Willson hadn't heard either name since returning to town. She tapped her finger on each of the names, one at a time, as though it were an internet link she could click to reveal the person's real history. *I already know something about Austin, and a little about Myers. Who are the rest of you, and what role do you play in this thing?*

Time to spend a few hours with Mr. Google and the police information database.

Despite her intention to start the deeper search, Willson spent the rest of the week preparing for a trio of court cases in front of the provincial court judge who came to Golden from Cranbrook a few times a month. She knew him to be friendly and fair, but his expectations were high for those appearing before him. The three files had been left a mess by her predecessor, so she'd invested many hours re-interviewing witnesses and reassessing evidence. In the end, it was worth her time; she got convictions on two out of the three cases. The third, a charge of illegal dumping, was tossed out by the judge because the evidence didn't directly link the dumped material and the alleged offender beyond a reasonable doubt. While disappointed that she hadn't gone three for three, Willson knew the judge had made the right call. Before her cases had come up, she had seen Benoit Fortier across the room, looking damn good in his uniform. He waved and smiled when she caught his eye. Never mind her success in court; that, she decided, had been the best part of her day.

After a debriefing in the hallway with the Crown prosecutor, Willson turned quickly and bumped hard into Fortier, who was standing behind her. He caught her shoulders with his strong hands, a grin on his face.

"Whoa, there!" he said.

"Sorry," said Willson, though she was far from sorry. "I didn't see you there." She took her time releasing her own grip on his waist.

"It's okay. As promised, I came to tell you we got the coroner's report back on Sue Webb."

"Cause of death?"

"It looks as if she died of smoke inhalation."

"Huh. It's such a small building. Why wasn't she able to get out when the fire started?"

"There's more to it," said Fortier. "She had a head injury that would likely have incapacitated her. The coroner's report suggests that it happened before she died."

"Really? You said you found her body under a collapsed wall. Could that have caused the head injury?"

"I wondered that as well," said Fortier, "but the fire investigator is convinced that the wall came down well after the fire had started, and that she was already dead by then."

"Webb was assaulted before the fire started?"

"It could be," said Fortier, "or she hurt herself trying to get out of the building. Unless we get more evidence, we'll never know for certain. But either way, this remains a homicide investigation. The Serious Crimes guys are involved, and they're now trying to figure out whether someone meant to hurt or kill Webb, then set the fire to cover it up ... or whether Webb was just in the wrong place at the wrong time and it was, as we first assumed, all about Stoffel and his research."

"Holy shit," said Willson.

"Exactly."

Two nights later, Willson sat in a worn armchair in her small house with a tumbler of Talisker Scotch in hand.

It was a crisp, cold night and the sky outside the window was full of stars. Through a gap in the trees, she could see the light from the restaurant at the top of the Kicking Horse ski resort twinkling like one more star.

She flipped through the local newspaper, skimming over stories about kids in trouble with the law, the successes of the local Junior B hockey team, and sales at local furniture and grocery stores. It was a typical small-town newspaper run on a shoestring budget with reporters who were either on their way up or had been there too long. It took only minutes to read, but it was a valuable snapshot into what made Golden tick. She'd read the front-page story about the ongoing investigation into Webb's death, but it had nowhere near the detail she'd gotten from Fortier. Her mind was still churning after their courthouse conversation. Who had been responsible for Webb's death? What was the link, if any, between the fire and the resort proposal? Was the ski area so important to someone that they were willing to kill for it?

Willson sipped the smooth Scotch, her left hand gripping the tumbler tightly, her eyes unfocused. She thought about Frank Speer and their agreement. What had at the time seemed like a simple conversation had evolved into something much more complex. This was a project with more questions than answers. Willson pictured an iceberg, most of its mass lurking out of sight below the surface, potentially deadly. And at the centre of it all was Stafford Austin.

CHAPTER 15

FEBRUARY 10

Stafford Austin watched the light of understanding click on in Hank Myers's face, as suddenly as it had for him in the darkened corner of the Red Deer restaurant. Austin had invited Myers to his rental house on the Blaeberry River Road north of Golden to fill him in on what he'd learned on his trip. He'd chosen this house because it was on a large rural property with a dramatic eastern view through the Blaeberry River valley, framed by peaks of the Rocky Mountains as it narrowed to form the gateway to Collie Creek, to the site of the project he hoped would be his opportunity to prove to members of the Terminal City Club that he belonged there.

The two men sat opposite each other in a pair of over-stuffed leather chairs, a single lamp illuminating a circle of the carpeted floor between them. Beside each chair was a small wooden table. Austin's right hand, resting on a table, held a crystal glass of bourbon. Myer's left hand did the same.

"You're telling me," said Myers, "that they're asking us to find investors for a highway through Howse Pass, a project that might also become a corridor for a pipeline?"

"That's exactly what I'm saying."

"Well, son of a bitch. We were wondering how we were going to finance a highway to the resort and now this falls in our lap. Unbelievable. This changes everything. Do you really think they're serious?"

"They sure as hell seemed serious," said Austin. "And if they are, it's a huge opportunity for us to cultivate a new group of investors and a new stream of income for the investment fund, not only during the design and construction phases, but also from the tolls on the highway and the pipeline. Or we could start a new fund. If we pitch it right, it could be a compelling story to tell existing and potential investors, a way to help them believe in what we're doing. And as I'm sure you've already realized, if we're successful, it could mean a shitload more money flowing to you and me."

"That never even crossed my mind," said Myers, smiling and raising his glass.

"But let's not fool ourselves here," Austin said. He stood with glass in hand and began pacing. "The more I think about what Thomas and Cummings told me, the more I wonder what's going on behind the scenes. There's got to be more to it." He traversed the carpeted living room, moving from the kitchen door to the fireplace and back again, his reflection passing across the darkened picture window.

"What are you worried about?" asked Myers. "This looks like the ideal scenario for us, better than we could have imagined. We'll have all levels of government behind us."

"That's exactly why I'm not sure what's going on. I have a million questions about what they're suggesting. And to be honest, a bunch of it makes no sense. And then there's the fact that two politicians approached us secretively — one of them elected, the other a back-roomer who normally hides in the shadows. It's odd. And it makes me nervous."

"What kinds of questions do you have? It seems pretty straightforward to me."

"Straightforward? Far from it. The first question I've had, right from the moment they started talking to me, is *why me*? The party in power is supported by big money and way bigger players than me. So out of all their possible choices, all the friends and cronies they could've tapped on the shoulder to make this happen, why did they approach me?"

"That's easy," said Myers. "Because you're the guy who's already stepped up to invest in a project right in the middle of the longest portion of the potential route. You're the one who's shown to be willing to make something big happen in that area. And maybe your lack of direct connection to them is useful. Maybe it just makes sense to them because who else has so much to gain if it goes ahead? Who's going to work harder to make it a reality?"

"Perhaps," said Austin. "But they've linked the highway, which will be controversial enough on its own, with a route for a pipeline. That I don't get. I mean, I understand how desperate governments and big companies are to get Alberta oil and gas to markets, but everyone knows that pipelines are a political nightmare. And a pipeline through Canada's best-known national park? They'd be walking into a hornet's nest, one where the hornets are already seriously pissed off because too many people have been poking them with sticks."

"But you said this Cummings guy was a senior adviser to the prime minister, and that the PM knew he was talking to you. That must mean something."

"These days, political involvement at the highest levels doesn't necessarily mean anything for the success of a project. There are too many explosive issues that could get in the way. Politicians shift back and forth like weathervanes. Look how many pipeline proposals have failed so far. They've tried to run them from Alberta to B.C. and failed. They tried one going south through the U.S., but our last president shot it down. They're trying to get one from Alberta all the way to Halifax on the Atlantic coast, and that's been an uphill battle."

"Okay, but this route is one of the shortest through the Rocky Mountains to the West Coast. Maybe it has a better chance of succeeding."

"That's the next question," said Austin. "A new piece of highway through Howse Pass makes economic sense for central Alberta. Instead of the long drive to the coast south on Highway 2, then west through Banff via the Trans-Canada, it's a straight shot to Golden that would reduce the distance by ninety-five kilometres. That's an hour less driving time for commercial and industrial traffic. But the idea of a pipeline makes no sense. It would be a pipeline to *nowhere*."

"What do you mean?"

"At the Alberta end, it could certainly connect to oil or gas fields and then flow through the mountains. That's fine. But the pipeline would end up north of Golden, near where we are now, in a valley that runs north-south, not east-west. That means someone would still have to build three hundred kilometers of new pipeline to ship oil or gas south to the U.S. border. Or they'd have to build more than five hundred kilometres of new pipeline to the B.C. coast at Vancouver, across four or five more mountain ranges. How is that going to help anything?"

"I see your point," said Myers. He took a slow last sip of the smoky bourbon, emptying the glass. "But maybe we don't care if it makes 100 percent sense or not," he said, standing to stretch. "If the federal government is behind it, we have an opportunity to make money. And even if it takes years for the idea to run its course through the maze of fucking review processes, what do we care? If the proposal dies a decade or two from now, so what? We'll make money at every step along the way, no matter what the outcome is. For us, it's no different than the resort project. Like you said earlier, all we have to do is convince people with money to believe in what we're doing, believe they can make *more* money by getting involved. To buy into the dream."

"And there lies our continuing challenge," said Austin. "But we're getting good at that, aren't we?"

"We sure as hell —"

The picture window exploded, interrupting Myers midsentence. He grunted and dropped to the floor as the crack of a rifle reached the inside of the house. Seconds later, there was a second crack. A corner of the fireplace blew apart, sending fragments of brick and mortar across the room, one piece tearing into Austin's right hand. He yelped and dropped the glass he'd been raising toward his mouth. Crystal, ice, bourbon, and blood joined the shattered glass on the carpet at his feet.

"Get down," croaked Myers, holding his left shoulder with his right hand. Blood was leaking through his fingers. "Get down!"

"What the ..." Austin was frozen in place. He looked toward the missing window, saw a muzzle flash, and at the same time heard a third crack. A chunk of the wooden fireplace mantle to his left spun up and embedded itself in the ceiling.

"Get on the fucking floor!" Myers yelled. "Someone's shooting at us!"

Austin dropped to the carpet and began crawling toward the kitchen, desperately trying to get as far from the shooter as he could.

"Turn off the lamp," yelled Myers. "Turn off the lamp! We're sitting fucking ducks in here."

Austin reversed direction and squirmed his way across the room on his elbows and knees like a swollen inchworm. Turning on his right side and keeping his head down, he slowly reached for the lamp with his left hand. But before he could touch the switch, the lamp flew off the table in a blaze of sparks, broken bulb, and shredded shade.

"Son of a bitch!" he yelled and began crawling back toward the kitchen. In the darkened room, he rolled like a barrel through the doorway, banging his head against a cabinet. Now prone, he peered around the door frame and saw Myers's dark shape crawling toward the open window, the outline of his 9mm pistol visible in his bloodied right hand. Austin's own hand was throbbing with acute pain.

When Myers reached the window, he sat with his back to the wall, turned onto his hands and knees, rose up quickly, and fired into the darkness, emptying the twelve-shot magazine two shots at a time. Then he slumped back to the floor, dropped the pistol, grabbed his shoulder, and groaned. Austin could hear his breathing, fast and shallow.

"Call 911," Myers croaked. "I don't know if I hit them. But I need an ambulance ..." He slumped onto his right side, leaving a streak of red across the wall.

CHAPTER 16

It was a cold afternoon for an outdoor rally, with a brisk north wind blowing directly at the backs of the locals huddled outside the provincial MLA office on 9th Street. Jenny Willson stood at the rear of the group, dressed in a toque, leather ski gloves, and a thigh-length down parka with the hood up, partly hiding her face. Even though she'd grown up in Golden, she was still unknown to many, and she wanted to keep it that way for as long as she could. She turned to count the crowd, twisting her body to the left and then to the right so the face opening in her parka hood followed her. Nearly two hundred people. That was a decent turnout on a day like today. *No doubt the president of the United States would claim it was half a million*, she thought.

Someone was tapping on the microphone of a public-address system. It took a few moments for the crowd to quiet down.

"Ladies and gentlemen," said a disembodied voice, "we're here to let our provincial government know that we want the Top of the World resort to go ahead — we want our local economy to grow. Please gather around nice and close so we can get started."

At five foot seven, Willson was by no means short. But she still couldn't see whose voice it was, though she noted the set of speakers mounted on the back of a red pickup truck. She shifted her position a few metres to the left and saw a man about her height standing on the far sidewalk holding a microphone. His tanned face, almost skeletal with its angles and hollows, was framed by a hand-knit toque with earflaps. Next to him was a small, mousy-looking woman with a fringe of curly brown hair showing under a Cowichan-knit hat, and behind them were others holding hand-drawn placards. Some were adults, some children. To Willson, they all looked cold and uncertain about being there. She scanned the signs: *Ski Top of the World*; *Ski Collie Creek*; *Wilderness or Full Bellies?*; *Grow Our Economy*; *My Dad Needs a Job*; *I Want to Raise a Family in Golden*.

She turned to a young woman standing to her right who was wearing a small beanie-style hat, with her long, brown hair pulled back in a ponytail underneath it. "Who's the guy talking?" she asked.

"That's John Theroux," said the woman. "He's head of the Collie Creek Ski Society. And the woman on his left is Sandy Trueman, his wife-slash-partner. She's on the executive of the society. They're the loudest supporters of the ski area. Everyone says it was Theroux's idea originally and that he was the one who encouraged the developer to come here and build it."

"Really?" said Willson, thinking about what she'd seen on the corporate records for Collie Creek Resorts Ltd. "I didn't know it was Theroux's idea. Do you know what he and his wife do here in town?"

"As far as I know, Theroux is a backcountry skier and works as a logger in the off-season. Trueman runs an online newspaper — mostly local news and gossip, a place for locals to rant and rave anonymously. It's biased toward things she believes in and very hostile about things she doesn't."

"Interesting," said Willson. "What do *you* think about the new ski area proposal?"

The woman looked around as though concerned about who was listening. "I ... I don't really know yet. I'm here to find out more about it. There are strong opinions in this town, both for and against. I don't want to be on the wrong side of any of them. My husband just started a home-based woodworking business, and we don't want to get involved in any of the controversy." Her voice softened. "He didn't want me to come here today." The last part of her sentence was drowned out by the screech of feedback from the sound system.

"Let's get started," said Theroux, his amplified voice bouncing off nearby buildings. "Like all of you, I'm excited about the Top of the World Resort being right in our backyard. It's what this town needs to diversify its economy and bring in more jobs and more investment. I hope you'll be loud and proud in letting our MLA know that we need her to take the message to Victoria: this town wants that ski area!"

Trueman, as if on cue, clapped her hands loudly. Her face was pinched as her eyes followed his every word, his every movement, as though she were a choreographer watching a performance of her creation. Others in the crowd began to applaud, nervously at first, and then the sound built to a first crescendo. Those with placards and signs raised them in the air, shaking and bouncing them in time to the clapping. *These guys are just getting started*, Willson thought. And this *was* all well-choreographed. She wondered how much media was here today.

"First," said a smiling Theroux, "I'm pleased to invite Stafford Austin up to say a few words. Many of you have met Stafford in Golden over the last few months. I'm honoured to call him my friend. As you know, he's the visionary who's bringing us the dream of a new four-season glacier resort."

From where she was standing, Willson hadn't seen Austin. She hadn't been sure he'd attend, after what had happened ten days earlier. That night, Benoit Fortier had phoned her from Austin's house to tell her there'd been a shooting. She'd gone out there to help look for evidence at the edge of the property — shell casings or footprints. But they'd found nothing. Austin and Myers were already on their way to the hospital by the time she arrived, so it was just her and Fortier after all the other officers had left the scene. She'd seen the carnage inside the house: broken window glass covering the living room floor, a smashed table lamp, pools of blood on the carpet, more blood on a wall, splinters of brick and wood scattered around the room. Without much effort, they'd found one bullet embedded in the wood mantle, another in the ceiling, and a third deep in the ash of the fireplace. By the time they'd left the house early the next morning, Austin had been released from the Golden hospital and Myers had been transferred to Calgary's Foothills hospital by ambulance, his condition unknown but with a bullet buried in his shoulder.

Willson was surprised to see Austin here, only ten days after being shot at. He took a few steps forward from the front row, shook Theroux's hand warmly, then turned and waved to the crowd with his heavily bandaged right hand. It was bold to make such a public appearance with the shooter still at large. Willson considered Webb's death alongside the shooting and found herself looking at Austin in a new light. Here was a man increasingly shadowed by controversy and trouble. And now violence. Despite Willson's initial digging into him, who he was, and what he was doing, she was still far from getting a clear picture. It was like trying to read a book from kilometres away with a telescope. Was Austin simply an innocent proponent who was the target of overzealous opponents, of someone who wanted him gone ... or dead? Or was this a consequence of something else, some other business he was involved in?

She watched him take the microphone and begin what was clearly a practised speech, likely one he'd given many times before to audiences large and small, not unlike what she'd heard from him at the open house. But here, in this bigger group that was clearly in favour of his project, he showed more enthusiasm, more flair for the dramatic, a sense of showmanship that came from a career built on trying to sell people things they didn't need.

"My friends," he said, his American accent strong, "I'm pleased to be in Golden, and pleased to be working in a community that is excited about its future. I want to be part of that exciting future." Again, the applause was led by Theroux and Trueman. A few shouted, "Yeah!" and "Right on!" She waited for a "Hallelujah!" but perhaps that was saved for later in the script.

"However, John has been too kind. It was John himself who first came up with the idea of a ski area in Collie Creek, and it was John who invited me to be part of it. I really don't deserve any of the credit." He lifted his right arm and gripped Theroux around the shoulder, grimacing as he did so. "I'd like you to give a warm round of applause to a man who cares deeply about his community, who wants all of you to have a better life." The applause was much more spontaneous this time, and Theroux's face showed that he was basking in the glory of the moment. His smile was wide, his eyes bright. Trueman stood on his other side, staring up at him as if he were a god.

Jesus Christ, it's the Collie Creek friggin' mutual appreciation society. What the fuck will they do if this thing doesn't go ahead? Who will they blame? She turned to look at the young woman beside her, afraid that she'd spoken aloud. But the woman was staring straight ahead, her hands buried deep in her pockets.

"We've got lots of work to do yet," Austin continued, "and there are many steps in the process to come. But you can do your part by making sure that your federal and provincial representatives know you want this project to go ahead. I look forward to making Top of the World a reality, with and for you. We can do this together." He again waved to the crowd and then returned to the front row, bumping fists with Theroux as he did so.

When Theroux reclaimed the microphone, the mood of the gathering immediately changed. "I think you all understand how Top of the World will benefit this community," he said. "That's why you're here today. But I'm going to be honest with you. Brutally honest. There are people among us who are opposed to it, who are working to see the idea fail. Some of them are outsiders who don't care about us or about this community. They'd rather save a few wolverines than see us have good jobs in this town. I suggest that they shouldn't be able to stand in the way of our progress. Don't let them stop Golden from moving ahead!"

He waited until a chorus of "No! No! No!" died down.

"Unfortunately, some of the people who're opposed to the project are also our neighbours. Your neighbours. They're supposed to care about this place, but apparently, they would rather see us stay where we are. They would prefer to see Golden stuck in the past. They don't seem to understand that if we're not growing, we're dying. They don't care about jobs for our young people. They don't care that we have trouble keeping doctors in this town. They don't care that we have to drive to Calgary or Cranbrook to shop because we our economy isn't large enough for us to have everything we need here. They don't care!"

Cries of "Shame!" came from the front row.

"Many of you know that just over a week ago, someone shot at Mr. Austin and his business partner. Was it an attempt to shut him up? To force him to drop the project and leave town? Was he really almost killed for believing in the future of this community? I applaud him, and so should you, for wanting to be with us today despite his injuries and despite the fact that his business partner is still in a Calgary hospital."

This time, the applause was loud and spontaneous.

"We can only do so much to make Top of the World a reality," said Theroux when the crowd was again quiet. "We're working hard. But, as Mr. Austin said, we need your help. We need you to tell the politicians that this town wants to move ahead. We need you to tell the people who oppose the project that they're wrong, that they should keep their mouths shut or move away if they don't like progress."

Someone yelled, "Shut up or move!"

"For too long, we've stood aside while these people oppose everything. We were quiet when they locked up more of our land in parks. We let them close kilometre after kilometre of roads and cut off access to the backcountry. We let them give more rights to wildlife than to people. It's time to tell them, in the loudest possible way, that we're mad as hell and we're not going to take it anymore."

A chant of "No more!" worked its way through the crowd like a wave breaking over the shore. "No more! No more!"

This was more like an old-time religious revival than a business rally, although Willson assumed that for people like Austin and Theroux, there was no clear line between religion and business. Today, Theroux was the preacher, the evangelist trying to lead his flock to economic salvation. Watching him with his fist in the air and a maniacal smile on his face, Willson wondered what was behind his devotion to the project. Was it a sincere and selfless belief in the community, or something more? Was Theroux addicted to the power and admiration — real or perceived — that his leadership of the "yes" side gave him? He was clearly savouring it. But beyond that, Willson wondered how Theroux would benefit if the project went ahead. Were he and others on Austin's payroll, as Albin Stoffel had suggested? If he was listed as a director, then he must be, in some way or another. What would he get if the project succeeded? What would he lose if it didn't? Willson pondered the firebombing of Stoffel's office. She had assumed the perpetrator was either Austin or Myers, or both. But perhaps she was wrong. How far would someone like Theroux go to make the ski resort happen?

The sound of breaking glass broke Willson's train of thought. To her right, she saw the front window of the Golden Coffee House explode inward in thousands of glittering pieces, like a blizzard of ice chips. She sprinted toward the shop, pushing past people frozen in place by the sudden violence. When she reached the front window, she saw a woman inside slumped forward on a table, blood streaming from her neck and head. It was the same young woman she'd spoken to just moments ago.

Willson stepped though the open space where the window had been, already on autopilot. Turning to a man standing behind by the register, she yelled, "Call 911 and confirm for me that you've reached them and that an ambulance is on the way."

"I'm a nurse," said a woman whose arms were filled with napkins gathered from the counter. "I'll help you until the ambulance gets here." The woman hadn't asked Willson if she knew what she was doing. It was obvious.

They worked on the young woman for the next ten minutes, careful not to push any shards of glass deeper into her body, and calmed her down, keeping their voices low and confident. The nurse held the young woman's hand. She had cuts all across the back of her head and neck — some deep and some superficial. As she edged toward shock, she kept saying over and over again, "My husband told me I shouldn't come today. I should have listened to him. I should have listened…." Like all head wounds, hers bled profusely. The pile of napkins quickly became soaked. The woman had been lucky to be wearing heavy winter clothes; the lack of a hood on her jacket explained the location of her injuries.

The ambulance arrived at the same time as Ben Fortier. He helped the paramedics load the woman onto a stretcher, and she was quickly transported to the hospital.

"Did either of you see what happened?" Fortier asked, notebook in hand.

"No," said Willson. "I was on the other side of the crowd when I heard the window break. I didn't see anything."

"I was inside," said the nurse. "Something broke the window, but I didn't catch what it was or where it came from."

"What was going on at the time?" Fortier asked Willson.

"It was the pro–Collie Creek rally," Willson answered as Fortier peered through the broken window. "They were finishing the speeches. John Theroux was challenging the audience to speak up against those who oppose the resort. I wouldn't say it was getting nasty, but there was an edge to it. And he certainly had the crowd whipped into a frenzy. All eyes were on him, including mine, so I didn't see what happened."

"There's a paving stone on the floor here," said Fortier. "Could Theroux have thrown it?"

"Definitely not," said Willson. "As I said, he was at the front, preaching to the crowd."

"Shit," said Fortier, staring at the blood and the broken glass. "I knew about the rally. One of my constables was supposed to be here to keep an eye on things. But he was called away to a motor vehicle accident south of town. I was just about to leave the office to cover for him when we got the call." He pulled off his cap and scratched his head. "I don't think it's a coincidence that someone would target a coffee shop that's known locally for being one of the project's biggest opponents." Fortier turned toward the now-dwindling crowd. "Where's Theroux now? I need to talk to him."

Willson pointed at a red pickup truck speeding down the street away from them. "You'll have to catch him first," she said.

Fortier stared at the truck until it turned onto the highway and disappeared. His gaze shifted back to Willson. "I'll find him," he said, his brow furrowed. "But starting now, it looks like you and I are going to have to work more closely. It seems some or all of this recent violence is connected to Collie Creek, or at least to people on one or other side of the issue. We need to find out what the hell's going on before someone else gets injured or killed."

With one person dead and three injured, the situation Willson had gotten herself involved in had become more dangerous than anticipated. It was time to come clean to Fortier.

"Let's go somewhere to talk," she said. "I've got some things to tell you."

CHAPTER 17

Willson sat in her small office in the parks compound west of Field. She'd spent most of the late morning reading every page of the Top of the World Resort submission, with cups of Kick Ass fuelling her focus. Her mind was filled with a haze of facts and figures, promises and projections, stats and statements, her desk littered with the binders Austin had dumped on the two governments like a load of foul-smelling manure.

Leaning back precariously in her chair (and ignoring the reprimands of every schoolteacher she'd ever had), Willson considered everything she'd read. What would happen to Collie Creek, the surrounding area, and Golden itself if the resort was approved? That wild place would be no more. It would become just like so many other valleys in North America and Europe. Edward Abbey had compared growth like that to a cancer that inevitably led to the death of its host. He'd written about the expansion of human communities and how it often destroyed the very thing that attracted people to them in the first place. In this situation, she completely agreed with Abbey.

She also thought about the breakfast meeting she'd had with Frank Speer. They'd met at the corner of a quiet café in Lake Louise and she'd told him about her investigation, recounting her discussions with Mike Berland in Boise and then describing the recent violence in Golden. When she told him about her decision to tell Officer Fortier what she was doing and why, she'd expected her boss to be angry. But she was surprised by his quiet acceptance of her decision.

"I thought you'd be pissed," she said.

"It's the right thing to do, Jenny. We've got no choice now. This is well beyond anything I ever imagined."

"What about Jack Church? He's going to find out what I'm doing."

"Funny thing about that," said Speer. "Frank phoned me last night in a real flap. In light of the recent events, and with it all being increasingly linked to Collie Creek, he realized that he's in over his head. He still wants the ski area to proceed, but he doesn't know what to do about the violence and controversy swirling around it. Like a good bureaucrat, I think he's worried it'll blow back on him. So he asked for my advice."

"And what did you suggest?"

"I said I would ask you if you'd be willing to work with the RCMP — very quietly, of course — to help in their investigations. I told him that was the best way for us to keep on top of what was going on."

"Did he agree?"

"Let's just say I made sure he saw no other option."

At that, they'd both had a laugh. Willson's original favour to her boss had just been repaid. But his smile had faded when he heard the next part of her plan.

"There is someone else I need to tell," she said.

"Who?"

"Mike Berland."

"And who is Mike Berland?"

"He's the Boise journalist I talked to about Stafford Austin when I was down there."

"A reporter? No way. We can't trust the media with something as sensitive as this."

"Normally," Willson had said, "I'd agree with you. But in this case, I believe he can do things I can't. And if he agrees to my rules — like only printing what I say he can print, and only when I say so — then I think he could be a useful avenue for releasing facts that might not otherwise see the light of day."

Speer had continued to shake his head. "I understand what you're saying, Jenny. But it goes too far. Even though we have some limited whistle-blower protection in Canada, you know how governments feel about employees going rogue when it comes to dealing with the press. Besides that, I think you're being naive here … you're gonna get burned." He pulled off his glasses and stared at Willson for a moment. "I know you think I'm wrong, but I'm assuming you're going to do it anyway …"

Willson didn't answer.

"You need to know that if you proceed down this path," Speer had said, "you don't have my approval. And I can't be there to back you up if things go sideways."

Willson had stared back at him. "Thanks for your advice today, Chief, and for squaring things with Jack Church."

She'd driven away from Lake Louise with the firm belief that she had to involve Berland if she was going to find out the truth behind Austin and his project. But she also knew that by going against her boss's advice, she was crossing a line — a line that would lead her in only one direction.

Willson's agitation was growing. The more she read, the less it made sense. As far as she could tell, the project embodied the *build it and they will come* theory at its worst. If Austin and his colleagues believed the claims they were making in the proposal, she thought, they were delusional. And if they didn't believe them, then they were intentionally misleading everyone. Just like her father amid the confusing world of railroad politics, Willson was frustrated with her own inability to understand what was happening behind the scenes, what drove wealthy people to consider these types of projects. What were they thinking?

For Willson, this was about the potential loss of another wild place and the animals that depended on it just so someone could get rich, or richer. But beyond that, she was also increasingly disturbed that no one was asking the community what it wanted. There were no predetermined objectives for an area like Collie Creek, no goals that being proactively developed and agreed to by the community through consultation or even civil conversation. And in her mind, that was the way things should work. Instead, the entire debacle was nothing more than a bureaucratic reaction to a proposal dumped in their laps by an outsider. It was a process managed by faceless government staff who controlled what questions were being asked and answered, what information was made available and to whom, and what timeframes it would all happen within. The people in the community were being treated as outsiders. All they could do was watch the process move toward what Willson saw as a pre-ordained conclusion: approval of the project.

With her feet up on her desk and her eyes closed, Willson realized that, in the last few days, she had turned an important corner. She was no longer doing this just because she had volunteered for it. For her, it was now a race to the truth. She was doing this for her community, for herself, and perhaps, ultimately, for her father. She was in a race to ensure that the project came to a screeching halt, that the lift towers and quad chairs and fancy overpriced condos and violence that came with it faded away like a nightmare dissipating in the light of day. There was too much at stake to do anything but.

Willson's reverie was interrupted by a knock at the door. She saw Tara Summers in the doorway, her red hair in a ponytail, a questioning look on her face.

"Hey there. Have you had a chance to read the proposal yet?" she asked. "Any thoughts or questions?"

Willson moved forward in her chair; the two front legs banged down on the floor and her own legs followed. The revelations of the last few moments had given her a spurt of energy, a refreshed commitment, and a clear path to follow. "I have and I do."

"Fire away. Like I said, I'm sure you're going to want to ask me about —"

Before Summers could go off on another rambling sermon, Willson interrupted her. "First, I believe even more strongly than I did before that this is a crazy-ass idea that should experience a quick and painful death. It's so bad that it doesn't deserve the slow and horribly polite demise that comes from government process."

"Uh, okay ..." said Summers, clearly surprised by the venomous certainty in Willson's declaration. She took a step back as though distancing herself from the straight talk she rarely heard in government. "You ... you said you had questions?"

"Yes. Why we're spending time and resources on such a ridiculous idea comes to mind. But consider that a rhetorical question. What I *am* wondering is why there's no financial information here other than some wild claims about the direct and indirect benefits that will flow from their investment?"

"Oh, the proponent was required to provide that. Along with the market analysis you saw, they submitted capital cost projections, an analysis of the economic feasibility of the project, and proof of their ability to finance it."

"I didn't see that anywhere in this stinking pile," said Willson, waving an arm at the binders.

"No, it's not there."

"Why not? Where is it?"

"Only a few politicians and senior government staff

have seen that stuff. To do so, they sign nondisclosure agreements with the proponent. I'm not in that loop, so I don't have access to the dollars and cents of the project. But from what I know —"

"How the hell is anyone supposed to develop an informed opinion on whether this project makes any sense or not?" asked Willson, interrupting again. "How's the public supposed to provide input?"

Summers chuckled, but her eyes showed neither joy nor humour. "C'mon, Jenny, you know that the folks who make decisions are under no illusions that they have to please the public. I haven't been in this job long, but even *I* know that's not the way it works. Like I said, the best scenario for them is that the public is divided, like they seem to be on this project. Then, the decision-makers can do whatever they want … whatever they were going to do anyway."

"Shit," said Willson, "you're right. Sorry I went off on you, Tara. This is completely fucked up." While she didn't always agree with Edward Abbey, she was quickly developing a much better understanding of why her hero had been a proponent of anarchy. In his mind, it was a truly serious approach to democracy. In situations like this, it seemed to Willson that democracy took a back seat to the driving frenzy of more business, more development. And government processes led by faceless bureaucrats only made it worse.

"Is anyone taking a run at this thing, Tara, anyone truly opposed to it and making a serious stink? Or is the project nothing more than rainbows coming out of unicorn butts?"

Summers chuckled again. She leaned against the doorway, clearly enjoying the conversation. "I wondered when you'd ask that. You won't be surprised to hear that the two lodges in the adjacent valleys have come out swinging. And the Canadian Mountain Club has already started a letter-writing campaign that's being noticed by key people in Calgary and Ottawa."

"So it should be," said Willson. "Our agency has screwed them something serious on this one."

"I agree. Like I said, they were blindsided by this after a long and very public fundraising campaign to finance the new hut. They have every right to be angry. From what I hear from my friends at the CMC, their lawyers are pursuing a court injunction. If they don't get that, and if the project goes ahead anyway, they'll be looking to Parks Canada to pay them back every dollar they invested in the hut, which was about five hundred thousand — plus interest."

"Jesus. I can't believe we let them go ahead with their project when this proposal was hiding in the weeds. Folks in Ottawa *must* have known."

"I guess we'll never know," said Summers, "but it's something we should all be embarrassed about." She peered around the doorway as if to make sure they weren't being overheard. "I also heard that the Town of Golden now opposes the project. Despite what Austin claims, they quickly realized that a resort located sixty-five kilometres from their town isn't going to provide them much in the way of benefits, not in the long term. But even that wasn't unanimous."

"I wondered when they would figure that out."

Summers nodded. "But most aggressive so far has been the Columbia Valley Environmental Society. Early on, they tried to throw a wrench in the works by submitting their own expression of interest not long after Austin's hit government desks. That had everyone in Calgary and Ottawa turning in frantic circles, at least until someone in the B.C. government decided that the Society's expression was not bona fide. Without discussion, they dismissed the submission, then gave the go-ahead for Austin to be the sole proponent. You've got to give the enviros credit. They tried, and it certainly slowed things down for about six weeks."

"Good on 'em," said Willson with a grin. "I like the way those folks think."

"Since then, the Society has persuaded a trio of American conservation foundations to fund environmental assessments of the area and the project, the kind of assessments the two governments will also ask the proponent to undertake. They've also got money for a media campaign. Collie Creek will soon be crawling with biologists and engineers and snow science experts and journalists. We'll end up with a battle of the studies — it'll no doubt be fought in the media. And there'll likely be a documentary film or two. It's only going to get more interesting."

"You got that right," said Willson. She paused for a moment, head bent over one of the binders, her hand tapping the cover. "I've got another question for you, Tara. Do you think any of the people you've met who are involved with any of these groups, either for or against the resort, would be willing to use violence as a means to an end?"

"Like I said, most of the participants on both sides are extremely strident in their views. No compromises. They don't *seem* violent to me … but I guess one can never be sure what someone will do when they're pushed.… The fact that you're even asking me this tells me just how screwed up this whole thing is. It's pushing people to do things they shouldn't, and it's tearing the community apart."

"You're right," said Willson, shaking her head. "It's a mess. And unfortunately, it seems like it might get worse before it gets better."

CHAPTER 18

The sun, which seemed to be rising higher in the sky with each passing day, shone through the large picture window of Sara Ilsley's kitchen. Her presentation finished, Ilsley circled the large table, pouring coffee from a pitted old enamel pot. Steam rose from mugs that were gripped, for comfort, warmth, or both, by five pairs of hands.

Over the rim of her mug, Ilsley looked at the faces of Columbia Valley Environmental Society's executive committee. Tom Bradley, the president, a bearded man in his late sixties, was a sheep farmer in the Blaeberry valley. The distinctive smell of livestock emanated from his clothing, his skin, and the shock of white hair on his head; he brought it to all Society meetings, no matter where or when they were held. It was, unfortunately, a smell that lingered long after his departure, like an unwanted guest overstaying his welcome.

To Bradley's left was Carol Kraft, the Society's vice-president, a thirty-something single woman who'd inherited a backcountry ski-tour lodge west of Golden after her parents were killed in an avalanche in the French Alps. She was fit and confident and always moved like a caged animal whenever she was indoors.

Beside Kraft, Bob Price held his mug to his face as if it would protect him from having to express an opinion. As the society's treasurer, Price's expertise lay with numbers and spreadsheets, but he seemed uncomfortable with loud discourse or vigorous debate. If asked any question that didn't involve the Society's finances, he would mumble and say little of value.

To Price's left, past president Wayne Warman sat smiling, perhaps with the knowledge that his time on the executive was coming to an end just as this controversial campaign was beginning to simmer.

"That's the strategy recommended by the campaign committee," said Ilsley, her right hand leaving her mug to indicate the flip chart facing the table. "As you've seen and heard, the proposed campaign slogan is Keep Collie Wild. The strategy includes a list of tactics, from social media to political advocacy and from working with First Nations to protest camps and legal challenges. We want the world to know that Collie Creek is a wild and special place that does not deserve to be spoiled by a ski resort that makes absolutely no sense. We've done a few things already, like trying to submit our own expression of interest to compete with Austin's. It's time to get smart and organized. As the society's executive committee, we're asking you to support the campaign committee's recommendation and sign the funding agreements with the American foundations I mentioned earlier."

"We thank you for your willingness to lead this, Sara," said Bradley, taking the lead after Ilsley's summary. "It's good work. My first question: Have we forgotten anything?"

"The committee tried to think of all possible scenarios and then plan for each," said Ilsley in response, "and I think we've done a good job of that. But the strategy can't be chiselled into a stone tablet, Tom. We must remain focused on stopping the project, but in doing so, we've also got to stay flexible ... we can't plan for everything. The review process could take a long time, and it might look very different five or ten years from now. The people involved may change, the proposal might be altered or evolve, and even the process may change. That's why fighting these big hairy projects can be so challenging."

"Fair enough," said Bradley. "I think you and your committee have done an amazing job in a short time. I move that we support the plan and officially launch the Keep Collie Wild campaign."

With a unanimous show of hands, the committee voted in favour of Bradley's motion. As always, Price's hand was the last to come up, slowly and cautiously, because he always supported the majority opinion. Bradley then signed the funding agreements with three family foundations from the U.S. This meant that hundreds of thousands of dollars would flow to their war chest over the next three years; it was an amount they all hoped would shift the balance of power away from the proponent. Price smiled for the first time that night.

"Thanks to all of you," said Ilsley, also smiling. "Now … there's one more thing we need to talk about." At that moment, a dark cloud covered the sun, the first sign of a storm boiling over the Purcell Mountains to the west. The light was flat and ominous.

"What's that?" asked Bradley.

Ilsley took her time. Her expression was dark. "Two days ago, I had a visit from RCMP Corporal Fortier and a Yoho Park warden named Willson. They wanted to talk about the shooting at Stafford Austin's place."

"Right. I heard the gunfire that night," said Bradley. "My sheep went crazy. Why did they want to talk to *you*?"

"They asked if I had any idea who the shooter may be, and whether the Society knew anything about it."

"What? You weren't involved, were you?"

"No, of course not. They didn't suggest I was. But they seemed to think that because we're so vocal in our opposition to the project, one of us might have decided to cross the line."

"That's crazy," said Kraft. "Why would they think you — or any of us — were involved?"

"They said we had the most to gain if the proponent was scared away from the project … or if he died or disappeared. And because they know that Albin Stoffel is working with us, they hinted that the shooting might have been retaliation for the firebombing of his office and the death of Sue Webb. From the look in her eyes, I don't think the warden completely bought that theory, but she sure as hell wants to find out who *is* responsible. As for Fortier, I've seen some poker faces in my business career, and his was as good as any I've seen. I don't know what he thinks."

"What did you tell them?"

"I told them that violence was against our bylaws and not a tactic we would ever use or condone."

"Good," said Bradley, the relief showing on his face. "I would've said the same thing, and I will if they interview me. Do you think that's the end of it?"

"No," said Ilsley, "I don't."

"Why not?"

"Because they obviously think that someone in our group, or someone linked to our group, may have been the shooter. And they haven't ruled anyone out yet for the arson."

"None of us would do something like that," said Warman, looking around the table as though searching for confirmation. "In fact, the first thing I thought of when I heard about it was that Austin somehow set up the shooting himself to discredit us, to keep us occupied with a police investigation."

"I did suggest that to them," said Ilsley. "They said they were looking at every angle. But I got the sense that they didn't believe someone would agree to be shot, or even shot at, as a distraction. They asked for our membership list," she added.

Bradley looked concerned. "Did you give it to them?"

"I had no legal reason to deny their request and it was sitting right on the desk in front of me, so I did. If I'd told them they needed a warrant, they'd be cranking up the heat on us even more."

"That's good, I guess," said Bradley. "We've got nothing

to hide. Does that mean they'll be looking at every one of us, though, asking us to verify where we were the night of the shooting?"

"It's likely they'll follow up with everyone." Ilsley paused, remembering the evening meeting at her house a few weeks earlier. "But we might have a problem."

"What do you mean?"

"Toward the end of our first committee meeting in early December, a young guy from Parson, Leo Springer, asked if our campaign had to 'follow the rules.' I asked him what he meant, but he didn't answer. Instead, he ranted about the process working only in favour of rich people. I think he called it an out-of-control steamroller or something like that. He suggested that our only option to fight the resort might be to 'put sugar in the gas tank of the process' or 'blow the fucker up.' I remember those words very clearly. He frightened me that night, and I sensed that others felt the same. But he never came to another meeting after that, so I didn't think anything more about him. At least until I heard about the shooting ..."

"Did you tell Fortier and Willson about him?"

"I didn't. In hindsight, I probably should have. But I wanted to talk to all of you first."

"Why didn't you just tell them?" asked Kraft.

"Because if Austin or the government finds out that one of our members was involved in the shooting, it will undermine everything we're doing. Our credibility will be toast. But more importantly, every person who was at our meeting that night will be at risk. Springer didn't seem like the kind of guy who would appreciate being turned in. I'm no psychologist, but he seemed a bit unstable. If they interview him, but can't find evidence to link him to the shooting, he might come after us, or do something to damage the campaign."

"I see your point," Bradley said. "This puts us in a tough situation." He paused. "You said Springer hasn't shown up to any meetings since then?"

"No, he hasn't."

"What if we revoke his membership?" asked Kraft. "Won't that put some distance between us and him, our views and his?"

"Perhaps," said Ilsley. "But maybe it'll just piss him off."

"Do you think he did it?" Kraft asked.

Ilsley remembered Springer's hooded eyes that night, the atmospheric shift in their meeting, abrupt and shocking, his profile as he had driven off into the darkness. She shrugged. "I have no idea. It was the first time I'd met the guy. He might have been blowing smoke, or simply trying to get a rise out of us … but he might have been serious."

"Shit," said Bradley, planting his elbows on the table and resting his forehead on his palms. "This is not the way to kick-start an important campaign." He lifted his head and looked around the table. "What the hell do we do?"

"There's only one thing we can do," said Ilsley, "and that's to meet with Fortier and Willson and be completely honest with them. We need to convince them that we don't promote or use violence to achieve our goals and we had nothing to do with the shooting. And we've got to tell them about Springer. They need to take a closer look at him."

"Does everyone agree with that?" asked Bradley. Once again, his gaze circled the table, searching for consensus. And once again, Price's head was the last to nod a cautious yes.

"This isn't the start I was hoping for," said Bradley. "We'll have to keep the campaign a bit low-key until this is sorted out."

Ilsley shared the disappointment and concern written on Bradley's face. The best laid plans ...

CHAPTER 19

APRIL 2

As Mike Berland unwound himself from his black Jeep on the street outside her house, Jenny Willson peered out through a narrow gap in her front drapes. The journalist stretched and gazed up at the Rockies to the east and the Purcells to the west. The valley here would be more dramatic than those Berland was used to in Boise; it was much narrower, the mountains on both sides more rugged. And there was no sagebrush this far north.

When she'd phoned Berland the week before and he'd agreed to drive north to join her on a tour of Collie Creek, Willson had felt the same thrill she got whenever she was in the midst of a major case. It was a tingling in her spine, a buzzing in her brain as her neurons fired with crackling energy. Part of that feeling was because Berland's presence was a critical next step in her investigation into Austin and his project. Despite Speer's direction to the contrary, she was ready to fill him in on almost everything she'd learned to date and to share her suspicions, theories, and concerns. Together, using their combined investigative talents, they might be able to make some progress with the long list of questions that swirled around the ski area proposal like mist on a mountain peak. But first he'd have to be willing to play by her rules.

Willson also understood that some of her anticipation was more than professional. It had to do with the unexpected connection she'd felt between them when they'd met, the sense of common understanding that had grown gradually and organically as they'd sat in that coffee shop, the world all but disappearing around them. Since Berland had agreed to come north, Willson found herself analyzing that new feeling at strange and unexpected times of the day and night, poking and prodding at it like a specimen in a lab. In the end, she hadn't come to any conclusion about how she felt about the American. That left her uneasy, on edge.

Before he caught her staring through her curtains like a peeping Jenny, Willson moved to the front door to welcome him. She opened it just as he was stepping onto the dilapidated front porch. He had a nylon computer case, blue and bulging, in his left hand, and a duffle bag in his right.

"Welcome to Golden," she said.

"Thanks, Jenny," he said, looking cautiously at a gap in the floor. "Nice place you've got here."

"One of the Government of Canada's finest heritage buildings ..." she said with a grin. "Come on in. But move quickly before your foot disappears."

When Berland reached the doorway, he dropped his bags and they both found themselves engaged in the uncomfortable dance of two people unsure of their relationship. It was part handshake, part hug, with awkward arm movements. They both laughed.

Willson closed the door behind him. "How was the drive?"

"It was fine. A Border Services agent gave me a hard time, though. I told him I was a journalist, but he didn't believe me when I said I was coming up to visit you. I had to go inside and answer a bunch of questions, and he went through my briefcase and laptop. I was there for an hour before he finally let me go. Maybe it's because I'm a persuasive guy … or maybe it was the long line of cars waiting to come north."

Willson laughed again. "So … beer or coffee?"

"Both sound good," said Berland. "Let's start with the coffee."

For the rest of the afternoon, they sat on battered couches on opposite sides of the small living room, talking about ski resorts, violence, Stafford Austin, and the cast of local characters who were linked to the project in Collie Creek, some of them directly, many indirectly.

"You're telling me," asked Berland, "that after an arson that caused a death in early December, there have been two attempted murders and the vandalization of a business? Since I spoke to you last? Wow."

"People from both sides of the debate are taking this very seriously. And because Austin's project seems to be the common denominator in all of this, I'm working closely with the RCMP on their investigation. I'll make sure you meet Corporal Ben Fortier at some point while you're here."

"Who do you think is responsible? Someone is crossing major ethical and criminal lines."

Willson paused. She needed to be honest with Berland if this was going to work. There was no doubt that the journalist could dig where she couldn't, and that his ability to get the story into newspapers and on websites across North America meant that it would be safe from the muzzles of politicians with a pathological need to control narratives, bury embarrassing information, or, as she'd seen with her poaching investigation, take credit that didn't belong to them. But she had to get his confirmation that he would be willing to work within her boundaries and agree that any reporting he did on the case not jeopardize the ongoing investigation with Fortier — not to mention Fortier's career, her career, or the retirement plans of her chief park warden. A lot was riding on getting this right.

"Before I answer," she said, "I want you to understand that I *do* want to work with you on this. That's why I asked you to come. But if I'm going to tell you more than I did in Boise, then I need you to agree to some ground rules first. Nothing personal, Mike, but I usually try to avoid reporters like the plague. There are clearly things you can do that I can't, and there will be things only I can do and information only I can access. In a best-case scenario, we'll both get what we need out of this. You're going to see inside information that no one else will, and you'll eventually be able to tell the stories that people in my own organization, and the proponent himself, won't want told, and in ways that no one else can. But I need you to agree to my rules right now, or you might as well go back to Boise."

Berland sat forward, his lanky knees sticking up. "As a journalist," he said, "I don't like the sound of that. But let's see where the discussion takes us. How about if you start with what's really going on and then I can decide whether I can or will agree to your rules."

Willson smiled. "Nice try, Mike. I need you to agree that nothing I tell you, nothing you learn while you're with me, will be printed by you, online, or in a newspaper or magazine, until I say it's okay."

"That doesn't really work for me …"

"Do you want to head back now, or wait until the morning?"

Berland smiled. "You really are a hard-ass, aren't you?"

"Hard-ass, kick-ass. You have no idea."

"All right, then," said Berland, waving a napkin as a white flag. "I give. I'll agree to your terms. But since I'm the writer and you're not, here's my condition: you can approve what I write about and when, but you don't get to edit *how* I write."

"That's fair," said Willson, reaching across to shake Berland's hand. "I'm not much of an editor, anyway."

Still holding his hand, Willson realized that this was the moment of truth. Time to lay it all on the line.

"When we met," she said, releasing her grip, "I told you that my being in Boise was simply part of our agency's due diligence on Austin's project." She wrapped her hands tightly around a now-empty coffee cup. "What I didn't tell you is that my investigation hasn't been formally sanctioned by Parks Canada. The chief park warden from Banff didn't know what to do about the project because he was concerned it wouldn't get an open and thorough review by folks higher up on the chain of command. I suggested being transferred here so we could both find out what was really going on. He reluctantly agreed, and we've only recently let my boss in this park in on what I'm up to. So I'm sure you can understand why I need to control the information flow."

"You're running a rogue investigation because of worries over political interference, due to concerns that the Collie Creek project might be crammed through review processes at the expense of the parks. Am I right?"

"That's it in a nutshell, although I'm not sure I would use the term *rogue*. If what you've heard concerns you in any way, I can understand if you don't want to work with me on this."

Willson lifted her eyes from her cup to see Berland grinning at her.

"What?" she said.

"That's it? That's the big secret?"

"That's what I couldn't tell you." She saw that his grin had widened. "You're not taking this seriously, Mike. Do you think I'm kidding you?"

"I don't think you're kidding at all. I think it's funny that you seem concerned about how I'd react to this. If anything, it makes me feel proud of you, for what it's worth."

"Why the hell do you say that?"

"Because I was worried that I was dealing with a do-gooder park warden who always follows rules and doesn't ruffle any feathers. Now that I know what you're *really* like, that you're willing to operate in the shadows with the rest of us to uncover the facts, we might actually get somewhere."

"You're not concerned?"

"Not at all," he said, leaning back again into the soft couch. "In fact, I wondered if that was what you were up to when we talked in Boise. Otherwise, it all seemed too pat, too sterile. I could tell there was something more."

"That's good, then. I'm glad that's out of the way." Willson felt relief, yet at the same time foolish for worrying that the truth might send Berland packing. She realized that their jobs had much more in common that she'd originally thought. Her idealistic, single-minded focus on protecting the parks at all costs had clouded her judgment. It was, as they say, a learning moment.

"Do your bosses know that you're proposing to work with me like this?"

"My Banff boss told me not to when I mentioned it to him, but he won't be surprised that I'm ignoring him. The other knows nothing besides the fact that I might work with the RCMP on their investigation. I hope like hell that my read on you is correct, Mike, because I'm going out on a limb here."

The only sound in the room was a clock ticking from the kitchen, measuring the passing seconds as Willson watched Berland.

"I'm not happy with it," said the journalist, "but you can count on me, Jenny."

"Excellent," she said, then stood and headed to the kitchen. "Let's get this show on the road." She opened the fridge, but paused for a moment. *That was easy*, she thought. *Almost too easy.* She grabbed two cans of Soggy Otter brown ale with her right hand, let the door bang closed behind her, and pulled two frosted beer mugs from the freezer. She walked back to the living room, her thick wool socks whispering across the wood floor, and passed Berland an icy glass and a can. After both glasses were full, they knocked them together with a satisfying clink. "To the success of our partnership," said Willson, staring into Berland's dark eyes.

"And may our combined efforts finally put Stafford Austin behind bars, where he belongs," said Berland in return, staring back at her. "Here's to the death of the project — slow and painful, or quick and excruciating, it matters not to me."

"I'll drink to that."

And they did.

"Now that's out of the way, you asked who was responsible for the violence," Willson said.

"I did. What do you think?"

"Well, we don't know yet. Ben Fortier and I have been over it a dozen times. We've looked at many scenarios. It could be Austin and his people trying to scare off or get rid of opponents. It could be any one of a number of anti-resort folks, trying to make the project go away. Or it could be some combination of the two, with both sides trying to dissuade, discredit, or scare the shit out of the other. With you here, we can focus more on motive."

"The list of suspects seems long."

"It is. Have you dug up anything more on Austin since we talked in Boise?"

"Not as much as I'd like, but I do have a couple of interesting things for you."

He reached into his computer bag and pulled a file folder out. "Remember when I told you I'd heard Austin had been involved in something in South America?"

"Yeah …"

"Well, I did some digging. It turns out that Austin was part of a group of businessmen who tried to set up a new ski area in the Andes, in Chile. It was going to be a major competitor to the area's other resort, Portillo." Berland handed clippings to Willson from the *El Mercurio*, the main newspaper in Santiago.

Willson flipped though the clippings. "I can't read any of this, but I see Austin's name mentioned once or twice. What does it say?"

"Here are the translations," he said, passing several typed pages to her. "I'll let you read them in detail later, but in short, it seems that Austin and his colleagues persuaded a bunch of investors from Chile, Argentina, and Uruguay to invest in the project. But it went belly up. Nothing was ever built, and all the money disappeared. Around that time, Austin moved back to the U.S."

"Really? Were charges ever laid … or whatever happens in the Chilean legal system?"

"Not that we can tell, from the newspaper reports. I tried to reach the federal prosecutor who was named in the articles, but he's retired. No one seems to have followed up since then. It's like it never happened."

"I bet the people who lost money don't feel that way …"

"I bet they don't. But it's been five years now and I can't find any information beyond the newspaper reports."

"What's your next step?"

"I only got these clippings last week," said Berland, "so one of the things I want to do now is to see if I can find any of the jilted investors. Perhaps they can tell me more about how the project was set up and what happened."

While Berland talked, Willson visited the kitchen again for a second round of drinks.

"You don't think Austin is doing the same thing here, do you?" she said, handing Berland another beer.

"I have no idea," he said after taking a long sip of the icy brown ale. "It's a different jurisdiction down there, with different rules and a very different legal system. But it sure raises a fascinating question, doesn't it?"

"It sure as hell does."

The sun had dropped behind the Purcells, and a light beside Willson clicked on; the lamp was on a timer. It bathed the room in a warm orange glow.

"What was the other thing you discovered?" asked Willson.

Berland smiled. "It was the lucky result of online sleuthing. I found the name and contact information for one of Austin's three ex-wives. She's in Salt Lake City. It took me a while to find her because she went back to her maiden name after the divorce. We've since traded emails and she's willing to talk. It's obvious that she doesn't harbour any warm and fuzzy feelings for her ex."

"Now we're talking," said Willson, raising her glass toward Berland. "You might bring some value to this partnership after all."

Berland laughed. "Your confidence in me is over-whelming."

"No problem." Willson stood and stretched. "How about I show you your room? I warn you, though, this is no Château Lake Louise. While you get settled, I'll order us a pizza. Any toppings you don't like?"

"Anchovies and olives disgust me, but other than that, I'm happy with anything."

"Extra anchovies and olives it is."

Three hours later, after they'd rehashed everything over pizza and more beer, Willson chose to call it a night. "We have to be at the helipad by eight a.m. for a safety briefing, so it's time to hit the hay."

"Helipad?"

"Yup, we're gonna fly in to get a good look at Collie Creek and the area of the proposed resort. That's why I asked you to bring winter gear with you. One of my colleagues is doing a field inspection of the area, so she asked me to come along. I told her I had a friend who wanted to join us. Lucky you!"

"Fly there? In a helicopter? I thought we'd be driving …"

"Most of it's inaccessible by road." She saw a new expression on Berland's normally calm face. It wasn't confidence. "You've been in a helicopter before, haven't you?"

"Uh, no … and I don't really like flying."

"Well, then," said Willson with a grin, "this should be a treat for both of us."

CHAPTER 20

APRIL 3

The Bell 206 JetRanger lifted off from the helipad, dropped its nose to gain airspeed, then climbed slowly, heading northeast. The silty waters of the Kicking Horse River passed below them, as did the old houses of the Swiss mountain guide's village on the bench to the north of town. The helicopter passed through a short patch of grey valley fog, the landscape disappearing and reappearing. It then headed up Hospital Creek toward Mount McBeath.

Willson sat behind the pilot and Tara Summers occupied the seat beside him, a topographic map spread across her lap. Willson could see only the back of Summers's toque-covered head; the headset gave her a set of giant mouselike ears. Willson's own earphones muffled the sounds of the roaring engine and the spinning rotors, but her thoughts were on her father's last flight to Golden, perhaps in this very machine. She'd been in helicopters many times over her career — rescuing injured climbers, searching for lost hikers, relocating problem bears — but no matter how hard she tried to focus on other things, her mind always shifted back to her father on the way to hospital after they'd pulled him from the icy river, lying on a stretcher on the aircraft floor, attended to by paramedics. Had he still been alive at that point? Had he been frightened, in pain? Did someone hold his hand to comfort him? Had he thought of her and her mother in his last moments?

Willson suddenly heard a loud gasp through the headset that roused her from her memories. She looked to her left to see Berland's eyes wide, his face pale, his hands gripping the seat on either side of him. She keyed the intercom with her left hand. "How are you doing over there, princess?"

"Holy shit," said Berland, "I was okay until we almost hit that mountain."

"No worries," said the pilot, chuckling, "that was Moberly Peak. It was at least five hundred metres off our port side."

"Jesus," Berland said. "I have no idea what a metre is, but that wasn't enough of them for my liking."

"C'mon, Mike," said Willson. "Sit back and enjoy the ride. You ain't seen nothin' yet."

Fifteen minutes later, the helicopter, now at an elevation of 2,700 metres, passed Amiskwi Peak on the left and entered the airspace over Yoho National Park. When the ground dropped to the headwaters of the Amiskwi River nearly nine hundred metres below them, Willson heard another squeak from Berland. "Almost there, Mike," she said. She smiled and patted his leg. "That's Mont des Poilus off our nose to the right, about one o'clock. It's right in the middle of where we're heading." Berland grimaced and looked down at the floor.

"We'll do a few circles of the whole area first so I can get some pictures," said Summers, her voice vibrating in synch with the machine, "and then we'll set down at the site of the proposed resort."

Summers directed the pilot through an aerial tour, stuck the lens of her camera out the open sliding window on the door, and snapped pictures of the area. Whether they wanted it or not, she provided a constant running commentary. Because her microphone was near the window opening, the passing air hissed loudly in their ears, at least until the pilot asked her to push the microphone to the top of her head. Willson basked in the welcome silence.

On their left were the pyramidal shapes of Arete Peak and Mount des Poilus, which shared the same ridgeline. From this elevation, it was hard to tell which of the two was taller, but Willson knew des Poilus won the competition by a hundred metres. It was one of the highest points in the area, and it was also the proposed location of the topmost lift tower in Austin's scheme. With a poke in the ribs, she tried to get Berland's attention so she could point out the Mountain Club hut on a spur below them. But with a shake of his head, he refused to lift his head or open his eyes. Instead, he slumped forward as if praying, hands clasped together, elbows on knees.

Shifting in her seat to look out the window on the right side of the aircraft, Willson blinked and then pulled on her sunglasses as the helicopter flew out over the blinding white expanses of glaciers and icefields that formed the north boundary of Yoho. Fittingly, the name meant "awe" in the Cree language. She saw a world of snow and ice, rocky ridges, and gaping crevasses. It was a wild world where winds blew cold and unfettered, a world inhabited by wolverines, mountain goats, hawks, eagles, and the occasional group of backcountry skiers on the multi-day Wapta Traverse.

In a gap between Mounts des Poilus and Collie, they got their first full view of the entire drainage of Collie Creek, from its upper headwaters to where it joined the Blaeberry River twelve kilometres to the north. The upper portions were rock and snow, the middle was a patchwork of subalpine forest bisected by avalanche paths, and the lower valley were roads and regenerating cutblocks, their rectangular shapes and dense greens differentiating them from the uncut forests around them. Willson tried to imagine Collie Creek scarred by paved roads, hotels, condos, lift towers, and, if Austin's proposal was to be believed, thousands and thousands of skiers. *I can't let that happen*, she thought. *I can't and I won't.*

At Summers's request, the pilot turned to the north, skirting Ayesha Peak, and then began a gradual descent down the path of the Ayesha Glacier. Circling to the left, they dropped into the upper basin of Collie Creek, and at about 2,200 metres elevation they landed beside a frozen lake. The blades threw huge circles of snow up around them. Using full power, the pilot moved the helicopter back and forth into the snow to stabilize it; the settling protectors on the skids ensured it wouldn't sink too deep. Willson and Summers knew what he was doing, but when Willson looked over at Berland, he looked terrified.

When the pilot was satisfied that the aircraft was safe and stable, he wound the engine down, but told his three passengers to keep their seat belts on until the rotors had stopped.

When all was quiet and the pilot had given them the thumbs-up, Willson opened the door on her side and stepped down, first to the step on the skid, then into the thigh-deep snow. She thrashed back to the cargo bay in the tail boom of the helicopter and pulled out their packs and three pairs of snowshoes. By the time she waded around to open the doors for Summers and Berland, the reporter had already leapt out of the cabin as if to get as far away from the machine as he could. He looked up at the two women from where he lay on his side in the deep snow, the relief in his face palpable. "I'm going to fucking walk back to Golden from here," he said. "Don't even *try* to talk me out of it."

Three hours later, the trio had tramped nearly the full length of a gravel moraine freed from snow by the sun, with Summers providing a running commentary on the locations where the lift towers, lift lines, ski runs, and resort base were being proposed. The west side of the ridge on which they stood, she explained, would be the site of an upper village, a small development with a restaurant and hotel beside the still-frozen lake, linked to the rest of the resort below by a gondola. Like many resorts in the border regions of the Alps, the lifts proposed here would rise to the peaks and ridges to the south of them, then continue down onto the glaciers beyond. In the Alps, skiers could start their day in Switzerland, ride a lift to the border, ski down into Italy or France for lunch, catch a lift back to the border again, and then ski back to Switzerland in time for dinner. In Collie Creek, skiers would move back and forth between Crown land in B.C. and Yoho National Park, similarly using lifts and ski runs on both sides of the park border.

As Willson and Summers worked their way along the ridge, talking and pointing and consulting maps, Berland followed behind them, casting suspicious glances at the waiting helicopter. He'd said little since they'd gotten out and seemed content to take pictures and scribble in a Moleskine notebook.

"What's up with all the shooting and writing?" Summers asked, glancing over her shoulder.

"I've never been in a place like this," Berland said, with a quick look at Willson. "I want to remember every moment. I can sure as hell see why these guys want to call this Top of the World."

Willson stopped when she spotted a set of tracks in the snow. "Wolverine," she said.

"How do you know?" asked Berland.

"From the size and shape of the tracks and their location, I'm guessing it's a male heading from the Yoho River drainage north into Collie Creek and the Blaeberry."

Berland looked at the wilderness around them. "What the hell is he doing way up here?"

"He's probably visiting one of his lady friends. This is his world — the bigger and wilder, the better. The biologists call wolverines an indicator species, because if they're around, it means things are still wild. But if Austin's vision comes to fruition," said Willson, shaking her head in disgust, "it's going to look like friggin' Zermatt up here. And it will be *no* place for wolverines."

"Zermatt *is* the model Austin's using," said Summers. "He says there's nothing like it in Canada, so people will come from all over the world to experience it. It'll have the greatest elevation difference from top to bottom of any Canadian ski resort, and where we're standing will be the highest on-hill accommodation. It will all be accessible by an interconnected network of lifts. According to Austin, that is."

Now back on snowshoes, Willson shuffled closer to the edge of the slope and looked at a large flood plain three hundred metres below them, where Austin was proposing to build the main resort village. It was a large and flat and gravelly, with a creek braided through it, and had clearly been under a glacier in the not-too-distant past. As she studied the narrow valley, she caught a flash of movement on a ridge on the far side. "Look!" she said, pointing.

They watched in awe as a collapsed cornice slid downhill, picking up speed and snow. It raced down the slope toward the valley floor. They saw the main mass of snow moving, along with the boiling cloud of white powder that rolled above, in front, and beside it. The speeding mass did not slow as it reached a narrow rib of trees, knocking them down and adding debris to the flow. Thirty seconds later, the monster hit Collie Creek with a roar. Some snow continued down the valley like a serpent, following the course of the creek, while the rest blew up the opposite side of the valley a few hundred metres before finally stopping. The white cloud continued up the hill toward Willson and her colleagues, dissipating around them in a momentary snowstorm.

"Holy shit," said Berland, his face dusted white, his eyes wide.

"That was a solid class four avalanche," said Willson. "In the Canadian classification system that means it was powerful enough to destroy a railway car, a large truck, several buildings, or a forest area up to four hectares."

"Or part of a resort townsite, and the people sleeping in their beds," said Summers, who'd caught most of the slide on her cellphone video.

"Exactly," Willson said. "And looking at this end of Collie Creek, I see few places where avalanches aren't going to be a problem. It's going to cost a shitload of money every year to keep this place safe, if they can do it at all."

"I agree," said Summers. "That's already been raised by our interagency committee, but this video will be compelling confirmation of the risk. We've already agreed to hire external avalanche and geotechnical experts to do a full assessment of the valley. Not that we don't trust what Austin says ..."

"No, of course not," said Willson, thinking back to Austin's sales job at the public meeting in Golden. "Have you got all you need up here, Tara? If so, why don't we circle back to the Mountain Club hut and see who's around? We can stop there for lunch. Maybe someone has coffee on."

"I'm good, Jenny," said Summers. "Let's do it."

Berland found his voice. "Does that mean getting back in that … noisy contraption that seems to defy all laws of physics …?"

"It does, Mike," said Willson. "If you tried to walk out of here, you'd either die in an avalanche or be wolverine food long before you ever made it back to civilization. Why don't you come back the easy way?"

"So, I have a choice, then?" he said with a grimace. "Let me think about it for a moment."

The next leg of their flight was short and uneventful. Willson watched Berland, despite his earlier whining, taking pictures through his window with his camera in one hand. However, she noted that the other still tightly clutched the edge of his seat.

They circled once above the Mountain Club hut, saw someone watching them from the front deck, then landed on a flat patch of south-facing moraine that was also melted free of snow. This time, Berland climbed out of the machine like someone who'd done it many times before.

The four of them carried their packs up a short slope to the hut and were met by a young man who looked surprised to see them. Standing at the bottom of a short staircase, he wore stained work pants, a beat-up Gore-Tex jacket, and a wool beanie. He was about six feet tall with broad shoulders.

"I'm Tom Yamamoto," he said. "I'm the hut custodian. Welcome to the Ernst Buehler Memorial Hut, the newest backcountry hut in the Canadian Mountain Club's network! I wasn't expecting any visitors today."

"Hi, Tom," said Willson, extending her hand. "I'm Jenny Willson, Yoho Park warden. We're in the area doing some fieldwork, and because none of us had been here before, we decided to drop in. This is Tara Summers, Yoho Park resource specialist. That's Mike Berland, a friend of mine. And over there is our pilot, Gerry."

"You're from Parks Canada?" asked Yamamoto, his smile quickly shifting to a scowl. He pulled his hand back, leaving Willson with hers awkwardly held out in front of her. She saw him eye the shoulder patches on her jacket. "Are you here to evict us?"

Willson raised her hands as if defending herself from physical attack. "Whoa, there, Tom," she said, "this is a friendly visit. We're simply here to look around."

"What ... so you can decide if the hut will become some fancy day lodge for the ski area?"

Willson was trained to deal with aggressive people who resented law enforcement and whose reactions were emotional rather than reasoned. She saw it almost every day. But this man's response, his overt agitation, was a surprise in this place. His fists were clenched tight at his sides, his knuckles white. Time to de-escalate.

"Tom," she said, "I get the fact that you're angry at Parks Canada. I understand why. Tara and I are here to gather information so we can advise our bosses on whether the proposed ski area should go ahead or not. I'll be up front with you, although I'm not really supposed to. Neither of us is convinced it's a good idea." She opened her arms wide and tilted her head. "We want to see what you've got here so we can communicate its value to the park and its users."

"You're from government and you're here to help? That's a fuckin' joke."

"Honestly," said Willson, "we'd like you to explain to us why this place is special." She watched a range of emotions flash across Yamamoto's face. None of them were positive and all of them showed his disbelief.

"Well, c'mon in, anyway ..." He turned and climbed up the front stairs. "It's not like I can stop you. You're the landlord."

Willson and Summers shared a look that said, *This ain't gonna be easy.*

Before they sat down to eat their bagged lunches, Yamamoto gave them a tour of the two-storey facility. He showed them the upper bunkroom, which slept eighteen people, the downstairs kitchen, communal space, and gear-drying area, the adjacent outhouse building linked by a covered deck. Then he explained how the electrical and mechanical systems worked, and how the hut was powered by solar and wind systems.

When the tour was complete and all questions had been asked and answered, Yamamoto led them to the communal space and reluctantly offered them coffee. Willson pulled her lunch from her pack and sat on a bench beside a long wood table. Through the window to her left, she could see the des Poilus glacier stretching to the south with the upper reaches of the Yoho Valley below it. Warden cabins and Mountain Club huts always had the best views.

"I'm sorry if I was rude out there," said Yamamoto as he poured steaming coffee into tin mugs. "We're all pissed off since we heard about the ski area. It's hard not to take this personally. A resort is going to change this whole place. We wouldn't have built this hut here, had we known. It was a huge volunteer effort — not only the fundraising, but the planning and construction, too. I spent a good chunk of last summer and fall up here. We had smoke from forest fires, a freakishly hot summer, and then rain and snow and inquisitive grizzly bears. We all feel tricked, cheated, like the Club should've spent its half-million dollars elsewhere."

Yamamoto stood while he talked, the coffee pot shaking in his hand, his anger and resentment translated into kinetic energy.

"Tom," said Willson, "it was neither Tara nor I who chose to accept the proposal. That happened above our pay grade. I understand how angry you and your colleagues must be. I'd feel the same if I were you. As I said outside, our job is to figure out what information we need from the proponent before it goes further. We'll advise the decision-makers on whether the project should proceed or not. That's the main reason we're here. As far as we know, Parks Canada is a long way from deciding anything yet."

As she spoke, Willson felt her own resentment rising, her cheeks flushing. She hated defending her own organization, even weakly, for acting in a way that was indefensible. She knew Yamamoto's anger was fully justified and that his sentiments were likely shared by many others. The faceless, nameless processes ran on and on, just as Frank Speer had described them. And the beautiful new hut in which they were sitting could be one of its many casualties.

"And what about the new highway and pipeline?" asked Yamamoto, banging the coffee pot down on the propane stove. "Are your bosses supporting that, too?"

"Say what?" Willson asked. She remembered Speer mentioning the highway, but it was the first time she'd heard about it from a member of the public. And had Yamamoto also said something about a pipeline?

He took a seat at the end of the bench. His voice started to rise again. "I mean the Howse Pass highway," he said, "and the fact that the road corridor could also be used as the route for an oil or gas pipeline from Alberta. First Yoho Park and now Banff. You guys are out of control!"

"Where the hell did you hear that?" asked Willson. Past trying to calm the situation, she shifted her gaze to Summers. She was as surprised as Willson. Berland's head was down while he scribbled furiously in his notebook.

"My oldest brother, Yas, owns one of the largest road construction companies in Alberta," said Yamamoto. "With the oil patch slow these days, the prospect for new projects is slim. Yas was recently approached by Stafford Austin, the proponent of the resort project. He told Yas that he's got a company started to make it happen, and the federal government supports the idea. He gave my brother the impression that if he invested in the project, he'd have a good chance of getting the primary construction contract — one that may be worth tens of millions of dollars. What do you say to that?"

"I say holy shit!" said Willson. "This is the first I've heard of it."

"Are you shitting me?" said Yamamoto. "Doesn't one part of government know what the other is doing?"

Willson smirked. "You don't know a lot about government, do you, Tom?"

"How can I contact your brother?" asked Berland, his head up, pencil poised over the notebook. "I'd like to talk to him." He missed or purposefully ignored the pointed look from Willson that said, *This is one of those things we'll need to talk about.*

Willson, in turn, ignored Summers's *Who is this guy?* look.

Yamamoto gave them his brother's contact information. Then they all sat in silence for a few moments, thinking, sipping coffee, staring out the window.

"Tara, Jenny," said the pilot, getting up from the table. "We better go. I see weather coming in from the southwest. I don't want to get stuck up here or have to fly home the long way."

The flight back to Golden was absent of conversation as the three passengers digested what they'd heard from Yamamoto. As they approached the airport, with clouds boiling down from the Purcell Mountains, Willson, who was now sitting beside the pilot, spoke over the intercom. "Un-fucking-believable."

"Yes," said the pilot, "it looks like a hell of a storm rolling in."

But Willson wasn't just talking about the deteriorating conditions.

CHAPTER 21

APRIL 3

The server set a plate in front of Austin, turning it slightly so the miso-soy-glazed salmon, framed by kale gomae and pickled vegetable, was closest to him. Ignoring her, Austin looked across the table at Matt Merrix, who was admiring his own entree: a twelve-ounce rib-eye buried in sautéed mushrooms and glistening with a café au lait sauce.

"Bon appétit," said Austin, raising his wine glass. Their glasses touched with the high crystal tone of a bell. The sound of soft voices and the gentle clinking of other guests' silverware at the Terminal City Club's restaurant, the Grill, filled the room.

"Thanks for setting this up, Stafford," said Merrix, a slice of bloody meat pierced on the end of his fork. "I'm pleased that my guys received their first quarterly dividend payments. Despite my assurances, they were still skeptical about the rates of return. But those cheques have calmed any lingering doubts. Nice work."

"Good to hear," Austin said, smiling. "It's important they're happy."

Merrix talked as he chewed. "I must admit that I was a bit skeptical myself. Mmmm, this is good. In our business, we don't see these kinds of returns so consistently. If this continues, it's going to work out very well, for both of us. I don't completely understand how you do it, but whatever it is, keep doing it."

"That's the plan," said Austin, nodding his head once solemnly. He hated his own reaction to such overt praise, like a schoolboy getting a teacher's approval for a correct answer. But it confirmed he was on the right track, that what he was doing was worth the effort. That he was respected and even admired. But this was less about praise than money.

Austin knew there was magic in his actions, and that he was the illusionist, the conjurer. Across the table, Merrix was his audience, seeing only what Austin wanted him to see. The man believed because he wanted to believe. And when the results matched the promises, like they did now, the audience's anticipation would only increase for what was yet to come.

Merrix lifted his wine glass by the stem and let the waitress top it up with the dark Chilean Carménère. "I did, however, get a call from one of my clients yesterday — Jarrett Taylor. He plays in the AHL on a two-way contract with the Flames. He took some business courses this past summer and he's asked me to explain the fund to him."

"What did you tell him?" Austin kept the smile on his face.

"I explained that while the ski area project was under review, you were investing most of the funds — the money that wasn't immediately needed to keep the proposal moving — in a range of opportunities. I told him that some are standard investments, while others are approaches that others have missed."

"Was he happy with that explanation?"

Merrix grinned. "It took a while, but I believe so … particularly because I'd just deposited your cheque into his account that morning. He did ask to see a current copy of his statement, though, and he'd like a more detailed explanation at some point."

"Not a problem," said Austin, taking a break from his salmon to make a note on his smartphone. "I can get a statement to him by next week." He chose not to respond to the request for further details.

"Thanks," said Merrix, tipping his glass toward Austin. "But what's most interesting is that my clients have started telling their teammates about the fund. Based on that, I'm getting calls from *other* agents asking me if *their* clients can get in on it."

"That's excellent." With his right hand, Austin reached for his own glass, trying to calm his excitement. Another toast. He looked at the inflamed scar at the fleshy base of his thumb, the spot where he'd lost a chunk of skin and muscle when he'd been hit by the fireplace fragment weeks earlier. It was a stark reminder of the risks he might face if he didn't keep the project moving in the right direction, if he disappointed his investors … or pissed off his critics too much. But this was a crucial time for him and his business. Happy customers were the best sales force, pitching his product to people he couldn't reach. Momentum builds, and investors feel a sense of urgency. This is a club they *need* to be part of. They don't want to be left on the outside looking in. "It would be fair to tell them that the fund is still open," Austin continued, "but it won't be for long. We're almost fully subscribed. If they want in, they need to get in soon."

Staring at Merrix across the top of his glass, Austin thought about his encounter with the senior politicians in that dark restaurant in Red Deer, the highway project that could become a pipeline, the new doors that could open for him. "If they want to call me, I can give them more information on the fund. Or — and this is something you and I haven't talked about, but you're one of the first to hear about it — I can fill them in on a new fund I've only just started."

"A new fund? Tell me more."

"To a degree, it's connected with Top of the World. But I've decided to keep the two as separate investments. I'll also keep this second opportunity low-key because the investment on which it's based is not yet public knowledge."

Austin watched Merrix move forward in his chair, eyes bright. As an experienced salesman, he knew he was close to setting the hook in the corner of the agent's mouth, like a fisherman persuading a cutthroat trout to rise twice to the same dry fly. Despite having seen it many times, he was always amazed at how little it took to transform supposedly sophisticated investors into hungry fish.

Austin kept his voice low. "I've been approached by people fairly high up in government to invest in a new highway through the Rocky Mountains. If built, it will go right past the ski area, so that will solve one of our major challenges." He surreptitiously glanced around the room as though worried about eavesdroppers. "As I said, this is *highly* confidential. But there's no doubt that it's a once-in-a-lifetime investment opportunity."

"A highway?" said Merrix, his eyebrows rising, his upper body moving subtly away from the table. "Geez, Austin. I don't know much about engineering or construction, but it strikes me that building a highway, a highway *through* the Rocky Mountains, would be hugely expensive, a massive dark hole you could throw money into for decades. I don't get it. Why'd they approach *you*?"

"I asked them the same question, and they gave me the answer I'll give you. Because I'm the guy who has already made a commitment to the area and because I'm the guy who's already built a core of smart investors to be part of it."

"Makes sense, I guess. But still …"

"It's not just a highway, Mike, not just a thirty-four-kilometre section of new road connecting two existing roads. It's also … a potential pipeline route from Alberta."

"A pipeline? That sounds even *more* expensive. And not just expensive, but risky. Pipelines aren't exactly popular right now. And I've shied away from them as investments because commodity prices can go up and down like yo-yos."

Austin thought again of the meeting in Red Deer and gave Merrix the same answer he'd been given by the PMO staffer, Cummings. It was an answer now bolstered by the results of additional research he'd done since then. "The highway and pipeline could be in the same corridor, which means less land involved in the project and lower cost to make it happen. And if it's approved, then it's about the tolls, Matt, all about the tolls." Austin smiled a knowing smile. "Right now, there's an average of ten thousand vehicles per day travelling through the Rockies on either the Trans-Canada or the Yellowhead Highway via Jasper. If we assume that 16 percent of the existing traffic, sixteen hundred of those vehicles, will use the new highway initially — a number that could rise to thirty-five hundred vehicles per day in twenty years — and if each of those vehicles paid a five-dollar toll, then the highway tolls alone would pay back more than one hundred million dollars to investors over those twenty years. And if you then add in a per-unit toll on anything moving through the pipeline, say ten cents a barrel, that amount could easily multiply five or six times. If we can make this happen, the current 12 percent return on the Collie Creek Investment Fund will look low compared to what this new fund would pay out."

"Wow," said Merrix, his body now tight against the table, palms flat on the linen, head and neck tilted forward toward Austin. "That's gonna be a *huge* project. What will it cost?"

"The 2005 estimates were two hundred and ten million dollars just for the highway. It's likely going to be at least double that now. Much more to build the pipeline."

"Jesus. My clients — most of the people in our world — don't have that kind of money. The only people who do are the billionaires who own the teams."

"Do you know any of them personally?" Austin said, chuckling. But then his mouth shifted to a straight line, his eyes serious. "I do understand, Matt. This isn't for everyone. I can tell you that I've begun talks with major Chinese investors who are as interested in the pipeline as they are the highway. They have a stake in oil and gas projects in Alberta and see this as a new way to get their products to market. If they decide to get in on this, it's likely they'll be investing in a big way, a very big way. That's why I wanted to raise this with you tonight. If your guys, or guys they know, want in early, even if it's only for small pieces of a very big pie, there's still time to do that. But I expect the door will close soon. The Chinese will demand to be majority players."

Merrix whistled and turned his head toward the other diners. Austin could almost see the wheels turning in his head. He'd firmly hooked his fish. He smiled. Getting positive feedback for something he'd already accomplished was one thing. But selling a new investment to a professional who was supposed to be business-savvy, whose job it was to represent the best interests of his wealthy clients, who described himself as shrewd and smart, was a whole different level of thrill. Austin knew that the story he would pitch to others about this new opportunity, one that he was still developing and practising, could attract more money than he had seen in any of his previous projects. It was an exciting time. Time to do some more casting with that juicy dry fly.

CHAPTER 22

APRIL 4

"Stafford's an asshole who cares more about money than anything or anyone. For him, it's *all* about the money, and always has been."

Willson looked across her kitchen table at Berland while they listened to Stafford Austin's third wife, Cheryl Paine, describing her ex. It was the day after their trip to Collie Creek, and they'd started the conversation with Paine by explaining their desire to learn more about the man behind the project. Even through the tinny speaker on Willson's cellphone, the woman's voice was bitterly reflective. She clearly had few good memories of her ex-husband and the way he treated those around him.

"In reality, though," Paine said, "I think money is only an avenue to power and prestige for him. He's an egocentric jerk who loves to manipulate others."

"Did he ever try to manipulate you?" asked Willson.

"Sure," Paine said offhandedly, "all the time. In the last few months of our marriage I recognized what he was doing, so I ignored most of it."

"You said he loved money. What do you know about where he got his money from when you were together … or even before that?"

"Not much. He was always extremely secretive about what he was up to, which right from day one was a problem between us. We kept separate accounts, so I never knew anything about his finances. When I snooped in his wallet one day, I found a business card from a banker in the Grand Cayman Islands. Of course, I immediately wondered if he had accounts offshore. I asked him about it later and he just laughed, like I'd told a joke. But he never answered. When the federal agents asked me what I knew about his mining scheme — which was nothing — they described the people who'd lost most of their life savings to his scam. That was the straw that broke this camel's back. We were done. When I confronted him, he denied it, of course; but didn't seem to have any remorse for the lives he'd ruined. Our divorce came through six months later, thank god. If he'd hidden any money, my lawyer couldn't find it. I got very little in the final settlement." They heard her sigh. "I guess I shouldn't have been surprised that it all unravelled. The marriage was a mistake from the start."

"How did you two meet?" asked Willson, less interested in their relationship than in keeping the woman talking and getting her to open up to them about Austin's financial past.

"It was at a Salt Lake Chamber of Commerce lunch meeting. We were at the same table. The guest speaker was a Chinese diplomat who talked about investing in mining and energy. Stafford was there to hear him speak, and I was there because my boss had taken three of us from the office to the lunch."

Willson heard a pause and another sigh. Perhaps there was at least one good memory in there somewhere. Or maybe she'd recounted her experiences once too often, and was now tired or embarrassed. Or both.

"We talked during lunch," she said, "and exchanged business cards. But once the meal was done, he left the table and introduced himself to the guest speaker. We didn't talk again that day, but he did phone me about ten days later. And the rest is history. Ancient history."

"How long were you together?" asked Willson.

"Only eighteen months. It seemed longer ..."

"You say he was secretive about his business dealings," said Berland. "When you were together, did you get the sense that he might be involved in things that weren't completely legit?"

"I didn't. I mean, I often wondered because he wouldn't tell me what was going on. And there was that card from the Caribbean banker. But then, Stafford was always an enigma, and not in a good way, so it was par for the course. At first, the mystery was interesting. But I soon tired of it. Even after a year and a half of marriage, I didn't really know the guy. I realize now that we never had any emotional connection — other than at first, maybe. In hindsight, anything I thought we *did* have was nothing more than an act on his part. It was like he couldn't make emotional connections with anyone, except when he was in selling mode. If he was trying to sell you something, he was your best friend. There was no doubt he was driven by money and what it gave him. No doubt at all. He loved to talk about money, about fancy cars and clothes and trips and people who wanted to talk to him. Important people. When the cops started asking questions about the mining scam, I wasn't at all surprised. Incredibly disappointed, angry, sad, yes, but *not* surprised."

Willson grimaced at Berland, her hands clenched. She refused to let the woman go without giving them some kind of lead. She despised dead ends. "Is there anything you *can* tell us about what he was up to? Anyone you can point us to who might know more? Business associates? Investors? Former partners?"

"The only thing I can think of is that there was a guy from South America who began calling, looking for Stafford, around out the time we separated. That was maybe a year or so ago? I might still have his name and contact information here somewhere in one of my files. He wouldn't tell me why he was looking for him or what he wanted. But I got the sense that he wasn't a big fan of Stafford. I don't know how I tracked him down; maybe he saw his name online in connection with the mining case. I told my lawyer about him, but as far as I know, she didn't find anything that helped my case. Just more questions."

Willson sat up straighter. "Have you got that contact information handy?"

"If I do have it, I can email it to you."

"I don't mind waiting," said Willson. "We'd like to follow it up, so if you can find it now, I'll stand by."

"Okay, I'll see what I can do. Hang on."

Five minutes later, she returned to the phone. "Sorry about the wait. I found it. First name Mauricio, last name Castro — like the Cuban president." She read them a phone number. "I remember asking him where he was from, and he said Santiago, Chile. He had an accent, but his English was good."

At the mention of Chile, Willson and Berland shared a quick fist bump. A potential link had just been made.

"Thanks so much for this, Cheryl," said Willson. "You've been very helpful and we appreciate your candour. If you think of anything else you haven't told us, or remember other people we should talk to, would you give me a call or drop me an email?"

"My pleasure," she said.

Willson gave the woman her cell number and email address.

"If Stafford's involved in a business in Canada," Cheryl continued, "I wouldn't be shocked if he ended up charged with something that involves stealing people's money. If that's what's happening, then your cops better build a hell of a case against that slimy bastard. He always finds a way to wiggle out of trouble and disappear."

"I understand," said Willson. "One more question. Was your ex-husband ever violent, either to you or to others?"

"Have you ever met Stafford?"

"I have."

"Well, then you know he's a big man. To many people, that's intimidating in itself. He knows it and he often uses it to his advantage to dominate, be the one in control. Sometimes he does it subtly, sometimes overtly. But did I ever see him lay a hand on someone? No. Did he ever physically hurt me? No. There were a few times when I felt he might, if pushed further. Would he turn to violence if someone threatened his power or prestige or money? I have no doubt. Would he hire someone else to do it? Absolutely."

"I appreciate you giving me the heads-up," said Willson. "I'll consider myself warned."

"Has he done something up there that led you to ask that question?"

"At this point, we don't know. Thanks again, Cheryl."

As soon as she'd hung up, Willson punched the number Paine had given them into the cellphone. "No time like the present," she said.

"*Hola*," a woman's voice said after two rings. "*Confiable Investigaciones. Dónde puedo dirigir su llamada?*"

"Uh, sorry, do you speak English?" asked Willson, momentarily flustered by the rapid Spanish.

"Yes, I speak English."

"Sorry … but what company is this?"

"You have reached Confiable Investigations. Who do you wish to speak with?"

"I'm looking for a Mauricio Castro?"

"*Si.* Señor Castro is in the office today. I'll put you through. Please hold."

While they listened to soft Latin music through the speaker, Willson looked at Berland, her face reflecting their shared puzzlement. "Investigations? If this is some kind of private investigator, this just got a whole lot more interesting." He nodded, clearly thinking the same thing.

The music ended and for a few seconds there was silence. Just as they began to think they'd been disconnected, a deep voice said, "*Buenos dias*, this is Mauricio."

"Señor Castro, good morning. My name is Jenny Willson. I am a park warden in Yoho National Park, in Canada. I'm here with my colleague, Mike Berland. Could we ask you a few questions?"

"About what?"

"About someone by the name of Stafford Austin. I understand that you spoke to his ex-wife a while ago and that you were trying to reach him."

"Why are you asking me about Señor Austin?"

Willson sensed the hesitation in Castro's voice. "I understand that you might be a private investigator?" she said. "You might have been looking for Austin, perhaps in the context of a failed ski area project in your country? Thing is, he's involved in a project of a similar nature here in Canada, and we're wondering if you have any information about him that would be of use to us."

"Yes, I *am* an investigator. Has Austin done something wrong again?"

Willson saw Berland grin. The man on the phone had asked the one question that was the clue to why he'd been searching for Austin. The fact that Castro was a private investigator was suddenly more intriguing.

"Not that we're aware of," said Willson. "At this point, our governments are early in the process of reviewing Mr. Austin's proposal. Would you be surprised if I told you that we weren't 100 percent sure that everything is as it seems with his project?"

"No," said Castro. "It's interesting to me that he's now in Canada. How did you say you found me?"

"I didn't say. We recently spoke to Austin's ex-wife in Salt Lake City and she told us about your call to her. She gave us your name and phone number."

"I see. Well, perhaps we have something to talk about. And perhaps we can help each other."

"Perhaps we can, Señor Castro," said Willson. "Are you willing to tell me about Austin and why you were looking for him?"

"First, please call me Mauricio. And second, I am *still* looking for this man, so your call is very welcome. I was hired by a pair of my countrymen to find your Mr. Austin. It seems he has some of my clients' money — a significant amount. They would like it returned to them."

"How much money are we talking about?"

"They're missing sixteen point four million pesos. That sounds very high, but in American dollars, it's approximately two point five million between the two of them."

"Two point five million U.S. dollars?" asked Willson, now reeling from the second surprise of the call. "That's still a very large amount."

"Yes. And that is why they are so interested in talking to Señor Austin and getting their money back from him. They're not the kind of men to accept refusal."

"How did Austin get their money?"

"He persuaded them to invest in a new ski area near Portillo. That's our most famous ski area in Chile. He did an excellent job of selling the project to them as an opportunity to make a significant return on their investment. They believed it was a benign way to get into the beginning of something big. I would not say this to them, but I believe their greed got the best of them."

"And the money disappeared?"

"It was not that simple. For the first year, they received dividends every three months that were very attractive. They were pleased. At the end of that year, when their money was due to be returned to them, plus some healthy interest, Austin persuaded them to reinvest the original investment amount back into the fund. Shortly after they did that, they discovered that the ski area application had been rejected by our government, Austin was no longer in the country, and their money had somehow left the country with him."

"Fascinating," said Willson. Berland's waving hand showed that he was keen to ask the Chilean investigator his own questions. His eyes were bright, and he was clearly no longer comfortable staying in the background taking notes. "My colleague has some questions for you."

"Please go ahead," said Castro.

"Mauricio, Mike here. Were you able to contact Austin after he left your country?"

"Eventually. As you heard from his ex-wife, I did, with some difficulty, track him to Salt Lake City and tried to contact him there without success. He did not return my calls. I'd heard about his legal troubles regarding a mining project in that area. I was ready to go there when I learned that he'd left town, quite suddenly."

"Were you able to trace any of the missing money?"

"I was not. I assume that our financial disclosure rules are very different than yours in Canada. Even the government prosecutors could not trace the money. I can only assume he was using offshore accounts — in Europe or the Caribbean — but I have no way of knowing for sure."

"And after Salt Lake City?" asked Berland.

"I found him again in Boise, Idaho. He wouldn't return my calls there, either. I did go there to talk to him and ended up following him for a few days. At dinner one night, I approached him in a restaurant. He was there with a young woman."

"What happened?"

"I simply sat down at the table with them and began to ask Austin questions about the money he owed my clients."

"Did you get any answers from him?"

"Not at all," said Castro with a chuckle. "He ignored my questions and had me thrown out of the restaurant. The woman he was with was clearly shocked by the incident. I bet he had to answer a few questions from her after I left."

Berland laughed with him. "You got nothing from him?"

"Nothing beyond the satisfaction that he knew I was still after him, and that my clients are *not* the kind of men to walk away from their money."

"Did you know he was in Canada?"

"I did not, not until your call today. I knew that he'd left Boise and have been trying, when I have the time, to track his movements from there. But because I'm not from the U.S., I don't have the same access to people and resources as I do here. I talked to an Idaho-based investigator only last week, hoping he could dig up things I could not. And then you phoned me."

"Were you surprised to hear from us?" asked Berland.

"Yes, I'm surprised to hear from someone in Canada. But I'm not surprised that he's involved in another ski area. I'm sure he learned valuable lessons here that he's putting to good use there."

Willson twirled a pen across her fingers. "As we continue our investigation, can we call you again?"

Castro's laughter was a deep rumble over the phone's speaker. "Please do," he said. "It seems that the three of us are chasing the same elusive man. As we say in Spanish, *Dos cabezas son mejores que uno.* Two heads are better than one. In this situation, we now have three."

"I agree," said Willson. With Fortier, Berland, and now Mauricio Castro working with her, she had an investigative quartet, a foursome with enough diverse talent to peel back more layers on the onion, and faster than usual. She'd never been a true team player, preferring to work on her own, and the way the quartet had come together was not something you'd find in any investigations manual. But in this case, four heads *were* better than one. "Based on what you know of Mr. Austin, Mauricio, do you believe that the ski area here in Canada is legitimate? Or is Austin up to his old tricks in a new location?"

"I can't say. But in my experience, jaguars don't change their spots, Miss Willson. I would bet that your concerns about his project are well founded. Assuming he's not using his own money for it, if I were one of his investors, I'd be extremely nervous about ever seeing my money again."

CHAPTER 23

The next morning, Willson sat at her kitchen table, a steaming cup of Kick Ass in hand and files piled to her left, waiting for Berland to get out of bed. They'd talked late into the night, about Austin and what they'd learned from his ex-wife and Mauricio Castro. After a third Scotch, their discussion had veered off the case and into their own backgrounds, families, and past loves. Both, it seemed, had had experiences that were equally pathetic. Willson had tossed and turned all night, wondering if she'd been too open with Berland, professionally and personally. And then there had been that long hug as they headed to separate bedrooms at the end of the evening....

Now, in the light of morning, she was embarrassed about what she might have said, embarrassed that she couldn't remember all of it, and embarrassed that she'd let the man get behind her defences, with his probing questions and apparent interest in everything she said. Damn him. Did he honestly want to know what she thought, she wondered, or was it nothing more than a skilled reporter building background for stories to come?

Willson's cellphone buzzed with an incoming text. It was from Fortier. Be ready in 10 min. I'll pick you up. Need to reinterview Sara Ilsley. She has more info for us.

Willson looked across the room at the closed bedroom door. She could hear Berland's snores. *Wake him or leave him?* Because she hadn't yet told Fortier about the reporter's presence in town or about their phone calls from the day before, the decision was an easy one. The trip to Ilsley's house would give her a chance to fill Fortier in on what she'd learned and what she was working on. And it would give her time to persuade him that having Berland, and perhaps even Castro, involved in the investigation, at least on the periphery, would be a good thing. At least, that was her intent.

After finishing her coffee, brushing her teeth, and running a brush through her hair, Willson scribbled a note to Berland and dropped it on the table. *Gone to do an interview w/ RCMP. Help yourself to coffee and breakfast. Be back in a few hours. J.*

She pulled the front door closed behind her and stood on the front porch. Nothing but clear skies over the peaks on both sides of the Rocky Mountain Trench. Much of the snow in town had melted, but the deep and brilliant white of the mountains was a dramatic counterpoint to the rich blue backdrop. She knew it would be a classic late-season ski day at Kicking Horse Mountain; she could see the gondolas crawling up the slope like a chain of ants, taking staff to their jobs and releasing early rising powder-hounds to their secret stashes.

An RCMP cruiser turned onto her street. She was there to meet it when it stopped in front of her driveway.

"Good morning, Ben," she said, climbing into the passenger seat and quietly closing the door. She grimaced when her knee banged the mid-dash computer console.

"Sorry," he said, waiting while she put on her seat belt. "Most people ride in the back." As he pulled away he asked, "Who's your visitor from Idaho?" He must have seen Berland's vehicle in her driveway.

"I've got lots to tell you. His name is Mike Berland, and he's from Boise. You remember I told you that I'd met a reporter from the *Idaho Statesman* when my mum and I were down there? This is the guy. Mike's interested in Austin and the ski hill, and he decided to come up here to do some digging for himself."

"Huh. And he's staying with you? Do you think that's a good idea?"

Willson looked over at Fortier before answering. The Mountie kept his eyes firmly on the road, his face blank. Was his concern professional or personal? What was with these men and their damn questions?

"He's staying in my spare room, if that's what you mean. And if that's *not* what you mean, then I think sharing information with him — some, but not all — about my investigation into Austin may help me ... help *us* find the truth. He can do things I can't do, and poke into places I can't poke without raising red flags with Austin or with my employers. But rest assured, I haven't told him anything about the criminal investigations. And I won't unless you agree. Happy?"

"For now. We're taught to never fully trust reporters, so I'm uncomfortable. As long as he stays the hell out of our investigations, then I can live with it. But don't expect me to get warm and fuzzy with him."

"Fair enough. And just so you know, my bosses don't know he's here or that I'm working with him. I'd like to keep it that way."

"You like to take chances, don't you, Jenny?"

"I find I make better progress that way."

"Well, I won't say anything … but don't say I didn't warn you."

Willson nodded. "Now that that's out of the way, let me tell you about two phone calls Mike and I made yesterday. There's no doubt in my mind that this all links together. We just have to figure out how." As they drove south of Golden toward the McMurdo Benches, the winter tires hummed noisily on the paved highway, and Fortier pulled the visor down after the sun rose over Mount Seven. Willson gave him a summary of the conversations with Austin's ex-wife and with Mauricio Castro.

Five minutes later, Fortier turned off the highway onto Horse Creek Road and pulled over onto the gravel shoulder. "That matches with the fraud charges I found in the system," he said, turning in his seat to stare at Willson, "and it indicates that this isn't Austin's first rodeo."

"Exactly," said Willson, smiling. "Based on what we heard yesterday, I'm even surer that something is rotten in the state of Denmark. I just don't have the proof yet."

"Geez, I've got to get our commercial crime guys in on this."

"Any chance you can delay that? Let me do a bit more digging with Mike? We're going to pursue a few new leads based on what we heard yesterday."

Fortier nodded. "I'm not sure how much help I'll get from our B.C. headquarters anyway, so you've probably got some time. But if we find *any* evidence of a link between Austin's business and prior criminal activities, I'm going to push hard to get our guys involved." A vehicle came down the hill toward them. The female driver slowed and stared at the idling police car as she went by. Fortier gave the driver a quick *Nothing to see here* wave and then turned back to Willson. "What I'm wondering is whether Austin is serious enough about what he's doing to murder someone, or to nearly get himself shot simply to shift our attention from him to someone else. Or whether he's just an innocent businessman trying to make an honest buck."

"The more I hear, the less inclined I am to use the words *innocent* or *honest* to describe that man."

"Agreed," said Fortier, as he put the police car back into drive and followed the winding route of Horse Creek Road uphill to Sara Ilsley's house on the upper bench.

Ilsley was standing on the front porch when they pulled up. Wrapped in a large blue flannel jacket, she leaned over the wooden railing, her greying hair in a tight braid that hung down her left shoulder. She looked as if she carried the weight of the world on her shoulders. She didn't move as they walked across the yard toward her. When they reached the stairs to the porch, she straightened and headed for her front door. "Come in," she said over her shoulder, with a resigned sigh. "I've got the coffee on."

Once they had mugs of coffee in hand, Willson and Fortier sat across from Ilsley, two uniformed bookends on an overstuffed leather couch.

Against her own nature, Willson let Fortier take the lead. "You said on the phone that you had something you wanted to discuss with us," he said. "We're all ears, Sara."

"Well … when you two were here a few weeks ago," she said hesitantly, staring down at the coffee table, which was covered in magazines, "I didn't tell you the whole story."

Willson and Fortier waited.

"I didn't tell you about Leo Springer."

Willson was less patient than Fortier. "Who's Leo Springer?"

"He's a young man from Nicholson who came to one of our Society's first planning meetings after we found out about the ski area. At that point, we hadn't yet decided how we were going to fight the thing, what our campaign was going to look like."

"And?" said Willson, her pen poised over her notebook, her eyebrows raised.

"And he asked how far we could go in opposing the project."

"What's wrong with a question like that?"

"In itself, nothing. But he went on to suggest that if we played by the rules — rules which were designed to benefit the proponent — then we'd get run over by the process.

It was then that he said, and I'm paraphrasing here, that our only option was to 'put sugar in the gas tank' of the process. Or, and I believe these were his *exact* words, 'blow the fucker up.'"

Willson saw Fortier's head come up. "And when he said that, what did you think he meant?"

"I was spooked by the comment," said Ilsley, twisting her hands around her coffee mug as if trying to strangle it, "so I didn't know what to think. But the more I've thought about it since, the more concerned I am in light of what's happened. The violence."

"Do you think he's violent?"

"I have no idea. But he sure as hell frightened me that night, and I could tell that others felt the same."

"And what did you say to him in response?"

"I reminded everyone in the room about the Society's bylaws, what they say about *not* breaking the law. And then I went into a bit of a rant about civil disobedience and violence not being part of that."

"How did he react?"

"He told me to 'chill,' but then said nothing more. I adjourned the meeting soon after because I was so alarmed."

"And why did you wait so long to tell us?"

"I guess because I hoped it wasn't him who shot at Austin and Myers, or who broke the window in downtown Golden, or burned down Stoffel's office in a dangerous attempt to point fingers at Austin. And because I was worried that, if he *had* done something illegal, the Society would be drawn into a controversy that would deflect our time and energy from fighting the proposal. That we'd be distracted from the campaign, or even worse, that our credibility would be shot. I also feared he might come after us."

"Why tell us now?" Fortier asked.

"Because," said Ilsley, looking at him with fear in her eyes, "I got home from town late last night after a movie and he was parked at the end of my driveway, sitting there in his pickup truck. My headlights lit up his face when I turned in, so I know it was him."

"Did he do or say anything?"

"He just stared at me. Whether or not he meant to, he scared the crap out of me." Ilsley stood and began pacing around the room. She ran her fingers down the spines of books on a massive bookshelf, as if checking for dust, then shifted a wooden bowl a few millimetres before turning back to them.

Willson could tell Ilsley was genuinely frightened. "What make of truck was it? And what colour?" she asked.

"No idea," said Ilsley, shrugging her shoulders. "I'm not good with vehicles. It was a dark pickup, that's all I know. And I've asked around and everyone has the same opinion of him. He seems to be a quiet loner who no one really knows. He works as a labourer at the plywood and veneer mill in town."

"Do you know where he lives?"

"His contact info is in the membership list I gave you. I looked at it again before you got here, and all we have is a PO Box in Nicholson and a cellphone number. That's it. So, no, I can't tell you where he lives."

"I'll find him," said Fortier. "And then Jenny and I will have a chat with him."

"*Please* don't tell him you got his name from me. That guy gives me the creeps. I live here all alone, and he knows that."

"No problem. We're talking to everyone on the Society's membership list anyway. His name just came up on our radar more quickly than originally planned."

Ilsley sat down again. "I hope I'm wrong about Springer. I really do. And I hope like hell this doesn't affect our battle against the ski hill and that arrogant prick Austin."

At the mention of Austin, Willson again took the lead in the conversation. She saw Fortier lean back in the leather couch, apparently content to watch and listen. "Now that you mention him," said Willson, "let's talk about Stafford Austin while we're here."

"Don't get me started …" said Ilsley, her disgust clear from her tone of voice.

"From what your group has learned so far, do you believe this to be a bona fide business proposal, Sara? Is Austin serious about this project?" Willson watched Ilsley's eyes rise in response to the question, slowly, as if realizing that the question was like an iceberg, with much more to it than what showed above the surface.

"Don't you?"

"At this point, we don't know. Let's say that there are people digging into his financial and personal history."

"I assume you're involved in the review process, too. The government seems to be taking the project seriously, aren't they?"

Willson couldn't tell Ilsley what role she *was* playing in the process, or what was going on behind the scenes. At the same time, she knew there was value in planting the right questions amongst those fighting the project. People like Sara Ilsley. One of those seeds might eventually grow into something substantial. "I'm somewhat on the periphery of the formal part of the process," she said, "but I'm always interested in learning more from folks on all sides of the issue."

Ilsley's eyes were bright as they bored into Willson, as though she'd stumbled onto something that might shed light on a problem that had seemed insurmountable. "And what have you learned?"

Willson paused, trying to decide what to say. She looked to Fortier but his face was like a stone, expressionless. She turned back to Ilsley. "You've heard, I'm sure, about the recent connection made between the ski area and a highway through Howse Pass?"

"That's not true, is it? We've heard some talk, but assumed it was nothing more than a rumour."

"It's real all right. It's a serious discussion. And then … there's the pipeline question."

"Pipeline?"

"There's talk about that same highway corridor through the park also being used as an alternate route for an oil or gas pipeline between Alberta and B.C."

"What?" The handle of Ilsley's mug broke off with a crack. She looked at her hands, mug in one, handle in the other. Her face showed confusion and horror, as if she'd realized that she was holding a grenade without a pin.

"At this point," said Willson, "there seems to be *some* truth to it. I've been told that it's being discussed at very high levels of the federal government. Way above my pay grade. And you didn't get this from me, but Austin appears to be in the middle of it."

"That changes *everything*," said Ilsley.

CHAPTER 24

APRIL 6

Stafford Austin gazed out the picture window of his rental home in the Blaeberry Valley. Outside, the peaks of the Rocky Mountains were bright and white in the morning sun. Fresh air flowed in from an open screen.

A sudden bang made him jump. He was still nervous after the shooting and only felt comfortable standing near the window during the day. Each night, before darkness descended over the valley, he would pull the thick drapes across the expanse of glass in case his assailant returned to finish the job.

Looking cautiously to his left, toward the source of the sound, he saw a pickup truck careening down the gravel driveway. In the dust behind the truck, held in place only by barbed wire linking it to adjacent posts, a fencepost swayed drunkenly. Austin watched as the truck slid to a stop in the yard and Sandy Trueman jumped out of the driver's seat, her arms gesticulating wildly. She was at the front steps before her passenger had time to undo his seatbelt.

"Jesus," yelled John Theroux through the open truck window. "You trying to kill us?"

Through the screen, Austin could hear Trueman's strident voice as she pounded up the front stairs. "We have to tell Stafford what's going on. That those goddamn enviros are sticking their noses into places where they don't belong and putting everything at risk."

Theroux followed Trueman up the wide wood steps to the front porch, where she'd already started banging on the front door. "We couldn't have told him anything if we'd ended up dead in a ditch," he said.

Hank Myers opened the door. "Come in."

Trueman pushed past him. "Where's Stafford?"

Austin sighed. "In here," he said. "What's going on?"

"What's going on," said Trueman, stomping into the room, "is that the Columbia Valley Environmental Society knows about the highway and the pipeline. They're going to raise a major media stink about it!"

Austin felt a jolt of anger and fear that clenched at his heart and his guts like a claw. "How did *that* happen? Was it one of you?"

"No," said Trueman, "it wasn't us. I don't know how they know ... but they know!"

She began pacing back and forth across the room like a caged animal.

In his world, Austin recognized that doing business with people like these two was a necessary evil. He couldn't succeed without them. However, they were often the weakest link in the chain and required the most care and attention.

Theroux spoke next, clearly trying to calm the situation. "Our contact in the group told me it was a female warden from Yoho Park who told them about it. She and a local cop showed up at the society president's house yesterday. I guess they're still trying to figure out who killed that researcher and who shot at you guys. But after that, the warden asked other questions about the project, and specifically about you, Stafford. This is third-hand information, of course, but it sounds like she's investigating you as much as she is the project."

"What warden are we talking about?" asked Austin.

"Her name's Jenny Willson. She's the park's law enforcement warden. She lives in Golden."

"Huh," said Austin, his eyes shifting to Myers for a moment, a silent message passing between them. "When we were interviewed after the shooting, that Mountie did tell me that someone named Willson was here with him that night after we went to the hospital. You think she's investigating *me*?"

"It sounds like it," said Theroux. "She apparently asked what the Society knows about your business background, where you came from before you arrived in Golden, whether they knew who your investors were … that kind of thing."

"That's what she was asking?" The claw gripped his insides tighter.

"Is there … something you haven't told us?"

Austin glared at Theroux. "I've told you everything you need to know."

Trueman continued her pacing. "Our guy told us that the Society talked about you and the project at a meeting last night after the warden talked to the president. Why doesn't she mind her own goddamn business? Her meddling could put the whole plan at risk...."

"Have they interviewed you yet, John?" asked Myers.

"The cop came and interrogated us the day after the rally in Golden, showed up at our house without warning. We talked to him for a half hour or so because I sensed we didn't have a choice. He asked me and Sandy about the fire at Stoffel's office, you guys getting shot at, the broken window at the coffee shop. He seemed to believe us when we told him we had nothing to do with any of it. I haven't talked to him since. And I've never spoken to this warden. I have no idea how she's involved, or why."

"Hmm," said Austin. He gazed out the window. "Same with us. We've talked to Fortier a few times, but I've never met this warden. Is your cousin aware of this turn of events?" he asked, referring to Brian Cummings at the PMO. Few people besides those in the room and Cummings himself knew of the family connection between Cummings and Theroux. And they wanted it to stay that way.

"I haven't talked to him for a few weeks, so unless he's heard about it from someone else, no."

"This is unfortunate. I'll have to advise him that someone in the federal government — this Willson woman — seems to be operating outside the review process. That's not good for any of us."

"Is there something you want us to do?"

"No. Stay low for now. I'm sure your cousin will want to know about Willson's activities. I'm betting he'll have a chat with her bosses in Parks Canada. If she wants to keep her job, that should be the end of it." Austin paused. "And I'm thinking that Hank and I should have a talk with her. She needs to understand that Top of the World is a bona fide project that's right where we want it to be and she shouldn't concern herself with anything other than that. I'm a simple entrepreneur trying to do something good for this community."

"And that's the truth, right?" asked Theroux, his head slightly tilted.

Austin took a step toward him. "Are you doubting me now, after all I've done for you?"

Theroux raised his hands, palms open. "Geez, Stafford, I just want to know the facts. I'm out on the pointy end of the stick for you and your project."

"That's what I'm paying you for … and paying you well. I can't afford for you to be anything but fully committed."

"Calm down, Stafford," said Theroux, stepping back, "I *am* fully committed."

"And so am I," Trueman said. "But I need to do something. I can't just sit on my hands while all this is going on."

"No!" yelled Myers, glaring at her. Even with his injured arm in a sling, he was still intimidating. "Nothing is *exactly* what you should do. Part of the reason we're in the middle of this is because of what you've done already. We don't need any more of *that*!"

"But we were just trying to help!" said Trueman, her stridency turning into petulance.

"If you want to do something useful," said Austin, his voice calm and quiet despite the frustration he was feeling inside, "focus on the ski society. Keep the group on track. Keep pushing the positive messages about the project. Keep looking for new members who want to see the ski resort move ahead. And be ready to counter anything coming out of the environmental groups."

He moved toward the front door, signalling the end of the meeting.

Through the window, Austin and Myers watched the couple return to their truck. Trueman was still talking and waving her arms. They saw Theroux pause, turn, and look back as if he wished he could stay with them rather than endure another life-threatening ride with his agitated wife.

"This is exactly what I was worried about," said Austin as the truck bounced away from the house. "Their impulsive actions are going to draw attention to us, the wrong kind of attention. Now we've got the cops digging into things … not just the Stoffel situation, or the shots fired at us, but into our business. We can't afford to let that happen. Not when money is flowing into both investment funds." He jammed his hands into his pockets, grimacing as he experienced a flash of pain from his injured hand. "What do you think?"

"I think we need to regain control of this. And it sounds like this warden, Jenny Willson, is the key to doing that."

"Do you think she's working on her own, or with the blessing of the government?"

"No idea. Cummings will have a better sense of that."

"I wonder how much she knows."

"We can't be sure until we talk to her. I know you've been careful, Stafford, but no one leaves a trail without any clues. We've got to ensure she doesn't dig up something she shouldn't."

"What are you thinking?"

"Like you said earlier, the first step is to meet her face to face. We should do that as soon as we can. If we can persuade her that she's barking up the wrong tree, everything might calm down again."

"And if not?" Austin asked.

"If using all our charm, good looks, and powers of persuasion doesn't work? Then we might need something more dramatic to get our point across."

"Like what?"

"Not sure yet," Myers said. "I'll need to look into Willson, find out what drives her, what her weakness is. Only then will we know how best to persuade her."

"And then?"

"And then it will be her choice as to how co-operative she wants to be."

"Hmm. I agree," said Austin. His anger and apprehension had now come to the surface. He felt it in the warmth in his cheeks, the unconscious clenching of his fists, the tension in his lower back. He'd experienced this kind of outside interference before, always forcing him to abandon his dreams and move on right when he was on the verge of achieving his goals. He refused to let it happen again. "I won't accept some park warden getting in my way," he said, "and destroying my relationships with investors and the government. This is too important for some low-level bureaucrat to screw up. We need to do whatever it takes to prevent that from happening."

"I understand," said Myers, his face absent of expression. "That's why you hired me, isn't it?"

CHAPTER 25

"Well, that was an interesting afternoon," said Berland, "and more than a bit painful. I need a beer."

Willson smiled. "I told you Albin was passionate about wolverines, didn't I?"

"Jesus. That's not passion. That's borderline obsession."

"When it comes to conservation, there's a fine line between the two. Those who toil in the trenches of research or advocacy drift back and forth across that line every day."

They were sitting in a Parks Canada truck parked in the pouring rain outside Stoffel's new office in downtown Golden. It had seemed small the last time Willson had been there, with just two of them in it. With three people, it had been downright uncomfortable.

"I've learned more about wolverines than I ever wanted to know," said Berland, shaking his head. "That guy would have talked the entire bloody day if we hadn't finally shut him down."

"If you're going to work with me on this, you need to understand the whole picture. And because I like to share, I didn't want you to miss out on that experience while you're here."

"Thanks a lot, Jenny. That was very generous of you." He returned her wry smile and looked down at his notebook. "Did you get anything new this time?"

"I did. Stoffel confirmed that Collie Creek is home to at least one wolverine den site, and that Collie Creek, along with the Blaeberry to the north and Yoho Park to the south, forms part of the home range of at least six different animals. That's significant in the world of wolverines."

"Why?"

"Wolverines cover large areas in low densities. Collie Creek and the Blaeberry are clearly a special area for them. In places like Yoho, the home ranges for males can be 600 to 1,000 square kilometres — half that for females, particularly those with young. The presence of a confirmed den site in the valley — and as you heard from Stoffel, those are often found at high elevations —means the female will leave her young there for a few days at a time to find food. At that time of year, in late winter and into the spring and summer, they're extremely vulnerable to any disturbance."

"And what are the implications of this knowledge for the ski area project, highway, and pipeline?"

"Because wolverines are classified as endangered under federal species at risk legislation, both levels of government must protect the animal's critical habitats. And recent research has shown that cutting the north-south connectivity between the animals with highways or other developments can cause population and genetic declines. That's bad news not just for the ski area, but for the other two proposals, as well. The animals and their habitats can't legally be ignored, not without going all the way to the level of the minister of the environment and the Cabinet. So, it puts the federal government, particularly Parks Canada, in a real quandary. Like we said when we were up there in the helicopter, if they allow a ski area to go ahead in Collie Creek, and at the same time approve a highway and a pipeline through the Blaeberry and Banff National Park, then those valleys will sure as hell be no place for any wildlife."

"Does that mean that Austin's proposal is doomed, then?"

"Far from it," said Willson. "What it means is that this thing is going to get more complicated, and a whole lot more political than it already is."

"And our friend Stafford is right in the middle of it all with his questionable background, a string of unanswered questions that follows him around like a marching band, and unhappy investors from previous projects."

"Exactly."

Willson's phone buzzed in her pocket just as she was about to pull out of their parking space on 9th Avenue. "Willson here."

"Hi, Jenny. This is Tara at the Yoho warden office."

"Tara, what's up?"

"This is strange. I just got a call from Stafford Austin. He says he wants to talk to you."

Willson looked at Berland, her eyebrows up. "Stafford Austin wants to talk to *me*?"

"That's what he said."

"Did he say why?"

"I asked him, but he only said that it was important he speak with you at your *earliest* convenience. He definitely put the emphasis on *earliest*."

"Isn't that intriguing? I was literally just talking about him, and then he crawls out from under his rock, demanding to talk to me. Did he leave a number where I can reach him?"

Summers read the number out to Willson, who scribbled it in her notebook. "Will you let me know what he says? We're keeping detailed records of every conversation we have with him." She chuckled. "Not that we don't trust him, of course. But we've been burned too many times by proponents claiming they'd been told things by Parks staff when, in fact, they hadn't."

"I will," said Willson. "I only met the guy once at an open house, and even then, I didn't tell him who I was. I wonder why he wants to talk to me now."

But her confusion was for Summers's benefit. Willson knew. She must have turned over the right rocks in the right places, asked enough questions of the people on the periphery of Austin's world, poked and probed and agitated just enough. In only a few months, she'd done enough to send him an unambiguous message: she was circling him, hunting him. Truly, it hadn't been a matter of *if* he would approach her, but when and how. The time had come. He'd received her message.

"Good luck, Jenny," said Summers before disconnecting.

"Unbelievable," Willson said, staring across the truck cab at Berland, a wry smile on her face. "How would you like to make the acquaintance of one Stafford Austin?"

Berland smiled back. "It'd be my pleasure to finally talk to that son of a bitch. Honestly, I didn't think it would happen this soon. You sure you want me with you?"

"Absolutely. He has met me before, although he may not realize it. And he might recall your name from his days of dodging you in Boise. Or maybe not. If he does, seeing us together should set him back on his heels. If he's feeling confident about what he wants to say to me, having you there should knock some of that out of him. And seeing that will be worth the price of admission."

"What about your Mountie friend?"

"Good question. I'll let Ben know that we're meeting with Austin and that we can play the tape for him after."

"We're recording it?"

"Yep. I'll have a world-class investigative journalist with me. He'll be recording the conversation so that his quotes are accurate."

Berland grinned. "You said 'world-class,' so you *must* be speaking about me. And I guess this means I won't get my beer quite yet."

Willson still had her cellphone in her hand, so she keyed in the number and put it on speaker so Berland could hear. It rang three times, then they heard a deep voice with a strong southern accent. "This is Stafford Austin."

"Stafford," said Willson, pausing for effect. "I understand you're looking for me."

"Who is this?"

"Jenny Willson, Yoho National Park warden. I was told that you'd phoned our office." She heard a pause at the other end.

"Ah, yes, Ms. Willson. I've been led to believe that you've been asking questions about me. I thought it would be worthwhile for us to meet so I could explain some things to you."

"That sounds like an excellent idea, Stafford. When and where would you like to meet?"

"Can you come out to my house on Blaeberry River Road? Does this afternoon work for you? I understand from Corporal Fortier that you were out here once before, although I didn't get a chance to meet you because I was on my way to the hospital. I expect you know your way."

"I certainly do. We'll be there in about an hour."

"We?"

"Yes," said Willson. She disconnected the call, hoping that she'd already put Austin on edge wondering who she was bringing with her.

Shortly after 5:00 p.m., Willson drove down the gravel driveway toward Austin's sprawling log home. The last time she'd been here, it had been dark, the house and yard illuminated by red and blue flashing lights. Now, with the valley illuminated by the bright spring sun, she could see more clearly how large the house actually was. It sat in a large open acreage with the trees cleared back for at least two hundred metres on all sides. As she had on her first visit, she was wearing her full warden uniform, including a bulletproof vest, and she had a 9mm pistol in a leather holster on her right hip.

"Nice place he has here," said Berland.

"Don't be too impressed," Willson said. "It's a rental."

When they reached the front yard, she turned off the ignition and faced Berland. "Let's have some fun, shall we? I won't tell him who you are unless he recognizes you himself." She also wanted to minimize the chances of Berland's presence being leaked to Speer or Church.

"Fine with me," Berland said, nodding. His eyes shone bright. "I've been waiting for this moment for at least a year."

They jumped out of the truck, and Willson placed her Stetson firmly on her head as they walked toward the front stairs. She noticed that Berland's attention was drawn to the snow-covered peaks around them; his head slowly swivelled from left to right. Willson paused and pointed to the east. "We're in the widest part of the main Blaeberry River drainage now. From where we're standing, through where it narrows in that direction, it's about fifty kilometres to the headwaters at the west boundary of Banff National Park. Collie Creek, where we were a few days ago, is up that way and to the right."

"This is quite the view. I've never seen anything like it."

Willson smiled and banged on the wooden door. It swung open to reveal a looming Hank Myers, one hand on the door, the other arm tucked in a sling. He said nothing, just nodded at them to come inside. Myers followed as they walked into the living room to the left of the front door. She recalled the chaos, the blood, the broken glass, and the upturned furniture from her last visit. Someone had done a thorough job of cleaning up, and the large picture window had been skillfully replaced. The pine floors shone in the afternoon sun.

"You must be Jenny Willson," said Stafford Austin, getting up from a chair and extending a meaty hand toward her. "Have we met?"

"I'm not sure *met* would be accurate," said Willson, trying but failing to exert as much force with her hand as Austin was with his. "But we did talk briefly at an open house in Golden a few months back. I'm hoping you'll answer some questions today that you wouldn't answer back then."

"Ah, yes, I think I remember. You asked me about my investors, but wouldn't tell me who you were. I'd wondered since then. And who is joining you today?"

Berland moved forward and stood beside Willson.

"This is my associate, Mike," said Willson. "He's here to take notes."

"Mike ..." said Austin questioningly, obviously prompting for a last name.

"That's right, Mike. Because you were so keen to talk to me, I've brought someone along who shares my interest in what you have to say."

Keeping her face free from emotion, Willson watched Austin. She could tell that the big man was struggling to control the situation. His eyebrows were moving up and down, he was shifting his weight from foot to foot, and his gaze was jumping between the two of them. From her perspective, it was an excellent start to the visit, better than she had expected.

"Shall we sit?" Austin said, "Hank will take your coats."

After giving their coats to his injured partner, Willson and Berland sat in adjacent seats opposite their host. Myers returned and stood in a far corner, watching silently, his good arm crossed over the injured one. At a nod from Willson, Berland pulled a digital recorder from his back pocket and placed it on the coffee table. With a click that echoed through the room, he powered it up and turned the small machine so that it faced Austin, then opened his notebook and slid a pen from his shirt pocket.

Willson sat back and crossed her legs. The leather couch creaked and squeaked beneath her. "Now that we're here, what would you like to talk to me about, Mr. Austin?"

"As I said on the phone," Austin said, moving forward in his chair, "I understand you've been asking about my project. In light of the formal multi-agency review process — with which I am co-operating fully — I'm wondering why you're asking these questions. I've never seen you at any of the project review meetings. What role do you play?"

"There are many people in Parks Canada, and in other federal agencies, I'm sure, working to ensure that we understand the full scope and scale of the project, its impacts and benefits, the capabilities, and *intentions* of those behind it. Not all of us are directly involved in the formal review process, but people like me are there in the background, offering our support. It's as simple as that."

"You're simply an average federal civil servant, toiling away in the background, asking questions that are a … *normal* part of the process?"

"Something like that. Are you suggesting otherwise?" She loved this part, when interviewer and interviewee were dancing a veritable verbal tango, sometimes twirling together, sometimes shifting in opposite directions.

"I don't know you well enough to be sure. For now, I'll have to take you at your word."

"Good," said Willson, nodding. "Mr. Austin, you asked me here. What would you like to share with us?"

Austin rested his elbows on his knees, steepled his fingers, and peered at Willson. She wondered if he had either forgotten about Berland or was ignoring him on purpose.

"I want to assure you, Ms. Willson," Austin said, "that we're very serious about the ski area. We have the necessary financial backing for the project and the team in place to make it a reality."

Willson waited, saying nothing, showing nothing. It was as if he'd said all he wanted or needed to say, and by making his simple statement, he had cleared up all questions and now expected her to cease her investigation. *Is he that stupid and arrogant*, she wondered, *or does he always get his way?*

"I hope that clears things up and allows you to move on to other duties." Austin shifted back in the chair.

Willson was quiet for a moment, then broke out laughing. "You're not serious, are you?"

"What do you mean? I'm very serious."

"You called me all the way out here to tell me that? A single sentence? Do you think I'm an idiot?"

"I didn't say that. I wanted you to hear my confirmation in person, in case you had any doubts."

"I've got a whole *valley* full of doubts, and those won't magically disappear just because you tell me that everything is fine. You *do* think I'm an idiot."

A smug smile came over Austin's face. "Again, I don't know you well enough to know for sure," he said. "Do you have any specific questions I can answer?"

"I certainly do, and I'm sure that Mike has some as well." She looked to Berland, who was nodding his head and smiling. "Let's start with the question I asked you at the open house. Do you have any of your own money invested in this project?"

"I do."

"How much?"

"Well, that's none of your business. It's private company information. What I can tell you is that I'm a consultant on the project, and because I want to see it go ahead, I'm not receiving my normal daily rate for a venture like this. Like others, I'm an investor."

"You're a consultant in the project, and you're *also* the president of the company? Probably the person who decides which consultants get hired? That sounds like double-dipping to me." She saw Austin's cheeks flush.

"You're showing your ignorance about how the business world works," he said, his voice wavering slightly. "Everyone involved in this is fully aware of the nature of my connections. There's no issue there."

"Hmm," said Willson, pausing to look at her notebook. "What about your investors? Besides you, who else has money in this project?"

"My investors will remain confidential. They refuse to be targets for those misinformed people who oppose the project. But the provincial government has documents on file that confirm my investors' commitments and their capability to finance the project."

Berland spoke beside her. "Are those investors aware of your past criminal activities, Mr. Austin? I'm referring to Chile, Salt Lake City, and most recently … Boise?"

Austin's eyes snapped toward Berland, his cheeks flushing a deeper red.

"What's your role in this, *Mike*?"

"As Jenny told you earlier, I'm her associate. That means I associate with her and take notes at meetings like this one."

"Well, Jenny's associate, I urge you to be very careful about making unfounded accusations. They could land you in court."

"Yes, I suppose they could, although that was just a question. I'm guessing that once a judge saw the hundreds of pages of court documents from those other jurisdictions we have in our files, he'd throw your case out. So honestly, I'm not really concerned about that. But I do wonder what your investors would say if *they* saw those documents. The affidavits and victim statements and, of course, the trail of fascinating, some would say disturbing, financial records. Perhaps then your investors' involvement with you would be just as short-lived as our appearance in front of a judge."

Austin glanced at Myers, still standing in the corner like a statue, then back at Berland. "You're treading on thin ice," he said.

"*I'm* on thin ice?" asked Berland, pointing dramatically at his own chest. "I wonder if the men looking for you, the ones from South America who want their money back, the money you absconded with in your *last* ski hill scam, have any idea that you're here in Canada now. I wonder what they'd do if they found out …"

Now Austin's face paled. It seemed Berland had found a weakness in the man's bravado.

"Let's shift gears for a moment," Willson said, attempting to keep Austin off balance. "What's your involvement in the plans to build a new highway from Alberta to B.C., through Banff Park and then down the Blaeberry? And what do you know about the plans to use that route for an oil or gas pipeline?"

Austin's eyes shifted back to Willson. "I'm certainly aware of it … and aware of the benefits it would bring to my project. But that's a federal government initiative, probably being discussed well above your level. At this time, I have no direct involvement in those plans."

"The stories I'm hearing are false, then? The ones that say that you've already approached at least one road builder in Alberta about the project?"

"I'm not sure where you heard that from, but as of today, that's definitely false."

"Did you have anything to do with the arson at Albin Stoffel's office and the death of his research assistant?" Berland asked.

"That was a sad and tragic accident. I've had numerous conversations with the RCMP, and they have no evidence to suggest that I was in any way involved."

"Interesting way to put it," Berland said. "Not a denial, but not admitting anything, either. To me, it seems a fortunate coincidence, for you and your project, that one of your main opponents experienced such a dramatic loss. Whoever did set that fire will soon be facing murder charges."

Austin exploded from his chair. He stabbed his finger at Berland, then at Willson. "The two of you have overstayed your welcome. Get the hell out!"

"That's fine, Stafford," said Willson, standing and moving toward the front door. "But I'm very disappointed. I'd hoped to learn more today, but it seems again you've left me with more questions than answers."

Austin stood holding the door, Myers lurking behind him, as they put on their coats. "Ms. Willson," he said, "I hope there's no question in your mind that I want you to shift your attention to other things. The same goes for you, *Mike*."

Willson turned in the doorway to face the two men. "There's no doubt in my mind at all," she said. "You said earlier that you don't know me well. That's true. Anyone who did would have no doubt that what *you* want doesn't matter to me. I hope there's no question in your mind about that."

"Does your mother approve of you having such an aggressive attitude?" Myers said, shaking his head. It was the first time he'd spoken since they'd arrived.

"What did you say?" asked Willson, taking a step toward Myers, her hand unconsciously moving to the gun on her belt.

Myers did not move, did not flinch. His face was a stone. "You heard what I said, and what Stafford said. You should think hard about how your misguided meddling could impact those around you."

Willson pushed her face closer to Myers's, her eyes blazing. "Don't you mention my mother ever again, do you fucking hear me?"

A mirthless smile spreading across his face, Myers slowly closed the door, leaving Willson and Berland standing on the outside.

CHAPTER 26

"Those are the most common options for businesses to attract capital, at least in a way that complies with our laws and, most importantly, meets the requirements of the B.C. Securities Commission," said Courtney Pepper, sitting at her desk across from Willson, Berland, and Fortier. The three of them were packed into the small office, which looked out on the main street of Golden. Outside, groups of skiers walking by looked like neon streaks as they headed to the Golden Taps pub a few doors down.

Pepper was a CPA who'd been a high school friend and teammate of Willson's before their lives and careers had diverged after graduation. Now, both were back working in their hometown, with Pepper owning and operating an accounting firm specializing in small and medium-sized businesses.

When Willson had learned from her mother that Pepper was back in town, she'd been excited to see her old friend again. That is, until the moment the three of them had entered the office and Fortier had kissed her, introducing her to the other two as his fiancée. Willson knew that her gaping mouth and wide eyes at the sight of the glittering chunk of stone on her old friend's finger had not gone unnoticed by anyone in the room, least of all Pepper. *Are you kidding me?* she'd thought. *Not again! Why the hell didn't Ben say anything when I suggested we meet here?* This wasn't the first time she'd been interested in someone only to discover that she'd badly misread signals and made an ass of herself. And Willson assumed that, with her luck, it wouldn't be the last.

"Thanks for putting that in layman's terms, Court," said Willson, the kiss still fresh in her mind, "so that even someone like me who gets a rash whenever I go anywhere near math can understand."

"No problem. Glad I could help."

"What if someone wanted to attract capital to a project ... in a way that didn't necessarily comply with those laws?" asked Berland.

"I'm not sure I understand what you mean," said Pepper, her head tilting slightly.

"Look," said Willson, "We're in the midst of an investigation, Court, and we're trying to figure out what's really going on behind the scenes with one of our persons of interest. That's the reason behind Mike's question. I need your commitment that you'll keep what we're talking about today to yourself."

"As long as we're not talking about one of my clients, and you can confirm that this is purely hypothetical, and I won't be required to testify to anything I've said, then no problem. Otherwise, I'm risking my designation."

Willson handed Pepper a copy of the corporate summary she'd received from the local government agent. "Is Stafford Austin, Collie Creek Resorts Limited, or any of the company's directors a client of yours?"

Pepper scanned the document. "No, none of those people are my clients, and I don't do any work for that company. Isn't this the group behind that ridiculous ski area proposal up in Yoho? The one they call Top of the World?"

"Yes, and I guess we know where you stand on it!" said Willson, chuckling. "Good. What I want to ask you is how an individual like Austin, who seems to have a track record of what might be called shady business deals, would or could run a project like this outside the law. I don't know if he is or isn't, but I'm trying to build a clearer picture, figure out what questions to ask, and of whom. Any advice you can offer would be much appreciated."

Fortier jumped in. "We do appreciate your help, Court. I'm just a small-town cop with no experience in business, so a lot of this is Greek to me. We don't have expertise in our detachment, and I've been trying to persuade someone in our commercial crime section to help me out, but I haven't had much luck so far."

"My pleasure, if this is all … hypothetical," said Pepper with a grin. "Do you know anything about the deals he's been involved with in the past? I could give you a better answer if I had a sense of what he's done previously."

Despite Fortier's protests, Berland (who had again been introduced as a colleague of Willson's) gave Pepper a summary of what they knew about Austin's previous business dealings in the U.S. and Chile. "He always seemed to act as a witness for the prosecution," he said, in conclusion, "or to leave town before he being charged with anything. As a result, the documents we have are less than complete."

"If his past is any indication of the present or the future," said Pepper, "then it strikes me that the situations you described could have been either pyramid or Ponzi schemes. Without more details, I can't say for sure. I'm no expert in forensic audits, which is what's needed to know for certain."

"I've heard of both of those," said Willson. "What's the difference?"

"I'll try to keep this simple. The Ponzi scheme is named after Charles Ponzi, who was notorious for first using it in the early 1920s. In essence, it's an investment fraud that promises high financial returns or dividends that are not available through traditional investments. The early investors don't know it, but their returns come not from legitimate profits, but from their own money, or from money invested by subsequent investors."

"So, it's a shell game," said Willson, "moving money from one person to another, making it appear to everyone as though the whole thing is legitimate?"

"That's one way of putting it," said Pepper. "In a traditional Ponzi scheme, like the one Bernie Madoff became infamous for, there's normally no legitimate investment at the heart of it all. The scheme unravels either when the promoter flees with everyone's money, when enough new investors can't be found to continue payment of the promised returns to existing investors, or when the scheme is discovered due to complaints from victims or from professionals like me who uncover questionable things in the financial statements."

"And what about pyramid schemes?" asked Willson.

"Based on what you told me," Pepper said, "that might have been going on with the mining deal in Utah, but it's hard to know. It could also have been nothing more than classic stock fraud, what they call a pump and dump. Pyramids are also known as multilevel marketing schemes. In those, participants earn money not so much from selling products, but by recruiting new participants to pay money to join the program. When they get others to sign up, they then get a cut of whatever the new members sell — either products or new memberships. In those schemes, the folks who get in early can do well. But those lowest on the pyramid often come in too late to get anything other than shafted."

"I think Austin might have been involved in one or both of these kinds of schemes in the past," said Berland. "I've, uh ... done research on both, and what you've said matches with what I've learned along the way. Both situations leave behind a trail of victims with less money than when they started. And they're often people who can't afford to lose that money — it's their life savings, money for their retirement."

Willson turned to look at Berland and knew from the anger on his face that he was thinking about his grandparents.

"Austin clearly has a questionable past," said Fortier, "but we have no idea if he's following the same pattern with the new business here, or if what he's doing is legitimate. There's a bunch of questions flying around but no solid answers. For me, the most important question is whether there's a direct link between the business and the recent violent crimes. We've got more interviews to do and we're still waiting on evidence reports. But maybe if we can better understand the business, the answer might become more clear. Are there red flags that we should be looking for as we dig deeper into the business aspect, Court?"

"There are," said Pepper. "I'm sure your commercial crime guys know these by heart, but I'll run through them in case you have to go it alone. First, the investment offers high returns with little or no risk, often in some form of guarantee. And those returns are often overly consistent, unlike other investments that go up and down with the vagaries of the market. Most Ponzi schemes involve investments that aren't registered with provincial regulators, which means that investors don't have access to information they should, or they're shown forged or fake documents. They're also commonly sold by people or businesses that aren't properly registered. And the alleged investments can be abnormally secretive or complex. From what I've read, the end of the scheme is likely near when you start hearing stories about missing or late account statements, late payments to investors, or if investors experience significant delays in getting their money back out."

"Shit," said Berland, tossing his pen on his notebook. After a single bounce, it disappeared under Pepper's desk.

"I think we need to talk to some of Austin's investors to truly get a sense of what's going on. And judging by our meeting with Austin, it won't be easy to get those names."

"How did, uh, journalists do it when they wrote stories about his crimes in the past?" asked Willson.

"When I asked them, they told me it was much easier then because law enforcement officials were already involved in the cases, so there were investigators willing to talk to me … I mean *them* … off the record."

Willson looked at Pepper, at Fortier, and then at Berland. "Maybe we can entice the investors out of the darkness like moths to a porch light."

"What're you thinking, Jenny?" asked Berland.

"There are two ways we can approach this. The most obvious is to get someone to pose as an investor, get on the inside of the project, and then look for those red flags that Courtney has identified."

"That would be a job for one of our commercial crime guys," said Fortier, "if I can convince them to help …"

"Agreed," said Willson.

"What's the other way?" asked Berland.

Willson smiled. "If a business story were to appear in the Calgary, Vancouver, and Toronto newspapers, and maybe online, that hinted at financial questions being raised about the ski project by 'unnamed sources,' how much would you bet that investors in any of those cities would come out of the woodwork to either push Austin for answers or simply pull their money out of the project? Or, better yet, get in contact with the journalist who wrote the piece to get more information."

"I'm not sure I'm comfortable with that second option," said Fortier, his brow furrowing. "That crosses an ethical line for me. But if it happens, such an article would have to be skillfully done so the writer didn't end up facing libel charges. I assume it breaks a number of rules of journalism, as well as sitting right on the line of defamation. Do you know of anyone who fits that description, has that level of skill?"

"I believe I do," said Willson, glancing at Berland. "There's a really good reporter at the *Calgary Herald* whom I dealt with in a previous investigation."

"I'm sure we can find someone better," Berland said, looking at Willson. "Based on what we heard last week from Austin and Myers, that kind of media attention is *not* gonna make them happy."

"And your point is?" asked Willson.

"My point is that it's a hell of an idea. And if your Calgary hack friend won't take the assignment," Berland said, "then I might know someone …"

"Either way, we should expect some blowback from Austin," Fortier cautioned. "I want both of you to pay extra attention to what's going on around you. If Austin and Myers *were* involved in setting that fire, then they've shown what they're willing to do to those who stand in their way."

"And I think I'll pretend I didn't hear *any* of that last bit," said Pepper, frowning, her hands over her ears. "I'll stick to my numbers and my spreadsheets."

"Good call, Courtney," said Willson.

CHAPTER 27

South of Golden, Ben Fortier turned off Highway 95 into the rural community of Nicholson, dropped down a hill, then crossed a bridge over the north-flowing Columbia River. From there, he steered the RCMP SUV onto McBeath Road and pulled over at a driveway entrance. He turned to Willson in the passenger seat. "The Yoho Park superintendent called you right after the meeting with Court yesterday. What did he say?"

"It seems Austin started making calls as soon as we left his house. As low man on the totem pole, the super was told to call me. He's in a tough position ... smart enough to realize that something's not right with the project, but experienced enough not to piss off his bosses. It's called multidirectional ass-covering. It's like yoga, but more challenging — and much less fun to watch on YouTube. He told me to keep working with you, quietly, but to back off of Austin."

"And?"

"And I tried to explain to him that based on what I've seen so far, the violence and the growing questions about the project can no longer be separated — the two are inextricably linked."

"Did he buy it?"

"Nope. He told me that *his* boss got a call from someone in Ottawa, who had received a call from the deputy minister, who had been dragged into the Prime Minister's Office to explain what I was doing and why. In a classic demonstration of the physics of shit flowing downhill, always picking up speed and volume, I'm being told to stop what they've called my 'rogue investigation into Stafford Austin and his project,'" she said, using air quotes, "and to leave any questions about the project to the review process."

"Your name was mentioned in the lofty halls of Ottawa? In our outfit, that's not normally a good thing."

"Not in ours, either," said Willson with a smirk. "Seems I've pissed off someone way up there. Can't help but wonder why …"

"Did Church actually tell you straight out to stop what you're doing?"

"He's too devious for that. He said he'd been told to tell me that government at the highest levels wanted me to stop. And that he was passing on that message. So I told him I heard the message and understood it."

"But you didn't say you were going to stop …"

"Nope. And I'm sure he suspects I'll keep going. He wants to keep his bosses happy, but he also doesn't want to be the guy who's later accused of trying to cover something up."

"You're not worried about what they'll do if you don't stand down?"

"Being on the wrong side of the bureaucracy isn't breaking new ground for me, Ben," she said, staring at Fortier with eyes like laser beams. "To be honest, I'm more concerned about what they'll do if I *do* stop. Who's got the balls to hold them accountable?"

"So, you're telling me you're not going to stop … even though your boss told you to, and even though Austin and Myers may have less than subtly threatened you."

"They *did* threaten both me and Mike, Ben. There's no question of that. But that just makes me want to dig deeper, although now I'll have to be more careful. I have no plans to walk away from this. Which is why I'm pleased that we're talking to Leo Springer today. I think he's a missing piece in this puzzle."

"Well, I do like your spirit, Jenny." Fortier put the car in gear. "Let's see if he's home."

"Wait," said Willson, putting her hand on his arm.

Fortier put his foot on the brake. "What?"

"Why didn't you tell me that you and Courtney were engaged when I suggested meeting at her office?"

"Oh … it didn't cross my mind. I thought everyone knew. You two are friends from high school, so I thought she would've told you."

"We hadn't talked in fourteen years. It was news to me."

Fortier looked at her blankly, like he had no idea what was going on. *He probably doesn't*, thought Willson. *Bloody clueless male.*

"It's not an issue between us, is it?" he asked, his face wrinkled in confusion.

"No," said Willson, turning away and feeling foolish about raising her discomfort. "No issue at all. I guess I wanted to congratulate you. She seems to have turned out nice."

"She wasn't nice when you knew her?" asked Fortier.

"Shut up and drive, Ben."

Once they were on the move again, Fortier began looking at rural addresses on passing mailboxes. "What's your friend Mike doing today while you're out with me?" he asked.

"I don't have Wi-Fi at my house, so he's going to the library to start writing the article we talked about. He seemed keen to put pen to paper ... or fingers to keyboard. I understand he's already contacted some media outlets about running it."

"And you still trust him?"

"So far, so good. He said he won't do anything until I tell him to pull the trigger."

"I'm interested to see how he pulls it off so he doesn't get himself in hot water."

"Me, too. Did you talk to commercial crime about making a covert connection with Austin?"

"I briefed an inspector in the section last night. All I can say at this point is that something *might* happen. I don't know if or what or when. Those guys are busy, and I may need to bring them more evidence to get them

excited. Oh, the joys of a small rural detachment ..."
He pointed at the last house on the left-hand side of the
road, tucked up against a steep hillside. "There," he said,
"that's the address we have for Springer."

The SUV bounced down the gravel driveway — its
surface was littered with potholes and tree roots. In the
main yard, a weathered single-wide mobile home sat in
a clearing, surrounded by equally weathered and seem-
ingly unmaintained outbuildings. A wooden garage
open on three sides was full of firewood cut and stacked
in rows. Across from it sat two aluminum sheds and a
large timber-frame building, its double doors open. A
very large bull mastiff was chained to a doghouse nearby.
As they got out of the truck, the dog stood, growling
at them and straining at the limit of its chain. For a
moment, Willson wondered if it would drag its house
toward them. But the chain held tight. For the moment.

Willson and Fortier heard the sound of a saw whining, so they headed toward the timber-frame building,
Willson taking an extra wide route to avoid the radius
of the chained dog, with her hand resting on her gun,
just in case.

Inside what they now saw was a workshop, a man
with his back to them was pushing a large board through
a shrieking planer. He wore tattered denim overalls over
a flannel shirt and was covered from head to toe in
sawdust. Because he was at least a foot taller than their
description of the suspect, Willson knew this was not
Springer. She waited until the board was through the
machine, then moved to where the man could see her.
Clearly startled, he dropped the board with a bang.

"Jesus Christ!" he said. He shut down the machine and pulled orange hearing protectors from his ears. His eyes were wide behind bulbous safety goggles. "You scared the shit out of me!"

"My apologies," said Willson. "I'm National Park Warden Jenny Willson, and this is Corporal Ben Fortier. We're looking for Leo Springer. Is he here?"

"Nope," said the man, wiping his hands on his pants. "You just missed him."

"And who are you?" asked Willson.

"Ben Jones. I own this place. Leo rents a room from me."

"What do you mean we just missed him?" Fortier asked, looking back up the driveway.

"He must have been expecting you. He drove in here in a hurry, grabbed some things, and then left."

"What direction did he come from when he came in?"

"I don't know."

"Shit," said Willson. "He must have seen us or passed us when we were parked out on the road."

"Did you see what he took with him?" Fortier asked, looking concerned.

"He had his rifle case and a canvas duffle bag."

"Was there a rifle in the case?"

"No idea. But he left in a hell of a rush."

"Which way did he go?"

"He turned left onto McBeath. If he saw you guys parked out toward the highway like you said, then he probably headed in the other direction, up the back road toward Cedar Lake and the ski hill. What's he done?"

"We just need to ask him some questions," said Fortier as he strode back toward the SUV. Partway across the yard, he paused and turned back to Jones. "What kind of truck is he driving?"

"An old Toyota Tacoma. It's got so many miles on it now it's more rust than metal. Used to be dark blue."

"Thanks," yelled Fortier. Willson was right behind him.

"He's probably only a minute or two ahead of us," said Fortier, "so let's see if we can catch him." He grabbed the radio microphone from the dash while he steered them out of the yard with one hand. "Echo Two-Four, this is Echo Five-Two. Are you around?"

The response came crisp and strong. "Go ahead Five-Two."

"What's your ten-twenty?"

"I'm pulling out of the office, heading downtown."

"I'm in Nicholson. Can you go up the ski hill road as quick as you can, lights and no siren, and keep your eye out for a dark-blue Toyota Tacoma, lots of rust? I need to talk to the occupant, a single male. I'm coming that way on the back road via Cedar Lake."

"Ten-four. On my way."

"If you don't see him when you get to the Dogtooth Forest Road turnoff, set up there. If you see him, stop him."

"Roger that."

"Thanks. The occupant may have a firearm, so consider it a high-risk stop. Understand?"

"Ten-four."

"Mr. Springer doesn't seem keen on talking to us," said Fortier. He dropped the microphone in his lap and put both hands on the wheel as he navigated the muddy, rutted hairpin turns of McBeath Road as it climbed the steep hill and became Canyon Creek Forest Service Road. "I wonder why."

Willson had her left hand on the dash while the right gripped the handle above the passenger door. "We'll have to ask him. The fact that he may have grabbed a rifle is disturbing, though."

"You got that right."

Fortier slowed as they reached the intersection of Canyon Creek and Dogtooth. From the fresh tire tracks in the mud, they could see that the vehicle they were chasing had skidded across the road to the right, almost hitting the ditch on the far side, before continuing north on Dogtooth. Fortier punched the gas pedal to follow and grabbed the microphone again.

"Echo Two-Four, this is Five-Two. He should be coming your way."

"Roger that," said the other officer. "I'm at the corner and can see a vehicle coming now."

After only a few seconds, the radio crackled again. "Five-Two, he saw me. He pulled a U-turn and is heading back in your direction. I'm behind him with lights on."

"Ten-four," said Fortier calmly. "We should see him any second." And he was right. The Toyota truck suddenly came up over a rise ahead of them, its tires off the ground. The pursuing RCMP cruiser was immediately behind. At the last possible moment, Fortier slammed the brakes and spun the steering wheel to the right, making the SUV slew across the road, blocking most of the two gravel lanes, with the front driver's corner facing the oncoming truck.

The old Toyota skidded for a second as its driver applied the brakes. But then it lurched and picked up speed.

"He's going to try to get by on my side!" yelled Willson. For a moment, she thought about opening her door, but quickly realized she'd be safer inside the vehicle.

Springer would have made it past them, but his back tire dropped into the ditch on the lower side of the road as he passed. The truck lurched again. This time, Springer apparently lost control, and the truck careened off into the trees behind and below them. Willson and Fortier jumped out of the vehicle and ran to the top of the steep bank in time to hear a loud bang. At the same time, a massive spruce tree shook violently, the leader at the top whipping back and forth. The truck's horn began blaring as though punctuating the end of a sentence.

Willson reached the truck first after punching downhill through patches of snow. She saw that Springer had been launched through the truck's front windshield and now lay still on the crumpled hood, spruce cones and broken branches still raining down on him. Moving to the downhill side of the vehicle, she raised the fingers of her right hand to the man's bloodied neck and held them there for a few seconds, gentle, practised, feeling for any throbs of blood still moving through his carotid artery.

"He's got a pulse! It's faint but it's there. Call an ambulance."

Fortier was already speaking into his shoulder microphone by the time he reached Willson and the truck, his police colleague on his heels. "Control, Echo Five-Two, we need an ambulance near the two-kilometre marker on the Dogtooth Forest Service Road, west of Golden. One male patient with serious injuries."

"Son of a bitch," said Willson, shaking her head. "I guess it'll be a while before Springer can answer any questions — if he even makes it."

When the ambulance arrived fifteen minutes later, it took the two paramedics, both Mounties, and Willson nearly half an hour to free Springer from the hood of the truck, get him onto a stretcher with a spine board and neck brace, and carry the unconscious man up the hill and into the back of the red and white B.C. ambulance.

After the ambulance left, followed by the other police car, Willson and Fortier stood in the middle of the road and stripped the bloodied blue latex gloves from their hands.

"Time to find out why he was in such a hurry," said Willson, heading back to the wrecked truck.

They methodically searched the truck's cab, but could not locate the duffel bag or the rifle case that Springer had allegedly taken with him. Knowing that the items, like the driver, could've been ejected in the crash, they expanded their search in an arc around the truck, peering behind trees, under logs, and through the dried and twisted stems of plants left from the previous summer. It was Fortier who found the duffel bag jammed under a large branch that had fallen from the spruce. Ten minutes later, Willson found the padded nylon rifle case, scratched and muddied, lying at the edge of a small creek ten metres below where the truck had landed. As soon as she lifted the case off the ground, she knew by its weight and bulk that it did contain a weapon.

After ensuring that the truck held no other useful evidence, Willson and Fortier climbed up the bank to the road and lay the bag and the case on the opened tailgate of the police vehicle. They slipped on fresh latex gloves.

With Willson peering over his shoulder, Fortier unzipped the canvas duffel first. From its dark interior, he pulled out pieces of clothing that appeared to have been tossed in quickly, followed by a small zippered toiletry kit and two boxes of ammunition.

"This was packed in a hurry. He was only at his place for a few minutes before we got there," said Fortier.

"It'll be a while before he can explain why he was in such a hurry," Willson said. "Let's check out the rifle." She unbuckled the straps of the black nylon case and slid the zipper down its length. Pulling apart the padded sides, she pulled out the rifle, pointing it away from Fortier. "I don't know rifles that well, but this looks serious." Its stock and barrel were white, with an overlying camouflage pattern. A large scope was mounted along the top, parallel to the barrel, looking like a weapon unto itself. There was a small dropout magazine on the lower side, just in front of the trigger.

Fortier whistled softly. "That *is* a serious hunting rifle. I think it's a Venture Predator bolt action. I've seen it at Cabela's in Calgary." He took it from Willson and carefully peered at the barrel, then at the stock. "It's set up for shooting .270 Winchester ammunition, which is what's in his bag. Nice gun."

"Unless this is a prized possession that he always took with him whenever he travelled," said Willson, watching Fortier look at the rifle with the same passion he'd shown for his fiancée, "I wonder if this is the rifle that was used to shoot at Austin and Myers?"

"That's exactly what I was thinking," said Fortier, running his hand slowly and lightly down the white stock.

"Jesus," said Willson. "Should I leave you two alone? Are you going to need a cigarette after this?"

"You're not a hunter, so I don't expect you to understand," Fortier said, smirking. He ejected a bullet from the chamber by sliding back the bolt handle, then removed the magazine before reluctantly inserting the gun back into its case. "With the magazine, I believe this will fire four bullets before the user has to reload, which matches Myer's claim that he heard four shots that night. I'll send this to the crime lab as soon as I'm back in the office to see if Springer's fingerprints are on it, and to see if there's a match with the bullets we found embedded in the wall and fireplace at Austin's. It's certainly the same calibre."

"If it is a match," said Willson, "that would provide us with a hell of a strong suspect in at least one of your investigations. Right?"

"Exactly. But we still don't know who burned down Stoffel's office. That's still my primary focus."

Willson stared down the road, her eyes unfocused. "Isn't it interesting that no matter where we look, the common denominator seems to be those two guys and their idiotic project? They're like the eye of a storm, violence and intimidation swirling around them, spinning outward like deadly shrapnel. We've got to find our way to the eye of that storm … and soon."

"Poetic, Jenny, very poetic. You know that before you reach the eye, you have to get safely through the storm, right?"

"Batten down the hatches, Ben."

CHAPTER 28

When Willson arrived home in the midafternoon, she was weary and hungry. She'd waited for the tow truck to come and extricate Springer's pickup, then gone to the station with Fortier to write up her statement about the chase and the accident. Leo Springer had been airlifted to Foothills Hospital in Calgary with serious back, neck, and internal injuries.

"Hi honey, I'm home!" she said, hoping that Berland might be back from the library, ready with a smile and a laugh and a cold beer. Or a burger. A big, juicy burger. But instead, silence. She paused for a moment, disappointed that she was alone in the house. And then she felt disturbed about being disappointed. It was a new and strange feeling after having lived alone for nearly ten years. Was she finally enjoying the experience of sharing space with someone, anyone, even if it was only temporary? Or did she simply miss the lanky reporter? Or was it both?

Pushing those thoughts aside, as she often did when it came to her emotions, Willson walked to the kitchen, pulled open the refrigerator door, and stood staring into the lit space, hating its emptiness. She slammed it shut and grabbed an overripe banana from the counter beside the sink, drank a glass of water to help her choke down the mushy flesh, then discovered a granola bar in the cupboard, the kind of bar that had a half-life rather than a shelf life and would still be edible after a nuclear war.

"Enough feeling sorry for yourself," she said aloud. "Time for a ride."

While chewing on bites of the bar like a beaver tackling an aspen, Willson hung her uniform on a hanger, locked her gun in the portable safe in her closet, and pulled on her mountain biking clothes. After locking the front and back doors, she bumped her bike down the back stairs and wheeled down Alexander Street. Despite her original intention to ride some of the Mountain Shadows trails south of town, she found herself instead heading toward the library.

Jesus, she thought, *what the hell has gotten into you? You're like a friggin' schoolgirl.*

Willson locked her bike to the rack in front of the library and jogged up the steps. Inside, she was heartened to see Mike Berland and her mother hunched over a table, laughing. When they saw her, they both looked up as though guilty of doing something subversive.

"What are you two plotting?"

"Hi, Jenny," said her mother, turning. "We weren't plotting anything. It's quiet now, so Mike was telling me about a race he was in two years ago … where he got lost in the middle of the course."

"How the hell did you get lost in a race?" asked Willson, grinning at Berland.

"That's what I was explaining to Anne when you walked in. It was a marathon in Coeur d'Alene. I was having trouble with my right knee, so I was overly focused on that. More than I should've been. I missed a turn, and about ten minutes later, I realized I didn't know where the hell I was. All I knew was that I wasn't on the course anymore. All my competitors had disappeared, as well as any local supporters along the side of the road."

Willson chuckled. "What did you do?"

"I approached some retiree watering his lawn in middle of an army of creepy garden gnomes. He pointed me back in the right direction. To say that I didn't set a personal best that day would be an understatement."

"What have you got against garden gnomes?"

"Don't get me started," said Berland with a shudder. "They're no better than clowns." Another shudder. "Let's talk about something else."

"You don't like helicopters or anchovies or olives, and now I find out you're scared of garden gnomes and clowns? You're one troubled guy, Mike."

"You say troubled, I say mysterious and unpredictable."

"I better get back to work and leave you two to your debate," said Mrs. Willson, placing her hand on her daughter's shoulder. "Thanks for the laugh, Mike. I needed that."

She walked back to the circulation desk, where an elderly couple was waiting to check out a stack of books.

Willson sat in the chair vacated by her mother. "Thanks for cheering her up, Mike. I think she likes you. How's the article coming along?"

"Your mother … I mean Anne … is great. I enjoy her company, too." Berland ran his hands rapidly back and forth across his shaved head, as though trying to get the blood flowing, or start a fire. "It's not ready quite yet, but I got a good start on it today. Anne was a big help finding research material. I've got solid historical background on the Blaeberry Valley, and she dug up a 2005 economic feasibility report on the Howse Pass highway. I didn't know it existed."

"I remember hearing about that. Does the highway make any sense at all?"

"Forget that," said Berland, shifting closer and glancing over at Anne. His eyes were wide. He clasped his hands in front of him as if begging. "I need to tell you something, and I don't want you to freak out."

"Oh, ye of little faith. Why so serious?"

"Hank Myers was here this afternoon, chatting with your mother."

"What?" said Willson, loud enough to make her mother turn and look.

"Keep it down, Jenny. I asked you not to freak out. He was here this afternoon and he spent quite a bit of time talking to her. Chatting. Flirting. Whatever you want to call it."

"Are you friggin' serious? You better be pulling my leg. And if you are, I'm going to pull one of *yours* right off."

"I am serious, and I need both my legs, thanks very much. They must've talked for a good fifteen minutes. He even waited off to the side while she served some customers."

"Did you do anything?"

"I did what I could. I was over in the corner where the light was better for reading." He pointed to a distant chair against the window. "I saw them talking. Myers didn't see me at first."

"You didn't stop it?"

"I went up and asked her a question about the Wi-Fi, to let Myers know I was there."

"And?"

"And he just smiled at me and waited for me to leave, like he was pleased that I'd seen him."

"What did you do?"

"I stayed there. It was like a standoff, me glaring at him, and him sneering at me. I'm sure your mum wondered what the heck was going on."

"Who blinked?"

"Myers did. He told your mother he'd enjoyed talking with her, said goodbye, looked at me one more time, and then left."

"Did you tell Mum who he was, that he'd threatened us?"

"And terrify her? Of course not. Anne seemed happy — she was laughing quite a bit — and she didn't seem to mind the attention. I simply told her that Myers was someone she might want to avoid."

"Son of a bitch, Mike. This is not good. From everything I've heard, Myers is dangerous — scary dangerous. I'm pretty sure Austin didn't hire him for his financial acumen."

"Maybe it's nothing …"

"Come on. You're an experienced reporter. Do you believe in coincidence? After what they said to us at Austin's place, do you really think this was a harmless chance encounter? I've got to assume Austin is trying to get to me through my mother. That's not good."

"You're probably right, unfortunately," said Berland, his face a mask of hurt and concern. "Which is why I told you about it. I'm sorry, I should have been more forceful. What are you gonna do?"

"I've got to tell Mum, persuade her not to see or talk to Myers ever again. She needs to understand how dangerous he is. I'd like to tell Myers to leave her the hell alone, but that would just confirm for them that they found my weak spot."

"Agreed. I can be there when you talk to her, if you'd like."

"Thanks, but no." Willson felt a single tear of anger and frustration run down her cheek. "Shit, shit, shit. If she was smiling and apparently enjoying whatever it was that Myers was saying, then it's going to be a tough conversation. She's so fragile and unsure of herself. If she realizes that she misread the situation, or maybe inappropriately opened up to that asshole, even just a little bit, it'll knock her back."

"I'm sorry, Jenny."

"It's okay, you tried. It's done now." She sat back in the chair. "We always knew they'd push back. I just didn't think it would come this soon, though, or in this form. They're obviously concerned about what we're doing. I better talk to her now."

"Wait," said Berland, putting his hand on Willson's arm like she'd done to Fortier earlier. "Why don't you wait until she's finished work for the day? Talk to her in private. It wouldn't be fair to her to say something now. With both of us here, nothing will happen."

Willson stared at her mother. She was smiling and laughing, interacting with the couple at the desk. It was a glimpse of the gregarious mother she remembered. "I guess you're right. We'll stay here until she's done."

"Good call. While we're waiting, why don't I tell you what I discovered today?" He opened his notebook, half full of scribbled notes and diagrams and bulging with photocopied pages from articles and books. He paraphrased the contents of the highway economic study, telling Willson that it suggested, while making many untested assumptions, that the highway would do better than break even. "But what was most interesting," he said, "was my conversation with the mayor of Golden. She came in this afternoon and your mum introduced us."

"Jo-Ann Campbell?"

He nodded. "She said she was a year ahead of you in high school?"

"That's right." Willson recalled a tall blonde who was confident and friendly with all of the disparate groups in her graduating class — a successful politician even then.

"What did you tell her about why you're here?"

"Just like I told your mother, I said you and I are friends from university, that I'm writing a novel, and I came to the library to do some research while you were at work."

"So you asked her about Collie Creek?" asked Willson. She glanced over at her mother again, still worried that Myers might return.

"I asked her what she thought about the new ski area and she told me the Town of Golden no longer supports the project. Apparently, at first most of the town councillors were excited, but that didn't last long. She said she was angry about the way the project has run roughshod over the community and divided it in two. She brought up a lot of the things you mentioned at the coffee shop in Boise. She was frustrated that the process didn't allow for rational discussion between the sides or take into account what the community wants. Austin did make a presentation to the town council, but it was glib, cagey, and avoided most of the tough questions. Without enough proof that the community would benefit from a project so far from town, the council voted to oppose the project. She seems exhausted by it all, and relieved that it's over, at least from Golden's perspective."

"What about the highway and pipeline?"

"Council discussed them, but because both corridors would connect to the Trans-Canada Highway nearly twenty kilometres north of town, they concluded that traffic and visitors and business would be diverted away from town rather than toward it. In the end, it wasn't that they supported the arguments of project opponents. They just realized that the projects would sideline the community, isolate it, and destroy its economic future."

Willson was shaking her head. "Jesus. These review processes are completely fucked up. They pit people against each other and tear communities apart. The winners celebrate, and the losers commiserate and keep fighting. Who believes that doing *any* of that is a good idea?" She looked at her watch. "It's closing time. I'll leave you to find your own dinner tonight, Mike. I'm going to walk my mum home and have a talk with her."

Berland began packing his documents, notebook, and laptop into his briefcase. "Not a problem. Unless you want me to stay, I was actually thinking I'd start back to Boise tonight. I was only supposed to be here a week, so my editor is expecting me tomorrow. If I can get back to the office by noon, he might not fire me. I can show him what I've done and finish the article there. It'll be ready when you give me the okay."

"Yeah ... I guess that makes sense." Willson spoke the words haltingly, looking into his kind brown eyes, that strange feeling of disappointment coming over her again in a wave. This time, she also felt an unexpected ripple of loss. *I thought we'd have more time.* She continued to stare into his eyes. "Travel safe, Mike."

From the sympathetic look on Berland's face, she could tell that he'd mistaken her sudden change in mood for worry about her mother. And that was fine with her.

Just as he had two weeks earlier, the tall American wrapped his arms around her in a warm hug that nearly brought tears to her eyes for the second time that afternoon. It was a hug that made her feel safe and appreciated.

"You're a hell of a daughter, Jenny," he whispered in her ear. "Your mother is lucky to have someone who cares so much. Don't ever let the bastards grind that out of you."

CHAPTER 29

APRIL 17

Austin's desk was littered with client statements, phone messages, and consultant reports. But instead of paperwork, his attention was on the business section of the day's *Vancouver Sun*. His phone was ringing; he let it continue until it fell silent. With his meaty finger rapidly sliding across the page, line by line, and his blood pressure rising at an alarming rate, he read the article under Mike Berland's byline. The article questioned the legitimacy of his investment fund.

"That goddamn son of a bitch!" Austin yelled as he reached the end of the page. "I thought he was another Parks guy, not a fucking reporter." The implications of what he'd just read came over him like a boiling thundercloud. "I told them to mind their own fucking business." He grabbed the edges of the newspaper and violently tore it in half.

"Mr. Austin," said his secretary, timidly poking her head into his office, "I have Matt Merrix on the phone. He's demanding to speak with you." She stared at Austin and the torn newspaper clutched in his hands. "Is everything okay?"

"A minor glitch, Carol. Tell him I'll call him right back."

"I tried that," she said, her voice trembling, "but he said that if you didn't take his call, he was coming right over here. He's very insistent."

"Shit!" he said, staring at the torn newspaper as though wondering how it had happened. "All right, put the call through."

The secretary disappeared more quickly than she'd arrived, then Austin's desk phone rang again. He picked it up after the second ring.

"Good morning, Matt. I hope you're well. Carol said you needed to speak with me?"

"Tell me there's no truth to what's in the *Sun* today, Stafford."

Austin recognized Merrix's opening to be as much a statement as a question. "What are you referring to, Matt?"

"Don't yank my chain about something this important, Stafford. You know what I'm talking about. The *Sun* article. The one that questions you and your investment fund, the investment fund into which many of my clients have put their hard-earned money. Two of them phoned me this morning before I'd seen it myself."

"My apologies," said Austin. "I'm looking at the article as we speak, Matt. I'm not sure where the reporter got his information from, but you have nothing to worry about."

"Nothing to worry about? If there's even a glimmer of truth in there about your background or about the fund, then it seems I do have a hell of a lot to worry about!"

"There's no truth in it at all. I met with the reporter the last time I was in Golden, and I sorted out his confusion. At least I thought I did. Frankly, I'm surprised and disappointed that he wrote this, and astonished that the paper printed it without fact-checking. I'll be on the phone to my lawyer as soon as I hang up."

"So you're telling me you weren't charged with any financial crimes in the United States or in Chile?"

"I've never been convicted of any financial crimes, Matt. I was chased a couple of times by some eager prosecutors who were too inexperienced to understand what I was doing with some complex yet successful investments. But I was never convicted of anything."

"Why does that not give me any comfort? Not being convicted is not the same as being innocent, Stafford. And it's certainly not the same as never having been involved in anything illegal, conviction or otherwise."

"Believe me," said Austin, keeping his voice calm and slow, projecting an air of professional confidence, "there's nothing to this, Matt. I'll certainly admit that the reporter didn't like me or the project. He must be in the pocket of the local enviros. This is nothing more than an overzealous reporter trying to scuttle the project, make a name for himself."

"And what's with the references to an investigation by the RCMP and the Parks department and possible links to arson and murder?"

"That's nothing more than crazy speculation. Fake news. That reporter is out of control, and I'll be directing my lawyer to immediately file a libel suit against him and the papers that printed the story. I've spoken with the RCMP and the warden about all that stuff. They've got no evidence connecting any of it to our project."

"Jesus, Stafford. This changes everything. I don't even know what to say."

"I'll deal with it, Matt. I'm sorry this reporter's incompetence has created a headache for you. You can tell your clients that you've checked with me, and everything is good. You have my word."

"I'm starting to question the value of that, Stafford. The reporter also seems to know about the highway and pipeline connection. According to you, that was supposed to be confidential. What's the deal?"

"Apparently someone in the federal government has a big mouth. I certainly can't control what they say. It could be some bureaucrat who doesn't like the idea, or a politician who wants to take credit for something before he should. Or maybe it's a smokescreen to divert attention away from other bigger controversies. Either way, this shouldn't affect our project. Don't worry, Matt. It's possible that having some of these ideas out in the open will attract more investment and interest."

"More investment might work for you, Stafford, but it doesn't necessarily benefit me or my clients. With an article like this out there — not only in the Vancouver paper, but in Calgary and Toronto, too — my guys are freaking out. They've all heard the stories or talked to players who were caught in the Bear Mountain situation on Vancouver

Island. And everyone knows how much money the players who were represented by Alan Eagleson lost years before that. They're not going to take my word for it."

"I'm organizing a flight up to the project site for some of my investors. Would you and some of your guys like to come along? Might help to calm the waters and get them feeling better about what they'll be a part of. Seeing the place, and seeing the plans for the place when you're standing in the middle of it, is very powerful."

"I'll ask, but I get the sense that won't be enough. They're spooked. And once they start talking to each other, their concerns will only build."

"What do you need from me, Matt?"

"I need up-to-date investment fund statements, preferably by end of day today, for *all* my clients. I want those statements to detail what they've invested, and in many cases reinvested, and what payments are due to them and when. And they're going to want to see something in writing that confirms they can pull their money out at any time. If all that can be authenticated by a third party, that would be even better."

"I've got a lot on my plate today, Matt, but I should be able to get those to you no later than the end of the week. As you know, we generate our statements on a quarterly basis, so I'll have to push to get them out of the system on a different schedule. Because of the concerns you've raised, and because of the strength of our relationship, Matt, I'll make that happen."

"Do it," Merrix said. The anxiety in his voice was palpable. "The sooner, the better. I'm expecting there'll be at least two of my guys who'll want to pull their money out right away. Their careers are almost over, and their investment with you is a big chunk of the money they've put aside for retirement. They can't accept *any* risk. Even a verified statement might not make them happy. This has put me in a very difficult position, Stafford. If I persuade my guys to keep their money in a bad investment, I'm done. And if I talk them into taking their money out of something that's given them solid returns to date, then they'll question my judgment from now on."

"I completely understand, Matt. I'll get those statements to you, and I'll try to sort things out with the reporter and the papers. I'll send you details of the site visit once it's set up."

"Right now, I'm sick about this. You're going to have to do a hell of a lot to get me to feel good again, not only about your funds, Stafford, but about you. And it's got to be bloody soon. I want those documents, and I want them yesterday."

Austin heard a dial tone. He slowly placed the phone back in its cradle. As soon as he'd seen the article by Berland that morning, he'd known immediately that things were on the verge of unravelling. His experience told him that, and the churning in his gut confirmed it. But after hearing Merrix's response, he realized that everything he'd worked for now sat at a critical juncture. Depending on the path he chose from here, he might get his plans back on track, continue to build the investment funds, and continue to push and prod and shepherd the projects toward government decisions. Or he might end up in a spiral that wouldn't end well.

He picked up the phone again and dialed.

"Hank, you still in Golden?"

"Yes," said Myers, equally curt in return.

"Have you seen the *Vancouver Sun* or the *Calgary Herald* today?"

"No."

"Grab a copy of either when you can. We told that warden and her sidekick to back off — I think we were very clear. But instead of listening, they ignored us. And it looks like that Mike guy was a reporter. There's a feature story about me written by a Mike Berland in the business section of both papers, and apparently in the *Toronto Star*, too. The article raises questions about what you and I are doing, mentions Willson's investigation into us, and hints at links between our project and the arson and murder in Golden. I just got an irate call from Merrix about it. If he's any indication of how our investors are going to react, we may have a huge fucking problem."

"Were you able to calm Merrix down?"

"I did my best, mostly by declaring my innocence and promising to send him verified statements for all his clients. But I don't know for sure. I get the sense he's right on the edge."

"If he pulls his clients' money out, will we be okay?"

"If it's only him, then yes, we can weather that storm. But if he starts talking to others, or if too many other investors see the article — which will probably spread like fucking wildfire on social media — then we're definitely screwed."

"How much did this Berland get right?" asked Myers. "Is someone talking to him who shouldn't be? Or was it mostly speculation?"

"More speculation than anything. But there's enough there, even when he quotes unnamed sources, for someone who doesn't know anything about it to assume that things aren't quite right. And if that someone is one of our investors, or if they're from the enforcement section of the B.C. Securities Commission, or the RCMP, then we've got an issue."

"What do you want me to do?" asked Myers. "Do you need a hand with the statements? Or setting up the visit to the site?"

"Nope. I'll start on those today. What *you* need to do is figure out what to do about Berland and Willson. If they keep digging, or if Berland writes any follow-up articles that get coverage like this one has, we will have a *major* problem on our hands. And as you know, Hank, that problem definitely is *our* problem. Not just mine."

"I understand that, Stafford. I do *not* need the reminder."

Myers paused. In that silence, Austin could sense the man's anger through the phone. He knew he had to be cautious. Myers was in as deep as he was, and he had as much to lose or gain, depending on what happened next. But he was also dangerous, a man you didn't want to piss off.

"Have you got any ideas?" Austin asked, trying to sound conciliatory and collaborative. "Any way we can get them to back off, even though some damage is already done? If we can do that, we might be able to salvage this."

"I believe I've found Willson's weak spot, at least one of them. I'll work on that. But my sources here tell me that this Mike guy left Golden a week or so ago. I have no idea where to, but we're clearly going to need a more aggressive approach. Apparently, his listening skills aren't so good. I need to turn up the volume."

"I'll leave that to you, Hank. We've got to get them *both* to back off. I don't need to know the specifics, but I appreciate you moving as quickly as you can. Time is critical."

"Don't worry, Stafford, I'll take care of it. After all, as you say, this is a shared problem."

CHAPTER 30

Careening out of the final turn, Willson squeezed the brakes of her mountain bike and slid sideways to a stop. The bike nearly slipped out from under her on the pine needles covering the trail. Beside her, Sue Browning did the same. They stood catching their breath after their aggressive ride on the single-track trails along the powerline, which looked down on the city of Cranbrook. Straddling their bikes, they stood on a rocky knoll, the city spread out below them to the west, the Purcell Mountains in the background. The late-afternoon sun was warm on their flushed faces.

"Who pissed in your corn flakes this morning, Jenny?" asked Browning, breathing hard. "I've never seen you ride like that. You kicked my ass on that last hill. And you weren't even in your lowest gear."

Willson stared at her. The two had been friends since meeting in a warden service climbing school eight years earlier. As a mountain guide, Browning had been the instructor, Willson the student. Shortly after, Willson introduced Browning to her university friend Jim Woods, the same Jim Woods whose photographs had helped her crack a major poaching case. Her two friends were now a couple, sharing a strong relationship that Willson envied each time she saw them together. Of the small circle of people whom Willson considered to be close friends, she trusted Browning more than she did anyone else. And today, she needed a confidant as much as she ever had.

"Was it obvious?" Willson asked with a stilted smile. She noisily sucked water through the tube leading to the reservoir in her pack.

"It was obvious as soon as we left the truck at the parking lot. You clearly had something to prove ... or some serious energy to burn off."

"Life sucks right now, Sue," said Willson, pulling her helmet off her wet head.

"What's going on?"

"I'm so friggin' pissed off that I don't even know where to begin."

"Start at the beginning."

"You know I took a temporary assignment in Yoho. What I couldn't tell you was that I was asked by the chief park warden in Banff to undertake a ... um ... clandestine investigation into the ski resort that's been proposed on the Yoho park boundary."

"That thing? You'd have to be asleep not to have

heard of that project. Everyone in our industry thinks it's ridiculous."

"I share that opinion," Willson said, laying her bike down beside the trail and sitting against a veteran Ponderosa pine, its bark like scaly puzzle pieces against her back. "That's why I accepted the assignment."

"Clandestine? That sounds unusual for the federal government."

"It is. But the stakes are high for the park and its wildlife. Once I understood what was proposed, I knew I couldn't stomach seeing it go ahead."

Browning sat beside her with her back against the same tree. "You're taking the assignment awfully seriously, even for a person as passionate and committed as you usually are."

"I am what I am. But that's not why I came down here. When I was in Idaho a couple of months ago, digging up background on the proponent, I connected with a local reporter called Mike Berland. He's an experienced investigative journalist who had some history with the ski resort proponent."

"Ah. Connected?" Browning's eyebrows went up and down in an impression of Groucho Marx. "Tell me about this mysterious Mike Berland."

"He completely and thoroughly screwed me," said Willson, "and not in the fun way."

"What happened?"

"My first mistake was trusting him. After he'd persuaded me that he was as interested in the proponent as I was, I stupidly agreed to work with him, let him in on what I was doing. I even told him the truth about my investigation and invited him to Golden to see for himself what was going on. The way I saw it, it was a way to shine a spotlight on a dumb idea: the ski resort. Now, I wonder what in hell I was thinking. I hate reporters almost as much as I hate poachers and ladder-climbing bureaucrats ..."

"And your second mistake?"

"Letting myself get too close to him."

"Uh-oh. You two didn't hook up, did you?"

"No. He stayed with me for about a week — in the spare room — and you know, I actually enjoyed his company. Sometimes he was came with me while I was working, like when we flew to the resort site, and he came with me to court a few times. But usually, he was off on his own during the day. We spent most evenings together and, I thought, became quite close. I exposed him to Canadian music — Great Big Sea, Blue Rodeo, et cetera — and he turned me on to the blues. Ironic, given how I'm feeling now."

Browning grinned. "You just used the words *exposed* and *turned on*. Are you sure nothing happened? You were together for a week in the same tiny house ..."

"That was it. But I'll admit to you, and only you, that I was beginning to think I'd found someone special, someone who brought out the best in me. He actually listened to me, he seemed to accept me for the crazy, intense, cutting person I can be."

"What the hell did he do to you, Jenny?" asked Browning, her eyes soft with concern.

"He left town, literally crossed the border in the dark of night, and a few days later wrote an exposé that appeared in newspapers across Canada. He started the article when he was in Golden, but when I asked to see it, he told me it wasn't ready. Now I know why the slimy fucker wouldn't show it to me." She shook her head. "It was a betrayal, pure and simple. Jesus, Sue, how could I have been so gullible? Even my mother liked him. I'm angry, embarrassed, and hurt. And I hate myself for being any of those things. Feeling all of them at the same time makes me want to puke."

"I can see why. Did he name names in his article?"

"Oh yeah, he named names, including me and my two bosses."

"Shit."

"Shit is right. Now that the story's out in the open, including what I was doing, the shit has hit the fan." Willson scooped up a cigar-sized bundle of tan pine needles in her hand and began breaking them into smaller and smaller pieces, a violent counterpoint to *he loves me, he loves me not.*

"How so?" asked Browning, concerned about Willson's agitated behaviour.

"The applicant for the resort, Stafford Austin, has complained to federal and provincial ministers that he's not getting a fair review process. As you can imagine, the shit is flowing downhill from there. My bosses are being pushed to 'get me under control,' and I even got a direct call yesterday from some asshole in the PMO who told me I could lose my job if I didn't 'get with the government program on economic development.'" Whatever the hell that means. Because of all that, I'm at risk of being shuffled into some kind of 'manager of special projects' position. In government, that's the kiss of death, one step away from being shown the door."

She angrily tossed the broken needles away. "I'll figure out my own situation, but I feel sick about my old boss in particular. While we both understood the risk, he trusted me with his career and his reputation. He told me not to trust Mike, I ignored him, and I was wrong. I don't know if he'll get axed because of this. And beyond that, the investigation has become a distraction from the real questions. Instead of focusing on the dubious resort project, the even more dubious proponent, and the project's finances, the free-enterprisers in government are in a frenzy over what they're describing as an out-of-control bureaucracy bent on wrecking Canada's economy. And for the moment, I'm their goddamn poster child. They're completely ignoring the fact that it's a stupid friggin' project to begin with, or that it might be some kind of scam. What a shit show."

"Jesus, Jenny, I'm sorry. Have you tried to contact this Mike to see why he did it?"

"I've left a bunch of phone messages and sent him a few nasty texts. No fucking smiley faces, that's for sure. He's ignored them all. I guess once he got what he needed from me, we were done." She leaned forward, hugging her knees, rocking, her chin on her forearms. "Wham, bam, thank you, ma'am, without the wham or the bam."

Browning put a consoling hand on Willson's back, rubbing it gently. "What are you going to do?" she asked.

"At this point, I have no idea. What I'd like to do is go down to Boise, find Mike, and then string him up by his short-and-curlies. But I won't. While it might feel good, it wouldn't help the situation."

Browning laughed, and Willson knew she was trying to lighten the mood, even if just for a moment.

"I'm guessing you're not going to stop the investigation. I know you too well."

"Hell no," said Willson. "I'm in too deep now. As my father always said, 'Where there's a Willson, there's a way.' I have to find the way."

Browning smiled. "I think there's a T-shirt out there somewhere with that saying on it, isn't there?" She knew there was because she, Jim Woods, and some of Willson's other friends had presented it to Willson after her successful poaching investigation.

But Willson wasn't smiling. "I've got some half-baked ideas that I'm going to sit on for a day or two. But first, I've got to get my head on straight. That's why I came down here for the weekend. I'm still furious at Mike for taking advantage of me like he did. I needed to see you, and I needed this ride."

"I'm glad you thought of me, Jenny. That's what friends are for."

Willson finally smiled and was about to say something more, but was interrupted by a muffled buzzing. She freed her cellphone from the small pocket on the back of her cycling jersey and slid her finger across the screen. "Willson here."

"Hi, Jenny, it's Heather from the Golden library."

"Uh … hi, Heather." This was the first time she'd ever received a call from her mother's boss. "What can I do for you?"

"I'm calling to see how your mother is doing."

"What do you mean?"

"She didn't come in to work today, and I assumed she was … under the weather. I know she was upset about the newspaper article you were named in. She showed it to me yesterday and seemed very worried about you."

"I … I saw her late yesterday afternoon before I drove down here. I'm in Cranbrook. She seemed fine when I left. As far as I know, she was planning to come in today for her Saturday shift." Willson felt a jolt of uncertainty, like the sudden onset of atrial fibrillation. At the lowest points of her mother's depression, Willson had become accustomed to her unpredictable behaviours, but missing work was out of character, even for her. The library was her safety line. She wouldn't miss work unless something was wrong.

"Oh. Anne was supposed to start at ten o'clock this morning. She didn't come in, and she hasn't phoned."

Another jolt, this time of fear. "And no word from her?"

"None," said Heather. "I had to come in to cover for her."

"Sorry about that. Did you phone the house?"

"It's okay. It's not your fault, Jenny. I did phone, but there was no answer. I thought maybe she was with you."

"No, she's not. I don't know where she is." Willson remembered Hank Myers's library visit not long after the veiled threats made by him and Austin. The discussion she had with her mother on the way home that day had been awkward and frustrating; her mother hadn't understood that she might be in danger.

"I'm sorry to have disturbed you, Jenny," Heather said. "I'm … I'm sure she's fine." But her pause betrayed that she was just as concerned as Willson was. "Is there anything I can do?"

"Please phone me right away if she shows up," said Willson, "or if you hear from her. I'm gonna head back to Golden right away." She looked at her watch. "You'll be well past closed by the time I get back there, though. Is there a number I can reach you at later?"

The librarian gave Willson her cell number. "Call me when things are sorted out, will you, Jenny? It doesn't matter what time. I won't be able to relax until I know that Anne's okay."

"I'll do that. Thanks again for phoning, Heather." Willson ended the call and then turned to Browning. "Shit, shit, shit. My mother's gone missing, Sue. She didn't show up for work, and I think that one of the people associated with the ski resort might be responsible. I hope to hell I'm wrong, but —"

"Jesus, Jenny. What kind of people are you dealing with?"

"The kind who prefer that people like me or Mike don't get in their way."

Willson searched for a number in her contacts and hit call.

"Jenny?" said a male voice.

"Sorry to bother you, Ben, but I'm in Cranbrook at the moment. I need a favour. Can you please go over to my mother's house and see if she's there? I'm not sure it's an emergency, but it could be."

"Slow down, " said Fortier. "What's going on?"

"Mum didn't show up to work today, and that's not like her. When I saw her yesterday afternoon, before I came down here, she said she'd be going to work this morning. But her boss just phoned to say she didn't come in, didn't call, and there's no answer at the house. After that threat from Myers and Austin, I'm worried." Willson gave Fortier her mother's address.

"I'm close, so I can go over there now. I'm sure everything is fine. Do you want me to phone you back?"

"No. I'll stay on the line."

As she waited, Willson could hear Fortier's police cruiser accelerating in the background. "I hope she's okay," she said, pacing amongst the trees as she spoke. "Myers showed up at the library the other day and spoke to my mother. And now she's missing. I'm not feeling good about this, Ben."

"Hang tight, Jenny. I'll be there in two minutes."

Willson continued pacing while she waited for Fortier to reach her mother's house. Over the phone, she heard him stop the vehicle and walk quickly to the front door; his steps crunched on the gravel walkway. The noise of his banging on the door startled her, even over the phone.

"Anne Willson," said Fortier, his voice tinny and distant, "this is Ben Fortier from the RCMP. Can you please open the door?" More banging, louder this time.

"No answer, Jenny," said the Mountie, back on the phone. "I'll check the back door."

Almost as if she was there, Willson could hear Fortier walk around the house, then knock again. "Anne?" And then the sound of a creaking door and more footsteps.

"What's happening, Ben? Is she there?" For Willson, every second was an eternity.

"Jenny," said Fortier, when he finally came back on the line, "the back door was unlocked and she's not here. I've checked all the rooms. She must have gone out shopping or something like that."

"No, she didn't, Ben!" Willson yelled. Browning stared at her with wide eyes. "She wouldn't miss work, go out shopping instead, and leave the back door open! She always locks the doors. Something's happened to her. Is her purse there?"

Another pause. "Her purse is here," Fortier said. "It's on the kitchen counter. Her cellphone, too."

"Shit," said Willson. "Either she's wandered off depressed, Ben, or that bastard Myers has somehow got to her. She never goes anywhere without her purse and phone. Is her car in the driveway … or on the street?"

"What does she drive?"

Willson heard Fortier walking again. "It's a champagne-coloured Honda sedan, about ten years old." She gave him the plate number.

"No. It's not in the driveway and I don't see it anywhere on the street."

"Okay …" said Willson, thinking out loud, trying to sort through the puzzle pieces. "I don't know if that's better or worse. If she was taken or persuaded to go somewhere, then it's unlikely she would take her own car. But if she was depressed and decided to go for a drive, she could be anywhere."

"Okay, Jenny, this is a small town. I'll get all our officers looking for her and the vehicle. Just get up here as fast as you can. Does she have any favourite places she might go to get some fresh air?"

Willson looked at Browning with dread in her eyes. "Just the library." She spun like a top, her free hand working like a claw in her still-damp hair. "The only other place you might look is the walking path along the Kicking Horse River. She and my dad always walked there when he was alive. But that's close to the house. I don't know why she'd take the car …"

"Okay. Leave it to me, Jenny. We'll find her. Get up here safely."

"Thanks, Ben." Willson disconnected the call, slammed her helmet back on her head, and jumped on her bike. "Let's go, Sue. I've got to get back." Before her friend could react, Willson rolled over the edge of the viewpoint and flew down the rocky hill toward the parking lot, her legs pumping, her mind churning.

CHAPTER 31

Sara Ilsley turned off Highway 95 onto Horse Creek Road, heading for home. She was exhausted but still shivering with excitement and a feeling of accomplishment, something that had been missing since she'd begun her work as the executive director of the Columbia Valley Environmental Society.

She knew that some of their campaign tactics so far — the protests and letter writing, the small but loud rallies in Victoria and Ottawa, the reports from their experts now appearing in popular and scientific media, and of course, the short-lived competing expression of interest — had gained attention for their cause. But she also knew that they were typical for situations like this, where local residents fought pitched and under-resourced battles against developments that were, in their opinion, jammed down their throats. Unfortunately, these tactics were expected, and while done with the best intentions, they were commonly ignored by decision-makers and politicians because they were so ... common.

It was an anonymous call three days earlier that had given her what she still thought was a brilliant idea. In that short call, she'd learned that Stafford Austin was planning to use a local helicopter to tour a group of investors around the site of the proposed ski area. Rightly or wrongly, Ilsley had immediately assumed that the visit was an attempt to counter the recent newspaper article, an effort to keep the money taps open and flowing. She and her colleagues had had very little time to react, but they had quickly chosen two dramatic courses of action.

Their first step was to fly a quartet of their strongest and most experienced backcountry skiers to one of the glaciers in the midst of the proposed resort area, a place where lift lines and chairlifts would desecrate the valley if this thing got off the ground. For maximum visibility from the air, they chose a wide west-facing glacier that ended in a dramatic corrugated icefall, its seracs tumbling like blocks to the valley below, its crevasses yawning and gaping like dry, weathered skin. With cans of green environmentally friendly paint and backpack sprayers, the four volunteers, three young women and one young man, skied from the heli-landing site to the target area and then created a welcome message for the investors in three-metre-high letters across the glacier: KEEP COLLIE WILD. Ilsley and her colleagues had debated using a remote glacier as a canvas, even though the paint was water-based. In the end, they'd decided that the hypocrisy was acceptable, given what was at stake. When they'd seen the images that the four skiers brought back at the end of their artistic expedition, the green message blaring across the white of the glacier like a garish alpine protest banner, it was a time for celebration. But they weren't done yet.

When the investor group, led by Austin, appeared at the Golden helipad that afternoon, they were met by a raucous, sign-wielding, belligerent group of protestors for which they were clearly unprepared. From her position on the edge of the fenced parking lot, Ilsley saw in Austin's group looks of surprise, discomfort, guilt, even anger. And she'd taken great pleasure in noticing that those looks were directed as much at Austin as they were at her and her noisy colleagues.

Just as the heli-safety briefing was complete, and seconds before Austin and his group began boarding the fourteen-passenger Bell 212 helicopter, Ilsley left the protestors to approach the investors through an open gate. "Before you go," she'd said, "could I please talk to you about the growing opposition to the project, so you understand why it's a bad idea and why it does not have the support of the community?"

At that point, Hank Myers had stepped in front of her and gripped her elbow to steer her back behind the chain-link fence.

But then a tall man with blond hair and a slight beard, dressed in a well-used two-piece ski suit and Sorel boots, stepped forward from the group circling the passenger side of the machine. "I'd like to hear what she has to say. We need the complete picture."

Ilsley smiled and turned to look at Myers, waiting for him to release her. She watched his face change as he realized that everyone was looking at him. For a second, he squeezed harder, then he removed his hand and stepped back.

Ilsley began her well-practised speech, an address she'd used in front of politicians, potential donors, and in public meetings where crowds were more often than not antagonistic. "We honestly believe that the Collie Creek valley, home to the endangered wolverine, and to grizzly bears, mountain goats, and many other wildlife species, is *not* the place to build a ski resort. It should stay wild. And we also believe that the project makes no economic sense —"

But that was as far as she got before she was interrupted by Austin. "Ladies and gentlemen," he'd said, shouting over her, "we could stand here all day listening to people who don't understand business. But if we do, we risk losing our weather window for our flight. I ask that you take your seats so we can start the tour."

Austin subtly moved his guests toward the open door of the helicopter, a hand on an elbow here, an arm across a shoulder there.

In a move that surprised everyone, including Ilsley, the tall man stepped toward her with a business card in his outstretched hand, his other gripping a pair of leather-palmed gloves. "Call me," he'd said quietly. "I'd like to talk to you." He smiled a painful smile at her, showing the discomfort and perhaps guilt that she'd seen earlier, and then he turned back to the group.

As she walked away, with Myers a step behind, she turned to see John Theroux and Sandy Trueman glaring at her. Both had venom in their eyes, Trueman most of all. Ilsley had no doubt that their anger was focused on her, and only her.

Once the sound of the rotors vanished, Ilsley and her colleagues had put their signs in their cars and calmly driven away, leaving Myers, Theroux, and Trueman standing alone, watching them go. Ilsley was confident that between the boisterous welcome and the glacial message that the helicopter passengers had yet to see, their point had been made.

Now, fresh from a celebratory dinner at the Golden Taps with her fellow activists, she drove the last few kilometres up Horse Creek Road, the fingers of her right hand touching the business card tucked in her left breast pocket: *Matt Merrix, Professional Sports Agent.* When she'd read the name for the first time, she'd realized that she now had a contact on the inside of the project, a link to the money. From her time in consulting, many years of reading people and trying to understand what they really needed as opposed to what they said they wanted, she had the strong sense that the man was looking for the truth, and had yet to find it. She thought about her last conversation with Jenny Willson, and how badly Willson had wanted to talk to the project investors. She'd call Matt Merrix and then, working together, she and Willson would help him find the truth he was searching for.

As she turned in to her driveway, she was startled to see a flash of light to her right, reflecting off the low clouds in the early evening sky. She gunned the engine and came around the last corner to see her stained-glass studio ablaze.

She parked her car well away from the burning building. The shock of what she was seeing momentarily stunned her. She stared at the flames, at the smoke boiling up into the sky. She jumped when a window blew out in a shower of glass. She thought about the projects she had been working on, the music she had accumulated over the years to accompany a hobby that, since her retirement, had become a small business. And she wondered why the building was burning. Coming to her senses, she pulled out her phone and dialed 911.

But it was already too late, she knew. One wall collapsed in a shower of sparks. It was only a matter of minutes before the building would be reduced to a blackened shell. No matter how good the local firefighters were, she knew they wouldn't get there in time.

Turning away from the disintegrating studio with tears in her eyes, she was shocked again when she spotted the brutal defilement of her house. *BACK OFF BITCH!* was scrawled across one wall in huge capital letters, the red spray paint still fresh and dripping, like blood from a wound.

As she stood in the chill of early evening, the fire behind her magnifying her shadow, she suddenly had the feeling she was being watched. She spun around, staring into the forest that surrounded her property, realizing that the individual or individuals responsible could still be nearby. She was in the open here, vulnerable. Panicking, she bolted up the front stairs of the house. Fumbling with the keys, her hands shaking, she managed to get the door open and get inside. Then she stood with her back against the locked door, breathing hard.

CHAPTER 32

APRIL 20, 9:00 P.M.

Jenny Willson was speeding through the small village of Parson, northbound on Highway 95, going well above the posted eighty-kilometre limit, when her cellphone rang. She answered over the Bluetooth system.

"Willson here."

"It's Ben."

"Did you find her?"

"No, we haven't found her yet, but everyone's out looking. I even asked the off-duty guys to come back on shift. Where are you?"

"In Parson, on my way." To her left, Willson could see the marshes of the Columbia River wetlands glowing in the last light of dusk. "I should be there in about twenty minutes. Why?"

"I'm at Sara Ilsley's house, and there's something here you should see."

"Why the hell are you there, instead of looking for Mum? Can't it wait?"

"Jenny, I have a small army out looking for her, but I got an emergency call to come out to Sara's place. I really think you should stop here on the way north. It may be connected."

"Connected to what?"

"Ilsley arrived home tonight to find her studio on fire and a message spray-painted across the side of her house."

"A message?"

"It says, 'Back off, bitch.'"

Willson's mind instantly jumped to Stafford Austin and Hank Myers.

"Why do you want me there?" she asked. "I need to find Mum."

"Because you need to see the video from the security camera. It's important."

"All right, all right," said Willson. "I'll be there in fifteen."

She pounded the gas pedal and watched as the dotted highway lines flew toward her like yellow tracer bullets, trees streaking by to the left and right. Her mind scrambled for answers. What was on the video that was so important? What could it mean to the investigation? Most importantly, with the entire Golden RCMP detachment still searching, where the hell had her mother gone?

When Willson reached the Ilsley house, she had to dodge two fire trucks to get up the driveway. The firefighters had already begun their mop-up, pouring water on the smoking hot spots and exposing the areas under the fallen walls to search for embers that might flare up later.

She stepped from her car and paused, her right arm

resting against the top of the door, as the scene in front of her transported her back to the burnt log building that had been Sue Webb's funeral pyre four months earlier. She remembered standing next to Fortier that morning, staring at the blackened ruins. She turned to see him staring down at her from Ilsley's front porch.

"Remind you of anything?" Fortier asked, his gaze shifting to the smoking building.

"I was just thinking that. Eerily similar, isn't it?"

The Mountie nodded once but said nothing.

Willson slammed the car door shut and followed Fortier inside.

Ilsley was sitting at the kitchen table, silhouetted against the illuminated screen of a laptop.

"Sara!" said Willson. "I'm so sorry about your studio. Are you okay?"

Ilsley turned in her chair. "A bit shaken up, but I'll be fine."

"What have you got for me to see?" Willson struggled to concentrate, desperately wanting to get back to Golden to find her mother.

"I arrived home at about seven-thirty and the fire was going pretty good," said Ilsley, "so let me scroll back to about thirty minutes before I arrived." She moved the mouse across the Calgary Flames mousepad until the time stamp on the screen indicated 7:00 p.m.

Willson looked down and saw a business card on the desk beside her. *Matt Merrix, Professional Sports Agent.* "Who's that, Sara?" she asked, pointing at the card.

Ilsley told them about the protest at the airport, and how the man whose card now sat on her desk had approached her. "He seems to be one of Austin's investors," Ilsley said, "or at least he represents some of them. I'm not sure."

"And he asked to speak with you?"

"He did, and I was more than a little shocked. It was unexpected, like he was looking for someone to talk to. He acted like he didn't want to be there."

"Did you talk to him?"

"No, that was it. They flew away and we left. I haven't had a chance to call him yet. I've been a bit busy since I got home," she said, grimacing.

"I need that number," said Willson.

"Take it," said Ilsley. "I expect to be occupied with insurance and restoration companies for a while. All I ask is that you send me an email with his contact info so I can call him later."

"Done," said Willson. She picked up the card and waved it slowly up and down, as though drying wet ink.

Ilsley hit play on her laptop. It wasn't HD-quality video, but it did offer a somewhat clear view of the driveway in Ilsley's yard, with the studio still intact in the background. "Here we go," said Ilsley.

"What did you say you used that building for, Sara?"

"It was my stained-glass studio."

"Ah," said Willson. She hadn't realized that people needed studios to make stained glass. "Okay," Ilsley said, "watch carefully now. I'll slow it down to quarter speed."

As she spoke, two figures, both in dark hooded jackets, moved across the screen from the driveway toward the studio, jerkily, furtively. Willson couldn't tell if they were male or female, but the taller of the two held something in a gloved hand. There was a flicker, a flash, and then the figure threw the object, now spouting flame from one end, at the studio windows. In the absence of sound, Willson imagined the high-pitched crash of the shattering glass. There was a larger flash as something inside the building exploded in a cloud of fire.

"I think that was my turpentine," said Ilsley, shaking her head.

The figures on the screen stood there for a moment as though admiring their work, two black silhouettes against the orange light of the flames. The pair then moved toward the house, the hoods still shading their faces. The second figure reached into a bag and pulled out a cylinder.

"This is where they painted the graffiti on the house," said Fortier.

"But we can't see who it is."

"Wait for it ..." Ilsley said.

And then, for what lasted two or three seconds on the slow-motion video but was likely only a blink of an eye in real time, the heads of both figures turned toward the camera. The fire's brilliance caught their features. One was fierce, manic, feminine. The other was also feminine, and clearly frightened. And then one pushed the other out of the frame.

"Holy shit!" said Willson. She stood back from Ilsley, in shock. She turned to Fortier. "Is that who I think it is?" But it was a question that didn't need to be asked. She already knew the answer.

"It is, Jenny," said Fortier, returning her gaze while zipping up his uniform jacket. "We need to find them. And *fast*."

CHAPTER 33

"I need to speak to Brian Cummings," said Austin, holding the phone to his ear. He glanced over at Myers, sitting across from him in their Vancouver office. Myers had his hands steepled, fingers tapping against each other as if counting the seconds, his eyes angry and dark. "He hasn't returned my calls."

Wendy Thomas's response was uncharacteristically soft, not at all like the confident, enthusiastic MP that Austin had met nearly a year earlier. "I know he's focused on a major project ... something to do with a senator and an underage parliamentary page," she said. "I spoke to him yesterday in the hallway outside the PM's office here in Ottawa. He told me he would call you."

"I need to explain something to him and to find out what the hell is happening," said Austin. "You folks probably saw that article about me and my investment fund. It was all bullshit. You have my word on that."

Thomas asked the question that Austin was most concerned about. "Is that the *first* article you're talking about … or the one that came out a few days later online, the one that named some of your investors?"

"I guess both," said Austin. "There's nothing to either of them. I'm assuming that everyone at your end understands that. But I want to make sure Cummings understands that. The second piece, written by the same American journalist, named a sports agent who's representing some of my investors. Because he and his clients are now all threatening to pull their money out of the fund, I've got to get confirmation from Cummings that the highway and pipeline projects are still on. And I need to know how close your government is to approving our Top of the World proposal. I might be able to persuade most of my investors to stay in, but it's going to take one hell of a Hail Mary at this point."

"I'll do what I can."

"I need more than that, Wendy. I need him to call me *today*. I've got a lot at stake here, and I don't need to remind you that you have just as much to lose as I do."

"No, you don't have to remind me of anything. My reputation and my career mean everything to me."

"Then we understand each other. Have you heard anything there to suggest that your government has softened its commitment to any of the projects?"

"Uh … *commitment* is a stronger word than I would use. All along, we've indicated an *interest* in these projects, Stafford. Committing to them, or approving them, is quite another thing."

"I don't like what I'm hearing, Wendy. It sounds like some serious political backpedalling."

"No, I'm just being honest, Stafford. I hope you haven't misunderstood anything that Brian or I have said to you."

"What about our conversation in the restaurant in Red Deer, or the many discussions since then? You both led me to believe that the federal government was committed to a partnership with me on these projects...."

"Again, Stafford, when you suggest a 'commitment to a partnership,' you've gone well beyond what I believe we ever said. That might have been your interpretation, but it's definitely not ours. When you deal with government, that kind of commitment only happens through written contracts, contracts that occur *after* the review processes are finished and only after a decision by the federal Cabinet. A highway through Howse Pass would have to go through the whole federal environmental assessment process. A pipeline would be the same, but then you'd also have to add into that equation the National Energy Board assessments and hearings. You understand that none of that has happened yet."

"I'm getting more and more pissed off with each sentence that comes out of your mouth, Wendy." Austin felt his blood pressure rising along with the volume of his voice, and again felt a prick of uncertainty, of fear. This vagueness was not what he wanted to hear. Combined with Mike Berland's recent articles, it was becoming a worst-case scenario for him. He could feel his plans caving in around him, not unlike what had happened in South America … and in Salt Lake City … and then in Boise. But this was like all of them happening simultaneously. And this time, he had much more to lose. And fewer options for moving on. He felt a red mist float across his eyes.

But then, just for a moment, he realized that his anger and desperation might be preventing him from hearing what the MP was really saying. "Wait. Are you trying to tell me something, Wendy, something that Brian Cummings is unwilling to tell me himself?"

"It's important for you to understand that I can't speak for the Prime Minister's Office. And I'm certainly not an official spokesperson for the Government of Canada on these projects. When Brian and I first met with you in Red Deer, we simply indicated an interest in them. Anything more than that is premature."

"And …" he prompted.

"And so, it appears that the trial balloon we sent up about the Howse Pass highway did what we wanted it to do. It showed us that, while there is strong support in my riding for the idea, there's an even larger amount of opposition to it all across the country. Punching a new highway through one of Canada's most popular and well-known national parks seems to be a non-starter with the public. At this time in the election cycle, I'm guessing it's *not* something the prime minister is willing to take any further."

"You're guessing? Is that a chickenshit way of telling me that the prime minister has already decided? That the highway idea is dead … and that bringing it to my attention, and leaking it to the media and others was nothing more than a fucking trial balloon?"

"Normally, I hang up when people use that kind of language. I won't now, because I understand the depth of your concern. What I'm telling you is that the idea of a highway through Howse Pass and down the Blaeberry River is unlikely to go further in the foreseeable future."

"And what about the goddamn pipeline?"

"Without the highway, it makes little sense. I'm sure you understand that, although you may not agree. But even if it *did* make sense, you may have heard that we recently approved another pipeline route from Edmonton across central British Columbia to the Pacific coast. As a result, the need for *this* pipeline no longer exists, at least not for the foreseeable future."

"So the pipeline along the highway was no more than a fucking diversionary tactic? A way to make the other pipeline seem more acceptable?"

"Those are your words, Stafford, not mine."

"And the ski area? Is that dead, too?"

"That I can't comment on. I know it's become the focus of some delicate, high-level negotiations between the Canadian and B.C. governments. I couldn't tell you what was happening there even if I knew."

"I've put a lot of time and effort and money into that project, Wendy, and it makes good sense on every level. I'm distressed to hear that people are negotiating its future without talking to me. This is not acceptable. What's the potential for it to be approved?"

"Well, I know there are many people, both inside and outside government, who don't share your opinion about how much sense it makes. What I *can* tell you is that, based on what I've heard, I would give it no more than a fifty-fifty chance."

"That's the best you can do? A flip of a fucking coin?"

"Your comment cheapens the depth of our review processes. I'm simply telling you the truth."

"The truth? Perhaps you should have told me the fucking truth at the beginning. Do you realize what you and your secretive backroom friend have done to my business, Ms. Thomas? You've yanked out from under us two of the key premises on which we attracted significant investments, and now the third seems to be hanging by a thread. To say that puts me in a difficult position is an understatement. I was told that your government was business-friendly, that it wanted to move the economy in this country for-ward, and that it wanted to work with people like us to make that happen. But obviously that's not the case. Obviously, that was nothing but a big steaming pile of horseshit. And that shit came out of your mouth. Did it taste good, Wendy?"

"I won't justify that with a response. I'm sorry you feel that way, Stafford, and that you appear to have so grossly misinterpreted what we said."

"I don't think I've misinterpreted anything. I don't think so at all. But what I think doesn't matter any-more, does it? It looks like I've been royally screwed." He paused to catch his breath before continuing. "You've left me to fix this mess, with no heads-up from you. Can you at least tell me when the media and the public will be notified about the decision for the high-way and pipeline?"

"Because of the nature of the feedback we got on these two ideas, it's my understanding that there will be no formal announcement."

"In other words," said Austin, speaking slowly, realizing how quickly the situation was unravelling, "they'll experience a slow and quiet death."

"Again, your words, not mine."

Austin glanced over at Myers, who was now leaning back in his chair, staring at the ceiling, and looking pissed, his arms crossed over his chest. "Cummings is not going to phone me back, is he, Wendy?"

"I can't say for sure. But if I were you, I wouldn't wait by the phone. I'm sure you have other things to do."

"I bloody well do!" said Austin, "but I haven't decided yet if that includes directing my lawyer to file a claim against you and Cummings and the Government of Canada, or going to the media to fill them in on your duplicity, or both. But I can assure you that there will be consequences, not only for you personally, but for your government. I will *not* forget what you've done, and you *will* be sorry." He slammed the handset down with such violence that it cracked into two pieces of cream-coloured plastic connected only by a trio of wires. Blood from the palm of his hand dripped onto the numbered buttons of the phone.

Myers's eyes were like black marbles, his face devoid of emotion. "Not good news, I take it?"

"Those fuckers have screwed us six ways to Sunday. The highway was a trial balloon, with no commitment behind it. The pipeline was a goddamn political diversion to make another pipeline look more attractive.

Our government contacts, who we thought were our partners, are now in full retreat and almost complete denial. And, of course, we're the ones left holding the bag. This is what happens when you get in bed with the government."

"What do you suggest we do?"

Austin blotted his palm with the back page of an environmental report, creating what looked like a red Rorschach test. "I don't fucking know. I guess we've got two choices. Either we pull the pin on everything, wrap up the funds, and move on, or we put our foot on the gas pedal and try to force the approval of the ski area. That'll hopefully keep some of our investors onboard and some new money coming in. To do that, we're going to have to make a hell of a compelling case."

"Neither of those options sounds very attractive."

"Have you got any better ideas, Hank? I'm so angry, I can't think straight."

"At this point, no, I don't. Seems like you've got us into a hell of a mess."

"Me? I thought we were a team here."

Myers moved forward in his chair and put his arms on the desk, one on top of the other, the one above less muscled after months in a sling. "I accepted this gig and played my role to bring money to the table, based on the promises *you* made about finding projects that would make investors foam at the mouth. In fact, I was approached by another prospective investor just this week. She seems keen on helping us build the ski area. But now I don't know. It seems like you've fucked up, Stafford, and fucked up big time."

Shocked at Myers's sudden reversal, Austin felt as though, in the last thirty minutes, he had been cast adrift on the sea in a leaky raft. Two of the three projects that were key to his investment funds had essentially vanished, the third was a crapshoot, and his main business partner seemed to have shifted from friend and confidant to accuser and potential defector — one with enough information to not only scuttle all his plans, but force him to leave the country or send him to prison for the rest of his life. Or he could tell the South Americans where Austin was. "Look, we've still got the ski area, Hank. I'll phone Paul DeSantos to see what he knows and push him to get us an approval. But I need to know: Are you willing to see this through … or are you giving up?"

"Based on what I've heard this morning, it's obvious that things have changed in a big way. I'm gonna have to give it some thought. What'll help me decide," said Myers, his eyes cold, "is whether or not there's a dramatic change in our financial arrangement. If I *do* stay, I'll be taking on more personal risk, you realize. To do that, I'll have to be better compensated."

"And what would that look like?"

"That's an excellent question." Myers rose and moved to the office door. "I'll have to chew on it." He looked back at Austin. "In the interim, I encourage you to think about what you're willing to offer, or maybe *afford* is a better word, to keep me on as a partner … a silent partner."

With that, Myers left.

CHAPTER 34

"What are the chances there'll be weapons in the house?" asked Willson.

She and Fortier were speeding down a gravel road north of Golden, Fortier driving a police SUV with the emergency lights flashing but the siren quiet. Two police cars followed, each carrying two more officers. They were near Donald on the old Big Bend Highway, at one time the main connection between Golden and Revelstoke before the Rogers Pass opened. It was now a dead-end road leading to a few cutblocks and backcountry lodges.

"No idea," Fortier said. "Let's assume they're there until we know otherwise. By the way, did you ever talk to that investor of Austin's?"

"Yes, I phoned him while I was waiting for you to get the warrants — which I must say took forever."

"I did everything I could, short of driving to Revelstoke or Invermere to find out where the duty JPP was. You know as well as I do that tearing out here without warrants would have been stupid. Your mother could have been hurt, and besides, then anything we found couldn't be used as evidence. Tell me about Merrix."

"Well, it turns out he's a Vancouver-based pro sports agent. He and many of his clients have invested with Austin. I was actually surprised at how eager he was to talk to me. I went over those questions that Courtney gave us, the ones to determine if something was a legit investment. He told me they'd been promised guaranteed high returns, but that the investment strategies seemed very complex and had been poorly explained. Most recently, he told me there were issues with the paperwork and that some of his clients were having difficulties getting their money back from Austin. We both agreed that they'd invested in a classic Ponzi scheme. From his responses, I think he already knew, but he was obviously hoping it was something, anything else. My call just confirmed his hunch."

"He must be pissed. How much money are we talking about?"

"Oh, he's pissed all right. And embarrassed and worried. I asked him about the money, but he wouldn't tell me exactly how much. But it was clear to me that they're in to Austin for a substantial chunk of change."

Fortier let out a low whistle. "Has he talked to the police in Vancouver?"

"He hadn't when I talked to him ... but I'm guessing he will."

As they moved on to rougher roads, Willson reached up for the grab bar with one hand while she gripped the centre console with the other, her fingertips inches from the shotgun bolted there. With each turn in the road, each thrust of the powerful engine, she fought to keep her body from sliding sideways on the vinyl seat. "Oh, and I meant to ask, did you ever hear whether or not the rifle we seized from Leo Springer matched the bullets from Austin's house?"

"Just this morning, and it did. It took over a week to get the results from the crime lab, but the bullets were definitely fired from that rifle. The Calgary Police Service arrested him this afternoon. He was still in hospital."

"So, can we assume he was the one who shot at Austin and Myers?" The vehicle hit a hole in the road and Willson's head banged against the ceiling. "Shit!"

"Sorry. Yeah, it looks like it. We've charged him with two counts of attempted murder, two of reckless discharge of a firearm, and two of careless use of a firearm. We have the rifle with his fingerprints on it and the bullets matching the rifle. But although the fact that he ran from us is incriminating, it doesn't mean shit. And we have no witnesses to the crime, nor do we have anyone who can place Springer at or near the scene at the time of the shooting. Without more evidence, it could go either way when it finally gets to court."

"In other words, it's a crapshoot."

"Exactly."

"Did he admit to anything?"

"Nope. When he was finally healthy enough a few days after our chase for the doctors to let investigators talk to him, he was eerily quiet."

"Gave them nothing?"

"Nothing. He was still a mess of bandages and casts and bruises. He just stared at the investigators from his hospital bed for the longest time, expressionless. And then he said the four words we all love to hear: 'I want a lawyer.' They tried the standard approaches to get him to talk, and a few new ones … but that was the extent of the interview with him."

"I wondered whether Springer might have been responsible for the arson and Webb's murder, too," said Willson, "but after the fire at Ilsley's place, and what we saw on the security video, it makes less sense."

"Agreed, but we made no assumptions, even though he was on the side of the anti–ski hill folks and had no obvious reason to burn down Stoffel's office. But I've seen stranger things happen. I still haven't ruled him out, but he's dropped way down the list." He pointed at lights in the trees to their right. "There's the house." A waiting RCMP cruiser posted there by Fortier since late last night was ready to block the road behind them.

Fortier switched off the emergency lights and the headlights, slowed the vehicle, and turned in to a gravel driveway.

Willson unbuckled her seat belt. "You've got the warrants," she said, her voice firm, "but I want the front door."

"Hold on, Jenny. We should have the element of surprise on our side tonight, but we'll both go to the front door. We'll keep two of the officers with us and send the other two around back."

In her impatience to enter the house and confront those inside, Willson had forgotten about the cavalry behind them. "I'm good with that ... as long as I'm first through the door."

Fortier nodded once and grabbed the microphone from the dash. "Echo Two-Four and Three-One, this is Echo Five-Two. Two-Four, you guys stay with us to hit the front door. Three-One, I want you at the back of the house."

There were two sets of double-clicks, indicating that the officers in the vehicles behind them heard and understood their orders.

They rolled up to the house slowly, furtively, their tires crunching almost imperceptibly on the gravel.

"You talked to them once before, right?" asked Willson, watching for movement in the house.

"I did. The day after the café window blew out. They didn't admit to anything. They seemed calm, like they were expecting me. I made it clear I was watching them."

When the SUV had rolled to a stop, Willson opened the door and moved toward the front of the house. It was a house in the loosest sense of the word, constructed of a mishmash of cedar shingles, recycled metal, salvaged wood, mismatched windows, and peeling paint. A lean-ing chimney belched smoke. There wasn't a right angle in sight, like a cartoon house drawn by a child. An older model Ford sedan was parked near the west wall, and the yard beyond was filled with junk.

Willson paused to let the two officers reach their position at the back. Each scurried low along the sides of the structure to avoid the windows. A few seconds later, she heard another double-click on Fortier's radio. They were in position.

Their hands resting on their weapons, Willson and Fortier walked quietly to the front door. Willson banged on it rapidly and loudly. When no answer came, she banged again. "Peace officers," she yelled. "Open the door!"

Finally, the faded door cracked open and a pair of eyes peeked out at them. Not knowing who it was and unwilling to wait, Willson swiftly pushed her way in, head down, shoulder against the door. Fortier, with his hand on her left shoulder, followed.

"What do *you* want?" said John Theroux, stepping back suddenly, his face a pale canvas of confusion and shock, his hand still on the door handle.

Fortier started to speak. "We have a warrant to search —"

With both hands, Willson grabbed Theroux by the front of his tattered flannel shirt. Below the shirt, he wore stained grey flannel sweatpants. His feet were bare. "Where's your wife? And where the hell is my mother?"

"What?" said Theroux, his eyes wide. "I don't know what you're talking about…. Let go of me."

Furious, impatient, Willson pushed him back two steps, shaking him like a dog with a chew toy. "I said, where *the fuck* are they?" She could smell his fear.

"Sandy's not here and I … I don't know anything about your mother. Why are you asking me?"

Willson shook Theroux again, this time tearing a piece of his shirt. "Stop stalling. I asked you where they were." She felt Fortier's hand on her shoulder.

"Jenny, let's take it slow here …"

But Willson ignored him. Her face was inches from Theroux's. "Where?" Her spittle hit his cheek.

"I don't know where Sandy is! She left two nights ago. I didn't see her all day yesterday, not until we met at the airport to greet Austin and his investors. She'd taken the truck, so I had to drive her shitbox of a car. As soon as the helicopter left, Sandy jumped in the truck and drove off again, leaving me standing there wondering what in the hell was going on. I haven't seen her since."

Willson gave Theroux one last shake, then relaxed her hold and stepped back. She glared at him, trying to decide if he was telling the truth or playing with her. "The officers with me will look around to be sure," she said. "But if your wife's not here, where else could she be? Where would she go?"

Willson watched as the two Mounties moved through the ramshackle house, checking every room for people and weapons. She heard the two at the rear of the house come in the back door. Fortier had moved between her and Theroux, perhaps to protect him from her rage.

"I have no idea where she went," Theroux said. "Like I told you, she drove off and left me standing there."

"No calls from her since?"

The RCMP officers called "Clear!" as they moved through the house.

"Nothing. When I heard your car in the driveway, I thought it was her coming home."

"Where does she go when she's not here?" asked Fortier.

"Nowhere special. Like I said, I don't know where she is. The truck's gone, so she could be anywhere."

"Do you have any other buildings on this property?"

"Or are there any other places she might go to? Friends? Family?" Willson asked.

"There's an old empty barn through the trees," said Theroux, pointing vaguely north. "We never use it. Other than that, nothing."

Fortier spoke to his colleagues as they came back into the room. "Anything?"

"All clear," said one of the officers. "We got one shotgun, one box of shells, but no one else in the house, and no other weapons."

"Good," Fortier said. "Two of you check the barn, please, and the others check around the property. Look in any buildings or sheds. Anywhere someone could be hiding, or being held."

After the four officers moved away, Theroux turned to Willson, his hands on his hips. "You still haven't told me why you're looking for my wife."

"We have your wife on a security video from yesterday evening," said Willson, "setting fire to Sara Ilsley's workshop down on the McMurdo Benches. She was also seen painting threatening graffiti on the side of Sara's house."

"Shit!" said Theroux, dropping his head before blowing out a loud breath through pursed lips. "Not ag— but what's this got to do with your mother?"

"My mother was with her," Willson said, not willing to say out loud that it was her mother who had thrown the Molotov cocktail, "and I'm goddamn sure she wasn't there willingly."

"You think Sandy forced her?" Theroux asked, incredulous. "I don't believe it. Why … why would she do that?"

While Willson could sense the man's confusion, she also saw a glimpse of the cockiness she'd observed at the rally. "You tell *me*, smartass."

"Wait," said Fortier. "John, a second ago you didn't finish your sentence. Were you going to say 'not again'?"

Theroux's cheeks flushed. "Uh … maybe … yeah."

"Why?" asked Willson. "Has she done this kind of thing before?"

Theroux's eyes were blinking rapidly back and forth. It was if his mind and body were at war with each other, using confidence and confusion as contrasting weapons. "Let's just say that Sandy's … an *intense* woman," said Theroux. "She takes things seriously and won't let them go. *Manic* is the word the doctors use. She scares me when she gets worked up over things like politics and religion and people she thinks are being treated badly by the system. The meds help some, if she stays on them …"

"She's on medication?" asked Willson.

"Her pills are still here … so not for at least two days."

"What is it about Austin's project that has her so worked up?"

"We created the ski society to help get the project approved. Austin's been supporting us financially and otherwise while we help him by building community support, getting people excited about it. Since then, it's like Sandy's been on a personal crusade, a one-woman mission to make the project happen. I mean, I'm committed to the project, too, but not like she is. Not only does she believe in it, I think she relishes the profile we get in the community. It's all she thinks about, all she talks about. It seems to give her a sense of power, so much so that she kinda loses it when someone threatens the project."

"Someone like Albin Stoffel?" asked Fortier.

"Anyone on the anti side. When Stoffel's office burned down and Sue Webb was killed in the fire, I asked Sandy the next day if she had anything to do with it."

"Why?" asked Willson, seeing the man's hands rolling and rubbing around each other like wrestling snakes.

"Because she came home late the night before, the night it happened, and went right into the shower. I smelled her clothes while she was in there, thinking that maybe she'd been out drinking, or with someone else. All I smelled was smoke."

"And what did she say when you asked her?" Fortier inquired.

"She wouldn't admit it one way or the other, but she said they got what they deserved."

"Do *you* think she did it?" asked Willson.

"I don't know. I guess she could've if she was mad enough. Those people who are against the resort should've listened to us."

Willson ignored his weak attempt to reassign blame. "Now that we have Sandy on tape starting a fire at Ilsley's house, what do you think?"

"I'm thinking you have a big problem."

"Why do you say that?" asked Fortier.

"Because she's completely unpredictable," Theroux said, looking at Willson with a mocking smile, the cockiness apparently returning, "and you don't know where she is."

Willson moved toward Theroux, ready to wipe the smirk off his face. "You smug little fucker ..." As Fortier moved between them, the other officers came back from their search of the property.

"We checked the small sheds. Nothing there, Ben," said the senior constable. "But there's a car in the barn. It's your mother's, Jenny, the one we've been looking for."

"Are you sure?"

"Positive," said the officer. "Goldish Honda, licence plate matches. The keys are in it, and the insurance and registration are still in the glove compartment, in your mother's name. Other than that, there's nothing in it, and no sign of any damage. No purse, no cellphone, no blood. Nothing. It's like she parked it there and walked away. Or someone did ..."

Willson turned to Theroux and saw in his eyes that he wasn't surprised by the presence of her mother's car in his barn.

"Okay," said Fortier. He pointed at the senior constable. "Chris, I want you to take pictures of the car inside and out, and then I want it towed to the detachment. I want *no* new fingerprints on it until we dust it and go over it with a magnifying glass. Please take that shotgun with you until we sort things out." He turned to Theroux. "Tell me what you know about the car and why it's on your property."

Theroux's crossed his arms across his chest. "I've got nothing more to say. I want to talk to my lawyer."

"You said your wife has your truck, John?" Fortier asked, referring to his notebook. "Is that the old Ford

F150, red, a white canopy on it, with the back panel on the driver's side in grey primer? The one I saw when I was here the last time?" He read out the licence plate number from his notes.

Theroux shrugged and smiled. Willson felt an urge to kick his teeth down his throat, but knew she'd have to get past Fortier to do it.

Fortier turned to the other constables, maintaining the demilitarized zone between Willson and Theroux. "Get on the radio and get this description out to all our guys, and to officers in Invermere and Revelstoke, just in case Trueman decided to take a trip. She could be travelling with Anne Willson. We'll assume that Willson is not with Trueman voluntarily. You already have Anne Willson's description. We're good here, so how about you three try to cover as much ground as you can to see if you can find them."

The officers quickly left the house.

"Could your wife have a gun with her?" asked Willson, still glaring at Theroux.

At the mention of his wife with a weapon, his eyes widened. "We have a loaded .38 revolver in a kitchen drawer, but I don't think she's crazy enough to take *that* with her."

Theroux began to move toward the kitchen. "Whoa," said Willson, putting her hand on his arm. "I'll get it. How about you point us to where it is."

They moved to the kitchen, Willson leading. Theroux pointed to three drawers to the left of the fridge, his hand shaking. "It's in the middle one," he said. "It's loaded and there should be a box of bullets with it."

Willson opened the drawer and pawed through a noisy spider web of metal utensils. "Not here," she said. After she'd checked in the remaining two drawers, it was clear the revolver was missing.

"It looks like she's armed," said Willson.

Theroux looked paler than he'd been when the officers first showed up at the door. "Son of a bitch!"

"Where did you get the gun? Is it registered?" asked Fortier.

"Sandy got it from Hank Myers. He said we might need it for protection because the people opposing the resort might try to scare us, or worse. As to whether it's registered or not, I doubt it."

Willson suddenly understood how Sandy Trueman had persuaded her mother to miss work, how she'd forced her to participate in the arson and vandalism at Ilsley's house. A gunpoint threat was a great encourager. And she suddenly understood the degree to which her mother was in danger, having been abducted by an unhinged fanatic with a weapon. Fear filled her veins like a shot of poison. She looked at Fortier, who had obviously come to the same conclusion. "We've *got* to find them, Ben."

"What was your wife wearing when you last saw her?" asked Fortier.

Willson saw that Theroux was almost in shock now, his face white, his body slumped. Whether he loved and was worried about his wife, or he was concerned about the trouble they both were in, she didn't know and didn't care.

"Uh," Theroux said, scratching his head, "I think she was wearing jeans, hiking shoes, and a purple fleece jacket. Sometimes she jams an old baseball cap on her head, but I can't remember if she had that on or not …"

Fortier called in the description of the missing truck and the missing women and relayed the fact that one of them might be armed.

"Again, John, what does your wife have against my mother?" asked Willson.

Theroux waited before speaking. He was clearly shaken. "Nothing that I know of. I don't know if Sandy had ever even met your mother."

"Then why was she with her at Ilsley's place?"

"The only thing I can think of is that she's furious with Ilsley *and* you, and she's using your mother to get at you. When Austin phoned a few days ago and told us about the articles that that American wrote about the project, and about your secret investigation, he said he needed our help. He sounded different than any other time we talked to him. Desperate. Angry. When Sandy heard that, she went berserk, throwing things, swearing. It got worse as each day passed. She was up all night a few nights ago, wandering the house, muttering to herself. And then when Ilsley showed up at the airport yesterday and Sandy saw her talking to one of the investors, it was as if something broke in her, like a dark cloud had come over her. She was quiet, which is rare. I think she must have thought that the project was unravelling, that everything we were working for was under threat, and that Ilsley had something to do with it. That's when she drove off in a cloud of dust. I'm betting she sees you two as being the cause of it all. So, in her disturbed mind, she's either trying to get you to back off, or she's out for revenge."

Willson's mind was reeling. "Is she violent, John? Would she physically hurt my mother if she's that angry?"

"Up until the last few days, I would have said no. Now, I'm not sure."

"I'll ask you one more time," said Willson, "where the hell would she go?" She grabbed Theroux by the shirt again. "It's my mother we're talking about here."

Like a rag doll, Theroux offered no resistance to Willson's shaking. "I told you, I don't know," he said, a tear dropping down his left cheek. "And I'm not saying another word until I speak to my lawyer."

Willson let go of him and stood back, her arms limp at her sides. As she stared at the dishevelled, tear-stained face of the man in front of her, she had a blinding flash of self-realization. She now saw that her obsession with the investigation had put in jeopardy the one person in her life she really cared about.

What the hell have I done?

CHAPTER 35

APRIL 22

"Paul, do I need to remind you about the photographs?" asked Austin.

"I'm telling you all I know, Stafford," said Paul DeSantos. "This project has moved beyond my level; I'm no longer in the loop on the discussions. I was told to put my work on the resort on hold until some key decisions are made. I'm like the meat in a sandwich here, being squeezed from both sides. This is a no-win situation for me. My hands are tied." There was a catch in the bureaucrat's voice. "Look, Stafford. About those photos. It would be great if you could keep them to yourself. Deleting them permanently would be the best. There's honestly nothing else I can do here other than tell you what I know. And it's not much."

Austin was doodling on a piece of scrap paper. The more he heard from DeSantos that was of no value to the situation, the harder he pressed down, eventually tearing through the paper to the wood desk underneath. He needed answers. "What *can* you tell me?"

"Our deputy minister is talking to her counterpart at the federal level. From what little I've heard, the feds seem to be doing an about-face on the ski area, shifting from general support over to the no side."

"What's changed their minds?"

"The word is there were two things making them nervous. The first was the release of Albin Stoffel's initial research paper. It was published in a scientific journal, but the popular press picked it up. The *Globe and Mail* did a big piece on it this past weekend. It says that Collie Creek and the Blaeberry area, as well as the wild northern parts of Banff and Yoho parks, are pretty much the epicentre for wolverines in the Canadian Rockies. It's not crawling with them, but compared to many other mountain areas in the West, it has more than its share. You already know they're on the species at risk list, so it's not a result anyone can ignore. The *Globe* article specifically referenced your project, again calling it a mega-resort, and quoted Stoffel saying it would have a dramatic negative impact on the species if it were built. Also, based on the research results, one of the First Nations groups in the area has announced its opposition to the project. The *Globe* journalist openly questioned why anyone in government was still giving it any consideration at all."

Shit, thought Austin. *I should have done something more about Stoffel when I had the chance. Fucking wolverines.* "And the second reason?" He waited, but DeSantos was silent for nearly ten seconds. "Paul?"

"The second reason is that they've all seen the articles by that American journalist. They're extremely nervous about the authenticity of your project funding. I've personally done three separate briefings for the deputy on that very subject, but no matter what I say, no matter what assurances I give her, I can't seem to convince her that this is a bona fide project with bona fide investors. The feds may feel the same."

Like a deflating balloon, Austin felt his body empty of any last semblance of hope that the deteriorating situation might be turned around. "So that's it, then?"

"It's not dead yet," said DeSantos. "Don't get me wrong. But in light of the questions and the fact that I've been told to focus on other things, it's not looking good."

"And the money I've invested to date in application fees, research projects, consultant studies, reports, and submissions for you?" If he couldn't get answers, Austin knew he needed all the money he could get his hands on. Even refunds would help, whether in the thousands or hundreds of dollars.

"You and I both know that was part of the process, Stafford. I'm not in a position to refund any of that if the project is denied … or if you pull out."

"What's the timing on the decision, Paul? When will I know one way or the other?"

"I have no idea."

"What if I *do* threaten to pull out if they don't give me an answer by a specific date?"

"You could do that, but an ultimatum like that might give them the very escape hatch they're looking for."

"I'm screwed if I push … and screwed if I wait."

"Unfortunately, that's about where you're at. I wish I could tell you different, but I can't."

"I thought I could count on you, Paul."

"I did my best, Stafford. Now, what about those photos?"

In a calm, deliberate motion that contrasted the storm of his emotions, Austin hung up the phone. He sat unmoving, his hand still on the receiver. With Myers pushing him from one side, now demanding an immediate larger share, and with the ski area project falling apart on the other, he understood that his situation matched DeSantos's: meat in the middle of a sandwich. In his case, he didn't have a career or marriage at stake. But he did have millions of dollars in play, which in his mind was much more significant. Unlike DeSantos, however, he did have an exit plan, developed months earlier with this very scenario in mind.

His thoughts were interrupted by a hesitant voice from the doorway. "Mr. Austin?" said his assistant. He looked up at the young man, who looked mildly confused, as if waiting for an explanation. "You have an appointment with Ms. Liang at two p.m. at the Terminal City Club?"

Austin looked at his Rolex. Ten minutes to two. "I didn't realize the time, Barinder," he said, with a thin, forced smile. "Thanks for the reminder."

Rain fell lightly during the short walk from his office to the club. Austin turned his attention to the meeting ahead. Suzanne Liang was an unknown, a referral via a text from Matt Merrix. His first thought when he'd read Merrix's message the day before was that Liang was an investigator from the B.C. Securities Commission or the police, and that Merrix had turned him in rather than wait any longer for his clients' money. After Berland's articles had come out, Austin had expected that the authorities would be onto him eventually, appear at his door either formally or covertly. After the investors' visit to Collie Creek, he had sensed in Merrix a man who'd made up his mind to pull his clients' money out. Thus it was surprising to receive his text suggesting Liang had funds that she wanted to invest, and quickly — that in itself sounded suspicious.

But Austin desperately needed cash. The next set of quarterly payments was overdue and he couldn't put them off much longer. If Liang *was* a legitimate investor, then he couldn't risk losing her money by refusing to meet with her. So he'd decided to proceed, but with significant caution. He'd been pursued by investigators in the past; he felt confident that he could pick up the signals of a person digging for details for the wrong reasons.

When the club's host pointed him to Liang, seated at a table by the window, Austin smiled and walked across the room toward her, his confidence returning. He was a salesman at heart and had no doubt that he could be persuasive when it came to pitching an investment. He would confidently and nimbly push her emotional buttons, moving swiftly from one plucked heartstring to another, most of them in the key of greed.

Liang was a slim woman who looked to be in her early forties. Her white pencil skirt and pink stilettos showed off her shapely legs to full effect, and her creamy, translucent blouse showed a hint of pink bra underneath. Her jet-black hair was pulled back in a ponytail, and her makeup was subtle yet enchanting, her eyes dancing in the light of the window. Instantly he decided that even if this woman was only acting the part, he would still enjoy the encounter.

"Ms. Liang?"

"That's me," she said, smiling. "Please, call me Suzanne. You must be Stafford Austin."

As he reached out to shake her proffered right hand, he noticed that her nails were painted the same shade as her shoes. Her left hand was resting on the table — a quick glance confirmed she was not wearing a wedding ring.

"At your service, Suzanne," he said, sitting down. He ordered a caffè Americano from the server, who was already hovering at his elbow. "I understand that you got my name from Matt Merrix. How do you know Matt?"

"He represented my nephew Simon when he played in the Western Hockey League for the Kootenay Ice."

"Ah … is Simon still playing?"

"No. He was drafted by an NHL team, but never really made the pros. After a month or two on some team called the Greenville Swamp Rabbits with only a tryout contract, he quit and came back to Vancouver to attend school. Playing in the minors was a horrible life, even if it was only part of a season — long bus rides, cheap hotels, empty arenas. He played four years for the UBC hockey team and now he's a chartered accountant, working for the family business."

Austin listened carefully; these were background details he could easily verify with a quick web search. "And what's the family business?"

Liang's lips, also pink, shifted upward in a barely perceptible smile. "For the sake of this discussion today, let's say it's an international import-export business."

"And what do you import or export?"

The smile remained. "Anything that will make a profit for us."

Austin returned the smile, then took a sip of his coffee, which had already been discreetly delivered. It was hot and fresh and strong. But his sense of urgency overrode his patience. He placed the cup back on the saucer — slowly, gently — trying to calm the slight tremble in his hand.

"Matt sent me a message suggesting that you might wish to invest in one of my funds."

"Good," said Liang. "I asked him to do that. He told me how successful you've been with your funds … at least until recently."

"We're still doing well. It is true that a journalist took a run at us a few weeks ago, tried to suggest something that wasn't true. But it was nothing more than speculation and exaggeration. My lawyer's dealing with it now. I'm pleased to confirm that the projects I'm investing in are indeed moving ahead, and that our investors are continuing to receive impressive and consistent returns."

Liang lifted a crystal glass filled with ice and a clear liquid. The cubes tinkled against the sides and she peered at him over the rim of the glass. "Matt suggested that there might be delays in dividend payments, and that some investors who've tried to move their money out of the funds haven't been able to do so. Is he right? Also, I need to ask: is there really no truth to the journalist's story?"

Austin paused before responding. If she was legitimately interested in investing with him, then these were questions any prudent investor would ask — due diligence. In his experience, he knew that wealthy people did not stay wealthy by being foolish, at least not the majority of them. But if she was something else, someone other than who she claimed to be, then she might be digging for details she didn't have or could only guess at, trying to catch him in a lie. In that case, he had to take great care in his answer. "I suggest that Matt is somewhat overstating the situation, despite my explanations to him to the contrary." Another pause, another sip of coffee. "The last round of dividends has been delayed slightly only because I'm focused on meeting government demands for more environmental information relating to the Top of the World project. Mine is a small company with very little overhead. I want my investors' money to work hard, not be swallowed up in administration costs, so I have to do most of the work myself. The government's requests come in waves, with very tight timelines. This short delay is only temporary, and I remain very confident. You have my word on that."

"I don't know you very well though, do I? How do I know your word is good?"

"I expected you to ask that question. I would ask the same. I can certainly give you a list of people who are pleased with what I've done for them."

"I'd like that," said Liang, sliding a business card across the table with one pink-tipped finger.

He picked up the card but didn't immediately look at it. There was strange logic at work here that did not make sense to him. "Allow me to ask *you* a question, Suzanne. If you *are* concerned about my funds, and about what you heard from Matt, rightly or wrongly, why did you ask to meet with me today? I'm sure there are many possible investment avenues for you."

"That's a perceptive question, Stafford." She moved forward in her chair and lowered her voice. "I can only say that the Canada Revenue Agency has been asking questions about … one part of our business … and I would prefer that some of our money be moved to investments that can't be touched, that are perhaps somewhat less visible to those searching for them, at least in the short term."

Now that she was closer, with only an arm's-length separating them, the smell of her perfume reached Austin's nose. It was sweet, slightly musky, almost animal-like, with a hint of vanilla. It raised his heart rate a couple of beats. She regarded him with slightly raised eyebrows. This was not the answer he had anticipated, and it was certainly not an answer he would expect from an undercover investigator. His worries began to recede.

"I see," he said, his thoughts racing, his voice barely a whisper. "Then perhaps we're not so different, you and I. Perhaps we can do business that will benefit us both."

"That's what I was hoping you would say, Stafford."

"How much would you like to invest?"

"For now, I have two million that I have to move quickly. If this works out, there will be more. Will that amount pose a problem for you?"

Austin hoped that his reaction wasn't obvious to Liang. It was no longer her perfume that was raising his heart rate. Two million dollars would solve his immediate cash-flow challenges and give him enough breathing room to implement his exit plan. It was almost too good to be true, and the timing could not have been better. For a moment, the worry returned. This *was* too good to be true. But he could check out her story before he made any moves. He felt like he had a cartoon angel on one shoulder encouraging him not to do it, and a devil on the other, urging him to go ahead. Austin made his decision. "That's not a problem at all, Suzanne. If you decide to proceed, I will put that money to very good use. I'm sure you'll be pleased."

"Excellent. And remind me of the interest rate you've been paying to your investors?"

"As Matt may have told you, we've been averaging 13 percent per annum over the last twelve months. We pay that out quarterly."

"That *is* very attractive. Given my situation ... and yours ... I'm comfortable with that for now. We can always renegotiate in future."

"That sounds reasonable."

Liang moved forward in her chair. Both elbows and her pink bra rested on the table, the contents of the bra pushing upwards enticingly. Inexplicably, Austin found that her perfume had a subtly different scent now, one that raised his anxiety level slightly. A hint of adrenalin mixed with high notes of fear. He unconsciously moved his upper body back from her.

"Let me make one thing *very* clear, Stafford," said Liang, her voice quiet yet steely. She slowly turned and looked across the room. Like a man under hypnosis, Austin followed her gaze. Two unsmiling men, one wearing sunglasses, both very large, sat watching them from a far table. Austin turned back to Liang. Her subtle smile had returned. But now Austin saw no warmth there.

"Those are my brothers," she said. "I mentioned that the money we've spoken about comes from a family business. I require your personal guarantee that our family will have immediate access to that money whenever we may request it. You must understand that we will not accept *any* delays. Failure to get the money to us upon my request will have significant negative implications for you. Do you understand?"

Austin stared at Liang, the ambient sounds of the restaurant drowned out by the rushing of blood that echoed in his ears. If this woman *was* an investigator, either with the Securities Commission or some police force, then she was extremely good, nothing like any of the bumblers he'd previously dealt with. She'd woven a story that was unexpected, compelling, and very different from anything he'd heard before. She could be setting him up for a very big fall. If he agreed to work with her, particularly now that she'd made the oblique suggestion the money might not be 100 percent legit, he was heading down a path of no return.

However, if she *wasn't* in law enforcement, and if she *did* have two million dollars to invest with him, then he'd hit a lucky break when he needed it most. If that was the case, however, she was far more dangerous than any investigator could ever be. He had no idea what the Liang family was involved in, but suspected that the products they were buying and selling didn't appear in local stores, and the Liangs would never be profiled in *B.C. Business* magazine. He understood that this could be a deal with the devil … a devil that would hunt him down mercilessly if she didn't get her money back. If that happened he'd lose more than just his soul. But he had no choice. He desperately needed cash for the final stages of his plan, and this might be his last opportunity to obtain it.

"I understand," Austin said, his voice weak, shaky. "Let me know when you're ready to proceed."

CHAPTER 36

"Case dismissed." The judge's gavel banged on the bench like an exclamation point concluding a sentence. But in this case, there would be no sentence. And no $4,000 fine.

The federal Crown prosecutor stood, sighed, and began returning files to her briefcase. Across the courtroom, the accused and his lawyer celebrated with high-fives. Seated in the front row, behind the prosecutor, Jenny Willson hung her head in disappointment. She'd been unable to help convict a young Alberta man of illegal possession of fossils from the world-famous Burgess Shale. Reluctantly relying on weak evidence gathered by a young Yoho warden, Willson and the prosecutor had failed to prove that this man had possession and control of the fossils, as opposed to one of the other two men who'd also been in the truck when the warden pulled it over on the road from Takkakaw Falls. Willson rose from her wooden chair, wondering if she should have pursued the case at all, whether lack of sleep was clouding her judgment. She had spent the last three nights driving the roads around Golden, looking for the truck used to abduct her mother. And while sleep was highly overrated at a time like this, it pissed her off that she'd let exhaustion get the better of her in the courtroom.

For Willson, it was scant consolation that a pair of rare lace crab fossils was back in the government's hands. And she felt no joy in knowing that the accused man had lost his chance to sell them for big money to a private collector.

"Warden Willson," said the judge, pulling his reading glasses from his face and staring directly at her, "the evidence you've brought in front of this court is usually more compelling."

"My apologies, your honour," said Willson. "I'm somewhat distracted. It won't happen again."

"The local officers have advised me of your ... personal situation. I was expecting a request for an adjournment, and would have granted it. But I wish you the best of luck." The judge offered her a warm, fatherly smile, then turned his attention back to the courtroom. "Next case."

Willson walked out to the hallway, preoccupied, angry at herself for making a rookie mistake. She turned left but looked right to watch the accused and his two friends smoking in the light rain outside. Not looking where she was going, she again bumped into Ben Fortier. His long, strong arms grabbed her.

"Geez, Ben. We've got to stop meeting like this." But then she noticed the serious look on his face. "What?"

"They found the truck, Jenny."

"Where? Did they find my mother?"

"Not yet. One of our highway patrol guys found it parked on an abandoned logging road off the Trans-Canada, a few kilometres west of Donald. There was no one in it but he says there were two pairs of footprints in the mud heading away from it, up the road."

"Holy shit. Did he follow them?"

Instead of answering, Fortier grabbed Willson's elbow. "Let's talk and drive, Jenny. I need you over at the detachment."

He slammed open the front door of the courthouse and they both sprinted to the police car. The gear on Fortier's belt clinked and bounced.

"And in answer to your question," said Fortier, as he sped along 10th Avenue North, "he didn't follow the tracks, and that's a good thing. Now that we think we know where they may be, we need to do this right. The officer is parked down on the highway watching the truck in case they try to leave."

When they reached the newly built detachment, Willson noticed a large blue van parked outside. Several black-uniformed officers piled out of the back. "What's this?" she asked.

"RCMP Emergency Response Team for the SE District happened to be running a training scenario near Invermere today. I spoke to the on-call critical incident commander about the situation, so he sent them up here. They just arrived."

Willson opened the car door and put one leg on the pavement. But instead of getting out, she turned to Fortier. "I want to go to the site now, Ben. I need to know that my mum's okay. It's great that these guys are here, but let's just go, please. I'm fucking tired of doing the right thing, tired of waiting."

"Jenny, I know you want to help … and you will. But we can't just charge in there like a pair of cowboys. We know Trueman's armed, and based on what we heard from her husband, she's unstable. That's a combination that could go very bad for *everyone* involved. We've got the access road covered, and we've got the pros here, so let's take advantage of them."

"This goes against what my gut's telling me to do, Ben," she said, reluctantly climbing out of the car. "I'll trust you for now, but my patience isn't limitless. That's my mum out there with that wing nut." She knew Fortier was right to hold her back, but that did nothing to quell her anxiety or her desire to race off and save her mother.

When they reached the small boardroom that was quickly and noisily being transformed into an ERT command centre, Willson didn't know whether to feel relieved or anxious. On the one hand, she saw a team of the fittest police officers in this part of B.C. — men and women who'd been selected, trained, and equipped to deal with everything from covert surveillance and rural tracking to high-risk arrests and barricaded sus-pects. But realizing that this expertise and weaponry had only gathered here because her mother had been abducted by an armed and clearly troubled woman bent on revenge caused her heart to race. This was as serious as things could get, and there was no way to guess how it would turn out.

Willson noticed a tall staff sergeant, dressed in a black uniform like the others, who appeared to be leading the planning. Fortier whispered in her ear: "He's the operational team leader." Willson saw the four gold upward-facing chevrons on his arm.

"Okay, folks," the staff sergeant said, "Gather round. Google Earth images show a trapper's cabin three kilometres beyond where the truck was found. I just sent a member to the airport to fly over it in a fixed-wing aircraft. The cabin's in the trees, so I'm not sure if they'll be able to see anything, but I asked them to do only one pass so as not to spook anyone on the ground. They should be reporting back in a few minutes to let us know if they spotted any activity, tracks, or other vehicles. As you all know, we're dealing with at least one suspect, Sandy Trueman, and one abductee, Anne Willson." He pointed to pictures of both women that had been taped to the opposite wall. The enlarged driver's licence photos, like all government identification, made them both look equally guilty of something. Their faces were dark and unsmiling in the grainy black-and-white reproductions. "You'll all get copies of these so you'll know who is who. For now, we're assuming these two women are at the cabin. There could also be other individuals there who we don't know about. We need to plan how we will approach the site to see what's happening, and if they're there, the tactics we'll use to free the hostage and peacefully arrest the suspect. Because it's so close to the highway, we will stop traffic in both directions until we know what we're dealing with."

Willson nervously observed the proceedings. These were trained professionals, and while she was comforted by their careful planning, her anxiety remained on a knife's edge. The shock of seeing her mother's unsmiling picture on the wall heightened her fears.

Willson felt her phone ping with an incoming message. For an instant, she wondered if it was from her mother, but then remembered that her mother had left her cellphone and purse at home. She stepped away from the long boardroom table, leaned against the wall, took her phone from her pocket, and looked down at the screen. It was a text from Mike Berland.

Jenny, sorry to hear about your mother. I hope she's okay. What's going on? M.

"You slimy son of a bitch!" said Willson, enraged, realizing too late that she'd spoken out loud. She looked up at a room full of questioning faces. "My apologies," she said, flushing.

"Anything we need to know about?" asked the staff sergeant.

"No. Sorry. Please continue." She knew the only reason she was being allowed to stay in the room after her outburst was that she was in uniform.

The officer turned back to his team and continued laying out the plan. Willson snuck a look at Fortier standing beside her. His face expressed concern.

"Are you okay?" he whispered. "Do you want to go outside and talk?"

Willson showed him the message. She'd told Fortier about the way the reporter had left the country and exposed her investigation. She hadn't, of course, told him about the empty space Berland had left in her heart.

"What the hell does *he* want?"

"I'm guessing information for another fucking story," Willson said, struggling to keep her voice down. "Jesus. What a dick. This whole thing is his fault, and then he sends me a text like we're still buddies? Does he think I'm fucking stupid?" She slid her finger angrily across the screen, deleting the message.

Thirty minutes later, Willson and Fortier, now in a police SUV, turned onto the Trans-Canada at the north end of Golden. With two police cars ahead of them and one behind, Fortier drove well above the speed limit with his red-and-blue emergency lights flashing. Like the others, his siren was silent. They did not want to announce their approach to the remote cabin.

"You okay, Jenny?" asked Fortier, his eyes on the vehicles ahead of him.

"I want my mother back, safe and sound. Having to watch someone else take control drives me crazy. When I know she's safe, I'll be fine." But Willson knew her mother wouldn't be fine. Far from it. Even if she hadn't been physically harmed by Trueman, the emotional toll on her already fragile psyche could be devastating.

She stared out the window at trees and houses and billboards flashing by as they raced north, then she raised both hands to the back of her head, interlaced her fingers, rested her head against the headrest, and stared at the roof of the police car.

"I fucked this up, Ben," she said, her heart pounding, her guts churning. "And my mother's paying the price."

"This is *not* your fault, Jenny," said Fortier. "We've got the best of the best involved now. If your mother is at that cabin, we'll get her out safely."

Willson dropped her head and noticed that they were passing a line of stopped cars. Fortier's highway patrol colleagues must have stopped the westbound traffic at the truck weigh-station at Donald. She stared at the faces in the car windows as they passed. Wide-eyed and wide-mouthed, they stared back at her and the quartet of police vehicles flying by them, fast and silent.

"It *is* my fault," she said. "I should never have let that fucking journalist into my life … into *our* lives. I may not ever see him again, but if I do, I'll kick his spineless ass from here to the border and back again."

"Hold that thought, Jenny," said Fortier with a chuckle. "I have no doubt you'll do exactly that if given half a chance. But perhaps do it *south* of the border so you're out of my jurisdiction?"

A minute later, they crossed the new bridge over the Columbia River near Donald and raced up the long hill toward the wide curve in the highway that brought them close to the trapper's cabin. Fortier pulled in to the temporary staging area set up at the junction with the old forest road. Around a slight corner to the right, they could see Trueman's truck parked twenty metres ahead on the rough gravel road.

Willson jumped out and began moving toward it.

"Hold on," said the staff sergeant. "You're not going anywhere." He was standing in front of a table that had been set up beside the blue ERT van. The table was covered with various maps, photographs, and radios. "In fact, I don't like that you're here at all," he added, glaring at Fortier, "but since you are, you'll do exactly as I say."

Willson felt Fortier's hand gently come to rest on her shoulder, but she shrugged it off. "My mother's in there," she said to the staff sergeant, stepping closer. "I'm not going to stand around here with my thumb up my ass when she might be hurt or in danger."

Willson saw that the officer wasn't fazed at all by her aggression. "You either stand here like I tell you to," he said, still leaning on the table with his head turned toward her, "or Corporal Fortier will put you in cuffs in the back of his car. It's your choice."

Willson again felt Fortier's hand, now less gentle.

"All right, all right," she said, arms out, palms up. "But what's happening? It looks like you're all standing around doing nothing, wasting time."

"For your information, we have a pair of two-man teams moving in to observe the cabin. They're close, but I won't do anything until I get a full situation report from them. And you won't, either. I have to know what we're dealing with."

"So we just stand here while my mother's in there with that wacko?"

The staff sergeant's mouth curled up in a joyless smile. "Yes. Let us do our jobs. We do this by the book. That's how we get her out of there safely, if she's in there at all."

In that instant, the man's index and middle fingers went up to his ear, to the tiny earpiece Willson knew was there. He tilted his head slightly as he listened.

She watched his face for a clue, a hint of what was happening at the cabin, some sense of whether the ERT members had observed her mother, whether she was still alive. But he gave away nothing.

CHAPTER 37

While the cabbie stowed his luggage in the trunk, Austin climbed into the rear passenger seat, happy to be out of the downpour. He'd stood at the corner of Granville and Hastings for five minutes, juggling his wind-blown umbrella, trying unsuccessfully to flag down passing cabs and ignoring his incessantly ringing phone. He'd almost decided to drag his suitcases and briefcase down the stairs to the Canada Line station two levels below the street when he finally managed to hail what might have been the only empty taxi in downtown Vancouver.

"Airport, please. Main terminal, Air Canada domestic," Austin said to the cabbie as the small man seated himself in the front. He hoped that his curt statement would dissuade the cabbie from trying to make awkward conversation with him.

To emphasize his desire to be left alone, Austin lowered his head to stare at the growing list of emails and texts scrolling and buzzing across the screen of his cellphone. Unwilling to engage with anyone right now, he tossed it onto the seat beside him.

The driver turned left on Howe Street and zigzagged through the downtown traffic, passing hotels and nightclubs and condominiums. The late-afternoon city lights, the traffic signals, the neon signs, the vehicle headlights, all streaked and blurred and ran in the rain.

Just as they reached the north end of the Granville Street Bridge, Austin saw the driver's eyes on him in the rear-view mirror.

"Expecting someone, sir?" the driver said in a heavy accent that hinted at a background in Eastern Europe.

"Sorry?" Austin replied.

"There's a vehicle following us, sir. It ran a second red light in that last intersection. That person there wants to be right behind us."

Austin twisted to look back. Through the wet hatchback window, he saw a pair of headlights close to their rear bumper. But he couldn't see the make or colour of the car, nor could he identify its driver. His heart skipped a beat. What if it was the police or the Securities Commission? If that was the case, however, why no red and blue lights? Or it could be Hank Myers. Or an investor, desperately trying to chase down their money. Or it could simply be a driver who was in as much of a rush to get to the airport as he was. Nothing to worry about. He shifted in his seat to face forward again.

"No," he said to the driver. "I don't know who that is. But I'm in a hurry to catch my flight. There's an extra twenty dollars in it for you if you can get me there fast."

"Yes, sir. I can do that, sir."

Fifteen minutes later, the taxi stopped in front of the domestic terminal at the Vancouver airport. Austin paid the fare and the tip in cash, then climbed out while the driver moved his luggage onto the sidewalk.

"Hey!" a voice yelled.

Austin turned around and recognized Matt Merrix just as the man grabbed him by his lapels. "Where the fuck do you think *you're* going?" said the agent, his eyes wide, teeth bared like a wild animal. "You owe me money!"

Behind Merrix, Austin could see the agent's Audi parked at an odd angle against the curb, its driver-side door open, the engine still running. Now he knew who'd followed them from downtown.

"Take it easy, Matt," said Austin. He looked to the cabbie for help, but the small man was frozen in place, his eyes wide. "I'm heading out on a quick business trip. I'll be back in three days." He tried to pull out of the man's grip without success. He had one hundred pounds on Merrix, but the man was clearly enraged.

"Fuck that," Merrix snarled, giving Austin an extra shake. "You're not going anywhere until you pay back the money you owe me and my clients. You keep promising to pay us out but I haven't seen a fucking cent of it, and I'm tired of your lies. I'm not waiting any longer."

"I told you I had to move some things around and that you would get paid," said Austin, aware of the curious stares of the people passing by them. "You just need to be patient, Matt."

"That's bullshit. I know what kind of scam you're running. I won't be the one who comes out on the short end of the stick while you fly off into the sunset with our money. I won't let that happen." Another shake. "I won't let you ruin me!"

By now, the cabbie had hustled back into his taxi and driven away as fast as his Prius would take him, clearly shocked by the sudden violence. Austin turned to see instead a young RCMP officer, his uniform full of muscle and confidence. He grabbed Merrix's left arm with his meaty hand. "Take your hands off him, sir. What's going on here?"

Both Austin and Merrix tried to speak at the same time.

"I don't know this guy at all," said Austin. "My taxi driver said he chased us all the way here from downtown Vancouver. I don't know if it's road rage or what. Get him off me!"

"This guy stole millions from me, and he's trying to get away!" Merrix said, his eyes still wide, spit flying, rain dripping from his nose.

"First off," said the Mountie, his hand now in the centre of the agent's chest, his eyes boring into him, "back off and don't touch him again or I'll place you under arrest." He looked at the car parked haphazardly behind Merrix. "Is that your vehicle?"

"Yeah, it's mine," said Merrix.

"You can't leave it like that," said the Mountie. "We immediately tow any vehicles that are abandoned this close to the terminal."

"But I'm trying to prevent him from leaving the country!"

The Mountie turned to Austin. "You say you don't know this guy?"

"I have no idea who he is, and I don't know what the hell he's talking about."

"Bullshit!" yelled Merrix. "His name is Stafford Austin. He talked me and my clients into investing money with him, and now he's trying to leave the country without paying me back."

"Calm down," said the officer. "I'll deal with this. I want you to go park your car properly, in one of the lots. Come back here and see me when you're done. What's your name?"

Merrix stood for a moment, obviously confused about what to do. "My name is Matt Merrix. Don't let him leave the country," he whined as he moved toward his car. Behind it, a line of taxis and limos sat waiting for the unloading space, their turn signals on and their wipers clicking impatiently in the rain.

"Go," said the Mountie. "I'll take care of this."

Austin and the officer watched Merrix reluctantly climb into his car and pull away from the curb. As he passed, the agent stared through the passenger-side window, then accelerated quickly.

"You don't know him at all? He seems upset with you. You haven't done business with him?"

Austin did his best imitation of a scared and surprised man. It wasn't difficult. "I've never seen him before. He really startled me. I think there's something wrong with him."

"Show me some ID." The officer reached into his uniform shirt pocket for a notebook. Austin pulled his passport from his suit jacket and handed it to the officer. "You're Brian Clarkson?" asked the officer, looking from the passport to Austin and back again. He wrote in the notebook.

"Yes," said Austin.

"Where do you live?"

My address is in there. I live in Maple Ridge."

"And where are you headed today, Mr. Clarkson?"

"I'm going to Toronto for a three-day business trip. Do you want to see my ticket? My flight leaves in just under an hour."

"No, that's fine." The officer looked at Austin's two suitcases for a moment. "But you're not planning to leave the country, are you?"

"No. Like I said, I'm going to Toronto on business."

"Why two suitcases? That seems a lot for a three-day trip."

"My son is attending the University of Toronto and will be staying out there for the summer," said Austin. "I'm taking him some extra clothes and care packages from his mother."

Austin watched the officer repeatedly tapping his passport against the notebook. "Why did Mr. Merrix suggest that your name is Stafford Austin?"

"I have *no* idea. I've never seen that guy before in my life. He must have me confused with someone else. He seems more than a bit unbalanced. Maybe he's off his meds or something …"

The Mountie paused for a moment, Austin's passport

still in his hand, still tapping it. He stared at Austin, then appeared to make a decision. He handed back the blue-covered document. "Do you want me to charge that guy with assault?"

"No," said Austin, looking and feeling relieved. "I just want to get to my flight. I'd left myself extra time, but after running into that crazy son of a bitch, I'm only just going to make it."

"I have your contact information, Mr. Clarkson, so go ahead and catch your flight. I'll contact you when you get back to Vancouver if I need to. Safe travels."

Austin moved like a man in a hurry. It wasn't difficult because he wanted to put as much time and distance as he could between himself and Merrix and the RCMP officer. He slid his laptop bag over his shoulder, pulled the handles of his two suitcases up, and then, rolling them behind him, he entered the busy domestic departures area without looking back, his suitcases leaving dual tracks on the wet sidewalk.

Less than an hour later, Stafford Austin — a.k.a. Brian Clarkson — was beginning to relax as his Air Canada flight for Toronto lifted off the runway at YVR.

Six hours later, Austin *fully* relaxed when his Air Canada flight for San José, Costa Rica, lifted off the runway at Toronto's Pearson Airport.

Staring out the window as the aircraft passed over Lake Ontario, gradually banking to the south as it climbed, Austin reluctantly accepted that his Canadian project was behind him. Like the other schemes he'd been forced to withdraw from, some of them very quickly, the concept of a ski resort in Collie Creek had ended before its time. He felt a sense of loss for what might have been. He could have taken it further, found more investors, if only he'd had more time. He could have finalized the investment fund for the highway and pipeline if the government had co-operated. That would have raised many more millions. He could have done more with the fake property title he'd created for the old sawmill site at Donald, a site he'd hoped to promote as an oil or gas refinery to Chinese investors. More millions again. But that was a lot of ifs, and all were irrelevant now.

However, unlike the previous times in the U.S. and Chile, Austin was abandoning Collie Creek with a very large sum of money waiting for him. It was money he'd moved to a Costa Rican bank via the Cayman Islands, his to use as he pleased, and if he was careful it would keep him comfortable for many years. For the first time in his adult life, he imagined himself calling somewhere home for a few years instead of months. This would be a new experience for him. He thought about the many willing, dark-haired *ticas* he'd met on his last trip to San José. From experience, he knew he'd be able to entice one of them to join him in his new life, agree to his becoming her *tio rico*, or "rich uncle." Money could do that.

He closed his eyes and anticipated the sights, sounds, and smells of his new hilltop house overlooking Manuel Antonio National Park, with the Pacific Ocean beyond: the rich, humid air; white-throated capuchin monkeys chattering and scrambling through the trees beside his expansive west-facing deck; in the afternoon heat, the constant tinny buzz of cicadas in the massive fichus trees in his yard. He imagined day's end, the sun dropping into the ocean like a stone, an ice-cold Guaro Sour in his hand, a barely clad young woman beside him, illuminated in the warm afterglow of —

A light touch on his shoulder broke Austin's train of thought. He turned to see a smiling flight attendant leaning over his business-class seat. "Would you like something to drink, Mr. Clarkson?"

"Yes," he said, smiling back. "It's time to celebrate. Bring me a glass of your best Scotch, please, with a bit of water. Make it a double."

CHAPTER 38

"Alpha team reports three adults at the cabin," said the staff sergeant. "All inside. Appears to be two females and one male. We've got eyes on them through a window on the south side. There's a dirt bike parked near the north side of the building, but no other vehicles present."

"Three?" asked Willson. "Who's the third?"

The officer listened to a broadcast on his earpiece. "No confirmed ID on any of the three yet, but they're thinking it *is* your mother and Trueman there. Any idea who the male may be?"

"No idea," said Willson. "I guess it could be John Theroux, although I think he would've told us if he'd found out where his wife was hiding. Maybe it's the trapper … maybe Trueman knows him?"

"It's not the trapper," said Fortier. "I called him earlier to get a sketch of the cabin for these guys. He was in Calgary with his wife. He doesn't know Trueman *or* Theroux. He says if someone's in there, they must've broken in."

Fortier and Willson walked toward Trueman's truck and then returned to the staging area. "There are no fresh bike tracks on the road there," said Willson. "Beyond the truck. So whoever it is must have ridden in from somewhere else. Is there another access road to the cabin?"

The staff sergeant pointed to the Google Earth image. "There's a rough track that leads from the cabin back to the Donald Forest Service Road. Here. The male suspect must have come in that way. I've got a team watching that spot, as well." His hand moved to his ear again. "Hang tough. Bravo team reports that the male has opened the cabin door and is moving toward the bike. He's wearing a coat, carrying a pack, and is putting on a helmet." A pause. "He appears to be leaving."

"Alpha and Bravo teams, this is command," said the sergeant. "If the male tries to leave the property, let him go. We'll either arrest him down here when he gets to us, or Charlie team will take him when he reaches the other road."

A moment later, they all jumped and turned their heads at the sound of gunfire. Two pops from the direction of the cabin followed by silence. Then four more pops.

"Sitrep!" yelled the staff sergeant over the radio. "What's happening out there, teams?"

Willson was already moving. The thought of her mother in the middle of a gun battle was more than she could stand. As she ran by Trueman's truck, she pulled her pistol from its holster and held it by her leg as she raced up the gravel road. She could hear both the staff sergeant and Fortier yelling at her to stop, but she was beyond listening to them. All thoughts were for her mother.

She'd run only a few hundred metres when she heard the sound of a dirt bike ahead of her, the engine screaming. She heard footsteps behind her as well, and assumed it was Fortier following her up the road. She ignored them, keeping her attention ahead. The bike was coming at her through the trees to her right. She hurdled over an overgrown ditch and crashed into the forest, her pistol out in front of her.

Catching a flash of movement, Willson changed her trajectory and saw the helmeted man on the bike reach the edge of an opening in the trees. He turned his head and saw her just as she saw him. He raised his arm, and she felt burning around her left bicep at the same time as she heard the crack of the gun. Grunting, she jumped and rolled behind a spruce tree. She peeked around the trunk and saw the man coming toward her on the bike, his head swivelling, searching for her, the helmet visor black and menacing.

Willson scrambled to her feet, stepped out from behind the tree, and fired three rounds directly at the man's torso just like she'd been taught, just like she'd practised hundreds of times on the range. With the impact of the bullets, the rider's hands lifted off the handlebars. He flew off the back of the bike. The engine raced for a second, and then, with a bang, the motor-cycle collided with a tree.

There was so much adrenalin in Willson's bloodstream that she barely felt the pain from the wound in her arm. She kept her pistol aimed at the now prone man. Breathing hard, she crossed the distance between them, carefully stepping over a downed tree.

She saw the man's pistol first, lying on the forest floor where he'd dropped it. She kicked it away from him. Standing over him, she saw three dark marks in the centre of his jacket. Normally she'd be pleased with her shooting. It had probably saved her life. But she was rattled by the sudden turn of events, and the reality of having needed to shoot another human being.

She knelt and used her injured arm to check for a carotid pulse, keeping the gun on the man with her right. No pulse. She yanked the helmet off his head and gasped when she saw Hank Myers's face staring up at her, eyes open but lifeless. "You son of a bitch.... That's the last fucking time you'll threaten me or my family."

She heard a sudden crashing behind her and spun quickly, moving her pistol in an arc as she turned. Just as she was about to squeeze the trigger, Fortier emerged from behind a copse of trees, his own pistol out in front of him.

"It's me, Jenny," said Fortier, gasping for breath, raising one hand as if in surrender. "Are you all right?"

Willson suddenly felt the sharp pain in her injured arm and dropped her pistol. "I think I've been hit, Ben, but you should see the other guy ..." She slumped to a sitting position on the forest floor, her back against a log.

Fortier knelt beside her and placed his hand gently on her shoulder above the injury. "Are you okay?"

"Like they say in the cowboy movies, I think he only winged me." She grimaced. "It hurts like hell. It might be a while before I can play the violin again ..." She smiled a weak smile, the effects of the adrenalin beginning to fade. She knew that shock would soon follow.

Fortier remained beside her, staring at the body on the forest floor beside them. "Is that who I think it is?" he asked.

"Hank Myers."

"What's Myers doing out here?"

"I don't know. He sure as hell can't tell us now."

"Is he dead?"

"Yes."

"Shit, Jenny. I can't believe you took off like that. The staff sergeant was yelling at me to get you back, but you were too damn fast, like a jackrabbit. What a crazy-ass thing to do!"

Willson started to rise. "Ben, we have to get my mother away from Trueman …"

"Take it easy, Jenny," Fortier said, his hand still on her shoulder, gently holding her down. "Sit for a moment longer. Your mother is okay, and you're going to need an ambulance. As soon as the first shots rang out, the ERT teams moved in on the cabin, arrested Trueman, and they've advised us that your mother is safe. She's shaken up, but she's fine."

Willson stood up shakily, with Fortier supporting her. "I need to see her. Let's get to the cabin. What the hell happened?"

"Myers tried to leave on his bike, up the back road. When he saw the ERT guys, he fired two shots at them, they shot back, and then he took off through the trees to here. Those guys don't miss, so I bet we'll find other holes in him. And then you ruined the rest of his day."

He looked down at Myers. "Dumb bastard. Let's go find your mother. She'll be happy to see you."

When Willson finally saw the trapper's cabin, it was not what she had expected. Rather than a rough log structure with a mossy roof and a pit privy, it was a large building, relatively new, with big picture windows, a steel roof, and even a new barbeque outside. It was obviously used for more than just trapping.

Desperate to see that her mother was indeed safe, she scanned the scene quickly. With the situation under control, most of the ERT members stood in a relaxed circle. The centre of everyone's attention was Sandy Trueman, who sat on the gravel in front of the building. Her hands were cuffed behind her back, the right side of her face was dirty and scratched, and her hair stuck up as if windblown. With a black-uniformed officer on each side of her, she looked like a wild animal after capture — wide-eyed, frightened, and clearly confused about what had happened.

When Willson locked eyes with Trueman, the woman struggled against her bonds and tried to stand. But two sets of gloved hands pushed her to the ground.

"You fucking bitch!" Trueman screamed. "You ruined everything!" She tried to fight off the two Mounties holding her down, but they were too strong.

Willson ignored the woman's rabid outburst. "Where is she? Where's my mum?"

Fortier pointed to a nearby firepit. Willson saw her mother at the same time that her mother noticed her.

She was sitting on a stump, rocking, hands clasped in front of her. A female ERT officer stood beside her. Mother and daughter moved toward each other at the same time, meeting with a hug in the middle of the yard. Willson grunted when her mother gripped her injured arm, but continued to hold her tight, ignoring the pain. Finally, she pulled back and looked into her eyes. "Are you okay, Mum?"

Her mother's eyes were brimming with tears. "I am so sorry, Jenny."

"You have no reason to be sorry, Mum. This wasn't your fault. I'm the one who should be sorry. I should have been there to protect you from these people. I should have realized that my obsession with taking them down could endanger you." She held her mother at arm's length, looking her up and down. "Did they hurt you?"

"I was so scared, but no, they didn't hurt me." Willson saw her mother's eyes drop and take in the blood on her arm. "Oh my god! What happened to you?"

"I'll be all right. Hank Myers and I had … a bit of an altercation in the forest back there. He got the worst of it."

Her mother began to cry again, deep sobs this time. Willson gripped her hard, letting her mother's head rest on her shoulder.

"I am so, so sorry, Jenny," said her mother, speaking in ragged, breathless sentences as tears poured down her cheeks. "I never should have trusted that man. I had no idea this would happen … I really thought he was a friend. I never wanted to hurt you."

"I know, I know. What happened, Mum? How did you end up with them?"

"I … Hank invited me for dinner. He seemed so nice, so willing to listen to me. It's been a long time since someone seemed so interested in me. I should have known better … and you warned me about him. Mike did, too."

"It's okay. You had dinner?"

"We went to that new restaurant on the highway. I enjoyed myself, although maybe I had one more glass of wine than I should have. We talked and laughed. And then that Trueman woman showed up."

"Was Myers expecting her?"

"He didn't seem surprised that she was there. Right away, she started talking about the ski resort, trying to persuade me that it was a good idea, that I should support it. She was really aggressive."

"But why was she trying to convince you?"

"She said you were getting in the way — I needed to get you to back off."

"What did you do?"

"I told them that I didn't know anything about it … that I didn't know anything about what you were doing. I said they should talk to you directly. But some of the things she said made sense, and she was awfully persuasive. After a while I started to get confused …"

Willson's stomach turned sour with guilt, realizing that her fervent investigation had victimized her mother. She had inadvertently put her mother in the centre of things and almost gotten her killed. "Then what?" she asked gently.

The tears flowed again. "And then I don't remember anything until I woke up here, in this cabin in the middle of nowhere, with a bad headache and no idea how

I got here … and that insane woman ranting about getting revenge on you for killing the project."

Willson thought about Myers lying dead in the forest. The bastard must have drugged her mother when they were at dinner, following through on the threat he'd made when they'd last met. Now, she felt even better about putting three bullets in his chest. She stared over at Trueman, fighting the urge to do the same to her. "I saw you on a security tape, Mum, setting fire to a studio south of town."

"She had a gun, Jenny! She made me do it. She said she'd kill me if I didn't, and then she'd kill you, too. I was still feeling groggy, and I was more scared than I've ever been my whole life!"

"Oh, Mum. Do you know why Myers came here today?"

"I think he came to ask Trueman if she knew where Stafford Austin was. He seemed to think that Austin had skipped town. They argued and yelled at each other. When Hank finally left, I thought Trueman was going to kill me. She was storming around the cabin, muttering, waving the gun around … I felt like it was all my fault, like I could have done something to change things. And I thought that Hank might be coming after you next …"

Willson hugged her mother again, holding her tight, ignoring the flashing pain in her arm. "It's okay, Mum. We're both safe. These people won't hurt us anymore."

She looked at Fortier, who stared back with deep compassion in his eyes. She dipped her head and whispered into her mother's ear. "I am so sorry I put you through this. It's over now."

CHAPTER 39

The aroma of freshly brewed Kick Ass coffee was wafting through the house when Willson heard a knock at the front door. Wiping her hands on a towel, she walked through the hall to open the creaky door.

"Is the coffee ready yet?" asked Frank Speer, a smile on his face. He was in civilian clothes, and his head showed the obvious white forehead of a man who normally wore a hat, like a rancher or a farmer. "I need a cup, bad ..." he said.

Behind him stood Jack Church, looking down at the gaping floorboards on the porch. "Jesus, isn't this thing condemned yet?" The Yoho Park superintendent smiled wryly at Willson. "And make that two cups. I like mine with milk and sugar — lots of both."

"Come in, gentlemen," said Willson, standing aside to let them in. "Make yourselves at home. Coffee's coming right up."

With one hand, Willson brought a cutting board back from the kitchen on which she'd placed three full mugs of coffee, a bowl of sugar cubes, a small jug of milk, and a trio of spoons. It was the poor woman's version of a fancy serving tray. The two men had already seated themselves in two mismatched chairs in the living room. Willson placed the board on the wobbly coffee table — really just rough plywood on four plastic milk crates — and sat in a lawn chair that had seen better days.

"Damn, that's good coffee," said Church, after his first noisy sip. "Kicking Horse?"

Willson smiled and nodded. "Where to start? A lot's happened in the last few weeks."

"You've been busy as hell, Jenny, since I saw you last," said Speer. "How's the arm?"

"I was lucky," she said, unconsciously touching her left arm, which was still heavily bandaged and in a sling. "The bullet went right through my tricep. Missed my deep brachial artery by centimetres. The muscle will take time to heal, and it probably won't ever be as strong as it was before. But it's better than if I'd been hit somewhere else."

"I'm relieved you're a better shot than Myers was," Speer said. Willson flashed back to the dead man lying in the forest, three bullets in his chest. She felt neither guilt nor sadness. The son of a bitch got what he deserved. "I'm glad you're okay. And your mother? How is she?"

"She's really struggling. She thinks what happened to me, to us, was all her fault. She talks about it every time I see her, keeps apologizing, no matter what I say. But she has been seeing a PTSD counsellor since we rescued her, so I hope she'll be able to work through it. It's gonna take a while, though. She was already suffering from depression, and this experience sure as hell didn't help."

"Give her my best," said Speer. "Let me know when she might be up for a visit."

"I'll do that. She and I are going out for dinner tonight."

Church put his cup down, but held out his hand for a moment, ready to grab the handle in case it toppled off the table. "So, what did you learn when you interviewed John Theroux and Sandy Trueman afterward?" he asked.

"Ben — Corporal Fortier and I spoke to Trueman first," said Willson. "That was an interesting conversation, to say the least. It turns out that she has bipolar disorder, and had stopped taking her medication. If she was having trouble managing it before this whole business, her involvement in the ski resort project made it even worse. But I used her anger toward me to get her to talk. I apologized for my role in what happened, and asked her to tell us why she was so upset. We didn't have to push her very hard to get her to admit to everything: starting the fire that killed Sue Webb, breaking the window at the coffee shop to try to shift blame onto the anti–ski area folks, abducting my mother and forcing her to burn down Sara Ilsley's studio and vandalize her house. She admitted to all of it, saying it was all justified because getting the ski area approved was so important. She firmly believes that the project's demise was because of my meddling, that I somehow made her do all those things. In her mind, it was all my fault."

"Do you think she acted on her own?"

"I think her husband knows more than he's willing to say. Trueman told us that Austin had offered them good jobs at the resort and a big payday if it was approved."

"How much money are we talking about?"

"Not much when you think of the millions that would be needed to build the resort. Maybe a few hundred thousand or so. But it was more than they'd ever had their hands on. It must have seemed like a fortune to Trueman."

"Do you think Austin and Myers knew? Did they maybe tell her what to do?"

"We'll never know for sure, with Myers dead and Austin out of the country. But I'm thinking that at the very least, Myers knew what was going on. They were using Trueman as a means to an end. She was like a rogue scud missile fired without a clear target in mind …"

"What did her husband say about it?" asked Speer.

"Theroux told us that once his wife saw the potential dollar signs and got a sniff of the prestige they might have in the community, she went off the deep end. He supported the resort, but he couldn't control her. He says that she did it all on her own, but he tried to stop her. He's got no loyalty to her after all, that's for sure. He seems willing to blame her for all of it. And because of her current mental state, it's an easy play."

"And Austin has definitely left the country? He's not just hiding somewhere?"

Willson shook her head. "He's gone. At Ben Fortier's urging, the RCMP put out an all-points bulletin for him. It turns out that he left Canada on a false passport. An officer actually spoke to him at the Vancouver airport, but let him go."

"Shit. Anyone know where he went?"

"I tracked him through Toronto, then onto a flight to San José in Costa Rica. I assume he's there because it's a non-extradition country. But he could still be travelling under yet another name, so there's no way to know for sure. For what it's worth, I let that Chilean private investigator know about Austin's movements. I'm betting he's hard on Austin's trail now. Costa Rica, or wherever he is now, may not be as comfortable as he thinks it'll be …"

Speer shook his head. "And what about the money?"

"I don't know yet. I've spoken with an officer in the RCMP's commercial crime section. She'd just begun to pose as a potential investor and met with Austin once. She thinks that he moved millions out of the country, maybe tens of millions, before he flew away. And I reinterviewed a sports agent who represented some of the money invested with Austin. He was particularly pissed off because he was one of the last people to see the guy before he left the country. He'd tried to talk a Mountie into detaining Austin at the Vancouver airport, but had no proof that he was anyone other than the guy listed in the false passport."

"Ouch," said Speer.

"Ouch is right," Willson said. "He and his clients' money literally flew away. Based on our interviews with him and other investors who've since come forward, I think our original estimate of the missing money is low. I'm no accountant, but I think it was a classic example of a Ponzi scheme on a very large scale. He left a string of furious investors behind. For his sake, he'd better keep one hell of a low profile. There *will* be people looking for him, from here and his previous escapades."

Church moved forward in his chair. "I understand from my sources in Ottawa that someone in the PM's office has somehow been implicated in all of this. Is that true?"

"Yep," said Willson. "In her desire to lay the blame on everyone around her, Trueman told us all about a man named Brian Cummings, who is, or *was*, before he was fired, a senior policy adviser in the PMO — as well as Theroux's cousin. Apparently, he was urging them to keep going because, according to Trueman, 'the Prime Minister wanted the project to proceed so he could justify building the highway through Howse Pass.' But of course, the prime minister is distancing himself from the whole thing. You'll see it in the news tomorrow. He said Cummings was acting without his knowledge or authorization. Now that the questions are out there, though, they'll only get louder. There's also a female MP from Alberta who's under investigation for taking money from Austin in order to get government contracts to build the new highway."

"That goddamn highway again," said Church, shaking his head. "What I can't figure out is how that American journalist got the inside information that led to all of this happening. Any ideas, Jenny? Or do I not want to know?"

Willson glanced at Speer, then stared at Church. "Would you like more coffee?"

"No thanks. If I have another cup, I'll be awake until next week," said Church.

"If you don't mind, I'd like to ask you two some questions," said Willson. "First, have you heard what's happening with the ski area application?"

"It's as dead as Hank Myers," said Speer, "pure and simple."

"For sure?" asked Willson.

"The funeral is well under way," he confirmed. "The federal and provincial governments jointly announced this morning that they've disallowed the project, claiming that their review showed it to be neither viable nor sustainable. The fact that the proponent skipped the country is almost irrelevant. The politicians are running away from that thing as fast as their scrawny little legs will carry them."

Willson was surprised — although perhaps she shouldn't have been — by the speed at which the two governments had closed rank and slammed the door on the project. "No mention of the Ponzi scheme, the violence, or back-room influence peddling?"

"Nope," Church said. "In fact, they're talking about re-amending the federal legislation so that no new ski areas in parks will be allowed."

Willson smiled. "Back to the future, then?"

"Exactly." Church nodded.

"Can they file charges against Austin?"

"They can, but if you're right about him being in Costa Rica, he's essentially untouchable."

"That leads me to my second question," Willson said. "Where does this leave us? The three of us, I mean?"

Speer and Church looked at each other for a moment. Church was the first to respond. "I'm being transferred to a national park in Ontario. I'm not being blamed for this mess, per se, but I should have listened to Jack when he tried to warn me, back at the beginning of this thing."

Willson looked at her old boss. "And you, Jack?"

"I'm pulling the pin at the end of July."

"Why? You weren't ready to go, were you?"

"No, I wasn't," said Speer. "But let's just say that this bullshit made me realize I had better things to do with my life than work for the federal government."

"And what about me? I know my actions caused you grief. And I know it's because of me that they're sending *you* east and making *you* retire early. I'm sorry about that. I truly am. Although at the same time, I know I've been a pain in the ass to those above you on the food chain, and I'm not sorry about *that* at all."

Speer laughed. "Jenny, I knew what I was getting into when I agreed to you doing what you did. I knew you would do what you thought best, despite whatever I might say. While you did go off script, I had no way of knowing where it would lead. I understood that letting you loose was for the best."

Willson sat back in her chair, appreciating the fact that Speer had not told Church about her connection with Mike Berland. "So I'm guessing you're here to tell me, perhaps as one of your last official acts, that I'm going to have to find another job?"

"Not exactly," said Speer.

"What, then?"

"The folks in Ottawa can't figure out if you're the hero in this for exposing the illegitimate scheme behind the ski area and saving their asses from huge embarrassment … or, if you win this year's prize for the most insubordinate employee in the entire federal government."

Willson smiled. "I'd be happy if both were true. So what happens?"

The two men looked at each other. With a nod from Speer, Church spoke. "What happens now is that we advise you that your request for the Namibian secondment has been approved, for up to twelve months."

"Are you friggin' kidding me? I assumed they'd never let me go after what happened."

"I'm not kidding. You can look at it as either being banished overseas for a year, out of their hair and hard for the media to find … or as a reward for a job well done."

Willson had worked for government long enough to know that it was never this easy. "What's the catch?"

"If you accept the secondment," Church said, "then I've been told to tell you that while you're away, you should think about if and how you'll come back to be part of the team, play by the rules, follow directions. In essence, to do as you're told."

"And if I don't accept those conditions? As you both know, that really doesn't sound like me —"

"Then I've been told to advise you that Namibia is off the table, and we have an opportunity for you to transfer to Gros Morne National Park in Newfoundland. It's not a voluntary transfer."

"Wow," said Willson. "They *do* want me to disappear. That's about as far east as I could be sent while still being in Canada."

Neither man said anything in response.

"Those are my choices?" asked Willson.

"They are," said Church. "What do you say?"

Willson grinned. Really, she had only one option. "I say 'Hello, Air Canada? I need to book a flight to Windhoek, Namibia.'"

* * *

As Willson drove toward her mother's house to pick her up for dinner, she understood that she was in a no-win situation. Pulling to the side of the road, she stared out the windshield, her eyes unfocused. She knew going to Namibia was the best thing to do in light of all that had transpired. She needed to get out of the country for a while, away from the bigwigs who were trying to silence her ... or move her. She needed time to think, to decide what she wanted to do with the rest of her life, to come to terms with her professional and personal challenges. And while she would have that time if she accepted the transfer to Newfoundland, she'd be separated from her mother by almost the entire width of a very large country. And she'd still be dealing with the same federal government, the same people at the top.

For a moment, Willson thought about Mike Berland. The anger and betrayal of a few weeks earlier had been replaced by a sense of melancholy. It was less about what might have been with him than about that short glimpse she'd had of having a supportive, attentive person in her life. It had felt good, as if it might soften some of her edges and make her less cynical about the world around her. But Berland was not in the picture and never would be. She needed someone she could trust. And she needed to move on.

At the same time, she understood that her mother needed her more than ever now, that she'd be devastated by the news that her daughter might move away for up to a year, perhaps longer. Would going to Namibia be smart … or incredibly selfish and thoughtless? She thought about alternatives. Her mother couldn't join her in Africa *or* Newfoundland; that simply wouldn't work. Would she consider leaving Golden and moving closer to her distant cousin in Kamloops? That wasn't a conversation they'd ever had.

Willson shook her head. She'd have to talk to her mother, lay out the facts as she saw them. Maybe they could come to a decision together. And because she had little time to make that decision, she'd have to start the conversation over dinner tonight.

A few minutes later, Willson pulled up to her mother's house and parked behind the Honda in the driveway. She walked to the front door, knocked once, and walked in. "Mum?" she called, looking first in the living room and then the kitchen. "Anyone home?" The house was silent. After checking the empty bathroom, Willson opened the door to her mother's bedroom. She peeked around the door and saw her mother in bed, the covers tucked to her chin, her thin greying hair spread across the pillow.

"Mum?" said Willson as she moved across the room. "Time to go to dinner …" Her mother did not move, did not answer. Willson touched her right cheek. It was cold. She moved her left fingers to her mother's neck to check for a pulse. Nothing.

Willson gasped, stood up straight, and looked around the room. Her heart pounded but she was too shocked for tears. She saw the pill bottle on the bedside table next to a glass of water. The glass was nearly empty. As if in a trance, she reached for the empty bottle. Norpramin. Her mother's antidepressant medication.

It was then that Willson saw the piece of paper on the dresser, neatly folded. She moved slowly toward it, frightened of what it might contain, terrified that it held a message from which there would be no return. Time stood still as she unfolded it. She saw her mother's writing, the cursive letters perfect and even, bringing back memories of notes in school lunches.

> *My darling Jenny —*
> *I am deeply sorry for the pain and trouble I caused you. I was searching for friendship, but I made the wrong decision. It broke my heart that I hurt you, and almost caused your death. I can never forgive myself, but I hope you can forgive me.*
> *I love you forever and will always be proud of you,*
> *Mum*

And then the tears came. They flooded Willson's eyes and ran down her cheeks, dampened her blouse. She slumped to the floor, her back to the dresser, her mother's letter gripped tightly in her hand.

CHAPTER 40

The Golden library was filled with flowers, with their mingled scents, the colours of thousands of books overwhelmed by a rainbow of carnations and daisies, marigolds and sweet peas, exotic gardenias and heliconias and orchids.

Willson stood in a circle of her mother's friends and colleagues, women whose children she'd grown up with. Her hands were wrapped around a mug of tea, despite wanting something much stronger. While she nodded her head from time to time, she wasn't truly listening. The conversation around her was nothing more than voices in a dense bank of grey fog, faceless, shapeless people who were hollow in their awkward attempts at comfort. This gathering, in a place that had meant so much to her mother, was a celebration of her life, a tribute to the unassuming woman and the quiet, low-key role she'd played in Golden for decades. At her mother's request, it was an afternoon tea party. No speeches, few tears, a story or two shared in small groups, friends meeting to recognize a life well lived.

But for Willson, her mother's absence was a massive, gaping hole. The most important person in her life was gone, the family of three she'd been raised in cut down to one. And it all came back to Stafford Austin, his deceitful attempt to start a ski area in Collie Creek, and the deadly chain of events that had followed. An innocent victim of a scam gone wrong, Anne Willson had paid the ultimate price for Austin's greed. Willson tried hard not to think about what might have been if she hadn't been so blinded by her own desire to stop the project. The guilt would be a permanent scar, deep and disfiguring, a constant reminder of the role she'd played in her mother's death.

In the days since her mother had taken her own life, Willson had operated on autopilot, moving around town like an impassive cyborg. She had settled her mother's legal and financial affairs, sold the Honda, and leased her mother's house to Ben Fortier and the now-pregnant Courtney Pepper. And most importantly, she'd made decisions for herself, for her future.

Her gaze wandered across the room without purpose. She saw women stealing glances at her, clearly wondering whether they should approach her, unsure of what they might say if they did. Standing in the shelves of the fiction section, she saw Ben Fortier, Courtney Pepper, Albin Stoffel, and the mayor, Jo-Ann Campbell. Ignoring the sad, questioning eyes around her, Willson worked her way over to that group.

"You know how sorry we all are," said Fortier, wrapping his strong arm around Willson's shoulder. Pepper moved in and gripped her old friend around the waist.

"I know," said Willson. "Thank you all for being here today. It means a lot to me."

The mayor smiled sadly at her. "We were just talking about how this community has been impacted by Austin's ridiculous idea. You and your mother paid the ultimate price, Jenny, there is no doubt. For that I am truly sorry. I've been thinking about it a lot these last couple of weeks, and I still find myself sad, angry, and confused. I feel like I should have taken the bull by the horns and shut this thing down earlier, as mayor. But in retrospect, I don't think I could have. At no time did we have any control. That bloody application cleaved this town like a giant axe; it may never come back together again. Now we're all left to pick up the pieces, find a way to heal. It's not right."

Willson nodded.

"You might think this inappropriate," said Albin Stoffel, "and if you do, I sincerely apologize — that's not my intention. But do you know who has benefited from this situation? The wolverines in Collie Creek. With the proposal disallowed, and the park legislation about to be changed, they will have the valley to themselves, hopefully for years to come. That's a good thing."

Willson thought back to the wolverine tracks she'd seen when she visited the Collie Creek valley with Mike Berland. She raised her mug toward the ceiling. "Here's to wolverines and wilderness," she said, "the only good news to come out of this whole friggin' mess." As she spoke, she felt a tap on her shoulder and turned to see Tracy Brown from the U.S. Fish and Wildlife Service. Her dark, curly hair framing her wide eyes and dark skin, the American agent was dressed in jeans, a white blouse, a dark-brown leather jacket, and hiking shoes.

"Sorry I'm late, Jenny," she said, after the two women had shared a long hug. "And I'm so sorry for your loss."

"I'm happy you're here, Tracy," said Willson, staring into her friend's eyes. "Thank you for coming this way so we could travel together." She introduced Brown to her circle of friends and colleagues, explaining to them why they were heading to Namibia.

An hour later, Willson found Brown talking to Ben Fortier in a quiet corner of the library. Like many curious visitors to Canada, she was asking him about the RCMP, about whether he always got his man, about his red serge, his horse, his log cabin.

"We have to go, Trace," said Willson, touching Brown lightly on the shoulder. "It'll take about three hours to get to the Calgary airport. Our flight to Frankfurt leaves just before six."

Willson turned to Fortier. In an instant, she was at a loss for words, not knowing what to say. She simply hugged him hard. Finally releasing him, she put her hands on his wide shoulders and stared into his eyes for a moment, long enough for it to be meaningful but not long enough to make him, or his fiancée, uncomfortable. "Saying thank you, Ben, is not enough. Meeting you and working with you meant more to me than you will ever know. I'll miss you."

"We'll all miss you, Jenny. Safe travels."

Willson turned and walked away. After saying a heart-felt goodbye to Heather, the head librarian, and sincerely thanking her for all that she'd done for her mother, Willson left the building, waved at Brown, who would follow her in her own car, and drove out of Golden.

As she headed up the hill to the east of town, she pulled over to a viewpoint on the side of the highway and climbed out of her Subaru. Brown steered in behind her, but stayed in her car.

Willson looked down at Golden, at the rushing milky waters of the Kicking Horse River that bisected the town, and the smoke rising from the mill at the north end. A train crawled northward along the main line. Cars zipped along the main street downtown.

At the southern edge of town, she could see the ceme-tery where, three days earlier, she had laid her mother to rest beside her father. A single tear fell down her cheek. She hoped they would both find peace in being together again, this time forever.

A warm wind blew at her from the west, and she could see towering cumulus clouds building and boiling and threatening there, signalling an oncoming storm.

As Willson stared down at her birthplace spread out below her, she couldn't help thinking that the real storm had, in many ways, already passed through Golden. It was time for people to come out from behind closed doors and work together to rebuild the community's confidence.

With her mother gone and her career with Parks Canada in question, at least for the next year, she recog-nized that the storm had passed for her, as well. There was nothing more to hold her here, and she had no role to play in the town's healing. She was not sad about that — it was simply her new reality. It was as if she and the town had completely and inexplicably changed, as if they'd somehow grown apart. It was time for them both to move on.

Willson turned away, slid back into the driver's seat, checked over her shoulder for traffic coming up the hill, and accelerated back onto the Trans-Canada Highway. As she entered the narrow valley of the Kicking Horse River, her mind was clearly focused on the road ahead.

ACKNOWLEDGEMENTS

It is a privilege to continue to share the adventures of Jenny Willson. While writing is mostly a solitary endeavour, I'm fortunate to be surrounded by a growing group of cheerleaders — family, close friends, fellow authors, and readers — who support and encourage me in countless ways. I truly appreciated the frank feedback I received on early versions of this novel from beta-readers: my wife, Heather, Darrell Bethune, Stan Chung, and Ian Cobb. It is a better story because of their efforts. Thanks again to my law-enforcement adviser, Sergeant Chris Newel of the RCMP. Despite his great advice, any errors in law or procedure are mine.

Thanks to the team at Dundurn Press. Dundurn is a leading independent publisher offering Canadian books from across the country, and I'm pleased to collaborate with this passionate and hard-working group. Thanks to editor Allison Hirst, "Dundurn's resident woman of mystery" (*Quill and Quire*), whose rigorous attention to detail and critical ear for tight dialogue and pacing make my writing stronger and more compelling. Thanks also to senior designer Laura Boyle, who creates kick-ass book covers! Special thanks to talented publicist Michelle Melski, who is patient and proactive and professional, and to assistant project editor Jenny McWha, copy editor Catharine Chen, and Beth Bruder, Margaret Bryant, and the many others at Dundurn.

I am in awe of libraries and booksellers across Canada, indies most of all, who strive to get good books into the hands of readers. I sincerely appreciate all they do for Canadian literature.

And finally, I would like to acknowledge that this novel was written and largely set in the traditional territories of the Ktunaxa and Shuswap First Nations.

I dedicate this book to my daughter Courtney and my son-in-law Curtis. You are amazing parents to Mason and Peyton, and you're both shining examples of Canada's accounting profession. Every day, I'm extremely proud of who you are and what you do.

MYSTERY AND CRIME FICTION FROM DUNDURN PRESS

Birder Murder Mysteries
by Steve Burrows
(BIRDING, BRITISH COASTAL TOWN MYSTERIES)
A Siege of Bitterns
A Pitying of Doves
A Cast of Falcons
A Shimmer of Hummingbirds
A Tiding of Magpies

Amanda Doucette Mysteries
by Barbara Fradkin
(PTSD, CROSS-CANADA TOUR)
Fire in the Stars
The Trickster's Lullaby
Prisoners of Hope

B.C. Blues Crime Novels
by R.M. Greenaway
(BRITISH COLUMBIA, POLICE PROCEDURAL)
Cold Girl
Undertow
Creep
Coming soon: *Flights and Falls*

Stonechild & Rouleau Mysteries
by Brenda Chapman
(FIRST NATIONS, KINGSTON, POLICE PROCEDURAL)
Cold Mourning
Butterfly Kills
Tumbled Graves
Shallow End
Bleeding Darkness
Coming soon: *Turning Secrets*

Jack Palace Series
by A.G. Pasquella
(NOIR, TORONTO, MOB)
Yard Dog

Jenny Willson Mysteries
by Dave Butler
(NATIONAL PARKS, ANIMAL PROTECTTION)
Full Curl
No Place for Wolverines

Falls Mysteries
by Jayne Barnard
(RURAL ALBERTA, FEMALE SLEUTH)
When the Flood Falls

Foreign Affairs Mysteries
by Nick Wilkshire
(GLOBAL CRIME FICTION, HUMOUR)
Escape to Havana
The Moscow Code
Remember Tokyo

Dan Sharp Mysteries
by Jeffrey Round
(LGBTQ, TORONTO)
Lake on the Mountain
Pumpkin Eater
The Jade Butterfly
After the Horses
The God Game
Coming soon: *Shadow Puppet*

Max O'Brien Mysteries
by Mario Bolduc
(TRANSLATION, POLITICAL THRILLER, CON MAN)
The Kashmir Trap
The Roma Plot
The Tanzania Conspiracy

Cullen and Cobb Mysteries
by David A. Poulsen
(CALGARY, PRIVATE INVESTIGATORS, ORGANIZED CRIME)
Serpents Rising
Dead Air
Last Song Sung

Strange Things Done
by Elle Wild
(YUKON, DARK THRILLER)

Salvage
by Stephen Maher
(NOVA SCOTIA, FAST-PACED THRILLER)

Crang Mysteries
by Jack Batten
(Humour, Toronto)
Crang Plays the Ace
Straight No Chaser
Riviera Blues
Blood Count
Take Five
Keeper of the Flame
Booking In

Jack Taggart Mysteries
by Don Easton
(Undercover Operations)
Loose Ends
Above Ground
Angel in the Full Moon
Samurai Code
Dead Ends
Birds of a Feather
Corporate Asset
The Benefactor
Art and Murder
A Delicate Matter
Subverting Justice
An Element of Risk

Meg Harris Mysteries
by R.J. Harlick
(Canadian Wilderness Fiction, First Nations)
Death's Golden Whisper
Red Ice for a Shroud
The River Runs Orange
Arctic Blue Death
A Green Place for Dying
Silver Totem of Shame
A Cold White Fear
Purple Palette for Murder

Thaddeus Lewis Mysteries
by Janet Kellough
(Pre-Confederation Canada)
On the Head of a Pin
Sowing Poison
47 Sorrows
The Burying Ground
Wishful Seeing

Cordi O'Callaghan Mysteries
by Suzanne F. Kingsmill
(Zoology, Mental Illness)
Forever Dead
Innocent Murderer
Dying for Murder
Crazy Dead

Endgame
by Jeffrey Round
(Modern Re-telling of Agatha Christie, Punk Rock)

Inspector Green Mysteries
by Barbara Fradkin
(Ottawa, Police Procedural)
Do or Die
Once Upon a Time
Mist Walker
Fifth Son
Honour Among Men
Dream Chasers
This Thing of Darkness
Beautiful Lie the Dead
The Whisper of Legends
None So Blind

Border City Blues
by Michael Januska
(Prohibition Era Windsor)
Maiden Lane
Riverside Drive
Prospect Avenue

Cornwall and Redfern Mysteries
by Gloria Ferris
(Darkly Comic, Rural Ontario)
Corpse Flower
Shroud of Roses

Book Credits

Acquiring Editor: Carrie Gleason
Developmental Editor: Allison Hirst
Project Editor: Jenny McWha
Copy Editor: Catharine Chen

Cover Designer: Laura Boyle
Interior Designer: Jennifer Gallinger

Publicist: Michelle Melski

Dundurn

Publisher: J. Kirk Howard
Vice-President: Carl A. Brand
Editorial Director: Kathryn Lane
Artistic Director: Laura Boyle
Director of Sales and Marketing: Synora Van Drine
Publicity Manager: Michelle Melski

Editorial: Allison Hirst, Dominic Farrell, Jenny McWha, Rachel Spence, Elena Radic
Marketing and Publicity: Kendra Martin, Kathryn Bassett, Elham Ali

dundurn.com   dundurnpress
@dundurnpress   dundurnpress
dundurnpress   info@dundurn.com

FIND US ON NETGALLEY & GOODREADS TOO!

DUNDURN